A Mercenary's Pilgrimage

By L.J. Nowak, PhD

A Mercenary's Pilgrimage

ISBN-10: 1523455845
ISBN-13: 9781523455843

Cover design by Barry Nowak

Contents

Preface

In 1062 A.D. the southern two-thirds of Hispania* is known as al-Andalus. For the past 350 years, al-Andalus has been populated and ruled by Muslims emigrating from North Africa. At its height, the region was a unified Caliphate, but now the Caliphate has eroded into autonomous city-states that constantly war amongst themselves. Meanwhile, the northern third of Hispania consists of small Christian kingdoms, which (incidentally) also war amongst themselves. When either the Muslims or Christians have excess time and energy, they fight each other. More often than not, the latter conflicts have less to do with religious differences than with the perennial pursuit of more land, wealth, and power.

* present-day Spain, Portugal, and Andorra.

Part 1 - You really shouldn't be here at all

Davides liked limes. They were more complex in flavor than lemons and oranges, their acidity ameliorated by a hint of floral sweetness, like lavender honey. Chopped lime and sugar cane mixed together in cool water was the closest thing he could imagine to ambrosia, especially after a long day under the intense Andalusian sun.

Today, the sun wasn't intense. It was autumn, and the temperature was correspondingly mild. However, the arid region through which they were riding wicked away all moisture, making Davides feel like a desiccated husk.

Enough about limes and ambrosia. He contemplated his depleted waterskin with distaste. They hadn't found a source of potable water since leaving their campsite that morning, which meant that the dregs of liquid in his resin-lined goatskin would now be infused with rancid nastiness. Still, it was wet. Suppressing his revulsion, he tipped up the bag and swallowed what was left.

His horse appeared similarly unimpressed with the pool of stagnant water he was offering her. After snuffling at the sticky, green scum on its surface, she turned her head away and nibbled on the grass near the water's edge. Davides gave her a sympathetic pat on the neck, then glanced over at Sajid, whose horse was grazing nearby.

It was one of those casual glances, which isn't meant to convey anything beyond acknowledgement of the other person's existence. For some reason, though, Sajid bristled.

"Don't worry," Sajid said. "We'll be in Salamanca before evening prayers."

Confused, Davides took a moment to consider the information. *Do I look worried? Should I be worried?* If Davides had had any reason to believe they wouldn't reach their destination on schedule, he wouldn't have just downed the last of his water.

"Yes," Davides responded, in a cautious attempt to appease the prickly, veteran soldier. "You mentioned that earlier."

"Well, you might want to reassure the ambassador and his attendants," Sajid grumbled. "They're carrying on like we're doomed to die in the wilderness."

That made more sense. Sajid's irritation stemmed from comments made by the Emir's perfumed and silk-swathed ambassador, who had been complaining about everything—the dust, the bugs, the bumps in the road—ever since leaving Seville. Davides was merely caught in the crossfire. Again.

Despite his young age of nineteen, Davides had quickly become the default intermediary between the ambassador and the four soldiers who were escorting him north. It stood to reason, he supposed, since the ambassador and the soldiers came from two very different worlds, while Davides had lived in both of them.

Davides had spent a good portion of his youth at the Emir's court in Seville and the colleges of Toledo. He could talk about history, philosophy, or jurisprudence, and could do so in several languages. He understood protocol at the highest echelons of society. His polished manners had won him the confidence of the ambassador (whether he wanted it or not), and his connection to General Haroun had cemented that confidence.

General Haroun was the Emir's most accomplished military commander and one of the most powerful men in Seville. Three years ago, the General had handpicked Davides to serve as one of his messengers, an occupation that involved riding hard, alone, on notoriously dangerous roads between increasingly unstable areas. Typically, the General's messengers had a short life expectancy, but so far Davides had beaten the odds.

Sajid and the other soldiers knew him by that reputation. They knew that, like them, he had often gone hungry and slept in the mud. His tanned, windburnt face and calloused hands were a reflection of their own. Those aspects had earned him a certain degree of respect from the soldiers, despite his polished manners.

While Davides had lived in both worlds, he didn't truly belong to either of them. He had been born into nobility, but had lost his title, his lands, and his wealth. The mail hauberk he wore and the sword strapped to his side were the last vestiges of his family's illustrious past. Now, he had to work or starve. To further complicate matters, Davides was a Christian. He had spent over half his life in al-Andalus, so his customs, style of dress, and fluent Arabic allowed him to blend in with his Muslim companions. In the end, though, he was still a *dhimmi* — a 'protected person' under the *qur'an*, but something akin to a second-class citizen. In a region ruled by Muslims, he was an outsider.

At times like this, when he was expected to mediate petty squabbles between the ambassador and the soldiers,

Davides would have liked to be even further outside. He took a deep breath and summoned a tight smile. He would talk to the ambassador. He would smooth things over.

It was only for one more night, and then his role would change.

* * *

A token knock, then the door to their room swung open. After their arrival in Salamanca, Davides and the four soldiers had been given a room to share in an old, vacant barracks. It was a little dusty and cramped, but considering their arrival had been unannounced, they were fortunate not to have been relegated to the stables.

They were expecting servants with fresh water. Instead, they saw a tall, young man with disheveled hair and a rumpled shirt standing in the doorway.

"God's peace and ..." their visitor yawned suddenly, and the rest of the standard salutation came out distorted, "... and blessings be upon you."

They had already been welcomed courteously (albeit with a certain reserve) by Abdur Rahman, the ruler of Salamanca. The greeting from this youth was neither courteous nor reserved. It was insulting.

"Peace and blessings," Davides responded, in a supercilious tone not at all in keeping with the usual sentiment behind the words. "I'm Davides. And, you are?"

"I'm Remir," he said, with a disarming smile, seeming to take no offense from Davides's deliberate haughtiness. "Remir ibn Rahman. Welcome to Salamanca."

So, this was Remir, heir to the small, frontier city of Salamanca and her surrounding communities. Davides studied him with new interest. By all accounts, the seventeen-year-old son of Abdur Rahman was a lazy, irresponsible sort. Unlike his father, the son had never bothered to study the art of war, had never bothered to study much of anything. Instead, Remir was rumored to while away his days—or nights, as the case may be—in taverns and *shisha* bars, drinking, gambling, smoking, and consorting with a variety of disreputable individuals. His current appearance certainly supported those reports, since although it was late afternoon, Davides got the impression that Remir had just rolled out of bed.

Except for his eyes. Instead of drowsy and vague, the dark brown eyes were keen and inquisitive as they scrutinized the Sevillian soldiers, who were beginning to shift uncomfortably under his gaze. The eyes lingered on Davides and narrowed a bit, as if registering that Davides's armor and accouterments were not exactly standard issue. And wondering why.

"If you were hoping to extend your greetings to the ambassador, I'm afraid you're in the wrong place," Davides said, in an effort to distract him. "We are merely the escort."

"Yeah, I know," Remir replied, insisting on addressing them informally. "But, I've always thought it was so unfair that you men do all the work, and the ambassador gets all the attention. If you need anything during your stay, anything at all, I would be happy to . . . er, find someone to get it for you."

Again, it was not what he said, but rather the way he said it: an offer of hospitality spun into mockery.

Feeling both affronted and just a little impressed by his gall, Davides said dryly, "You're too kind."

"Don't mention it." Remir took a moment to stretch. Despite his allegedly indolent lifestyle, well-defined muscles rippled under the wrinkled shirt. Remir might be a slacker, but he was a strong, athletic slacker, a relevant detail that had somehow been omitted from the information Davides had received before leaving Seville. "I'll let you get back to unpacking, but maybe I'll catch up with you later? I'm dying to hear all about Seville."

Good God, he can't be serious.

"It would be a pleasure," Davides said, with his best fake smile.

After Remir had left, Davides continued to stare at the doorway, mulling over the implications of the encounter. One thing seemed certain: this was going to be a more difficult job than he had been led to believe.

* * *

By early evening the close confines of the barracks had become intolerable for Davides. Anticipation, anxiety, and tense boredom filled the room. By now, the ambassador would be dining with Abdur Rahman, but there was nothing for Davides and the soldiers to do except wait.

He hated waiting.

Ignoring Sajid's sharp, questioning look, Davides tossed his sword and belt on a cot, grabbed his cloak, and left the barracks. He needed to walk, to be in motion. He didn't care where his feet took him.

He crossed the practice yard, followed some narrow steps up to the catwalk of the battlements, and began walking the perimeter of the *alcázar*. The guards watched him warily as he passed. He didn't blame them for keeping an eye on him. He really shouldn't have been up on the battlements.

You really shouldn't be here at all.

As he reached the section that looked out over the city, he slowed and stopped, inadvertently captivated by the shimmer of the setting sun against the buildings below him. For a few, brief moments, when the sun was just right, Salamanca transformed into a city of gold.

It wasn't an original thought, he knew. Everyone since the Romans had admired the gleaming, flaxen hue of Salamanca's stonework.

The Romans had also admired the city for her strategic importance as a gateway to the North. Nearly a thousand years ago, the Romans had built the bridge that still spanned the Tormes River. They had constructed fortifications that had endured to this day. They had invested heavily in Salamanca in order to expand their empire.

And now, the Emir had similar ideas . . . without the investing part.

An approaching voice invaded his thoughts, a voice that joked with the guards in a familiar fashion. With a shock of disbelief, Davides realized that he recognized the voice. He steeled himself, then turned to face Abdur Rahman's son, Remir, who was strolling towards him.

"It's better up close," Remir said to him without preamble.

"What?"

"Salamanca. Not much of a view. It's better up close." Remir paused, then added, "It's Davides, right? I was about to go out for awhile. You want to come along?"

Davides stared at him in consternation. How could Remir be going out? Abdur Rahman's son was of an age where he was expected to spend the evening with his father and their very important guest, the Sevillian ambassador. Remir's absence would be a serious breach of etiquette. More to the point, his absence would put a disastrous hitch in the General's plan, since without Remir, there was no plan.

"Look," Remir inserted into the pause, "if you need to get permission—"

"I don't," Davides interrupted, not bothering to worry about whether that was strictly true. He was still trying to figure out a way to keep Remir within the confines of the *alcázar*. "I hate to point out the obvious, Remir, but won't you be missed?"

Remir shrugged, unconcerned by the prospect. "Your ambassadors sing the same song every time they come here: 'Join forces with Seville and attack Castile-León!'. It's gotten really tedious. But, my father will hear him out anyway, before finally telling him to go—" He stopped himself, smiled diffidently, and censored the remark. "Telling him to go back home. So, what do you say? Let's avoid the mind-numbing boredom and have some fun, instead."

Fun? Hardly. More like a special kind of torture. But, Remir would be going out on the town, with or without him. It had better be with.

"I would be honored to accompany you," Davides said, resorting to stilted decorum to mask the lie.

Remir laughed. "You might want to leave your honor behind when you see where we're going."

* * *

They started at an unpretentious *shisha* bar that was little more than a sturdy tent, the course fabric of the sides and roof waxed stiff to protect against wind and rain. Most of the clientele appeared to be commoners who stopped there to share a pipe and catch up on the day's gossip before heading home. No one seemed astonished by their appearance, which led Davides to believe that Remir was a regular. The establishment's keeper arrived, smiling, with a sebsi pipe and a bag of smoking herbs. Remir gave him a friendly clap on the shoulder, asked about his children and his children's children. Then, he introduced Davides as a friend who was visiting from out of town. Davides drew from the long-stemmed pipe and hoped that whatever they were smoking wouldn't completely addle his brain.

To his relief Davides felt alert and energized when they left the *shisha* bar. They moved to a more boisterous part of town where merchants and travelers gathered for entertainment. The narrow streets abounded with jugglers, dancers, and musicians playing lively music, all vying for space amid the crush of people.

They finally disentangled themselves from the street and went through an arched doorway, down a hallway, and into a large patio filled with people. Sputtering oil lamps hung from the second story balustrades and provided faint illumination. As they made their way through the crowd, Davides felt the crunch of discarded sunflower seed hulls beneath his feet and decided this must be some kind of open-air tavern.

A cheer arose from one corner, and a group of young men from imprecise backgrounds converged on him and Remir. Some friendly soul handed Davides a long-spouted, green glass bottle. After a moment's hesitation, Davides lifted the decanter and drank. He tasted the dry, citrus flavor of pardina grapes, followed by the bite of alcohol typical of fresh wines. Apparently, Salamanca's denizens held a liberal view on the Muslim policy regarding alcohol consumption. Without comment, Davides held the bottle out to Remir.

"Oh, I never drink," Remir said, suddenly serious, and for a moment Davides thought that he had been misinformed about Remir's reveling ways. Then, raucous laughter and jeers erupted from the group. "On Fridays," Remir amended, his face breaking. "But, since this is a Monday, ..." He accepted the bottle and expertly sent a stream of pale gold liquid into his mouth.

Going out for 'awhile', in Remir-speak, meant staying out all night. Gambling, dancing, drinking. They took a brief respite at another *shisha* bar, and, urged by his friends, Remir recited some poetry. He was a gifted storyteller with a fair repertoire of folkloric ballads, epics, and lyrical *moaxajas*. That evidently sated the group's need for higher forms of entertainment, and they went back to their gambling, dancing, and drinking.

Larks were trilling merrily when Davides and Remir finally wound their way back up the hill towards the *alcázar*. Stupid birds, Davides thought. Where was a crossbow when he needed one? The larks were innocently celebrating the coming of dawn, but Davides had now gone without sleep since about this same time yesterday morning. His head felt as if it were stuffed with cotton wadding, and his legs slogged along, erratic as those of a string puppet.

When they passed through the inner gatehouse, one of the guards stepped close to Remir and said in a low voice, "Your father has been asking for you. He wanted to see you as soon as you got back. Him, too," he added, jerking his head in Davides's direction.

In the dark shadow of the gatehouse, Davides couldn't read Remir's expression, but his verbal response was characteristically nonchalant. "See, Davides? I told you we shouldn't have stayed out so late."

Davides wasn't feeling flippant enough to produce a suitable comeback. He knew that, whether or not everything had gone according to the General's plan, the immediate future was going to be distinctly unpleasant. Concealing his dread the best he could, he followed Remir into the residential part of the *alcázar*. Everything was quiet and dark. Most of the household was still asleep. Eventually, they reached a set of double doors, elaborately carved with flowers and entwining vines. Remir pushed the doors open and stepped into the room with Davides close behind.

They had entered a sitting room that connected to Abdur Rahman's private chambers. Heavy drapes had been drawn over the windows, probably to mask the atypical sounds and light that would have emanated from this area earlier. Several cross-frame chairs were arranged around a low table, where spent cups of tea attested to the length of time that Davides and Remir had kept the room's occupants waiting.

The space seemed entirely too small for the number of people currently filling it. Upon seeing them, Abdur

Rahman rose, candid relief wiping out lines of worry. The Sevillian ambassador remained seated, looking smug and unconcerned. Behind him were four more men, their enveloping black robes broken only by the silver glint of their weapons and the dispassionate boredom in their eyes.

Remir glanced around the room, his head tilted slightly. "Sorry we're so late. I was showing Davides here around town. Must have lost track of time."

Abdur Rahman started to respond, but was preempted by the ambassador. "No harm done," he said, in a honeyed voice. He gave Davides an approving nod. "In fact, I'm glad you two had a chance to get to know one another, since you will be spending quite a bit of time together."

Remir's jaw dropped. "Father, you didn't! How many times have I said, 'No arranged marriages'?"

Abdur Rahman's face flushed, but it was impossible to say with what emotion. "Remir," he said hoarsely, "this is serious."

"I'm serious, too. I mean, I like Davides and all, but he's not really my type."

Davides's eyes went wide, and he barely checked himself from giving Remir an elbow in the ribs. How could Remir be so irreverent? Didn't he realize what was happening?

Remir's father tried again. "They are taking you to Seville. They are keeping your sister here. And, they are planning to use Salamanca as a staging area from which to attack Castile-León."

That was a succinct way of putting it. Abdur Rahman might have added that the Sevillian ambassador had been a distraction to focus attention inward while an

16

elite band of North African mercenaries infiltrated the *alcázar* under cover of darkness. Davides had not been privy to all the details, only that the ultimate goal was to take Abdur Rahman's son and daughter hostage. Abdur Rahman would then be unable to retaliate, even though he ostensibly remained in charge of an entire garrison of soldiers.

As it turned out, Remir had not become a hostage until this very moment. But, Abdur Rahman would have believed — may have been led to believe — that Davides had already seized his son and was holding a knife to his throat.

Instead, Davides had spent the night carousing with Remir. In retrospect, it was a cruel trick to have played on the father. Never mind that Davides had not instigated the outing or that the end result remained unchanged. Remir was right where the General had wanted him to be.

The long term success of the ploy depended on Remir being removed to another location, far away from his father's reach and any possible rescue. That was why Davides and the four Sevillian soldiers who had ridden north with him would be conveying Remir to Seville, while the North African mercenaries would remain in Salamanca to guard Remir's sister, Amira. She would guarantee Remir's good behavior and vice versa. If Abdur Rahman balked at cooperating with Seville, either or both of his children would be used as leverage. This was the Emir's twist on wardship: the tried-and-true practice of sending a son off to be raised by an ally as a gesture of good faith. The fact that Abdur Rahman was not participating voluntarily was a minor technicality.

Remir couldn't possibly know all of those details yet, but after the briefest pause he said enthusiastically, "Seville, huh? That's great! I've always wanted to go there."

A short, stiff silence followed this remark, as the different parties sought to discern how fully Remir comprehended the situation. Chancing a furtive glance at Abdur Rahman, Davides thought he detected a spark of paternal pride rather than the flare of exasperation one might have anticipated. Remir understood what was happening, all right, but had intuited that open defiance would gain him nothing.

"Excellent!" the ambassador declared with an oily smile. "Then, everybody gets what they want. You'll leave with an escort this morning."

"Okay," Remir replied, with what seemed the first hint of hesitation. "But, I'll need a bath and breakfast first. And, I'll have to pack." He turned to the aloof mercenaries with a hopeful look. "Unless you guys already did it for me? I hate packing."

* * *

Remir's bath seemed to take forever, especially since every moment they spent in Salamanca risked having the whole scheme unravel. Davides waited for him in a small patio adjacent to the bathhouse, where water splashed musically in a fountain and vibrant purple flowers cascaded from their pots. The citrus smell of verbena infused the air around him.

After a while, Davides was joined by Sajid, who handed Davides his sword with a silent glower. For some reason, the soldier was even less friendly than usual.

Maybe he'd been chastised for Davides's disappearance last night. Or, maybe Sajid was catching wafts of pipe smoke and alcohol over the verbena, and was wondering just how useless Davides would be today.

When Remir emerged from the bathhouse, he appeared annoyingly relaxed and refreshed. Davides and Sajid followed him across the patio, up some stairs, and along an open gallery to his chambers. Someone had already brought up a breakfast tray loaded with orange sections, hard-boiled eggs, and slabs of bread fried in olive oil and garlic. It smelled wonderful.

"You hungry?" Remir asked Davides, as if reading his thoughts, and tossed him an egg without waiting for an answer. "Dig in. Hana always brings enough for a small army."

Startled, Davides nearly dropped the egg on the floor. Why on earth was Remir offering him food? He should have been cursing Davides, or possibly punching him in the face. Not sharing his breakfast. And, the egg couldn't even be poisoned, Davides reasoned, since it was still in its shell, and any poison on the shell would have affected Remir, too.

Remir was tucking into the food on the tray with an appetite. After another doubtful moment, Davides shrugged mentally and began peeling the egg. It wasn't as if he had any other options for breakfast, and it was going to be a long day.

After a not-so-hasty breakfast, Remir donned some leather armor and then began throwing things haphazardly into a large trunk.

"Oh, no," Sajid said firmly, and tossed Remir some saddlebags. "We're traveling light."

Remir regarded the saddlebags with raised eyebrows. "You've got to be kidding."

Sajid just looked at him, so after a moment Remir began stowing essentials into the saddlebags. "I can bring my sword, right?" he asked, reaching for the tooled leather scabbard that housed the item in question.

"Yes," Davides interjected, before Sajid's scowl could turn into another 'no'. In case it had escaped Sajid's notice, Remir was taller and more muscular than either of them. All things considered, Davides would rather face Remir down the length of a sword than in hand-to-hand combat. If it ever came to that.

Remir strapped the sword on, then stopped to study Sajid and Davides in turn. "I'm a little confused," Remir confessed at last, with a vague smile. "Which one of you is in charge?"

After a quick glance at Davides, Sajid replied, "I'm in charge of your escort."

"So, you're the one who kills me if anything goes wrong?" Remir's casual tone hadn't changed. He might have been asking Sajid if he should bring snacks for the trip.

"No, that's my job," Davides answered, his voice sounding strangely remote.

Remir's gaze cut back to him, and Davides felt like the lowest form of treacherous bastard. Last night, they had been drinking together, and now . . . Then, Remir blinked. The reproof, if there had been one, vanished.

"Good to know," Remir said quietly, as he tied the saddlebags shut.

They left Remir's quarters and retraced their steps to the patio, where the other soldiers — Basir, Adi, and Hatim — were waiting for them. Without breaking stride,

Remir tossed his saddlebags to a surprised Hatim and turned in the opposite direction from the stables.

"Where are you going?" Sajid demanded.

"To say 'good-bye' to my sister," Remir replied, as if stating the obvious. "You can go ahead and saddle the horses, though. I won't be long." Paying no heed to Sajid's look of outrage, Remir continued towards the harem, where the women and the children of the household resided.

"I'll have to accompany you," Davides warned Remir, as he caught up with him. Men who were not members of the family did not just barge into the residences of Muslim women, even when the general climate seemed as relaxed as it did in Salamanca.

Remir quirked an odd smile at him. "Don't worry. I'll protect you."

As they reached the intricately carved screens that partitioned the harem, they heard a loud crash from within, followed by men cursing. Moving faster than Davides would have thought possible, Remir darted through the door and into the room beyond. Davides followed, his hand reflexively grasping the hilt of his sword.

It took a moment for his eyes to adjust to the relative darkness inside. Two hulking figures had turned towards them, weapons half-drawn. They were the brawny eunuch slaves, acquired by the General for the express purpose of guarding Abdur Rahman's daughter.

"It's just my brother, you moronic thugs." A slight figure stood beneath a horseshoe archway on the other side of the antechamber. In each tightly clenched hand, she held a colorful clay plate.

21

"Amira," Remir said in a choked voice, "what are you doing?"

"I was just demonstrating for my new watchdogs the superiority of Salamantine ceramics," she replied in a dulcet tone.

Davides contemplated the shattered remains of several plates on the floor. "Superiority?" he asked aloud, and immediately wished that he had kept his mouth shut as her flinty eyes alighted on him.

She flung one of the plates through the air. Davides ducked, and the plate crashed into the ornate screen behind him. "As a projectile," she snapped. "Its superiority as a projectile."

Remir hastened forward and drew Amira back into the adjoining room. Davides crossed the antechamber but stopped when he reached the archway, reluctant to further invade such an intimate space. A few other women from the household hovered in the background, ignoring him as completely as possible. After a few minutes of discourse — impassioned on Amira's part, reassuring on her brother's — Remir kissed her lightly on top of the head and turned back to Davides. Amira trailed after him, her head bowed.

As the brother and sister reached the archway, Amira stepped close to Davides, tilted her head up so that she could look him in the eye, and said, "If you harm so much as a hair on my brother's head, I will see to it that you get staked out for the crows. And, when you are too tired to struggle any longer, they will peck out your eyeballs and dig through your chest to feast on your still beating heart!" She smiled sweetly, turned on the ball of her foot, and faded back into the adjoining room.

"*Nossa!*"   Davides said and stared after her, wondering when exactly he had become 'that guy' — the one who merited a slow, agonizing, and imaginative death rather than your run-of-the-mill execution.

Remir nudged him. "Shouldn't we be going?"

Davides gave him a sour, sidelong glance.   "I thought you said you were going to protect me."

"Yeah, I lied."

* * *

Sajid was anxious to put miles behind them.   They were mounted on different horses now, having exchanged their Andalusian chargers for North African barbs brought by the mercenaries.   The barbs were known for their speed and stamina, and Sajid put those traits to use as soon as they were out of sight of the city's outer walls. Hatim, who seemed to have the best hand with the horses, was ponying a spare mount in the event that one of the animals should pull up lame.   For the first couple of days, they were going to stay off the highway as much as possible and away from towns and inns.   They didn't want any complications with people who might recognize Remir.

The landscape was unremarkable: vast plains filled with parched grasses and occasional groves of holm oaks. A little after dusk, they reached a small woods fed by a trickle of a stream.   Drinkable water.   Sajid picked their campsite, and they swung down from the horses.

Except for Remir. He stayed on his horse, looking about with a certain trepidation.   "Wouldn't it be better if we went back to the road and stayed at an inn for the night?" he asked.

"Better for whom?" Sajid retorted, as he picked up his horse's feet, checking for any stones.

"You must have heard about this area." Remir's mount shifted uneasily and tossed her head. "It really would be better if we kept riding until we got out of these woods. Or found an inn," he added.

"No inns," Sajid said firmly. "And, no fire. We'll have a cold camp tonight."

"It may be colder than you think," Remir continued. "If you were from around here, you'd know: these woods are cursed."

Hatim dropped the saddle he had just pulled off his horse and stared at Remir.

"What do you mean, 'cursed'?" Basir demanded.

"I mean cursed. Perfectly healthy people are struck down while they sleep. All because of the Curse of Gabirol."

They were all ears now: Basir, Adi, Hatim, even Sajid. Davides might have been more interested in what Remir was saying if he hadn't been so crushingly tired. He plucked a piece of sackcloth from his saddlebags and began rubbing down his sweaty mount.

Remir leaned forward and crossed his arms over the pommel of his saddle. "Nearly a hundred years ago, a small group of cavalry got into a skirmish, and their leader, Abdul Nasser, was struck by an arrow. They were forced to retreat, and their guide, a Christian *dhimmi*, led them to these woods. When Nasser's condition worsened, the guide went to the nearby village in search of a famed physician named Gabirol. With the promise of a rich reward, Gabirol followed the guide back to the camp and treated Nasser, who quickly improved. Nasser was so grateful that he gave the physician all of the gold he was carrying as recompense for saving his life.

"The guide was supposed to escort Gabirol back to his village, but along the way, he was overcome with greed. He stabbed the physician and stole the gold. In his last moments, Gabirol tried to place a curse on the deceitful guide, but something went wrong. The curse did not limit itself to the man responsible for Gabirol's death. Instead, a sinister murk still roams these woods, hungering for the warmth of the living."

Remir's voice fell until it was almost a whisper. "Travelers speak of a low-lying shadow, deeper than darkness itself, that steals into campsites at night. Frigid air settles over the ground, chilling to the bone, and then some foul shroud wraps itself around its chosen victims. They're found dead in the morning, mouths stretched wide in a soundless scream. Shepherds, soldiers, scholars: it kills indiscriminately, although, …" Remir paused, as if reluctant to finish. Finally, he forced the words out with singular slowness. "It is said that the Curse of Gabirol is drawn to those who travel with followers of the Cross."

Silence ensued. Davides looked up from his task, sackcloth in hand, to find all of them staring at him with varying degrees of recrimination. For a moment he didn't know why. Then, he backtracked the details of Remir's story: a Christian (like himself) responsible for the initial curse and the presence of Christians (like himself) responsible for its subsequent attacks. Nice. He turned an inimical eye on Remir, who had the audacity to smile wickedly back.

"Should we finish making camp, Sajid?" Davides inquired with exaggerated politeness, "Or, would you prefer to move to the open plains, where there are no shadows to jump at? You do realize he spent the whole day concocting that story just to mess with us!"

As Davides had anticipated, the attack on the soldiers' courage held more sway than Remir's ghost story. Sajid's brow darkened and he said gruffly, "We'll make camp here. Hatim, see to the horses. Basir and Adi, you two take first watch; wake Hatim and me for the second. Davides and Remir," he finished, with a curl of his lip, "sleep well."

* * *

Davides awoke with a sharp intake of breath. His subconscious was clamoring an alarm, but he had no idea as to why. In the stillness of the night, his heart thumped a couple of anxious beats. Nothing else moved.

Letting out his pent-up breath, Davides berated his imagination for overreacting to Remir's story of killer shadows. A sliver of moonlight trickled down through the foliage, barely allowing him to make out where Sajid, Hatim, and Remir were sleeping. Just as he was convincing himself that nothing was wrong, he heard a gusty, alarmed snort in the distance, and a tremulous voice yell, "Something's out with the horses!"

A *whoosh* reverberated through the camp, and an arrow sliced into the ground inches from Davides's nose. He recoiled and kicked off his blanket. Still prone, he slid his sword free from its scabbard and scrambled over to where Remir was lying. Only, Remir was gone. The blanket, either by chance or design, bulged where Remir's head and body should have been. Davides looked around frantically, trying to pick out Remir's shape or shadow from among a host of others in the gloom. Basir and Adi were now kneeling among the packs. Sajid had pulled his sword and, with Hatim on his heels, rushed out in the direction of the horses.

To hell with the horses. Where was Remir? Another *whoosh,* and another volley of arrows hit the campsite. They seemed to be coming from every direction. He saw Adi spin and fall.

Davides ran in the opposite direction of the horses, which were, he was betting, just a diversion. The leathery leaves of the smaller holm oaks slapped at his face as he dodged from one tree to the next. He heard another volley get loosed and let himself slam into the relative safety of a tree trunk. Chancing a look around the tree, he spotted someone nocking another arrow. Davides sprinted forward, hoping he could reach the dark silhouette before the arrow was readied.

The silhouette materialized into a man who, upon seeing or hearing Davides's sudden approach, shot wildly. Davides swung his sword, and the man made a clumsy and ineffectual attempt to block the blow with his bow. The archer fell with a muffled cry, clutching his wounded leg. Davides raised his sword again, but stopped when he heard a whisper of voices somewhere in the distance. His sword still poised, he tried to sort out a word or two, but the figure at his feet gasped and tried to shift away from him.

"Be still!" Davides hissed, but by then shouts from the campsite drowned out any further chance of hearing whispers.

Davides looked down disgustedly at the fallen archer, who stared back at him with wide, terrified eyes. No armor, no sword, and no skill in direct combat. This man hadn't been sent by Abdur Rahman . . .

The sound of a screech owl broke through his tenuous train of thought, making him start nervously. It was obviously some sort of signal, since the hum of bowstrings was replaced with the furtive sound of running feet fading into the distance. Both he and the archer scanned the darkness, searching for any sign that someone was approaching them. When it became evident that they were alone, Davides twisted his hand into the fallen man's collar, jerked him to his feet, and shoved him against the nearest tree.

"Who sent you?" he demanded.

Confusion competed with fear on the man's face. "Sent me?" he squeaked.

Still holding the front of the man's jerkin, Davides leveled his sword at his throat. "I don't have time for this," he muttered, and flexed his sword arm back slightly, as if preparing to drive the sword home.

"Hisham!" the man said. "It was Hisham's idea! He thought your prads worth nimming."

Now, it was Davides's turn to be confused. He spoke Arabic, Castilian, Portuguese, Latin, and some Greek. But, none of those languages were helping him understand what this man had said.

"He says they were after the horses," a voice commented from behind him.

Reacting instinctively, Davides swung his blade towards the newcomer. The tip of the sword stopped a hand's breadth from Remir's nose. Davides stared at Remir in astonishment: he had been so sure no one was nearby. Yet, here was Remir, materializing out of thin air like some kind of jinni.

Remir regarded the sword, and then blinked at him, seemingly unperturbed. "Did I forget to mention that there've been reports of horse thieves in this area? Most people are safe because they stick to the highway and spend nights at inns or way stations."

Davides grimaced. He was not in the mood for Remir's incendiary sense of humor. "Where have you been?"

Remir's eyes widened innocently. "Oh, I hid. It all looked so very dangerous when the camp was attacked. In fact, I think Adi got shot."

Davides looked from Remir to his captive and back again. What was he missing? The archer was either a consummate actor or truly was scared out of his wits. Nor had he appeared to recognize Remir. "What should we do with him?" Davides asked, indicating the alleged horse thief but watching for Remir's reaction.

Remir shrugged. "String him up, I guess. He confessed to being a horse thief. In so many words."

Remir was the picture of complete indifference. The 'horse thief', sweat beading on his face, was appropriately aghast. Was it possible that things really were as they seemed, that nothing more had happened tonight than prosaic banditry? Davides found it hard to believe, but if the group that had attacked them had been after Remir, they had had ample opportunity to take him.

"Davides!" Sajid bellowed from somewhere in the darkness.

"Here! Everything's fine!" he called back, before Sajid starting shouting Remir's name to the four winds. The only thing that really mattered, he decided, was that they still retained possession of Abdur Rahman's son.

Davides pulled the horse thief away from the tree and gave him a hard shove in the direction the fading footsteps had taken. "Get!" he said, in a soft, menacing voice.

The man stumbled backwards, bewildered. Then, when it appeared that no one intended to impede him — or impale him — he hobbled out into the night. Davides picked up the discarded bow and arrows, and started back towards the camp.

Walking alongside him, Remir remarked, "You know, for a hired sword, you're not very good at killing people."

Davides stopped short, a flare of temper on the tip of his tongue. He wasn't sure which he resented more: the appellation of 'hired sword' or the suggestion that he wasn't good at it. He drew a steadying breath and reminded himself that Remir specialized in provocative statements. "We're trying not to draw attention to ourselves. A body hanging from a tree draws attention. So does taking a bandit to the nearest magistrate, which is probably what should have been done. All in all, I don't care if Salamanca's environs are beset by horse thieves as long as they leave us alone. What do you want to bet that they will from now on?"

Without waiting for Remir's response, Davides stalked back to camp where he found Basir squatting low to the ground, trying to start a fire. Huddled nearby, Adi sat shivering, a dark stain splashed across his right side. A little further off, Davides could hear Hatim's quiet voice reassuring the horses — or, more likely, the horses' calm demeanor reassuring Hatim.

"Where's Sajid?" Davides asked Basir.

"Still out," Basir replied, and struck flint against steel a few more times, sending sparks into the kindling. "We lost two horses, you know. Where were you?"

"Doing your job," came an unexpected retort from Sajid as he rejoined the group. "You and Adi were on watch, and you managed to lose track of Remir and let two horses be stolen, all in one night. Good work."

Adi, undoubtedly stung that his wounded status hadn't saved him from blame, protested through chattering teeth, "I s-s-said from the beginning he should be tied up. How can we be expected to guard someone who's not even restrained? We never should've listened to Davides and his s-s-stupid—"

"Hold on!" Davides cut in, not liking the direction of the discussion. "I didn't find Remir; he found me. If he had wanted to get away from us, he easily could have. As far as I can tell, we were attacked by a bunch of bandits, who fled when they saw we'd fight back."

Sajid surprised him by agreeing. "Davides is right, I think. I killed one and wounded another, but there were still plenty of them left to finish the job if they'd chosen. Instead, they scattered like a flock of chickens."

"With two of our horses," Basir reminded them, as a small flicker sprang up from the sparks in the kindling.

"What if they were sent to slow us down?" Hatim piped up from the darkness. "Now, we'll have to go to a town, try to buy at least one decent horse before we can keep going."

It was a good point, and one that Davides had not considered. Adi being injured would also slow them down. However, he reflected, the archers wouldn't have been able to see precisely at whom they were shooting. Even if Remir had known to get out of harm's way when the attack came, it was still a huge risk to run if the objective was merely to slow them down. Unless, the attack had not started until Remir was already out of harm's way. Something had awakened Davides from a sound sleep. What was it? And then, there were those whispers he had heard . . .

"Abu Hamden raises some nice horses," Remir mentioned in an offhand manner. "His stud farm is only about five miles northeast of here."

Sajid's frown and its accompanying glare showed what he thought of that helpful suggestion. "We can't do much tonight. Basir, tomorrow morning you and Hatim will walk to the nearest village and get another horse or two. If anyone asks, keep it simple: you're working for General Haroun, you're riding to Seville, your horses were stolen. Don't get carried away with details, and don't mention the rest of us."

* * *

Though bloody, Adi's wound turned out to be superficial. The thick padding of his gambeson had kept the arrow from penetrating too deeply. Sajid cleaned it and packed it with a poultice, while Adi whined more about the treatment than he had about being shot.

Basir and Hatim returned around mid-day with a horse and a mule. The horse was a skittish bay mare that had had little training. Hatim assured Sajid that she was sound, fast, and just needed a few miles put on her, to which Sajid pointed out that they would be heading into rougher territory today, and that the damn fool mare would likely back herself right off a cliff. But, in view of their options, the mare would have to do. After a brief lunch of lentil stew, they headed south once more, with Hatim volunteering to ride the new horse.

32

Their pace today was unavoidably slower as they ascended the foothills of the Gredos Mountains. Lush, green valleys alternated with increasingly steep hillsides, and dense forests of chestnut trees replaced the scattered oak groves of the meseta. As the afternoon wore on, the air became crisper and the wind picked up, bringing the faint scent of pine.

Eventually, they were forced to pick up the Via Delapidata as the only navigable way through the mountains. The road, paved during the time of the Romans, had once served as an important commercial highway. Then, some 350 years ago, Tariq ibn Ziyad had used the still functional Via Delapidata to send his Muslim armies north, and had managed to conquer most of Hispania before the disorganized Christian rulers even knew what was happening. Since the dissolution of the Córdoban Caliphate nearly thirty years ago, the paved surface of the Via Delapidata had been slowly crumbling apart, yet it remained the fastest way north or south, especially for those mounted on shod horses.

As long as they had to be on the Via, Sajid was taking advantage of its relatively smooth surface to push the horses a little faster. He was determined to get past the village of Béjar before stopping for the night. Béjar was situated near high peaks, where a dusting of snow could already be seen against a sky that was now grey and brooding. During one of their short breaks, they broke out fur-lined cloaks and woolen scarves to ward off the chill. The accessories would have the added benefit of concealing Remir's features when they passed through the village.

As it turned out, they needn't have been concerned about someone recognizing Remir. When they rode through Béjar, it was locked up tight against the approaching storm. The village inhabitants, wiser than the little group of riders, were snug in their homes. A few freezing raindrops splashed down and skated across Davides's face. He hunched his shoulders and looked wistfully at the puffs of smoke coming from stone chimneys and the faint glow behind shuttered windows. Wherever and whenever they stopped, they probably wouldn't even be able to find dry kindling to get a fire going. It was going to be a long, miserable night.

They made it another couple of miles before the storm hit. A roll of thunder seemed to shake the air around them. It was followed by a crackle of far-off lightning. Sajid cursed luridly and pushed his mount faster, scanning the surrounding area for decent cover.

The tempo of the thunder and lightning gradually accelerated, and in the distance searing slices of light cut through the grey. They came to a wide stream, and, after a moment's hesitation, Sajid's horse splashed into the cold, dark, belly-deep water. Basir and Adi followed him, then Remir and Davides. They had already climbed the far bank when Davides looked back and saw Hatim still on the opposite side of the stream.

Hatim's mare stood braced at the water's edge, staring bug-eyed at its surface as if it were some unfathomable abyss. Hatim cued her forward again, turning his spurs into her sides for emphasis. She wove back and forth, muscles bunched, but just as she seemed ready to take the plunge, she spun away from the glassy, black surface and bolted in the opposite direction. Hatim kicked his feet out of the stirrups and vaulted to the ground, using himself as an anchor to stop the mare's headlong flight. She fought him, half-dragging him a good twenty feet before he got her back under control.

Someone was going to have to go back across to help Hatim. *"Merda!"* Davides swore and then called out to Sajid and the others, shouting to make himself heard over the wind and grumbling thunder.

They stopped and were turning their horses around when Adi's gelding shied violently at something hidden on the hillside. Caught by surprise, Adi lost his seat and fell to the ground. His frightened horse spun away and galloped off into the grey mist, while the source of the animal's terror lifted slowly out of the rocky outcroppings.

It was a bear, Davides realized. A very large and irate bear. It loomed high above Adi, who lay on the ground with the wind knocked out of him. Before anyone could act, it dropped down on the helpless soldier.

Davides jumped from his horse. Even if he could have relied on her not to panic, the terrain was ill-suited for a mounted charge. Enough rain had fallen to make the rocky ground slippery under shod hooves, and the steep slopes on either side of the road meant that space was limited. He pulled the enarmes taut on his shield and drew his sword.

"Can't you just shoot it?" Remir yelled over the sounds of the storm.

Davides indicated the bandit's bow and arrows. "You shoot it! And, stay clear!" He turned away without waiting for Remir's reaction and pelted up the road towards the bear. Enough arrows might eventually kill it or drive it off, but mostly they would just make it mad. And this one was pretty stirred up already. He had helped kill a bear once before while on a hunting trip with

35

General Haroun, but they had used a pack of dogs to harry the beast, specially trained horses, and long spears. The only thing this group had was swords.

Sajid had likewise abandoned his horse, and had rushed back to where the bear straddled Adi's prone form. Sajid slashed into its right flank with his blade. Just as Davides reached them, the bear turned towards Sajid and stood up again on its hind legs, its colossal form making Sajid shrink by comparison. It reached out almost casually and slapped at Sajid's round shield. The blow, which connected with the force of a battering ram, sent Sajid sprawling to the ground.

An arrow peppered into the bear's exposed shoulder, making it snarl and snap its massive jaws. Spying Davides, it blamed him for this newest source of aggravation, and it came down on all fours with a lunge. Davides skipped back and began backpedaling up the slope. The bear's face was roughly the same size as his shield, he realized, and the animal had at least twice his reach. Suddenly, Remir's idea of shooting it from a distance sounded like really good advice.

They had successfully drawn it away from Adi, but the creature was fully enraged now, and there was no hope of merely driving it off. Davides dodged and scrambled upwards, desperate to avoid the sweeping paws and crushing maw. Another arrow plunged into the bear's side, distracting it momentarily. Seeing an opening, Davides stepped in close and swung hard. He felt his blade go through layers of fur, hide, fat, and muscle. For all of that, the bear seemed unfazed by the blow. Its jaws clamped onto the rim of Davides's shield, and it whipped its head furiously back and forth.

Davides, unable to break away, felt a sickening wrench in his left shoulder. Too late, the shield's enarmes came loose, freeing him. Davides fell back with the bear practically on top of him, its teeth still gripping the shield.

Then, the bear's head jerked up, and it spun away from Davides to confront Sajid, who had attacked it again from behind. Davides struggled back to his feet. Using all the strength he could muster, he plunged his sword down between the bear's shoulders. He tried to hold on and drive the sword deeper, but his left arm wasn't cooperating in the effort. Another lurch from the bear made him lose his grip altogether. He saw Sajid leap sideways to avoid the bear's throes as it tried to dislodge the sword and half-rolled, half-lumbered to the bottom of the slope, where it lay still.

The storm was right on top of them now, with the rain falling in sheets and brilliant flashes of light surrounding them. Davides finally spotted his scarred shield, but when he bent down to retrieve it, pain ripped through his left shoulder. He dropped to one knee, gasping and clinging to the shield. Finally, the pain ebbed and he carefully got to his feet. Sajid stood a little ways off, watching him through narrowed eyes, and Davides wondered vaguely what he had done wrong this time.

Remir! Where is he?

Davides scanned the darkness in the direction of the stream until, in the brief illumination of more lightning, he saw a familiar figure holding a bow. That was all right, then. Relief — or something — made him weak in the knees, and he wobbled his way down the slope, intent on recovering his sword. Cautiously, he approached the bear's recumbent form, watching for any sign of life. After prodding it a few times with his foot, he grabbed the hilt that still jutted out from its back and tried to pull the sword free.

An ear-splitting crack sent concussive waves throughout the area as lightning struck something nearby. Davides hunched down next to thick, wet, brown fur, suddenly wondering about the wisdom of holding a long, metal object in the midst of a storm. Not to mention the mail hauberk he was wearing . . .

Someone took hold of his arm — mercifully, his right arm — and pulled him up. It was Sajid, who then yanked the sword out of the bear, grabbed Davides's arm again, and propelled him a short ways to where the others were already assembled. Hatim had somehow made it across the stream with his mare, Remir was holding their two horses, and Basir held the other horses and the pack mule. Adi was draped across the latter.

"What's wrong with Davides?" Basir asked, with his usual tact.

"His shield arm's screwed up," Sajid replied. "And, I expect he's going through some shock. He'll snap out of it. C'mon, let's move."

Shock? What was Sajid talking about? Davides felt fine. His shoulder didn't even hurt now; it was just a little numb. And, he was perfectly lucid. He took the reins of his horse from Remir, who was watching him with curious eyes. "I'm fine," he insisted.

* * *

Later, Davides would have given just about anything to return to that lovely, anesthetized state. The rush from the fight had subsided, and his shoulder was throbbing with a vengeance. He kept his arm tucked close to his side, since any movement it made, no matter how minimal, sent jabs of pain into him. He had also come to the depressing realization that Adi was dead. The others had already known, had loaded the body on the mule. He should have known, too, he supposed. They wouldn't have tossed a severely wounded man across the mule like that.

They sloshed along dispiritedly, searching for anything that resembled shelter. The thunder and lightning had diminished by that time, but the chilly rain was still falling, carried sideways by a stiff wind. At last they found a small, crumbling stone structure with half its roof caved in and a dark slit where a door once had been. After leaving the horses on the lee side of the building, they stumbled inside. It was pitch black and smelled musty, like a damp cellar. Davides edged along the wall, sliding his feet carefully over a packed floor that was strewn with debris. He found a clear space and sank down, his back pressed against the wall.

In the darkness he heard someone rummaging through a pack, then came the sharp *chink* of flint and steel. In a rare moment of foresight, Basir must have squirreled away kindling in his saddlebags, and was now in the process of trying to light a fire. The flame that danced up from the thin strips of bark illuminated their surroundings surprisingly well. Not that there was much to see. Whatever it used to be, the building had been abandoned a long time ago. The part that was still standing didn't even have enough space for them all to lie down.

Basir nursed his little blaze along while Sajid and Hatim scavenged some of the beams that had come down with the roof and were dry enough to fuel the fire. Before long, chunks of broken beams were burning brightly.

Davides thought that the fire was one of the most beautiful things he had ever seen. It was small, but they were in a small space, and soon they were stripping off sodden cloaks and boots. Basir heated water for tea, and they passed around bags of almonds and dried fruit.

After they had warmed up a bit and had had something to eat, Sajid looked over at Davides, his face set with grim resolve. "We might as well get this over with," he said.

Davides raised his eyebrows. "Get what over with?"

"Your shoulder. The longer we wait, the harder it will be to reset."

"Reset?" Davides didn't much like the sound of that.

Sajid nodded. "I think your arm's out of its socket. That's why it won't move right. If I can reset it, you should be able to start using it again in a couple of days."

Remir stirred. "Are you a physician?" he inquired.

"No, but I've seen this done," was the unconvincing reply.

"Ah." Remir caught Davides's eye, a tempered glint of malicious amusement replacing the somber weariness on his face.

Davides glowered back at him: nice to know his injury offered Remir some entertainment value. "What exactly are we talking about doing?" he asked Sajid.

"You just lay down flat and try not to tense up," Sajid explained. "I'll sit next to you, brace my foot in the pit of your arm, and pull on your wrist until the arm snaps back in place."

Snaps back in place?

"Gee, that sounds like it might hurt," Remir commented, chewing methodically on some dried figs.

"That's probably not going to be the worst part," Sajid went on, sounding almost apologetic. "The worst part will be getting your hauberk off first. We can't do this with it still on."

Davides tried to envision rotating his arm far enough to pull the mail armor over his head. He swallowed hard. "Does anyone have anything resembling alcohol?" he asked, with the faint hope that one of his Muslim companions carried some for medicinal purposes.

To his surprise, it was Remir who turned and withdrew a flask from his saddlebags. He tossed it to Davides, who made a graceless, one-handed catch. Davides studied the flask for a moment: funny, he didn't recall seeing Remir pack this.

"*Obrigado,*" Davides said reflexively, still pondering the flask.

"Don't mention it."

Davides gave himself a mental shake and decided that now was not the time to ask immaterial questions. He unstopped the flask and took a swallow. Then shuddered. It was some kind of cheap *aguardiente*. Revolting but, on the positive side, very strong. He quickly downed a few more swallows until the alcohol warmed his body and blurred the pain in his shoulder. "Okay, let's get this over with."

* * *

They made quite a spectacle riding into the sleepy town of Ambroz the next afternoon. They had wrapped Adi's body in blankets, but it was still unquestionably a

41

dead body. Davides's injured arm was strapped tight to his side, immobilizing it, and his armor hung like another casualty behind his saddle. To complete the picture, Adi's gelding, which had turned up in the middle of the night with a deep, oozing gash in his shoulder, limped along behind the mule. They were muddy, bloody, and probably looked like they had just straggled in from the front lines of some battle.

Sajid was counting on them to be far enough south to risk staying in town. Or, he was just past caring. In any event, they needed to arrange Adi's burial, and, since tomorrow was Friday, they would stay so Sajid and the others could attend prayer services. In Davides's case, he could use the day for rest and recuperation.

They rode to the mosque and sought out the local imam, who agreed to do the funeral for a small fee. Next, they went to the large but unpretentious inn on the outskirts of town. They left the animals with the hostler and then, despite the fact that the inn already had a number of travelers staying there, Sajid was able to requisition one large room for their private use. The innkeeper, impressed by the steady stream of coins that Sajid shelled out, supplied them with pallets to sleep on, relatively clean blankets, and warm water for washing. He also sent servants to bundle up their laundry and to find them fresh shirts. They certainly couldn't attend a funeral looking as they did.

Washing up and changing clothes proved to be an arduous process for Davides. He finally tore out the seams of his old shirt, rather than trying to pull it over his head. The new shirt, which had all the tailored grace of a burlap sack, at least allowed him to slip his left arm through the sleeve without undue acrobatics.

He wasn't even sure why he was going to the funeral. The only thing Adi and he had ever shared was a mutual dislike for one another. He supposed it was more to cultivate a sense of morale than anything else. Sajid had been making an effort to be more civil to him; the least he could do was return the favor.

No sooner had that thought crossed his mind than Remir, lounging on a pallet, announced his intention of remaining at the inn. "You can't be serious," Remir scoffed, when Sajid remonstrated. "Do you really want *my* thoughts accompanying Adi to the hereafter? Let's have a little respect for the dead, shall we?"

A frozen silence followed this outrageous statement—outrageous more for its derisive delivery than for its sentiment. The sentiment was justified. Why should Remir mourn if one of them died? It was more a cause for his celebration.

Now that Davides thought about it, maybe the delivery was justified, too.

"He's right, Sajid. He shouldn't be there," Davides said, in an attempt to diffuse the tension in the room. "I'll stay with him, and the rest of you can give Adi a proper burial."

Sajid's rigid anger relaxed slightly. He cast a critical eye over Davides. "Are you up to it?"

Davides nodded. "You should go. It'll be dark soon."

Sajid, Basir, and Hatim filed out. Remir waited a few moments, then hopped up from the pallet.

"You owe me," he said brightly.

"For what?" Davides asked, pretending not to understand his meaning.

"For getting you out of that funeral. You didn't want to go, either."

"I had convinced myself that I did," Davides replied, in what he hoped was a convincing tone.

"Ha. Come on. Let's go to the bar."

"What? No!"

"Why not? I'm hungry, your shoulder must be hurting like hell, and I'm all out of alcohol."

And Davides did owe him for that, damn it. Of course, there was still the question of where that alcohol had come from in the first place. Perhaps a better question was why Remir had chosen to give it to him, of all people. Wouldn't Remir rather have watched him suffer as much as possible? Crows eating his eyeballs, and all that.

"Where did you get that flask, anyway?" Davides asked casually.

Remir glanced over at him while pulling on his boots. "From one of the horse thieves. When they attacked, I thought it was some ill-conceived plan to liberate me. I caught up with one of them, found out they were just bandits, and let the guy go. But, I asked for his flask."

That made sense. It also explained why someone like Remir would be carrying what was essentially by-product brandy. It might even account for those whispers Davides had overheard. "Okay, so why give it to me?"

Davides thought he caught a spark of resentment in Remir's eyes, but Remir answered with his usual repartee. "Maybe you were in too much pain to notice, but that stuff was nasty. For all I knew it was going to leave you permanently blind or something. You ready?" Remir stood up decisively, ending the interrogation.

44

"I don't have much money," Davides warned Remir, as they started out into the common room.

"What, they don't pay hired killers like they used to?"

This time, Davides did not take the bait. "I don't get paid until the job's done," he shot back pointedly.

Remir paused and gave him an appraising look. "And, that would certainly put a damper on our ability to go drinking together." He waved the topic aside. "No matter. We won't need much money tonight."

"What do you mean?" Davides demanded, but Remir ignored him. Instead, he turned into the common room, and called for food and drink. Davides followed, wondering uneasily what Remir was up to now.

The inn was bustling. Their arrival earlier that afternoon had been duly noted, commented on, and speculated about. Now, in addition to the travelers staying at the inn, the good townspeople of Ambroz were showing up in force, eager for more substantial gossip.

Remir was in his element. Accustomed to being the town darling, it took him no time to be embraced by this crowd. When enough people had gravitated about him, he revealed what had befallen him and his 'friends'.

He didn't just tell them about the bear attack. In the space of a day, and by borrowing shamelessly from other works, Remir had concocted a full-blown epic poem about their encounter with the bear, one which painted Davides as the lone slayer of a gigantic, mythical beast. While the other men huddled in terror, the mighty Davides pried the jaws of death (alas, too late!) from the lifeless body of his dear friend. Armed only with a dinner knife, Davides then engaged the creature in a grueling battle, culminating in a blow that opened the bear from stem to stern.

The crowd loved it and bought them drinks. The innkeeper loved the crowd and gave Remir and Davides their meals on the house. Davides tried to interrupt Remir, and when that failed, tried to correct the story. But, the audience just seemed to find his 'modesty' endearing and bought them more drinks. They weren't interested in facts; they just wanted to be entertained. New people filtered in and demanded a re-telling, so Davides had to suffer through it again, this time with more embellishments. One of the other travelers produced an *oud* and began plucking out melodious background music. Davides gave up and started drinking.

Night fell and so did the temperature outside, but the inn's common room was pleasantly warm. As was the reigning attitude towards Remir and him. Since Remir had turned them both into local celebrities, they were positively awash with folksy goodwill.

Davides was feeling quite happy and relaxed when a flat voice in his ear demanded, "Where is Remir?"

The perennial question. Davides, unconcerned, gestured towards a corner table where Remir was deep into the fourth spinning of the story. This time, there was a girl. Davides wasn't sure where she had come from, or where she would go after the bear attack, but she was flouncing and fluttering her way through the poem in all of her barefoot and buxom glory.

Basir grabbed him by the sleeve. "Is this your idea of guarding him?" he hissed.

"Is this your idea of being discreet?" Davides asked, and smiled around at his fans, some of whom were watching the exchange. "Back off, Basir," he said between his teeth. "I may be drunk, but I'm not the one being stupid."

So much for cultivating a sense of morale. Basir's anger was palpable, and for a moment Davides thought the disgruntled soldier would take a swing at him. How could Basir be so dense? Even with one not-so-proverbial arm tied behind his back, Davides was pretty sure that he and, say, nine or ten of his newfound friends could take Basir.

Basir's eyes shifted as he finally grasped that Davides was not here *alone*. He took a step back just as Sajid and Hatim wended their way through the crowd.

"What's going on?" Sajid inquired in a neutral voice.

Which was Sajid's way of saying *why the hell didn't you stay in the room*? However, Davides didn't feel inclined to apologize or explain himself, so he simply responded, "Basir disapproves."

Sajid's tight lips showed that he concurred with Basir.

"Hey," said an impressed Hatim, who had been listening to the conclusion of Remir's tall tale. "How'd I end up with a girl?"

Davides started to laugh, and Hatim grinned sheepishly back at them. At least Hatim had a sense of humor. Sajid rolled his eyes and drew Davides a few feet away from the locals.

"You're supposed to be handling him," Sajid began.

"Sajid," Davides interrupted in a low voice, "I assure you, this is handling him. Let Remir have some fun, blow off some steam, get rid of some of his frustration."

Sajid furrowed his brow and looked over at Remir, who was doubled up with laughter at some joke the *oud* player had told. "Frustration?" he repeated skeptically.

Davides felt his own happy buzz evaporating as a kaleidoscope of memories spun briefly in his head. "Yes, frustration. Why do you think we don't need irons on him? They're up here," he tapped at his temple. "His heart is clamoring for him to do something, but his head keeps insisting that he mustn't. That he can't. One false move, and his family pays the price. So, yes, there's probably a little frustration there!"

"You give him too much credit," Sajid muttered. "Just because you reacted that way, doesn't mean that he has. Whatever else you might be, Davides, you are not a shiftless, no-account princeling. You don't think like one. You and Remir are not the same." Sajid enunciated the last part distinctly, as if explaining a difficult concept to a small child.

Somewhere in there, Sajid had buried a compliment, but his overriding message was *you're being an idiot*. Davides drew himself up, eyes snapping, and Sajid's usually steady stance faltered as he realized he had crossed a line.

"Are you really telling me," Davides began, in a chillingly quiet voice, "that you know more about what's going on in Remir's head than I do? That my experience makes me *less* capable for this job? All right, Sajid, since you're an expert on Remir, explain something to me: why did he shoot the bear?"

Sajid blinked at him, uncomprehending.

"He didn't need to get involved; he wasn't even being threatened. Yet, he saved your neck with the first arrow and probably mine with the second. Why?" Sajid just shook his head, so Davides continued, "I don't have an answer, but I've at least bothered to ask myself the question! Why did he shoot the damn bear?"

"Who says I was shooting at the bear?" interjected Remir, who appeared unexpectedly next to them. He looked at them both, giving them a moment to consider the alternatives. Then, with one of his engaging smiles, he pushed a tankard of ale into Davides's hand. "Sajid, I hate to interrupt, but the crowd's getting restless. Now they want to hear how Davides single-handedly fought off forty bandits. You don't mind if I borrow him for a bit?"

Sajid did not look at all sorry to be interrupted or to see Davides borrowed. Davides took a long drink from the tankard and let himself be drawn back towards their adoring fans. Stupid, he thought. He usually wasn't so volatile, but Sajid had hit a nerve. That was no excuse, though. The last thing they needed was for Remir — or anyone, really — to see Sajid and him at odds. He wondered how much Remir had overheard.

"Forty bandits, Remir?" Davides said with a short laugh, trying to get back into the spirit of things. "You're seriously going to tell them there were forty?"

"Well, I thought fifty would sound like an exaggeration."

* * *

Davides woke to the muezzin's call to morning prayers. Sajid and Basir were already awake, since they had taken second watch — or whatever was left of it after Davides, Remir, and Hatim had stumbled in last night. They goaded a groggy Hatim out of bed, but similar efforts to rouse Remir failed completely. The three soldiers left for the mosque, saying they would check back before midday prayers.

After splashing some cold water on his face, Davides felt more or less alert. Moving carefully, he unwound the scarf that held his injured arm in place and tried flexing the arm backwards, forwards, and sideways. The pain was still pretty intense, and he wondered for the hundredth time how long it would be before he could wear armor or use a shield again.

To take his mind off that depressing thought, he started cleaning and oiling their equipment. Unfortunately, the routine nature of those tasks did nothing to occupy his mind. Sajid had definitely hit a nerve last night. Not the part about him being an idiot (that assessment was looking to be woefully accurate). Rather, in his attempt to make a point, Sajid had dredged up Davides's past: *just because you reacted that way . . .* That's all it had taken. The memories associated with that one defining event in his life had gnawed at him all night and were well on their way to consuming the morning.

By the time Remir awoke, Davides had fallen into a pensive quagmire. Remir, remarkably unaffected by a river of ale and little sleep, decided that Davides's funk was due to lack of nourishment. They went downstairs, and Remir charmed the innkeeper's wife into making them a late breakfast. They sat in the empty common room, munching on crusty bread smeared with soft, sheep's milk cheese. Remir was carrying the conversation, chatting easily about nothing in particular.

Davides, only half-listening, found himself wondering how long it would be before Sajid and company returned. It had to be getting close to midday.

50

Remir and he might never get another chance to speak privately.

Remir was in mid-sentence about something or other when Davides blurted out, "How much do you not want to go to Seville?"

Remir blinked a few times, sat back in his chair, and cocked his head. "I do want to go to Seville. I've always wanted to."

"Knock it off, Remir. Don't tell me you want to go to Seville while the Emir uses your home as a staging area for war."

Remir's features hardened. "What exactly do you expect me to say, Davides?"

Davides held his gaze for a moment, then took the plunge. "I'm pretty sure I can fix it so that you could stay with General Haroun's army. We'll be meeting up with it in a few days. That would keep you close, at least, and might even get you back to Salamanca."

"How exactly would you 'fix' that?"

"Well, it would involve saying some uncomplimentary things to General Haroun about your father," Davides began. Remir's eyes flashed, and Davides hastened to explain, "Not like he sleeps with sheep! Just that he's out of touch with today's politics. That his ties with King Fernando and the counts of Castile-León make him weak and ineffectual. That you've spent your life genuflecting to the North and you're sick of it. That you are eager to go to war with the infidels, and you don't want to be sent away to Seville."

"You're an infidel," observed Remir.

"A landless infidel; I don't count. And, you're getting off track."

"Okay. Why would he believe me?"

"Because General Haroun expects people to agree with him. In his mind, agreeing with him is part of the natural order of things. It would make sense to him that you would want to join Seville in this war. People like your father are the irrational aberrations. In fact, the General probably thinks he's doing you a favor by getting you away from Abdur Rahman's pernicious influence."

The last statement prompted a half-smile from Remir. Then, it faded. "That explains how. Now, why? Why would you do this?"

Why would I do this? It was an excellent question, and one for which Davides should have had an answer before he broached the topic. It was so easy to forget that Remir had a sharp mind hiding behind that carefree exterior. Since Davides had no intention of telling him the real reason, he voiced the first logical alternative that sprang to mind. "Money."

"Money," Remir repeated.

"Sure. If I take you to Seville, my job is done, and I get compensated for a few weeks of work. But, if you stay on with the army, you'll require protection and training, and I'm confident the General will give that job to me. I can drag that out for months."

"Oh." Remir nodded thoughtfully. "So, this has nothing to do with the fact that you were made a hostage when you were a kid?"

Davides felt like his legs had been swept out from under him: dizzy disorientation followed by a hard *smack* on the ground. "The official term is 'ward'," Davides said coolly, trying to mask his disconcertion. "Yes, I was also a ward of Seville. How did you know?"

Remir's dark eyes shone with mischief. "I didn't know for sure until just now. However," he added, leaning forward and crossing his arms on the table, "there's a frontier ballad about the Emir's raid on the Portuguese city of Coimbra—what was it—about ten years ago? Coimbra became a tributary of Seville, and the young son of Lord David was taken to Seville as collateral. Curious coincidence, I thought. Everyone calls you 'Davides', which, as I understand it, means 'son of David'. You're about the right age. And, you have a tendency to slip into what sounds like Portuguese when you get rattled."

"Do I?" Davides could think of a few choice words he'd like to use now.

"The song is mostly about the Emir's inspiring victory," Remir went on. "You're just a footnote."

"How appropriate," Davides murmured.

"I don't know. There's obviously more to your story, and I bet I would find it a lot more interesting than that frontier ballad."

Remir paused expectantly, but Davides sat in stubborn silence, studying the whorls on the plank table. How had this conversation become about him?

"I suppose I could always make something up," Remir drawled ominously. "For entertainment tonight, I mean. 'The Tale of Sisnando Davides: from Lord to Hapless Mercenary.' Think about it, Davides. Do you really want to leave that to my imagination?"

"Good God, no! Fine. I'll fill in some gaps for you, if you give me your word that you will leave my narrated exploits to bears and bandits. Deal?"

"Deal," Remir replied, with a triumphant smile.

Davides took a moment to organize his thoughts. "I was nine when I was taken to Seville. Once I adjusted, I had a good life. They treated me like a prince, educated me like a prince, gave me the best of everything. Most people even seemed willing to overlook my regrettable condition of being Christian. As long as the money kept rolling in.

"Three years ago, the Almoravids came up the coast to Figueira da Foz, then inland to Coimbra. They weren't interested in exacting tribute; they had more serious goals in mind, like conquest and conversion. They razed Coimbra and killed, well, everyone associated with the ruling of the city. Suddenly, in addition to being an orphan, I became worthless to the Emir. He was quite annoyed at the loss of tribute from Coimbra, but magnanimously decided not to sell me into slavery or execute me on the spot.

"That was probably due to General Haroun. The General wanted me to work for him, mostly as a messenger, sometimes as an interpreter. Lately, he's even had me acting as an envoy. And, since Seville's forces drove the Almoravids out of Coimbra last year, the General has been lobbying for the Emir to let me buy back my family's homestead. Which means that I do need money, lots and lots of it."

Remir frowned. "Shouldn't he just give your lands back to you? They belong to you, don't they?"

"They belong to whoever holds Coimbra, and right now, that's the Emir." Davides kept his voice impassive. He had accepted the situation a long time ago. It had been hard at first, when he had lost his family, his wealth, and his status in one fell swoop. But, with a little help from General Haroun, he had learned to make his own way in the world. And he had been genuinely pleased when Seville had won back Coimbra, not because he expected to be reinstated but because it had served as retribution against the Almoravids. The possibility of buying back his family's homestead had not entered his mind until recently, when the General had brought it up in the course of discussing this mission.

A mission you are putting in jeopardy.

Davides brushed the thought aside. "Let's not worry about me and Coimbra. We're talking about you. I can try to convince General Haroun that you're enthusiastic about the war, but a lot will depend on you. You'll have to follow my lead and say the right things."

At that moment, the outer door opened, and Sajid, Basir, and Hatim filed in. Spying Davides and Remir, they started across the room.

"Deal," said Remir under his breath.

Part 2 – I believe it's called collusion

The next morning, Sajid kept them on the Via Delapidata in order to recuperate lost time. During their infrequent breaks Remir evinced a budding interest in all things military, plying them with questions and putting on a convincing display of latent hostility towards Castile-León. He even broke through Sajid's stiff wall of reserve with his wide-eyed curiosity regarding the veteran's past campaigns. His inquiries continued that evening, after they had stopped in the town of Cáceres.

At the rate he was going, Davides thought wryly, Remir was in danger of actually learning something significant about politics and warfare.

Sunday morning, Davides rose early and found his way to the small church in the Christian Quarter. It was a squat, unadorned building laid out in the simple plan of a Latin cross. With its thick walls and small, high windows, the church looked more like a fortress than a place of worship. Inside, it had the dark, echoing quality of a cavern and, in like manner to a cave, had tons of rock blocking out the sights and sounds of the outer world. It was peaceful, and as he started down the nave, Davides caught the familiar aroma of incense laced with myrrh. Nostalgia, as comforting as a heavy cloak, wrapped around him, and he slid into one of the long, wooden benches near the back.

"*In nòmine Patris, et Filii, et Spiritus Sancti,*" chanted the priest.

"*Amen,*" he responded with the congregation, making the Sign of the Cross.

It had been a while since Davides had had the opportunity to attend Mass and even longer since he had confessed. He'd have to skip confession again—he wouldn't have known where to begin, and he certainly didn't have that kind of time—but he sat through Mass, listening with faint amusement as the parish priest intoned the Latin liturgies with a pronounced local accent.

"*Credo in unum Deum, Patrem omnipoténtum ...*"

As the Mass went on, Davides's thoughts turned inwards: he had some serious soul-searching to do. How had he gotten himself into such a predicament? Somewhere along the way, the dividing line between right and wrong had gotten blurry, and for the life of him, he didn't know which side of the line he was on anymore. He had offered—offered!—to mislead General Haroun. The man who had been his benefactor for the past three years. The man who had pulled strings and stepped on toes to get him this high profile and lucrative assignment. And, he was going to show the General his gratitude by lying to him? *Gratitude for what?* challenged the critical voice in his head. *For being made an accomplice to kidnapping?* Okay, he probably shouldn't have taken the job in the first place, but how could he have said 'no' to General Haroun?

"*... et ne nos indùcas in tentatiònem; sed libera nos a malo.*"

Besides, if he hadn't accepted the assignment, someone else would have. Remir and Amira would still be hostages, and he would only have succeeded in offending his patron. *And in the future, when the General wants you to murder someone, you can console yourself by saying 'if I don't do it, someone else will'.* The critical voice had a point: Davides felt like he was on the edge of a slippery slope. How far would he go, should he go, to keep the General's favor?

"Agnus Dei, qui tollis peccàta mundi; miserère nobis."

Davides had always considered General Haroun to be an honorable man, and he knew that the General had devised the current plan in an effort to avoid bloodshed. It wasn't exactly a diplomatic solution, but compared to some of the alternatives that had been presented, sequestering Remir and Amira was a relatively nonviolent way to co-opt Abdur Rahman's unwilling support. *What if something goes wrong, though, and General Haroun orders you to kill Remir? Where will your line between right and wrong be then?* He closed his eyes: in Hell, of course, along with his doomed soul.

"Ite, missa est."

Mass was over, and people were filing out of the church. Instead of following them, Davides went in search of a deacon. He needed to buy some candles to light for his family and pay for prayers to be said on their behalf. His own soul might be a lost cause, but at least he could help theirs get through Purgatory.

* * *

Davides and Remir didn't revisit their arrangement. There was nothing to discuss, since they had no plan, no specific goals, only the rather hazy objective of altering Remir's status as a helpless pawn. At least, that was Davides's objective. Who knew what might be swimming around in Remir's head.

The sun shone brightly as they continued their journey south, and its warmth quickly overcame the early morning chill. A light breeze pushed fat, lazy, cumulus clouds across an azure sky that spanned the rolling plains. Flocks of fluffy white sheep drifted across the grasslands, occasionally goaded or regrouped by vigilant, energetic dogs.

The sun had moved to midday when one of those sedate flocks of sheep on the horizon suddenly broke apart. Sajid drew up short, scanning the far rise that blocked their view of what lay beyond. Once stopped, they could hear and feel the growing tremor of hoof beats. Lots of hoof beats. The riders, thirty in all, crested the far rise and cantered down the slope towards them in a double column formation. A thin green banner, as long as the lance to which it was attached, bobbed and fluttered with the rolling gait of the standard bearer's horse. It drooped, nearly touching the ground, when the leader of the small cavalry unit called a halt.

The two groups eyed each other across the short distance that separated them. Odds were good that this was part of Seville's vanguard, sent ahead to scout the road, but since the Emir had never adopted the obvious heraldic devices popular with Christians, it was impossible to be sure. While their little group of five didn't constitute much of a direct threat, the fact that they were so well armed would be raising the scouts' suspicions. Sajid motioned for Davides and the others to wait while he went forward and conferred with their leader. The conversation was brief, and when Sajid returned, his usually dour countenance had brightened.

"The main army is camping at Alcuéscar, which is only another four miles or so from here," he reported.

It seemed that General Haroun's army was making good time. The mounted scouts continued on their way, and Sajid quickened their pace, anxious to reach the symbolic goal of Seville's lines. He probably figured that, once the army was between them and Salamanca, the most dangerous and unpredictable part of their assignment would be behind them.

As they neared the village of Alcuéscar, they stopped a moment to take in the panoramic view of Seville's military forces. The troop projections that Davides had heard back in Seville estimated a combined army of between seven and eight thousand, depending on the troops mustered at the last minute by less-than-enthusiastic supporters of the Emir. Judging from the hordes of soldiers teeming around Alcuéscar and swarming in every direction, they had come close to their mark. Brightly colored pavilion tents, representing the many captains and their corresponding companies, were being erected in a pattern that radiated out from the central command post like spokes on a wheel. In the far distance, the long lines of the supply train trickled towards the sprawling encampment.

Davides shot a quick look at Remir. In all likelihood, Remir's experience with 'war' was limited to what could best be described as skirmishes. On the frontier, fielding a force of a few hundred men was sufficient for most battles or for the defense of a city like Salamanca. This was a serious army, probably the largest that this region had seen for more than a century.

The sight of that vast field of soldiers, all primed for conquest, seemed to rouse the patriotic fervor of Sajid, Basir, and Hatim. Their expressions verged on exaltation.

They cantered ahead, oblivious or indifferent to Remir's reeling incredulity.

Instead of following them, Davides lifted his waterskin from the saddle's pommel, as if he were pausing for a drink. "You know, we could still just ride to Seville," he commented.

Remir, sitting like a stone on his horse, turned vacant eyes towards him.

"We could go on to Seville," Davides repeated. "You could spend the next year or so in bars, bathhouses, and brothels. If you've changed your mind, that is . . . or lost your nerve." Davides tipped the waterskin up and took a long drink, confident that the cheap dig would provoke some kind of reaction.

Remir did indeed react. Speaking in Portuguese, he articulated an obscenity that suggested precisely what Davides could do with himself. Caught in mid-swallow, Davides inhaled too fast, choked on water, and had to cough violently before he was able to breathe again.

"So I know a few useful phrases in Portuguese," Remir remarked. "Don't act so surprised."

"Useful for what?" Davides blinked tears out of his eyes. "Getting yourself into bar fights?"

Remir thought back for a moment. "Well, yes, now that you mention it, but also handy for making a point. I did make my point, didn't I? 'Cause, if you need me to elaborate …"

Torn between amusement and exasperation, Davides rolled his eyes, then started down the slope after Sajid. "You will be able to control that smart mouth of yours around the General, won't you?"

"Why? Doesn't the General like smart people?" Remir countered.

Oh, God, Davides thought helplessly. Maybe a dumbstruck Remir wouldn't have been so bad, after all.

They caught up with the others, who were navigating their way through a sea of men, mules, wagons, and tents. As a seasoned soldier, Sajid enjoyed a certain renown among the rank and file. He nodded out terse greetings along the way, not wanting to stop until they reached the central command post. Davides was known to a different echelon within the army: couriers, captains, and the General's cohorts. One young courier, whom Davides recognized but whose name escaped him, rode up and greeted him eagerly. Undeterred by Sajid's glower, he offered to take them directly to General Haroun, who (he informed them in confidence) was out arbitrating a dispute between the captains of Huelva and Utrera.

Although relatively inexperienced, the courier obviously had a nose for urgent intelligence. Davides's little group would be the first to report the outcome of the Emir's gambit in Salamanca, but the courier couldn't know that. Instead, he was extrapolating an important update based solely on the unexpected appearance of an injured and travel-worn Davides.

Sajid looked over at Davides, deferring the decision to him. The timing was bad, since the General was bound to be in a lousy mood after refereeing some petty argument. However, General Haroun was not a patient man, and rumor of their arrival would reach him soon. Davides nodded his assent, and the courier happily took the lead.

They could hear the General's stentorian voice from a distance as he upbraided the captains, lieutenants, and anyone else who might have had anything to do with the clash between companies. As they drew nearer, they saw a semi-circle of mounted men with crested helmets and *adarga* shields, the General's bodyguard. In their forefront, sitting high on his powerfully muscled warhorse while formerly stalwart men cringed before him, was General Haroun.

Davides's group had almost reached the outer ring of mounted bodyguards before anyone bothered to notice them. At a murmured word from his aide-de-camp, the General broke off his diatribe, and his sharp eyes swept over them, finally stopping on Davides. Much to the relief of the malefactors from Huelva and Utrera, General Haroun dismissed them and turned his full attention to the newcomers. Or, more precisely, to Davides. The General didn't give the others a second glance.

"What happened to you?" General Haroun shouted and beckoned him forward. "I expected you sooner. And, you're a man short. And, you look like hell."

"Yes, sir," Davides answered and maneuvered through the semi-circle of guards, close enough so he could lower his voice. "We ran into some bad luck."

The General snorted scornfully. "There is no such thing as luck. You know that! It is as God wills it to be."

"Yes, sir. Then, God willed unforeseen obstacles into our path," Davides amended.

The taut lines of General Haroun's face relaxed reluctantly. "And, I can't very well complain about God's will, can I? I suppose that means I'll have to hear you out first, before I criticize your response to those obstacles. Let's take a ride, shall we?" The General turned to his aide-de-camp. "Get Davides a horse that doesn't look like an overgrown gazelle hound. Then, take the boy to the central command post and wait for us there."

One of the bodyguards immediately offered Davides his horse: a spirited, steel grey charger with a billowing mane and tail. Davides smiled appreciatively and switched horses. He did sometimes miss the finer things in life.

Once the two of them had ridden out of idle earshot, General Haroun inquired, "Has he given you a lot of trouble, then?"

"You mean Remir? No, sir. He has demonstrated some finely honed taunting skills, but he hasn't caused any real trouble. And, everything went according to plan in Salamanca," Davides reassured him. He proceeded to recount their initial reception in the city, his night out with Remir, their early morning conference with Abdur Rahman and the Sevillian ambassador, and Amira's volatile reaction. Then, he reached the part of the debriefing where things had gone awry: the horse thieves, the violent storm, and the freak bear attack that had left Adi dead and Davides injured. Compared to Remir's portrayal of those events, his report lacked panache, but it satisfied the General.

"You had a rough couple of days," General Haroun acknowledged. "No more bizarre incidents after Ambroz?"

"No, sir," Davides replied with a short smile. "Nothing that slowed us down or tried to kill us, anyway." He paused, as if weighing the importance or relevance of another 'incident'. "I did have a rather curious conversation with Remir a couple of days ago. He expressed some frustration regarding his father."

"That's not 'curious' for someone his age, Davides, that's normal."

"Granted, but at the time we were discussing Abdur Rahman's policies with the counts of Castile-León." He stopped there, giving the General time to cogitate and draw his own conclusions.

General Haroun frowned. "I was under the impression that the boy had no interest in politics."

"As was I. Lately, though, he's been talking favorably about the Emir's goals, and he's quite knowledgeable for someone who's supposedly disinterested."

"Remir is in favor of war with the Castile-León?" General Haroun raised speculative eyebrows. "If he is as popular in Salamanca as you say, and he endorsed this war, do you think they would back him?"

Davides felt his heart leap in his chest. He didn't like where this was going. The General had arrived at the desired conclusion, but then had sailed right past it to a scenario in which they supplanted Abdur Rahman with Remir. "Would who back him, sir?" Davides asked, opting for obtuseness.

General Haroun scowled at him. "The guards! The townspeople! The other noble families!"

Davides shook his head. "I didn't see Remir interact with the other nobles, so I couldn't say. And, if *they* didn't back him, the rest would be irrelevant."

The General nodded grudgingly. "And, he has no military training. Or, does he?"

"No, sir, although he has a lot of natural talent. Just going to waste."

General Haroun paused, his shrewd eyes searching Davides's face. "Could he be playing us? Pretending to support an attack on Castile-León, but having an ulterior motive?"

"He's certainly capable of it," Davides replied, with feeling.

The General nodded and scanned an imaginary horizon, while he considered Davides's revelation. "Whether Remir is deceiving us or is genuinely supporting our aims, it sounds as if I should get to know him a little better. I want both of you to join me for supper tonight."

Davides relaxed. They were off to a good start, almost ideal, and he had managed to keep prevarication to a minimum.

"And, Davides," the General added, eyeing him critically, "have the Field Marshall get you and Remir some decent clothes — something that doesn't make you look like a couple of vagrants."

Ah, the finer things in life. "Right away, sir."

* * *

If Davides had hoped that Remir would exercise some restraint when they dined with the General and his staff, he was soon disillusioned. Before they even finished the soup, Remir had taken his impudence to the limits of their forbearance. But, just when Davides thought that Remir was doomed to languish in Seville, Remir began lacing his speech with the warlike sentiments he had cultivated on their ride from Ambroz. Both amazed and appalled, Davides watched in silence as Remir verbally presented an alternate version of himself: a rebellious son, callously ready to break outdated agreements with Castile-León, and more than eager to drive back the encroaching infidels.

It was quite a performance, and by the end of the meal, Remir had somehow persuaded General Haroun that it was in everyone's best interest if he be allowed to stay with the army. At least for a short time. As anticipated, the General gave over Remir's military training to Davides, with the additional charge that Davides keep their political asset out of mischief.

The latter task would almost certainly be more challenging than the former, Davides thought with good-humored cynicism. Nothing about Remir's new role required him to leave off needling those around him, all of whom owned sharp weapons and were inclined to use them. Even so, the new arrangement felt like a godsend.

The next morning, Davides broke the news to the other members of Remir's escort. For reasons quite different than Davides's own, they seemed content with the change of plans. Sajid and Basir gladly washed their hands of the two annoying, young nobles and rejoined the ranks of their old company. Hatim, on the other hand, volunteered to stay and help with Remir's training, since, in Hatim's words, Davides wasn't going to be good for much with that bum shoulder.

From what Davides had seen, Hatim didn't have a malicious bone in his body. His remark was therefore not intended as an affront. Davides looked at Hatim levelly while he suppressed a knee-jerk reflex to defend his honor. After all, Davides told himself, Hatim was just being sensible: Davides was wearing armor again, but he still couldn't use a shield, shoot a bow, or even tack up his own horse. It was unrealistic to think that he wouldn't need someone's help until his arm and shoulder were fully functional again. Swallowing his pride, Davides accepted

Hatim's offer as amiably as he could, and Hatim beamed innocently back at him.

The main army spent two days in Alcuéscar waiting for the Emir's politicians to smooth out the details of their passage through Cáceres. The lull in travel gave Davides, Remir, and Hatim the chance to spend a significant amount of time training, rather than squeezing it in at the beginning or end of the day.

At first, Remir acted as if he hardly knew how to grip a sword, but he caught on fast. Really fast. Too fast? Other people had to practice for months to learn the skills that Remir was picking up in two short days. Maybe his natural athleticism made all physical endeavors easy for him. Or, maybe Remir had had more martial instruction in Salamanca than he had let on. In either case, Davides found himself wondering, only half in jest, if improving Remir's ability to kill someone was such a good idea, after all.

On Wednesday, the army marched to Cáceres, and Davides, Remir, and Hatim went with it, retracing their steps northwards. They were riding with the forty-odd members of the General's retinue, blending with his bodyguards and personal retainers. When the rest of the army made camp outside the city walls, General Haroun beckoned them to accompany him and his retinue to a nearby villa belonging to a local ally.

Late afternoon found them cantering down a dusty two-track bordered by loosely-mortared, sandstone walls. Behind the low walls, freshly harvested fields of flax shimmered in the sunlight, and a distant herd of cattle grazed contentedly on expansive pastures. The main house and major outbuildings of the villa were enclosed by tall, stucco walls. At the moment, the perimeter's heavy wooden gates stood open, and a small army of servants and slaves hovered inside, waiting to attend them. They dismounted just outside the gates, leaving their horses and ancillary equipment with the servants, then entered the compound.

Their gracious host, Abu Haydar, came forward to greet them. Short of stature and broad of girth, he bowed and recited gushing expressions of hospitality, putting his entire villa at their disposal.

Glancing about, Davides noted that Abu Haydar's tastes leaned heavily towards the functional. The house looked like a giant mud brick, without curved lines or carvings to relieve its blocky frame. The wrought iron *rejas* protecting the windows could withstand an armed assault if the need arose, but they had no decorative merit to them. The central water feature was a simple stone well and water trough. And, the gardens — while offering an array of herbs and vegetables — did not include so much as a daisy for adornment.

Whatever Abu Haydar might have lacked in aesthetics, he more than made up for with his notion of an evening meal. A veritable feast, it must have cost their host a small fortune: shredded purple and yellow carrots in vinegar, rice with minced chestnuts, skewers of marinated beef, and a *turrón* of almonds and honey. Davides hadn't eaten that well since leaving Seville, and he was agreeably stuffed and sleepy by the time they were shown to their accommodations.

As it turned out, Davides, Remir, and Hatim were staying with some of the General's bodyguards in a large shed adjacent to the villa's brick oven. Normally, the shed was stocked with dry firewood, which was used to keep the oven at a steady temperature for baking bread. In

69

anticipation of their arrival, the firewood had been cleared out, and fresh straw pallets had been moved in. Thanks to the oven, the space inside was pleasantly warm and smelled constantly of freshly baked bread.

Given their recent experiences, being warm and full and lying on something soft were luxuries they didn't take for granted. Davides pulled off his boots and armor, then stretched out in the fluffy, flax straw. He drifted off almost immediately but was vaguely aware of the arrival of some of the off-duty bodyguards.

One of them nudged him with a foot. "Davides, the General wants to see you," he whispered.

Davides pried his eyes open. "Now?" he asked in a pained voice.

The bodyguard looked both amused and sympathetic. "What do you think?"

Davides groaned, turned out of bed, and pulled his boots back on. Then, he followed the bodyguard to a small room in the main house that served as Abu Haydar's office. Like everything else at the villa, it had gotten pressed into service for General Haroun, and its desk was now covered with a detailed map of Hispania. Oil lamps dimly lit the desk's surface, but much of the rest of the room was in heavy shadow.

The General began by asking about Remir's training. Although he nodded in the right places and interjected the occasional *good, good!*, Davides could tell that he was distracted. Obviously, a progress report was not the compelling reason for summoning him at such a late hour. Davides wrapped up his briefing and waited expectantly. He didn't have to wait long.

"While you're here, Davides, I'd like you to take a look at something that came in today, see if you can make heads or tails of it." General Haroun unfolded a large piece of parchment until it covered most of the map and placed weights down on the corners.

Curious, Davides moved an oil lamp closer and studied the text for a few moments.

"Can you read it?" General Haroun asked in a casual tone, but when Davides glanced up, he saw an eager light in the General's eye.

"It's in Greek," Davides answered noncommittally.

"You know Greek."

"A little, yes, but I mostly studied the philosophers. This is some kind of alchemical formulary." Davides tried to read it again, then shook his head. "Honestly, sir, I don't think I could understand it even if it were written in Arabic."

General Haroun didn't appear disappointed. Quite the contrary. "But, I bet you know people who could understand it," he said. "Tell me, do you still have that scientist friend in Toledo?"

Davides had a number of 'scientist friends' in Toledo, but there was only one whom General Haroun would have bothered to remember. "Yes, but Ishaq is an astronomer, not an alchemist."

"Right," the General agreed, not put off in the least. "You mentioned he was working on some kind of maritime astrolabe."

"Yes, sir," Davides replied, feeling now as if he were being led down some premeditated conversation.

General Haroun drummed his fingers on the parchment. "Davides, I have a proposition for you. I'd like you to go visit your friend Ishaq in Toledo, and let him know that we are interested in his astrolabe. That we'd like to acquire a few for a fleet being built in Huelva."

Davides frowned. There was no fleet in Huelva. Not to his knowledge, anyway.

"We'll pay him well," General Haroun continued. "Even invest in his research, if his progress was curtailed last spring. And, while you're in Toledo, maybe you could get this translated." He jabbed a finger at the parchment. "And explained. And understood. Discreetly."

Davides's mind scrambled to assimilate what the General had just said—and left unsaid. Like Seville, Toledo had a Muslim ruler, al-Mamun. Last spring, King Fernando of Castile-León had sent a large army to camp outside Toledo's gates, and had advised al-Mamun that the city was in need of his 'protection'. It was an increasingly common scheme, with peaceful, wealthy communities trying to avoid armed conflict by buying off aggressive neighbors. Ironically, the tribute paid by these peace-loving (or, at least, peace-desiring) regions funded armies exactly like the one under General Haroun's command.

Rather than face a protracted siege, al-Mamun had decided to contribute to King Fernando's war chest. With the promise of annual tribute, the big, bad army had gone away. But, it had undoubtedly left behind a few key administrators to oversee King Fernando's interests; and there were bound to be informants skulking about, looking to curry favor or to pick up their thirty pieces of silver.

General Haroun didn't need to spell it out: Davides would be acting as a spy, getting Castile-León's allies-by-association to make sense of something that was somehow important to Seville's war effort. And, he wanted Davides to do it by using his contacts in Toledo.

"A lot of people know me in Toledo," Davides reminded him, "and not all of them like me. Or you. Or Seville."

The General nodded. "That's why you front with the astrolabe. It's a perfectly legitimate reason to send you — especially you — to Toledo. Nosy people will have something to sink their teeth into, and they'll take that back to their master."

Or, they'll sink their teeth into me and take me back to their master.

"We'll also lay some false trails for you. They'll expect us to send this document to Seville or maybe Córdoba. They shouldn't be looking in Toledo. Still, it could be dangerous," General Haroun said with an arched smile, as if 'dangerous' were some kind of incentive in his book. "When King Fernando's people figure out what happened, they're going to want this back."

Back? Want it back?! Davides almost laughed out loud. "Sir, are you telling me that you want me to ride into hostile territory, leak misinformation about a nonexistent fleet in Huelva, and get a stolen document deciphered without the other side noticing?"

"That's it in a nutshell, yes." The jaunty smile faded, and the General sighed. "Davides, you have always done excellent work for me, and you've performed many valuable services for the Emir. Understand, then, that this is beyond a job or a service; this is on the level of a favor. You are the only one I trust to do this, or I wouldn't be asking it of you."

Hopelessly swayed by what he knew to be a verbal pat-on-the-head, Davides's misgivings faded into the background. "Okay," he heard himself say.

General Haroun gave him a tight-lipped smile and a nod of approbation. He re-folded the parchment, slipped it into a stiff envelope, and placed that in a set of worn saddlebags that sagged heavily in his grasp. "I'm going to send this with you now, so there's no odd exchange tomorrow in broad daylight. I've allotted enough gold, I think, to make a respectable bid for your friend's astrolabe; pay translators, alchemists, or whomever for the document; and allow you and Remir to live, not lavishly perhaps, but at least—"

"Remir?" Davides cut in, aghast.

The General showed mild surprise. "You haven't finished training him, have you?"

"No, sir, of course not, but—"

"And, I'm not ready for him to be back in Salamanca. This way, I don't have to be rude about it."

"But, sir ..." Davides trailed off. How could he explain that Remir was the last person he should take to Toledo on a covert mission? Remir gave new depth to the word 'sneaky', which would have been great if he had actually wanted Seville to win the war. As it was, though, Remir was more likely to use his craftiness against them.

General Haroun held up a placating hand. "Now, Davides, I know what you're thinking."

Davides blinked. He certainly hoped that wasn't the case.

"If King Fernando's moles figure out who Remir is, they'll try to get their hands on him and use him as reverse leverage against Abdur Rahman."

Yes, that could also be an issue.

"But, first they have to be looking for him, don't they?" the General said. "Odds are, they still don't know of our arrangement with Salamanca. Even if they do, they'll assume we're whisking the boy off to Seville, which means that Toledo might actually be safer for him than traveling south."

Right. Safer. Forget the part where Remir sabotages the mission and reveals Salamanca's situation to the enemy.

"On top of everything else," the General went on, oblivious to Davides's glazed expression, "I can't delegate Remir's custody to just anyone. These past few days have shown me something of his character. He's high-spirited. He'll run roughshod over those he doesn't respect — which means practically everybody but you. I'm not sure how you did it, but you developed a good rapport with him."

I believe it's called collusion.

"Any other reservations?" General Haroun asked, holding out the saddlebags.

"No, sir," Davides replied and accepted the bags, the gold, the document. The proposition.

* * *

When Davides stepped out into the crisp night air, his thoughts were ricocheting so fast that he couldn't keep track of them, much less sort them out. He had crossed about half the distance to the bread oven when an irregularity in the darkness near the outer wall made him shy back and reach for his sword.

His hand closed on nothing, and his heart skipped a beat as he remembered that his sword was lying next to his bed. He hadn't anticipated needing it.

"Wow, are you jumpy," a quiet voice observed from the shadows.

"*Pelo amor de Deus*, Remir!" Davides exclaimed harshly. "What are you doing here?"

"You brought me here," Remir replied, and coalesced out of the gloom. "Don't you remember?"

"I mean, why are you wandering around in the middle of the night . . . alone?" Davides looked around with mounting disbelief and outrage. "None of the bodyguards thought to stay with you?"

"They're not my bodyguards," Remir pointed out, disregarding the first question. "Besides, they were sleeping. They looked so comfortable, curled up in their little beds, I hated to disturb them." Remir's eyes fell on the saddlebags. An eyebrow went up. "Those look heavy."

"You have no idea," Davides muttered, and struck off towards the bread oven.

Remir didn't move, and after a few strides, Davides stopped. Remir had every right to be concerned by the late summons, since at this point, whatever affected Davides affected him as well. Davides glanced around, but the night was so dark that it was impossible to know if other ears were listening in. More to the point, he hadn't had a chance to decide what he could tell Remir and what, if anything, he could keep concealed.

"General Haroun wants us to spend some time on mounted combat," he said finally, choosing his words with care. "Tomorrow we'll find a spot, somewhere off the road, and practice for awhile."

Remir moved close enough to make eye contact, and a ghost of the familiar smirk returned to his face. "Tomorrow should be interesting. Is Hatim practicing with us? Sajid? Basir?"

"Just Hatim." Davides thought he noticed Remir's tension go down another notch. "Now, if you don't mind,

I'd like to go to bed." *I have some serious lying-awake-all-night to do.*

* * *

The horses were puffing and lathered with sweat before Davides called a breather. Charging at targets, weaving through poles, making sudden starts and stops, and jumping random obstacles had taken a heavy toll on their mounts. The drills had taxed the riders, too, physically and mentally. As with many forms of combat training, one side of the body had to know how to attack with a weapon while the other side defended with a shield. When fighting on horseback, the rider also had to guide a spirited and unpredictable animal through irregular terrain using primarily his seat and legs. Bringing all of those elements together required sharp focus and superb body control. When a rider's concentration got fuzzy, he usually wound up on the ground, looking up at the sky, wondering what had just happened.

Davides recalled his own initiation into cavalry training. Real cavalry training. Not the pretty horsemanship he had learned when he was still too valuable of a commodity to risk on the battlefield. He had spent the entire morning in the blistering, Andalusian sun, going through several mounts in the process. By the end, he had been bruised and battered by numerous falls, the inside of his knees had been rubbed raw by the stirrup leathers, and heretofore unknown muscles had been sore beyond comprehension. Davides had since dedicated an enormous amount of effort to becoming an accomplished mounted soldier.

His commitment was not unique; it was standard. Everyone aspiring to that occupation had to devote a similar amount of time and energy to their training. Everyone except Hatim and Remir.

From what Davides had heard, Hatim had progressed from humble stable boy to upwardly mobile man-at-arms by virtue of his preternatural link with the equine species. He possessed a God-given gift that not even he could explain. During their drills, Hatim's newly assigned warhorse was always right where Hatim needed her to be, which was a definite bonus when it came to mounted combat. He still had a lot to learn about offensive and defensive maneuvers, but he made the part about controlling the animal look effortless.

Remir was all about less effort, but much to his frustration, he did not share Hatim's facility with horses. He was riding a black mare with a crooked white stripe down her forehead, and he affectionately dubbed her the "Harpy from Hell" since she went faster when he wanted to slow down, swerved when he needed to go straight, and slid to a stop when he expected her to jump. He quickly learned to compensate for the miscues with his extraordinary balance and reflexes, and the few times that the Harpy did manage to unseat him, he demonstrated an uncanny ability to land on his feet.

A useful skill, always landing on your feet.

Davides pulled himself out of his reflections and looked around. The last supply wagons were wobbling their way north. Remir was stretched out in the tall grass, soaking up sun and well on his way to falling asleep. Less nonchalant, Hatim sat with his arms wrapped around his knees, glancing occasionally at Davides in anticipation of new instructions. The bulging saddlebags lay nearby, crushing the grass in a rough circle.

"We'll wait a bit longer before readying the horses," Davides told Hatim. "I need to discuss something with you and Remir first."

"Here we go," Remir murmured from his prone position, eyes still closed.

Davides ignored him and kept his attention on Hatim. "I have a new assignment—an additional assignment, I should say—and you two are stuck with me for the duration. General Haroun needs me to take a document to Toledo and get it translated." Out of the corner of his eye, Davides saw Remir slowly ease himself up on one elbow. "I don't know where the document came from, but I got the strong impression that other people might be searching for it, so it's not something we want to talk about, not amongst ourselves nor with anyone else."

Hatim bordered on guileless, which was the reason Davides had wanted to lay that much out clearly. When it came to Remir . . . well, Davides hoped he wasn't outsmarting himself. The Greek text should have been the most secret part of their mission, but while ruminating last night, he had arrived at two basic conclusions: first, that Remir would automatically assume that he was withholding the real reason for their trip to Toledo; and second, that Remir would snoop through the saddlebags at some point and find the damned thing anyway. When they reached Toledo, Davides's pursuit of the astrolabe would then appear to be the real reason they were there, and the document should fade into the background. It was a bit convoluted, but then again, so was Remir.

"Toledo?" Hatim asked with a concerned wrinkle of his brow. "Isn't there an army there, as in, not one of ours?"

Davides gave a short, humorless laugh. "No, not anymore, but that army will have left behind people who aren't exactly friendly towards Seville. We'll have to be cautious."

"I don't understand," Remir broke in, as curiosity overcame languor. "Why take the risk of going to Toledo?"

"As opposed to heading for Seville? Well, for one thing, General Haroun thinks the roads south will be watched, which makes traveling east less hazardous by comparison. Second, Toledo probably has the best translators in Hispania. Third, I happen to know some of those scholars personally because I studied in Toledo for a time. I know the city, and I know the right people to get the translation done."

"Wait." Remir sat up, staring at him in disbelief. "People *know* you in Toledo? Are these people aware that you work for General Haroun?"

"Yes," Davides said, and stifled his own reservations on the matter. "The General sent me there with a message for al-Mamun last spring."

"In other words, countless people in Toledo know who and what you are. You're going to be about as inconspicuous as a Pict in a parade!" Remir exclaimed.

A disturbing visual flashed through Davides's mind of a naked, tattooed man marching through Toledo's Bisagra Gate. With an effort he blocked it out. "I'm sure they'll keep an eye on me, but it would take a lot of gall for someone to lay hands on me. Seville isn't officially at war with Castile-León." *Not yet, anyway.*

Remir snorted. "From what I've heard, King Fernando has plenty of gall, and then some." He paused for a moment, debating something. Then, in a strangely hesitant tone, he asked, "Davides, is it possible that the General is setting you up? Deliberately using you as bait?"

Hatim gaped at Remir as if he had just committed some kind of sacrilege, but it was a logical question, one that had crossed Davides's mind the night before. General Haroun had said that he would lay false trails to Córdoba and Seville, but what if he had assured the other couriers of the same thing, throwing Toledo into the mix, so that none of them knew who was carrying the real text? That would be the smart thing to do. Nevertheless, Davides had good reason to believe that his mission was the genuine one.

"It's possible, but not likely," Davides responded. "Even though General Haroun would have no qualms about using me as bait, something tells me that he wouldn't stick *you* on a hook, Remir. And, he's the one who told me to take you with me. It sure as hell wasn't my idea."

Remir raised eyebrows at his last statement. "Gee," he drawled with searing sarcasm, "I am so sorry to be complicating your life."

"Don't be," Davides retorted. "I just assume I'm doing penance for past sins."

That prospect seemed to revive Remir's sense of humor. The corners of his mouth twitched. "In that case, I guess you'll be stuck with me for quite a while."

"But why?" Hatim burst out. Then, abashed, he clarified, "Not 'why are you stuck with Remir', but why did the General tell you to take Remir along?"

81

Davides had prepared himself for the question, so he was able to answer matter-of-factly. "Because General Haroun doesn't want Remir back in Salamanca yet. Even after the document is translated, we're supposed to wait in Toledo until he sends for us. If we feel like either the document or Remir is in danger, we fall back to Ávila."

"Why would I be in any particular danger?" Remir inquired with a puzzled frown. "You're the one with the giant bull's-eye painted on your back."

Davides gave him a long look. "Because that bull's-eye could transfer to you if King Fernando's agents were to figure out who you are, what your strategic relevance is with regards to the upcoming war, and just how much that might be worth."

Remir quickly put two and two, three and three, and four and four together. "They would try to use me the same way that Seville is," he mused aloud. "My father would be forced to make a choice."

Only they all knew there was no real choice involved: Abdur Rahman would have to save Remir, his male heir, over Amira.

"Listen, Remir. Given the distances involved, odds are that Castile-León still hasn't figured out what's going on in Salamanca." A peculiar expression flitted across Remir's face, not exactly one of relief; he was taking the whole 'reverse leverage' concept harder than Davides had anticipated. "Even if we've grossly underestimated them, and they do have information about your ... um, situation, Toledo is the last place they will expect you to turn up. Again, they'll assume that you're being taken south."

"And, that you're a prisoner," Hatim chimed in. "Not riding with us of your own free will."

Davides didn't trust himself to speak. His mind was weaving crazily back and forth between the inherent flaw in Hatim's observation and its paradoxical truths.

Remir, on the other hand, directed an approving nod at Hatim and said solemnly, "You are absolutely right, Hatim. Seeing me with you two, no one would guess that I'm some kind of prisoner." He uprooted a tuft of grass, lobbed it into the air, and watched as it plummeted to the ground a little ways distant. "Still, just to be on the safe side, maybe I should start going by a different name."

"'Remir' is a bit unusual," Davides agreed, happy to move away from the whole 'free will' topic, "although I've heard variations: Arimir, Ramiro, ..."

Remir brightened suddenly. "Now, there's an idea."

Coming from Remir, those words inspired a certain level of apprehension. Davides braced himself.

"I could be Ramiro," Remir continued, "a cousin of yours who is interested in studying in Toledo. You could be showing me around, introducing me to people. It would be a great cover, especially if I pretended to be Christian, like you."

"What? No!" Davides said.

"Why not? I can act like a Christian." Remir shrugged. "What do I really need besides a Latin cross, an overdeveloped sense of guilt, and a martyr complex?"

Flabbergasted, Davides fumbled for words. "There are practices. Stuff you do and don't do. Prayers you recite."

"*Pater noster, qui es in caelis, sanctificetur nomen tuum.* You mean like that one? I have Christian friends, Davides, and I've even been to Mass a few times. I just don't do the confession and communion parts." He smiled wickedly. "Something tells me you don't do them either."

"That's beside the point," Davides began, between gritted teeth.

"Not really," Remir interrupted, serious once more. "It keeps us from being separated. This way, we go the same places, do the same things, at the same time. C'mon, don't look at me like that. It's not as if I'm converting in my heart and soul; I'm just playing a part for this trip to Toledo. God will understand."

"It's not God I'm worried about! I have more earthly concerns, like what your father or General Haroun would do to me if they found out that I had you posing as an 'infidel'."

Remir's expression reflected a mixture of pity and amusement. "Face it, Davides: my father can't be any more angry with you than he is already, considering you helped abduct his only son. As for General Haroun, he's the one who initiated a cloak-and-dagger operation, for which disguises are just a logical precaution." With that, Remir cast an appraising eye in Hatim's direction.

"Oh, no!" Hatim protested. "I can't pass as Christian. All I know about them is that they eat pork, get drunk a lot, and go to temple on Sunday instead of Friday."

Remir let out a hoot of laughter, and Davides glared half-heartedly at both of them. He was still pondering the pro's and con's of Remir's original idea. Laying aside his initial shock—and his probable evisceration by the General—Davides had to admit that playing a Christian cousin of his would make for a good cover and that Remir could almost certainly pull it off. All in all, he decided, the benefits of the disguise outweighed the risks.

Hatim's cover was an entirely different matter, but he had already given it some thought, before ever requesting that the young soldier accompany them. "Relax, Hatim. You don't need to resort to anything so drastic. I was thinking that it would be pretty easy for you to pass as Remir's—"

"Ramiro's," Remir corrected.

"Fine. As *Ramiro's* servant. Anyway, you already take care of the horses. Just carry our equipment and throw in a few 'yes, sirs', and no one will look twice at you. That's good for you because it's an uncomplicated role, and you don't have to change your name; and it's good for us because you'll be able to watch our backs."

Hatim nodded eagerly, and Davides smothered a smile. He had never seen anyone so happy to be relegated to servitude.

Davides stood up and brushed at the dirt and dried grass clinging to his pants. "We should head out. There's a fair-to-middling sized town about thirty miles east of here. Considering we have no equipment or provisions for traveling, it behooves us to get there before nightfall."

* * *

As the crow flies, Toledo wasn't that far from Cáceres, but a substantial natural barrier lay squarely in their path: the Montes de Toledo. They weren't the tallest mountains in the peninsula; in fact, Davides had always thought they looked kind of old and tired. Nonetheless, their lack of navigable passes or convenient plateaus forced travelers to move and camp at a constant forty degree pitch. It got tiresome, so much so that armies and merchant caravans generally considered it easier to go around.

Having spent the better part of his life among the comforts of one metropolis or another, Davides wasn't about to argue with conventional wisdom on the matter. The night before, he had used the General's maps to plot a course that, while slightly roundabout, avoided crossing the mountain range, camping under the stars, or wandering aimlessly through the wilderness. Roads and inns, all the way. He hoped.

While they rode, they discussed their cover story in a little more detail. Davides had to go as himself. If he assumed a disguise, and someone saw through it, they would *know* he was up to something, instead of just suspecting it. To keep things as simple as possible, they decided that Hatim had only been in Ramiro's service for a few weeks, which would excuse any inconsistencies or gaps in knowledge between master and servant. After further discussion, they determined that Ramiro should be Davides's second cousin: the grandson of Davides's mother's aunt. Such a kinship ought to confound anyone who bothered to investigate.

They spent Thursday night in Trujillo, a town whose economy depended on the production of cheeses: sheep's milk cheese, goat's milk cheese, cow's milk cheese, and mixtures of any of the above. Apparently, the cheese business was booming, since the local landowners were erecting a large, austere fortification on the hill that overlooked the town proper: a place of refuge for the townspeople (and the aforementioned sheep, goats, and cows) the next time an indiscriminate army showed up on their doorstep.

In the morning, Hatim went to the mosque for prayer services, while Davides and Remir asked around and found a placid mule for sale. They had decided that if Hatim's cover was going to be remotely credible, they needed to downgrade his steed. Servants, even ones with wealthy, indulgent masters, didn't ride chargers. From the standpoint of their cover, an aspiring student and his guide shouldn't have been astride warhorses, either; but, Davides was counting on Seville's reputation for flamboyance to explain away the powerful, majestic bearing of their mounts.

From Trujillo they followed a well-traveled road north to the wide, westward-flowing Tagus River. The Tagus made a great landmark, since it cut through most of Hispania, dividing the peninsula into northern and southern halves. If you were trying to find Toledo, you could just follow the river east, and eventually you would bump into the city.

This time of year, clumps of white and purple heather dotted the river's long, sloping, green banks, creating an enchanting, rippling effect when the wind blew. Looking down at the river, they saw a small, single-sailed vessel using the light breeze to tack its way methodically upstream.

They followed the road east, keeping roughly parallel with the river. Soon, the geography changed from buff-colored stratum to outcroppings of mottled grey granite. The ever-present holm oaks now mingled with taller cork oaks. Some of the latter showed evidence of cork harvesting: the cortex of the lower trunks had been neatly stripped away, revealing their russet brown interior.

They stopped for the night at a drafty, overpriced inn on the banks of the Tagus. The shrewd innkeeper had situated his establishment where the main road on the south bank ended at the river. Most travelers would spend the night before fording the Tagus or being ferried across. Then, they would pick up the road on the far bank and continue northeast to Talavera, the largest town in the vicinity.

Despite the exorbitant rate, the inn was nearly full when they arrived. Davides made a quick scan of their fellow lodgers, who were mostly merchants and teamsters transporting goods to Talavera. A couple of the merchants had brought men-at-arms with them for protection, an indication that they were dealing in more expensive items, like spices, wine, or textiles. There did not appear to be anyone of Davides and Remir's social status, which meant they could keep to themselves without drawing attention.

Davides must have forgotten that he was traveling with Remir, for whom an inn was merely another name for a tavern that stayed open all night. In the past, the fact that it was a Friday night might have restrained Remir. Now, embracing his new role and religion, he immediately called for ale and began mingling with the other guests.

One merchant had a crudely made *alquerque* board, just a round of unfinished wood with deeply etched lines marking the possible moves, and light and dark pebbles for markers. Bright-eyed, Remir watched the end of one game, bought the loser a drink, and challenged the winner to another match. With a typical nobleman's bias, Davides preferred chess, and he had always considered *alquerque* one of the lesser strategy games. Under Remir's tutelage, however, he quickly discovered that *alquerque* — when combined with copious amounts of ale — took on intriguing degrees of complexity.

* * *

Davides didn't know how long he had slept when it finally filtered through his overly tired, slightly intoxicated brain that he was in a room full of strangers and didn't have a clue where the saddlebags were. He awoke with a start. His hand shot out, fumbling blindly, and made contact with the thick, well-oiled leather of the bags, under which he could feel the dead weight of coinage. That only provided a small measure of reassurance. Intent upon checking inside, he sat up, but as he did so, his chest felt oddly constrained. He padded the front of his shirt, then reached inside. Thoroughly bemused, he pulled out the document — or, at least, the rigid envelope that was supposed to contain the folded piece of parchment.

For a long moment, he just stared at it. Try as he might, he could not recall taking the precaution of hiding the envelope on his person. He *should* have thought of doing so, but he didn't think he had. Still fearing the worst, he peered inside: there was the Greek text, safe and sound.

He glanced around. It seemed like everyone else who had bedded down in the spacious common room was fast asleep, including Remir and Hatim. From the dim, grey light penetrating the cracks in the shutters, he gathered that it was still early morning. No clanking of pots from the kitchen; no neighing of horses or braying of mules, anxious for breakfast.

He slid the envelope back into his shirt and laid down again, closing his eyes and pressing the heels of his hands into his aching forehead. He must have drunk more ale than he had realized. How could he have been so careless? Curse Remir's infectious, happy-go-lucky attitude! Although, how happy-go-lucky was it, really, if Remir was the one who had hidden the envelope on him? And, who else could have or would have? Not Hatim. If Hatim had been concerned about the security of the saddlebags, he would have roused Davides or taken it upon himself to guard them.

Such cheery thoughts kept him awake until the rest of the inn started to stir. It turned out that it was not so early, after all. The chill, morning air had created a dense fog that rolled off the Tagus and suffused the inn with a false, pre-dawn gloom. The other travelers were content to have a slow morning, since they would wait until the sun burned through the thick haze before attempting to cross the river. Unlike the merchants and teamsters, Davides was in something of a hurry and had no intention of crossing the Tagus.

By the time they got underway, the fog was beginning to lift, but occasionally, almost impenetrable pockets obscured the ground beneath them, making forward progress a nerve-racking act of faith. Hatim and his surefooted mule took the lead, following what was little more than a deer trail along the south bank. Davides trailed behind. He knew he needed to bring up the document at some point, but he had not yet figured out how to go about it without sounding like a complete idiot. He was still mulling over possibilities when Remir slowed his mare so that the two of them were riding abreast of each other.

In a voice so soft it barely carried above the creaking of their saddles, Remir said, "Thanks for giving me a chance to look over that stuff last night."

Had Remir really just thanked him for drinking too much and leaving the all-important document unguarded? Davides started to face him, an indignant response ready on his lips, but a low-hanging branch loomed out of the fog, and he had to bend over his horse's neck to avoid being scraped out of the saddle. By the time Davides straightened, he had had a chance to reconsider his reaction. In essence, Remir was offering him a little pact: Davides didn't have to admit his own blunder, and Remir sidestepped any reproaches for his actions.

"Sure, no problem," Davides replied sourly. "Did it make any sense to you?"

Remir chuckled and shook his head. "I couldn't even tell if I was holding it right-side-up." He loosened the reins and let the Harpy retake her spot, single file between Hatim and Davides's mounts.

Mystery solved. Except for the part that explained how Remir had put the envelope inside his shirt without waking him. Davides may have been more groggy than normal last night, but he hadn't been falling-down-drunk. Somehow, he didn't find it comforting to know that Remir was capable of placing something on him — or lifting something off him — without his noticing.

They traversed a rugged, lonely stretch, splashing through a number of creeks that fed into the Tagus. Around midday, the sun finally cleared away the last of the mist, and they were able to pick up their speed. Eventually, they veered southeast, keeping the Montes de Toledo on their right shoulder in order to dip slightly south of Toledo. The river would have led them right to the city, but Davides wanted to create the illusion that they were approaching from the direction of Seville instead of from the west.

He had been hoping they could reach Sonseca, a village with which he was familiar that lay about twelve miles south of Toledo. However, by the time they were far enough south to turn due east, dusk was nearly upon them. They would have to settle for whatever inn or way station they happened across next.

* * *

The village wasn't exactly a shining example of civilization, but it was the closest to it that they had seen for some time. The scattering of mudbrick dwellings suggested a farming community of a couple hundred residents. The only stone structures were a crumbling church and a rectangular building with a high, peaked roof. A few other businesses were huddled close by, but several of them appeared abandoned: windows and doorways yawned open, last season's thatched roofs had rotted, nothing remained to reveal the trade or wares that had once given them purpose.

The town was quiet. Not so much as a stray dog ventured forth to bark at them as they rode in. Given that it was harvest season, it was likely that all the able-bodied townspeople were out working in the fields. For lack of anything better, Davides headed for a split-rail fence behind the large stone building, hoping the corral might serve as a place to keep their horses while they worked out where to spend the night.

From the corner of the fenced-in lot, a couple of black and tan dairy goats stared at them suspiciously with their eerie, yellow eyes. The goats were the only sign of life until a boy of perhaps twelve years appeared from the barn. He greeted them—somewhat breathlessly—in a colloquial Arabic mixed with Castilian that made it sound like he had mush in his mouth.

"We were hoping to find lodging for the night," Davides replied in the Castilian he had picked up while living in Toledo. He didn't want to alarm the boy by sounding like an exotic foreigner.

"We take lodgers. My grandmother is inside," the youth said, nodding towards the nearby stone structure. "She can get you supper and beds for the night. I can take your animals."

Hatim looked at the boy dubiously and in one easy motion hopped off his mule. "I'll just give him a hand with the horses, sir."

The youth's eyes fell, and he shrugged. "As you wish."

Somewhat amused by Hatim's protective nature regarding their animals, Davides swung down and handed the reins over to him. He shouldered the saddlebags but, in keeping with their new roles in life, left the rest of their equipment for Hatim to fetch in. There wasn't much. Their shields, the bow, and a few odds and ends they had picked up in Trujillo.

The pale grey building had seen better days. Ivy grew up the sides, slowly ripping out bits of mortar with its sticky fingers. For some reason, the usual, wrought iron *rejas* had been removed from the windows, and now thickly woven blinds were all that shielded the interior. Davides and Remir circled around to the front, where a weathered door stood partially ajar in the center of the building's façade. Raised flowerbeds, which now displayed only a confused mixture of herbs and weeds, flanked the entrance on either side.

The heavy door opened into a narrow corridor. Despite a thick layer of grime, they could feel the cold solidity of paving tiles beneath their feet. The stucco of the interior walls was cracking and flaking, allowing dull mudbrick patches to show through. The corridor opened into a sizeable room in which the ceiling went all the way to the peaked roof. A few solid, square tables were set up with a motley assortment of chairs and stools placed around them. To their right, an open staircase led up to a loft, which overlooked the common room and served as the ceiling for the corridor they had just traversed and the rooms on either side of it.

"One moment!" called a high-pitched voice from the closed area to the left of the corridor. Perhaps the kitchen, since the fireplace in the common room didn't appear to be set up for cooking.

Davides and Remir sat down at the nearest table. They pulled a couple more chairs close to use as footstools and put their legs up.

The woman who finally bustled into the room had dark hair streaked with grey, which poked out from beneath a scarf of homespun cloth. Deep lines crinkled the corners of her hazel eyes and bracketed a tight-lipped smile. As she put two chipped, earthenware cups down, her hands shook, and water sloshed onto the table. She dabbed at it absently with her apron. "Clumsy me! I'm so sorry." She spoke in the same odd dialect of Arabic crossed with Castilian as the boy had. "The water is fresh and sweet. We have an artesian well here. Of course, we have other drinks, too. How 'bout some ale?"

Davides made a face, and Remir grinned. "Oh, dear!" she exclaimed. "I meant no offense! I thought . . . that is, I took you for—"

"No offense taken," Davides said. "But, I doubt we'll be drinking any kind of alcohol tonight."

Her voice dropped to nearly a whisper. "I'll get you some cider, then. Just pressed today."

Davides blinked at her in confusion. "Okay," he replied, in a similarly soft voice. "We'll need room and board for three."

"Well!" she said, her voice suddenly loud and carrying. "I don't understand you big city types, always in such a rush. The best I can do is maybe fry up some eggs and onions. If you were at least staying the night, I could roast a nice, fat hen for you."

She was staring at them intently. Davides stared back, utterly befuddled. Was the woman senile? Was he not speaking the right language? Did the local water give you some kind of mental disorder?

"Fried eggs would be fine," Remir assured her, before Davides could formulate an adequate response to her bizarre prattle.

Her hazel eyes turned watery. She ducked her head and scurried off from whence she came.

"What was that?" Davides asked.

"I think she's scared and wants us gone," Remir answered, similarly perplexed. He cast about the room, as if searching the nooks and crannies for clues. "I don't usually have that effect on women."

"It can't be us. Why –"

Booted feet thumped down the corridor, and a burly man strode into the room, wearing a studded leather cuirass and carrying a two-handed battle axe. Behind him, three more men filtered in, all bearing swords and shields.

"Good evening, friends," their leader began, speaking Castilian with an accent Davides didn't recognize. "My name's Jahwar; I'm the constable here. You are welcome to stay the night, but I want to make it clear we are a peaceable community. We have laws about folks carrying weapons. While you're here, we'll keep your swords and any bows you might have. They'll be returned to you when you leave, of course."

They had to be joking. In any large city like Toledo, it was common courtesy for nobles and soldiers not to walk around armored and armed to the teeth. One might scare the civilians. Or try to overthrow the government. But here, in the middle of nowhere? A mere commoner had no right to ask for their weapons, even if he was the constable. Come to think of it, why did a community this size need four peacekeepers, let alone ones who carried anything more impressive than a heavy stick?

Davides and Remir stayed seated: Remir, plucking at a loose string on his shirt, as if that were more interesting than the situation at hand; Davides, inspecting the four men and trying to figure out what was really going on. The constable had the look and swagger of a bully, from his outthrust jaw to his puffed-up stance. Of the three deputies, one had small, squinty eyes that darted from Remir to him and back again, reminding Davides of a rat which had become entirely too bold. The second was a lanky fellow who instinctively flexed his shield arm when he felt Davides's eyes on him. The third deputy, a young man with a shock of auburn hair, avoided his gaze and shifted his feet uneasily.

Not only were these men not joking, but they obviously had other things on their minds besides 'peacekeeping'.

Irritation and contempt brimmed over Davides's initial incredulity. "Don't be absurd," he responded, not bothering to hide his sneer.

The constable's brow darkened, and he dropped any pretense of politeness. "We'll have those weapons. Now."

Before anyone else could move, Remir toppled his footstool into the constable's path and hopped nimbly onto the tabletop. He took two running steps and launched himself towards the loft. His chest and elbows hit the edge, which gave him enough purchase to swing a leg up and lever himself onto the second story.

Davides took advantage of the general astonishment to kick his own chair back out of the way and draw his sword. He was a bit surprised by Remir's sudden departure, but mostly relieved that he wouldn't have to protect Remir while fighting these yokels. He pivoted enough to put his back against the wall that Remir had just scaled. With the table in front of him, only two opponents could effectively attack him at once. Unless one of them had the common sense to heave the table aside.

The constable remained where he was, blocking the way out. He sent the first two men around to flank Davides and ordered the third deputy, who was looking longingly at the exit, to take the stairs to the loft.

For Davides, what happened next was a lot like a training exercise — except with considerably more blood. He knocked aside the first roundhouse swing from the constable but directed his own attack at the overly eager rat-man, who had already circled the table. He cut across the deputy's unprotected right leg. When the man cringed and let his shield fall, Davides slashed at the exposed neck. Before the deputy even hit the floor, Davides had brought his sword back across his body to block another attack from the battle axe.

The second deputy stepped up, but had to straddle the form of his fallen comrade to do so. Sensing he was off-balance, Davides used a backhanded blow to sweep the man's feet. For a brief moment, the long arms and legs flailed like a crazed marionette, after which he fell heavily atop his shield arm. In anticipation of the constable's next attack, Davides sidestepped right into the tangle of arms and legs on the floor. And none too soon: the edge of the axe skittered across his mail hauberk. At the same time, the gangly man on the floor tried to twist his body enough to strike at Davides's leg, but his lifted sword arm gave Davides a clear shot through the open armpit and into the chest cavity.

In retrospect, that thrust might have been a mistake. A jet of blood sprayed into Davides's eyes, blinding him. He jerked back, holding his sword in front of him defensively and swiping an already blood-soaked sleeve ineffectually across bleary eyes.

Before the constable could exploit his advantage, however, a limp body tumbled down from the loft and slammed into him. The shock of having a body fall on him only slowed him for a moment, but that was time enough for Davides's vision to clear. Davides spared a brief glance at the body to make sure it wasn't Remir's, then landed a brutal blow to the constable's right arm.

That should have been the end of the fight. After losing three men and having an arm nearly severed, a rational person would have surrendered or fled. Instead, his stalwart opponent redoubled his attacks. Davides gave ground to a rapid succession of irate slices, mindful of the fallen bodies and slippery paving stones all around him. Flagging quickly, the constable used his not inconsiderable weight as impetus to attack again. Davides ducked the wild swing and drove his sword deeply into the muscle of the man's inner thigh. More blood. Lots more blood. And, the constable crumpled to the floor.

Davides drew back a few paces to catch his breath and scan the room. What he spied first made him look twice. The red-headed deputy was still standing on the bottom step of the staircase, transfixed by something in the loft. Davides had assumed that he was the one who had been tossed down on top of the constable. He followed the man's wide-eyed stare up the flight of steps and discovered Remir, crouched low, with a loaded crossbow leveled at the alleged peacekeeper.

"I don't really know how to use one of these," Remir said. "Tell me, do I just point and shoot?"

"*Nossa!*" Davides exclaimed in disbelief. "They had a crossbowman planted in the loft?"

Remir quirked a smile, but kept his eyes on the deputy. "Yeah. From the way you were acting, I didn't think you'd noticed him."

Davides shook his head and turned back to the man with the mop of auburn hair. "Drop your sword," he suggested curtly. "Unless you're planning on using it."

The deputy transferred his horrified gaze from Remir to Davides. An instant later his weapon clattered to the ground, followed closely by his shield.

Without obstructing Remir's line of sight, Davides used a foot to slide the sword far out of reach. "Kneel and stay put," he ordered.

The red-head closed his eyes, hunched his shoulders and dropped to his knees. Keeping one eye on their captive, Davides stepped back to the area by the table to check for survivors.

In the meantime, Remir stood up and came about halfway down the steps. After surveying the room, he muttered, as if to himself, "I guess now I know why they sent you."

"What?" Davides asked. The crossbowman from the loft was still alive, but not conscious. The others all appeared to be dead.

"You're quite good, aren't you?"

Something in Remir's voice made Davides stop and look up. The words themselves might have been a compliment, but the way he had said them sounded more like a reprimand. He wasn't sure how to respond. Being skilled with a sword really didn't seem like the sort of thing he should have to apologize for. It was then that a corollary thought came to his mind, and sheer annoyance overrode everything else. "I've been training you for a week, and *this* is the first you've noticed?" Davides demanded.

Remir spread his arms wide to indicate the carnage in the room. "Well, you obviously were holding back! Besides," he added, his voice sounding defensive, "half the time I was sparring with Hatim."

They both froze, struck simultaneously with the same alarming thought. Hatim should have heard the sounds of the fight. Which meant that he should have been there by now.

"Go on. I've got this," Remir said, with a nod toward the cowed deputy.

In a few quick strides, Davides reached the back wall of the inn. He ripped down the heavy blind from the window. Fading sunlight slanted in, but that didn't obscure his view of the corral. The horses and mule were nowhere to be seen. Instead, several crossbowmen lingered in a group while another searched a motionless body on the ground. Hatim.

Seeing the blind come down, the men started in surprise and then hastened to bring their weapons to bear.

With a shout of warning to Remir, Davides stooped beneath the window ledge as a volley of bolts sped towards him. He felt one skim the top of his head. The others bit into the stone wall, sending a spray of chips and mortar through the open window.

Crossbows take a while to reload. If those men had been well trained, they would have shot in pairs and kept him pinned down. However, since none of the visible crossbowmen had a weapon ready, Davides dropped his sword out the window—so he wouldn't do something stupid, like impale himself—and vaulted through the opening head first. He fell out the other side, rolled as his shoulder hit the dirt, grabbed for his sword, and scrambled to his feet. The crossbowmen, apparently having no contingency plan, scattered in various directions.

The bold approach was working so far, but he knew that he only had a few moments before they got behind cover and reloaded. He rushed to Hatim, seized an inert arm and bowed his head under Hatim's mid-section. Grunting as he took the body's full weight on his right shoulder, he stood and wrapped his sword arm securely around Hatim's legs. He moved as quickly as he could back to the relative safety of the building. Remir was waiting at the window, hands reaching to pull Hatim inside. Davides followed, going through the window in the same awkward fashion as he had before. This time, though, he stayed on the floor, chest heaving as he sucked in air.

He didn't have to check Hatim to know. He had felt it when he had lifted the body: too heavy, too limp, too . . . empty. Hatim was dead.

Davides didn't remember getting back on his feet. Or moving across the floor. He barely registered shoving an astonished Remir aside when the latter interposed himself between Davides and the deputy cowering on the floor.

"Davides, don't!"

The voice was distant. Irrelevant. He ignored it.

Something dragged at Davides's left side. He flicked his arm, trying to shake it off, but Remir held on tightly and spun him around.

"He surrendered," Remir objected.

Davides yanked free of Remir's grasp. The dissonance of rage was swirling so loudly in his head that the only thing he understood was Remir's interference. "Stay out of my way!" he snarled, and started to turn.

"Go ahead. Show your back to me again. See what happens."

The soft, not-so-subtle threat made itself heard in a way that loud protestations had not. Davides stopped and finally looked at Remir. The dark eyes were troubled, but resolved: Remir wasn't going to back down.

Davides's bitter gaze swung to the deputy, who hadn't budged and whose face bore the same blank, doomed expression as a rabbit being toyed with by a lynx. He was pitiful. And harmless. And ridiculously obedient. And he didn't deserve to die any more than Hatim had.

Davides swallowed hard, still seething inside but trying to channel his anger more constructively. "If he doesn't explain what the hell is going on here, *then* can I kill him?" Davides inquired between gritted teeth.

"Absolutely."

First things first, though. Davides scooped up the constable's battle axe and headed for the front door. He shouldered it shut, dropped the axe across the open cleats to serve as a crossbar, and hastened back to the common room.

Remir had pulled a chair close to the kneeling deputy and had sat down so that they were at eye level. "What's your name?" he asked.

"Mateo."

"Okay, Mateo. Tell me, how many more people are out there trying to kill us?"

Rather than joining Remir in his pleasant chat, Davides crossed to the door that the proprietress had gone through. He nudged it, expecting it to be locked, but it swung inwards freely.

"There's Attab," Mateo began.

Remir stopped him. "Who is he?"

"The leader . . . er, mayor, I guess. And, two more of his men. Plus, however many of us were rounded up. Usually six."

"*Usually*? You mean to say this happens a lot around here?"

"Umm ..."

Davides peered cautiously into the kitchen. It had the typical assortment of pots and dishes lining the shelves, links of blood sausage and chorizo dangling from the ceiling. A cooking hearth. Bags of dry beans, rice, and barley. Casks of ale and cider. To the right, he saw a narrow door leading outside. Like the front door, it opened inward, but this one didn't have any visible means of locking it.

The congenial grandmother who had brought them water was standing behind a heavy table, holding a knife. Next to her was an enormous mound of sliced onions. Her eyes flitted about the room but never quite landed on him. "Supper isn't ready yet," she said.

Davides wasn't buying 'crazy and oblivious', but 'frightened and desperate' was still a possibility. He stepped forward and held out his hand. "The knife, please."

She placed it on the table and edged away. Davides took the short blade and drove it into the crack between the door and its frame. Then, he got behind the table and pushed. With a horrid *shriek*, it slid across the stone floor until it was up against the door. Such precautions wouldn't hold indefinitely, but at least no one would be able to get in without making a tremendous racket.

"Let's go," Davides ordered, motioning for the woman to lead the way back to the common room.

They found Remir on his feet, obviously alarmed by the sounds that had emanated from the kitchen. Seeing them emerge, he dropped back into his chair and gave the innkeeper — who had come to an abrupt halt upon entering the room — a watered-down smile. "Sorry about the mess."

Davides pushed past the woman, stepped over a couple of dead bodies, and opened the door to the remaining room. It was a bedroom, with a bench, a couple of beds, several baskets, and a row of hooks holding various garments. Another side door with a simple, ineffectual latch gave to the outside. He cursed to himself, thinking that securing this place was like trying to stop water from going through a sieve.

"What do we know?" Davides asked, turning back to Remir.

Remir gave him a long look before answering. "If I understand him right, the mayor and his men have a habit of killing well-to-do travelers and taking their stuff. They've done it maybe a dozen other times."

"You're kidding," Davides stated in disbelief. In other words, the attack was not a premeditated attempt to recuperate either Remir or the Greek text. It was completely random. That would have been more reassuring were it not for the part about the gang's homicidal tendencies. "This has nothing to do with ...?"

"Nope. Primordial greed, plain and simple."

"What will they do next?" Davides shot the question at Mateo.

The deputy looked stricken. "I dunno. No one's ever fought back before. Folks usually just handed over their weapons; some of 'em tried to run."

The woman spoke up hesitantly, "They'll probably send the *alanos*."

"What are *alanos*?" Remir asked.

"Dogs," she said. "Awful dogs, trained to hunt people down and kill them. Attab brought a whole pack with him. I think there are seven left."

Davides looked around at the three large windows. The north- and south-facing ones were still covered with blinds, the one looking west towards the corral was wide open. From outside they heard an excited yelp. "Can they go through the windows?"

"He trained 'em to," was the disheartening reply.

Remir looked at Davides. "Loft?" he inquired.

"Loft," Davides agreed.

Remir pulled Mateo to his feet, sent him and the woman up the stairs, and followed on their heels. Davides picked up the saddlebags, Mateo's shield, and a chair. He made it to the loft just as the first dog, unhindered by the blinds, burst through the north-facing window.

It was a heavy-boned, muscular brute, only two and a half feet tall at the shoulder but weighing in at a good hundred pounds. It had a short, brindle coat, blocky muzzle, and uncanny, violet eyes. Spotting movement in the loft, it ignored the bodies on the ground and dashed towards the staircase.

Davides was familiar with this kind of dog. They were impressive animals, used for bull and bear baiting, as well as other forms of pit fighting. Pain meant little to them, and once they had their jaws locked on something, nothing short of a crowbar could get them to release it, even after they were dead.

He dumped the chair over at the top of the stairs and readied his shield. The *alano* charged up the steps and attempted to go straight through the overturned chair. The force of its body hitting the chair's legs jarred Davides back a step, even though he was braced for it. The whole chair shook, lifted in the air, and listed sideways. The dog's massive shoulders had gotten stuck. Slavering at the mouth, it snarled and growled and bit at the chair, while it drove with its hind legs and tried to force its way through.

Four more *alanos* came through the windows. Davides hurriedly killed the first dog, then used a foot to shove the chair — with the animal's body still lodged in its legs — back into position. The other dogs lunged up the stairs, but in their frenzy to reach their prey, they kept pushing each other off the open staircase. Falling to the floor did little to diminish their bloodlust, but it at least kept the number of snapping jaws at the top of the stairs manageable. Davides held the shield defensively and waited for opportune moments to strike. He felt like a butcher, as he killed one single-minded creature after another.

Once the fifth dog had fallen, Davides glanced over his shoulder. Remir had taken up a post at a small, shuttered window that overlooked the front door and central plaza. Mateo and the woman were huddled together in the far corner, backed up against the sloping ceiling of the thatched roof.

"There's been movement in the church," Remir informed him. "I haven't seen anything else."

"That's where Attab stays," Mateo offered.

"Is he a priest?" Remir asked.

"Dear Lord, no!" Mateo exclaimed. "But, when our priest didn't come back, Attab moved the constabulary there."

Davides and Remir exchanged glances. "Back from where?" Davides asked.

"From Toledo. He went to try to help our cobbler, who got arrested there last spring. Something to do with the *jizya*."

"Your cobbler," Davides repeated, trying to make a connection between shoes and the *jizya*, the special tax levied against Christians and Jews living under Muslim rule.

"He was also the mayor," the woman clarified. "Before Attab came here, our cobbler was our mayor."

"Ah." Things were starting to make sense now — warped, evil sense, but sense, nonetheless. Attab had probably killed the mayor for the village's taxes. Then, seeing an opportunity, he had taken over the position, claiming the former mayor had been arrested. The only other official voice in town, the priest, was subsequently silenced as well. No one had come to investigate the village's failure to pay the *jizya* since Toledo had had more pressing problems last spring, namely King Fernando's army.

"Is there any chance they would try to fire the roof?" Remir inquired, still watching through the shutters. "I only ask because I see a little parade of torches coming from the back of the church and circling around to the north and south of us."

Davides crossed to the window and peered outside. Dusk had settled, morphing the buildings and surrounding landscape with its long shadows and gauzy blue film. Flickers of light, three to the left and three to the right, winked in and out of sight as the torchbearers tried to move into position without coming too close to the inn. He swore luridly, his anger and frustration mounting. He had known that escorting Remir to Seville would be dangerous; he had had no illusions about the risks involved with getting the Greek text to Toledo; but, who would have thought that staying a night in some wretched little village would prove to be such a nightmare?

He took a deep, calming breath, then addressed Mateo again. "What does Attab look like?"

"Fair hair, blue eyes. About your size."

Davides handed the saddlebags to Remir. "Would you do me a favor and watch these?"

Remir frowned. "While you do what?"

"Go after Attab. I don't think the rest will fight with him out of the way."

Remir looked mutinous, and for a moment Davides thought he was going to argue the matter. Then, his expression smoothed out, and he accepted the saddlebags. "Okay. Have fun."

Such bland acquiescence, coming from Remir, filled Davides with a profound sense of foreboding. "We don't have time to discuss this," he insisted, as much to himself as to Remir.

"You're the one talking. Go already."

Davides gave him a final look of warning before moving to the edge of the loft. Avoiding the slick and slippery stairs, he dropped his sword and shield to the floor, then followed them by using the table as an intermediary landing. He snatched up the weapon and shield, moved into the adjoining bedroom, and left the inn through the side door.

A loud shout went up from a nearby, concealed position. An instant later, a crossbow bolt slammed into Davides's shield, the force of it staggering him into the side of the building. Since stealth was not going to be an option, Davides switched to a more direct approach. He charged the short distance to the crossbowman, who continued hollering for help and trying to span his crossbow until Davides summarily cut him down.

Then, Davides turned to face the three torchbearers who had responded to the man's cries, spears in hand. They appeared about as happy to confront him as Mateo had been. Acting on impulse, and using the pure Arabic of the court, Davides said, "I'm the new constable here! Sent by al-Mamun himself. Dowse the torches and go home, or I swear I'll have you slow-roasting on spits before the sun sets!"

Their response was gratifying. After one confused moment, they threw down their torches and spears, and fled.

Once they were out of sight, Davides released his grip on the shield and let it drop to the ground. His left shoulder was aching again, aggravated by the force of the bolt striking his shield. He kicked dirt over the pitch-fueled torches and reconsidered his original plan.

Attab was running out of men. Maybe going after the leader wasn't the best way to finish this. If the other so-called attackers were as easily intimidated as these had been, he could leave Attab squatting in the church while he cut all his support out from under him.

Davides checked his surroundings again, then picked up the crossbow, its gaffle, and some bolts. He put his foot in the stirrup and spanned the string to reload.

Jahwar. Attab. What kind of names were those, anyway? Slavic, maybe?

A muffled sound from the back of the church broke his train of thought. It was followed by an explosion of barking.

Seized by a dreadful premonition, Davides ran across the open plaza and skidded to a halt next to one of the church's long, narrow windows. Inside, he glimpsed an ash blonde man, his arm pointing east towards the altar; a crossbowman bringing his weapon to bear in that same direction; the two remaining dogs, whose enthusiastic yowls made it impossible to hear anything

110

else, likewise launching themselves towards the far end of the church. Davides still couldn't see what was causing their agitation, but he had a pretty good idea of what — or who — it might be.

For the first time since this whole incident began, Davides was scared. He swung the crossbow up with his left hand and pulled the trigger lever. The bolt missed the other crossbowman by a mile, but it at least caused the man to drop his aim and dive for cover. Davides discarded the crossbow and dashed to the back of the church, taking the corner so fast his feet nearly slipped out from under him. The back door stood wide open. He hurdled a body that was lying across the threshold and wove his way through the sacristy into the chancel.

Remir had closed with Attab. He was wearing Mateo's coarse woolen cloak, perhaps as a rough disguise to get him in the back door. How he had eluded the *alanos*, Davides didn't know, but he was now entwined with Attab on the floor, both of them with knives drawn. Remir was employing some impressive wrestling techniques, but at the moment he was expending all of his skill and strength to keep Attab superimposed between himself and the vice-like jaws of the *alanos*, who were snapping randomly at the tangled bodies.

Scarcely pausing, Davides went for the crossbowman, who couldn't seem to decide between loosing a bolt or drawing a sword. At the last minute, he threw the crossbow itself at Davides and ran for the back door. That was fine with Davides, who picked up the weapon and threw it, in turn, at the teeming pile of men and dogs.

One of the *alanos* yelped, snarled, and leapt for him. It took three, frustrating slashes to bring it down. Davides turned back to the fray, which was still going strong. He was afraid to use his sword on the last dog since it was leaping over and onto the two men struggling on the floor. Finally, he kicked it hard in the ribs. In a flash its teeth were deep into his right boot. Davides tried to pull it away from Remir's vicinity, but the muscle-bound dog yanked hard at his leg. He lost his balance and fell.

Seeing its prey on the ground, the animal released his boot and went for his throat. With the dog's front paws planted on his chest, Davides lacked space to effectively swing his sword. Instead, he punched the pommel repeatedly into its muzzle. The blunt force finally backed it off enough for Davides to apply the blade in a more conventional fashion. By the time the second *alano* was dead, however, the frenzied struggle between Remir and Attab had also subsided.

Heart hammering at his chest, Davides looked over in time to see Remir shove the other man away from him and spring to his feet. Remir's face was twisted in aversion as he stared down at Attab, who was clutching feebly at the hilt of a knife protruding from his side.

Then, Remir looked over to where Davides was still sprawled on the floor, saturated in canine blood. The dark eyes widened. "Are you all right?"

Relief, beset by several other emotions, rendered Davides temporarily incapable of speech. He responded with a short, mirthless laugh and a few bobs of his head.

Remir raised a skeptical eyebrow, offered him a hand, and hauled him to his feet.

Attab was still alive but wouldn't be for long. Remir's knife must have punctured a lung, because he was rapidly choking on blood. Before Davides could decide whether he deserved a mercy killing, the fingers quit grasping and the gurgling stopped.

Glancing at Remir, Davides noted with renewed alarm that he seemed to have paled. "Are you hurt?" he demanded.

Remir blinked at him several times, then finally registered what Davides had said. "Am I hurt? Good question." He took a step back and inspected himself. No gaping wounds. He had a slash through his left sleeve from Attab's knife, but it had barely left a scratch. Of greater concern was an ugly rent behind his knee where one of the dogs had successfully sunk its teeth into him. It was bloody, but not gushing. "I think I'll live," he declared, "assuming that beast wasn't rabid, and that our hostess has some *aguardiente* stashed away someplace."

"That might keep it from getting infected," Davides acknowledged, thinking to himself that he needed to get Remir to a decent physician — in other words, to Toledo — as soon as humanly possible.

"What? Waste perfectly good alcohol on a wound? Hell, I was planning to get drunk." The familiar twist of a smile was back in place, leaving Davides to wonder if he had imagined the earlier pallor.

"Speaking of the inn," Davides said, "we probably should go stop the others from burning it down. Where's your sword?"

Remir glanced vaguely about the nave. "'Round here somewhere. I gave it to one of the dogs to play with on my way by. Ah, here it is." He lifted one of the overturned benches and retrieved the weapon.

He didn't reclaim his knife.

* * *

113

The remaining torchbearers were easy to find, dissuade, and disperse. They were unenthusiastic participants in Attab's scheme, and they weren't keen on setting one of their own roofs ablaze in the first place.

With that small matter taken care of, Davides helped Remir hobble back to the common room of the inn. No sooner had he deposited Remir in a chair than Mateo shoved the saddlebags at him, as anxious to be rid of them as if they were pet vipers entrusted to his care. At the moment, Davides couldn't have cared less about the saddlebags. He dropped them on the table and demanded firewood, fresh water, and linens. Remir demanded alcohol.

Mateo and Eldonza, the innkeeper, scampered off in opposite directions. Eldonza returned almost immediately with squares of linen. A short while later, some townspeople filtered in with armfuls of wood and buckets of water. Davides had them build up the fire in the hearth and start some of the water boiling. Meanwhile, he tore the linen into strips, and tossed the makeshift bandages into the pot. Linen soup, he thought wryly, as his stomach rumbled with hunger.

It took Davides a moment to realize that his stomach was responding to the actual smell of food cooking in the kitchen. Moments later, Eldonza appeared with eggs, onions, brown bread, and cider. Soon thereafter, their new best friend, Mateo, came back with a small cask of amber-colored *aguardiente*, part of Attab's private cache. Remir and Davides both took a stiff drink (or two) while they inhaled their food and waited for the water to boil.

Davides didn't know much about the art and science of healing. He had never studied Abu al-Qasim's famous medical encyclopedia, the *Kitab-al-Tasrif*, compiled when Córdoba had possessed the best physicians and hospitals west of Damascus. However, he was aware of some of its basic principles for treating open wounds, principles which had become common knowledge among the educated elite of al-Andalus. He was just a little fuzzy on the details.

After letting the linen boil for awhile, Davides fished the strips of cloth from the pots and hung them near the hearth to dry. Then, he pulled two tables together, and Remir stretched out facedown on them, cradling his head in his arms. Working slowly and carefully, Davides cut the material back from Remir's wound and blotted away the dried blood with warm water. Pure, dumb luck. Given its location, the dog bite should have hamstrung Remir, but instead, it seemed to have only torn through skin and muscle. Davides filled a cup with the *aguardiente*. How strong did alcohol need to be to effectively block sepsis? Considering that he could have lit this libation on fire, he was hoping it would do the trick.

"Ready?" Davides asked Remir.

"Ready for what?"

If Remir didn't already know how much the alcohol would sting, then there was no point in warning him. Davides dumped the contents of the cup over the wound. He heard a sharp intake of breath from Remir, followed by a steady litany of obscenities, most of them directed towards Davides, his immediate family, and the late, great Abu al-Qasim.

"That's all I can do until the bandages dry," Davides said, speaking over the colorful invective.

"Thank God!" Remir breathed emphatically, his face shining with perspiration. He pushed himself up and rolled over, so that he could sit at the edge of the table.

"If it's any consolation, the pain tells you the alcohol is working," Davides assured him.

Remir cast a withering look in his direction. "And, when I punch you in the nose, what does that pain tell you?"

"That I'm awfully slow, if I can't keep clear of you in your current, gimpy state."

Davides hopped back out of reach as Remir feinted a jab in his direction. "Hmph," Remir grumbled, settling back onto the edge of the table, "Rather than mocking my pain, how about getting me another drink?"

"Pretty sure I can do both at the same time." Davides replied. He sloshed another finger's worth of *aguardiente* into Remir's cup and handed it to him.

It wasn't until he turned to check on the bandages that he realized they had an audience: Mateo, Eldonza, and about half a dozen other villagers who had not had the sense to make themselves scarce. They were staring at Davides like he was some kind of sorcerer engaged in the practice of strange magicks. Or, maybe their wary fascination was simply due to the sticky spattering of blood that was coating him from head to toe. He really needed to wash up.

Mateo cleared his throat and stepped forward. "They was wondering what you want done with the dead," he explained.

Aside from Hatim, Davides couldn't see how the dead were his concern. "I don't care. What do you usually do with the dead?"

"Well," Mateo shuffled his feet, "Attab would burn 'em."

Burn them? Something jangled in the back of Davides's mind. The practice of burning bodies was forbidden among Muslims and heavily discouraged by the Church. Some cultures, though, burned their dead as a matter of course. Some Slavic cultures, in particular.

"Bury them," Remir said. "Put them in the church for now, and bury them in the morning. Except for Hatim. He stays here with us." He shot back the *aguardiente* and grimaced. "Maybe you should go with them," he suggested to Davides. "Make sure Attab's men are accounted for. Make sure our horses are accounted for, so we can get outta here tomorrow."

"What? You can't leave!" one of the villagers protested frantically, looking straight at Davides. "You're the constable!"

* * *

Even after Davides had clarified that he was not, in fact, the new constable and that he had no intention of staying in their fleapit of a village, the townspeople continued to act as if he and Remir were officially in charge. It soon became apparent that they were desperate for direction and aid. They had lost all of their town leaders—the mayor, the priest, and anyone else with enough conviction to stand up to Attab or to try to get help. Gone. Disappeared. Dead.

Remarkably, only one villager had died that night at their hands: the gangly fighter who had accompanied the axe-wielding constable. The guard from the back door of the church had a broken nose and a sizable lump on his head, compliments of Remir, but he didn't appear to be holding a grudge. Lots of dead bodies — the guard's not being among them — must have put things in perspective for him.

Attab's men had fared worse. Attab, Jahwar, and three others were dead, including the sniper from the loft. Either he had been more seriously injured than Davides had thought, or his death had been precipitated by a disgruntled villager. The only member of the band to escape was the one who had thrown his crossbow at Davides and fled. No one seemed to know where he was, but they soon discovered that a horse was missing.

Not one of theirs, though. When Davides had gone to check, following Mateo to a blind corral outside of town, he found their horses and mule calmly eating hay. With them were another mule and a short, stocky draft horse. According to Eldonza's grandson, who had been in charge of watching the animals, the man named Mishwar had come at dusk, saddled a horse, and ridden out without a word of explanation.

"Where was he going?" Davides asked.

The boy shrugged.

"Which direction?" Davides specified impatiently.

The boy pointed east.

"Probably to Toledo," Mateo said. "That's where they went to sell the stuff they filched. Jahwar would go 'bout once a month. Sometimes traded for weapons; sometimes money. But, I also heard talk of a village north of Toledo called Alferia and another to the east called Yepes. Attab had ties with all of 'em."

Which meant that, regardless of his destination, Mishwar was heading for familiar territory, a place where he could lose himself in the crowd. Davides wouldn't

118

have cared so much except that it sounded like Attab and his men had strong connections in Toledo, a fence that was capable of easily liquidating random articles of value and just as easily providing controlled items like crossbows and swords. If Attab's fence was anything like the criminal organizations in Seville, its leader could well be an unscrupulous, local noble. Or, perhaps, a visiting dignitary from King Fernando's court?

"Great!" he muttered. As badly as he wanted to ride after Mishwar and keep him from telling his associates about the two *dhimmis* who had so rudely disrupted their quaint operation, Davides knew it would have constituted a foolish undertaking. The sun had set quite a while ago, and Mishwar had probably holed up somewhere. In the darkness, Davides would either ride right past him or become the target of an ambush.

Maybe they could catch up to him tomorrow. Maybe Mishwar was heading for one of the other villages Mateo had mentioned. Maybe Davides was being paranoid, and the fence in Toledo had no ties with the powers-that-be.

Or, maybe he should stop aspiring to optimism and instead prepare a plausible explanation as to why 'Ramiro' and he had been this far off the main highway.

* * *

"You want us to do *what?*" Davides must have misunderstood. He had stayed up all night keeping watch, unwilling to trust anyone very far in this rural madhouse. Now, as the morning sunshine streamed in, he decided that the madness was contagious and that he was beginning to hallucinate.

He thought Eldonza had just asked Remir and him to help the village appease the Toledan exchequer by delivering their overdue *jizya*, but he must not have heard her right. It was an outrageous favor to expect of them, especially considering that last night, half the villagers had been trying to kill them.

"They won't give us the chance to explain," Eldonza lamented. "But, you speak their language, follow their ways. And, you're *hidalgos*, of the nobility. They'll listen to you!"

Davides had been right not to trust them. They must have had a secret town meeting last night and elected Eldonza spokesperson, realizing that she was the only one who wouldn't get her head bitten off for making such a request. Crafty villagers.

"We figured out how much to send and added something extra to satisfy them. The rest of it belongs to you."

"The rest of what?" Remir asked, with a quizzical half-smile.

Davides knew what Remir was thinking: the community wasn't exactly overflowing with wealth. Perchance they'd be the proud, new owners of the dairy goats?

Eldonza turned eagerly to Remir, encouraged by anything that wasn't a flat refusal. "Attab's money and weapons. We already got everything ready, out by the corral. Mateo can drive the wagon. You can ride in front with him, so's your leg can rest. And, we left space in back for your servant, if you were wanting to bury him in Toledo." She blinked hopefully at Remir, who sighed, shook his head, and arched an eyebrow in Davides's direction.

Davides bristled, then glowered at the assembled townspeople, who had obviously put some forethought into the best way to persuade them. Needless to say, he felt obligated to give a decent burial to Hatim in a Muslim cemetery — in other words, not here. Yes, it would be better if Remir didn't try to ride a horse today. And, while Davides didn't know how much money a rural bandit could have set aside, the crossbows and swords were worth a fair sum, in and of themselves. Of course, Remir and he could just take the wagon, weapons, and money. The villagers had no right to expect *quid pro quo.*

Deep down, though, Davides knew that these people had reason to be concerned. It was entirely possible that some officious secretary would review their taxes, turn a deaf ear to their excuses, and recommend that the town be punished as an example to others. From what Davides knew of al-Mamun, Toledo's ruler was a reasonable, tolerant individual; but, this case would never make it to his audience chamber. The exchequer had its own enforcers, who could either compel the village to convert to Islam or enslave the male population as a penalty for not paying the *jizya* on time.

Furthermore, the townspeople couldn't know that the favor they were asking of Davides and Remir was a lot more complicated than it seemed. A contentious meeting at the exchequer would draw attention, and someone was bound to recognize Davides. And ask questions, directly or indirectly, that could compromise his task and Remir's safety.

No. They had done enough to help the village, the name of which Davides did not know and, frankly, did not care to learn. They absolutely could not be involved.

* * *

The village was called Manantial, named after its delightful, ever-flowing spring. They found out that and more regarding its inhabitants and its recent subjugation by Attab as they plodded their way east: Mateo and Remir on the wagon, with Hatim's mule tied behind; Davides on one of their horses, while trying to string along the other two. He didn't have Hatim's knack for it, though, and more than once, they got themselves wound into a snarled mess. It was like a little allegory of his life.

Around mid-morning, their small cavalcade pulled into Sonseca, the town south of Toledo that had been Davides's original destination. When Sonseca's imam heard that they had been attacked by highwaymen on their way from Seville to Toledo, he was appropriately sympathetic, but not surprised. It was a fairly common occurrence.

The funeral rites took several hours. Towards the end of the proceedings, while gravediggers filled the shaft, Davides stood in silence and, as was customary, prayed for God to forgive Hatim—although he was hard pressed to imagine what Hatim would need forgiveness for. Hatim had been one of the most selfless and honest souls that Davides had ever met.

Afterwards, Remir and he headed back towards the tavern where Mateo awaited them. They had reached the outer fringe of the cypress-lined cemetery when Remir broke the silence. "If I haven't said so already, I'm sorry about Hatim. I rather liked him. You know, in spite of everything."

The comment almost stopped Davides in his tracks. It wasn't Remir's condolences that Davides found shocking—who hadn't liked Hatim?—but the 'in spite of everything' tacked onto the end. Somewhere along the way, Davides had forgotten that he and Remir were not exactly on the same side, that Remir was an unwilling associate whose cooperation depended on the continual threat of violence to him and his family. Hatim had formed part of that threat, although not nearly so large a part as Davides himself.

"He had a good heart," Davides acknowledged awkwardly to cover up his lapse. "May God show mercy on him."

Part 3 – The smart thing would be to bury you

Before rolling into Toledo, they had to make one more stop, since the guards at the main gate would not appreciate the collection of swords and crossbows in their wagon. In order to avoid lengthy delays and possible detainment, Davides had determined that it would be best to stash the weapons outside the city walls.

When they reached the vast olive groves that grew in the clay hills south of Toledo, Davides took the lead. The landscape was familiar to him now, and incipient nostalgia nudged at him as he guided them off the highway. They followed an overgrown two-track, crossed a rocky creek, passed a twisted tree, and skirted a steep bank. When they got to the ruins of an old, Roman aqueduct, Davides swung down from his horse.

"This'll only take a moment," he told them, as he hefted the two bundles of weapons: the swords wrapped together in oilcloth, and the crossbows bulging at odd angles from inside a burlap bag.

He followed the aqueduct up the hill, loose stones rolling under his feet as he struggled with the awkward load. At the top of the slope, under one of the supporting arches, there was a recessed area that was protected from the elements and concealed from the casual passer-by. He had found the spot during his schoolboy days, when he had had the leisure to roam and be inquisitive, and had used it to hide all kinds of worthless treasures. Now, he was counting on the cache to keep an actual treasure hidden, at least until they figured out how to liquidate it.

* * *

Toledo was a proverbial sight for sore eyes. The sense of intimate familiarity that Davides had been resisting hit full force as he looked up at the city, perched high atop her promontory. Her crenellated walls accommodated the rough terrain in such a way that the walkways on top ran nearly level while the height of the bulwark ranged from twenty to nearly fifty feet. Below the solid walls, the pitch of the land varied considerably, sometimes falling straight down to the river, sometimes sloping gently enough for grass, bushes, and small trees to grow. From her towering battlements to her narcissistic reflection in the mirrored surface of the Tagus River, Toledo was magnificent.

They made their way to the Alcántara bridge and crossed the Tagus under the shadow of the fortified *alcázar*. Then, they turned uphill and went through the gates into the city proper. It would have been less expensive to stable the horses in the sprawling settlement north of the walled city, but Davides didn't know that area well, and he was not in the mood to be adventurous. Besides, with the dinars and dirhams that Attab had put away, they had a little extra coinage to spare.

Mateo stayed at the livery stable so that he could watch over the wagon and its contents. It was too late for them to go to the exchequer today. Plus, if Davides wanted to be taken seriously, he at least needed clean clothes and some boots that hadn't been chewed on by a dog.

As they stepped into a crowded, triangular-shaped plaza, Davides glanced at Remir, whose eyes were sparkling as they took in the hustle and bustle of the city. "Do you think you can contain yourself for one or two nights?" Davides asked.

"Contain myself?" It was hard to tell whether Remir was questioning the need to carry out the request, or his ability to do so.

"I'm planning for us to stay with an old friend of mine from when I was a student here."

"I promise to be on my best behavior," Remir said, with an unconvincing smirk. After a few strides, however, the smirk faded. "Are you sure you want to drop in on him like this, with no warning?"

Davides winced. "No. Not at all sure. But, those who know me would find it exceedingly strange if I stayed anywhere else." He shrugged the saddlebags into a more comfortable spot on his shoulder and led the way into the narrow, twisting streets of the upper city.

Ishaq's house was at one of the highest points in town, which made for a long, tedious climb. It was a newer, two-story building with a terrace on the roof. Half of the ground floor was devoted to a smithy, with a large furnace off one end. A pleasant warmth seeped out of the smithy's open doors, taking away some of the chill from the evening air.

Davides tapped at the front door of the residence, using its ornate, wrought-iron knocker.

"Your friend is a blacksmith?" Remir asked, as he leaned against the stucco wall, resting his injured leg.

"He crafts precision instruments for the scientific analysis of the heavenly bodies," Davides clarified.

"Oh. So, your friend stares at the stars while pounding on an anvil," Remir mused, evidently trying to wrap his head around the concept. He peered into the open door of the smithy. "Are you certain he's not a blacksmith? 'Cause that sure looks like a forge."

Davides sighed. "Ishaq comes from a family of blacksmiths, but not the kind that makes a living from fitting horseshoes or repairing armor. They have a reputation for fashioning small, complex mechanisms, like locks and hinges. A few years before I was a student here, al-Mamun commissioned Ishaq to contrive some tools for the study of astronomy. Ishaq understood the physics behind the tools so well that he was invited to do research with Toledo's intellectual elite. Now, he's considered one of the principal authorities on all things astronomical."

From behind the closed door, they heard the patter of soft-soled shoes crossing the vestibule. The peephole's visor slid back, and an unfriendly eye peered through it. The eye widened, and an earsplitting shriek resounded through the door. Remir, sore leg notwithstanding, jumped about a foot in the air. There was a rattle of latches being drawn back, and the door flew open.

A tiny, elderly woman stood in the doorway, all wrinkled skin and missing teeth. "*Sisnando! Benditos los ojos!*" Her frail figure grabbed Davides in a fierce embrace, then drew his dirty, scruffy face down to her level and showered him with kisses. By the time he could pull away, Davides was blushing furiously and grinning like an idiot.

"*Me alegro mucho de verte, Josefina,*" he mumbled self-consciously.

Alerted by the woman's cries, a wiry man was hastening to the door. Ishaq didn't fit the burly,

127

blacksmith stereotype, but then again, he wasn't that kind of blacksmith. He hadn't aged much in the five years that Davides had known him. His light brown hair and closely trimmed beard showed no signs of graying. There were some faint creases in his broad forehead, but the lines cleared when he recognized who was at the door.

"Sisnando? Sisnando! It *is* you!" Ishaq stepped forward to shake Davides's hand and give him two quick kisses on the cheeks.

Still smiling, Davides offered the traditional, formal salutation: "Peace and blessings upon you and your household." Then, he added, "It's really good to see you, Ishaq." Remembering himself, he turned towards Remir, who had been observing the exchanges with interest. Davides swallowed hard and forced the words out: "May I introduce a cousin of mine from Salamanca, Ramiro Méndez. Ramiro, this is my good friend, Ishaq al-Zarqali."

Remir moved forward to greet Ishaq, but as he put weight on his wounded leg, it buckled beneath him. He half-fell against Davides, who grabbed his arm to keep him upright.

"*Dios mío*, he's hurt!" Josefina exclaimed. "Sisnando, why do you just stand there? Bring him in! I'll send for the doctor." She turned back into the house, calling loudly for one of the other servants.

Ishaq took Remir's other arm. "We can put him in your old room," he suggested, "if you think he can make it up the stairs?"

"I suspect so," Davides said, somewhat callously. True, it had been a tough, uphill walk for someone with a bad leg, but Davides couldn't help wondering if some of

128

Remir's sudden debility was feigned. He had been fine just a moment ago.

"What happened? How did he get hurt?" Ishaq asked, as they navigated the stairs to get to the bedrooms.

"We were set upon by bandits last night. They had attack dogs, and one of them managed to get through his armor."

Ishaq shook his head in disgust. "It seems like the roads are becoming more dangerous by the day. I've heard horror stories of what happens to travelers who aren't well-armed, or who are taken by surprise."

Like Hatim.

Davides didn't want to talk about Hatim at the moment, so he remained silent as they climbed the last few steps. His old room was right at the top of the staircase. It faced westward, and when Ishaq threw open the split doors that gave to the balcony, the early evening sunshine lit up the inside.

"I'll ask Yasmin to bring up some mint tea," Ishaq offered and headed back downstairs.

Davides eased Remir onto the bed, then asked, "What are you doing?"

Remir eyed him with mild exasperation. "Dispensing with painful, social amenities. Let them fuss over me. After the physician leaves, I'll plead exhaustion—which won't really be a stretch—and go to sleep. That leaves you to renew acquaintances with Ishaq and his family without having me in the middle."

"Oh. All right." That might indeed make things easier. Davides glanced around the room, which had changed very little since his student days: the bed and its overabundance of pillows (Josefina's contribution); the wardrobe, with its intricately carved cedar screens on the sides; the writing desk, a dark stain spread across its surface from when he had knocked over an entire inkwell; the olive wood washstand, currently missing its jug, basin, and towel; even the bright red carnations in the flower pots on the balcony.

He turned abruptly back to Remir, who was making himself comfortable amidst the pillows. "Maybe we should start discussing these plans you concoct in advance — you know, so the dim-witted members of the group can keep up."

Remir laughed. "There's your first mistake, thinking that this is some kind of a plan. I'm just —," Remir broke off as Ishaq came back in the room. "Tired," he finished, then addressed Ishaq. "I appreciate your generosity in welcoming me into your home, but I don't really need a physician. A little rest, and I'll be fine."

Ishaq smiled sympathetically. "I don't blame you for not wanting a doctor, but we have some of the best here in Toledo. It can't hurt to have one take a look at your leg."

"Ah, but it can hurt," Remir said with a sage look at Davides.

Before Davides could respond to the implied accusation, they heard footsteps on the stairs. Ishaq's wife, Yasmin, appeared bearing a pot of steaming water and tall glasses stuffed with mint leaves and sugar. She was a handsome woman, with thick, black hair, strong features, and a proud bearing. Yasmin's greeting was cordial, but she observed the standard decorum of Muslim women around men: no shrill cries, hugs, or kisses from her.

Josefina, who had already shown that she had no such inhibitions, was the next to arrive. Accompanied by the cook, who was carrying a large jug of warm water, she puffed into the room with a basin and some towels. "*Sisnando, favor de quitarle las botas y la armadura al pobrecito.*" She poured some of the rosemary-scented water into the basin and dampened a towel.

Remir's eyebrows shot up, and he shrank back in the bed. "Davides," he said, an edge of panic on his voice, "tell her I can wash up on my own. That I'm feeling much better now."

It was kind of refreshing, not to mention amusing, to have Josefina's maternal instincts focused on someone besides him. "She understands you just fine," Davides said. "Getting her to listen might be another matter."

Ishaq, however, took pity on Remir. He ushered everyone out of the room, leaving the two of them to remove their armor and wash away the worst of the day's travel without an audience. "We'll let you know when the doctor gets here," he said, and shut the door behind him.

* * *

Somnolent darkness permeated the room, except for a line of bright white under the split doors. Sunlight. Davides pushed himself up from the pallet on which he was lying, rubbed bleary eyes, and looked around. Remir, who had slept in the bed, was already up and gone. Yawning, Davides got to his feet. On the chair by the desk, he spied one of Ishaq's long cotton robes, its cuffs and collar elaborately embroidered in Josefina's expert hand. Nearby, a pair of kidskin slippers had also been laid out for him. His own clothes had apparently been confiscated, destined either for laundering or (more likely) burning. He shuffled over to the washstand. The water was cold.

After plucking a drowned sprig of rosemary from the basin, he began to wash up, thinking about his long conversation with Ishaq the night before.

Normally, they would have gone to the rooftop terrace and gazed at the stars while they talked; but last night, Davides had asked to go to the smithy, where they could converse with less chance of being overheard. He had told Ishaq everything. He hadn't meant to reveal so much, but he was sick and tired of misleading people. It hadn't been a particularly cogent narrative. Still, Ishaq had listened patiently, the creases on his forehead deepening as Davides's account unfolded.

"I don't want you or your family to be put in danger," Davides had said at last, "but I was afraid it would look suspicious if we didn't come to your house, at least at first. Since 'Ramiro' is pretending to pursue studies here, we'll need to find him long-term housing, anyway. We can look tomorrow — "

"Nonsense!" Ishaq had interrupted. "If you are in danger, all the more reason for you to remain here, where you have some security." Before Davides could object, Ishaq continued, "What explanation did you come up with for being off the main highway?"

"That we were attacked by bandits *on* the highway. They killed Hatim, which made us very angry, so we followed them back to Manantial to finish the fight. Manantial then asked for our assistance with the overdue taxes. The main points of the story stay the same, we're just avoiding the part about us riding in from the west. Ishaq, I still think — "

"You would offend me and dishonor my house by staying anywhere else," Ishaq had declared, thus putting an end to any notion Davides had had of relocating.

Davides finished washing and got dressed. Then, he opened the doors to the balcony. The sun was high — higher than he had expected. In fact, the muezzin's call to mid-day prayers must have been what had finally awakened him.

"*Merda!*" How could he have slept so long?

He grabbed a knife off the desk and slid it into his belt on his way to the door. As he reached the stairs, he slowed and stopped. What was he forgetting? His mail hauberk was in the smithy, waiting to be repaired by one of Ishaq's apprentices; his sword was in the wardrobe, keeping the saddlebags and their contents company. Mateo had the tax ledgers. All Davides needed was himself. He supposed it just felt odd not to be carrying all that weight around.

The terrace was Ishaq and Yasmin's main extravagance. It offered an amazing view of the city, the river, and the olive groves to the south, as well as providing a place for Ishaq to conduct his astronomical calculations. The low wall that surrounded the rooftop was decorated with glazed tiles in soft hues of blue and green. Potted lemon trees were interspersed with a myriad of shrubs and flowers. A dedicated gardener, Yasmin had once assured him that each variety had its own distinct name, just as it had its own special needs in order to thrive. For his part, Davides generally referred to them all as 'plants'.

A few details had been pounded into his head, however. For instance, the pergola that ran along one edge of the terrace was draped in purple flowers called bougainvillea, which climbed the columns and crossbeams to create a pleasant, shaded walkway. It was there that he found Remir, reclining on a bench and telling a scary tale to two of Ishaq's children, Isa and Yaqub. As Davides approached, however, he noticed that they didn't appear at all frightened by the story: Isa had covered her mouth with both hands in an attempt to hide an impish smile; and Yaqub, the youngest, was bouncing up and down excitedly. Davides broke off in mid-greeting. "Where's Tanim?" he asked, referring to Ishaq's oldest boy.

There was a rustle in the curtain of purple flora covering the pergola, and an agile nine year-old leapt on Davides's back, wrapping his arms tightly around Davides's neck. Davides staggered in dramatic fashion, then spun round and round, trying to get Tanim to lose his grip. After nearly careening into a lemon tree, Davides toppled over dizzily, and Isa and Yaqub cheered while Tanim did a victory dance.

"My turn! My turn!" Isa exclaimed.

Davides picked himself up and examined his robe ruefully. "I can't right now, Isa," he said, brushing the smudge of dirt off as best he could, "but, I'll make it up to you later, okay?"

Isa's outthrust lower lip indicated that it was not, in fact, okay. However, the children's nanny interceded, shooing her protesting charges off to another part of the house.

Davides turned to Remir, who had been watching them with a complacent expression on his face. Like Davides, Remir was borrowing one of Ishaq's robes, but given the difference in size between the two men, the normally voluminous garment fit Remir more like a tunic. "How's the leg?" Davides asked.

"Still stiff. The physician is going to stop in this afternoon and dress it again. He uses an ointment that he

134

claims has special healing properties, but to me it reeks of pine tar. Oh, and Josefina arranged for a tailor to come by later and measure us for some new clothes."

"I can't stay," Davides said. "I need to get this business with Manantial taken care of. I meant to go this morning, but …"

"But, you were sleeping like a rock. Yeah, I noticed. Don't worry. I asked Ishaq to send word to Mateo that you'd be along this afternoon. In the meantime, I'll be a good patient and wait here for the physician."

Davides hesitated. He was so used to constantly guarding Remir — keeping him safe and secure on the one hand, and out of mischief on the other — that the thought of leaving him alone at Ishaq's was a bit unnerving. Overall, though, it did make more sense for Remir to stay here and rest his leg than to traipse all over town. "Okay. Do you need anything before I go?"

Remir shook his head. "Nah. Josefina comes and checks on me regularly, so I'm sure I'll manage to get through the afternoon. I can deal with the tailor, too, if you like. Order a few things for you."

"I would appreciate that," Davides said guardedly, unaccustomed to such smooth cooperation from Remir.

"No problem," Remir assured him. Then, as Davides started to turn away, he added, "You fancy sequins, right?"

That sounded more like the Remir he had come to know. Davides made a rude gesture and kept walking.

Remir laughed. "Maybe something gauzy, to show off your legs?"

* * *

135

As Davides had expected, the line at the exchequer crept forward at a snail's pace. Actually, he would have bet on the snail to win. The wait was made worse because he knew that the longer he stood in the expansive hallway, the greater the chances that someone would happen by who knew him. At least Mateo's presence gave him some cover, since past acquaintances of his wouldn't expect him to be keeping company with a farmer.

A couple of guards recognized him early on and joked about him being 'disguised as a civilian'. He laughed merrily at their wit — ha, ha — then recounted the edited version of what was bringing him to the exchequer in Toledo. Later, a scribe spotted him and gossiped for awhile, until Davides gently reminded him that someone, somewhere was awaiting his services. Soon after, a supercilious nobleman who had never much cared for him strutted by with a small entourage. Davides did a slow about-face and asked Mateo for the tax ledger. The man swept past without noticing him, and Davides went back to shifting his weight from one foot to another.

By the time he was able to speak to the bureaucrat in charge, that individual was bored and bitter. Or, maybe he had been born that way, and the time of day had nothing to do with his disposition. In any event, he didn't even listen to Davides and was already brushing them aside when Davides planted his hands on the table that separated them and changed his tone.

He reminded the official that under Muslim law, Toledo had an obligation to protect communities in exchange for their taxes. Since Toledo had neglected to shield Manantial from malefactors, it had no right to expect any taxes from the village. The fact that Manantial

136

was offering to pay the *jizya* now was a gesture of their desire to restore their relationship with the city.

It didn't work. Davides hadn't really thought that it would. As a couple of guards stepped forward — the same ones with whom Davides had spoken earlier — Mateo was already tugging at his sleeve, trying to get him to abandon their petition. By then, however, Davides was thoroughly annoyed: why did some people have to be so heartless and difficult? The guards were looking from the bureaucrat to Davides, but they didn't try to take hold of him. Perhaps it wasn't so bad having a small level of renown.

With a respectful nod at the guards, Davides backed off a step and smiled unpleasantly at the sneering civil servant. Using fulsome language to express his appreciation for the man's careful consideration of Manantial's request, he then insinuated that he had a pressing appointment with Domingo Ansúrez, King Fernando's representative in Toledo. Davides went on to speculate how Lord Ansúrez and his sovereign might react to the knowledge that Toledo was mistreating her Christian subjects, how al-Mamun would react to a lowly minion at the exchequer causing a political nightmare.

Where reason, mercy, and jurisprudence had failed, blackmail worked wonderfully.

* * *

Davides bade Mateo a heartfelt *A Dios*, and headed for the center of town. As he strolled along, his thoughts turned to the real reason he had come to Toledo: the translation. He knew he couldn't go to anyone who was closely affiliated with the government. Al-Mamun might

137

sympathize with Seville, but officially he was allied with Castile-León. That made scholars who frequented the palace off-limits. Also, while a number of people were capable of translating Greek to Arabic, he suspected that he first needed an alchemist who happened to read Greek. Even in a city like Toledo, such individuals were scarce, but Davides remembered one from his days as a student.

Bendayan was a Jewish alchemist who had migrated to Toledo from Córdoba, after the Caliphate fell. Davides had never taken lessons from him (alchemy not being one of his primary areas of interest), but Bendayan was one of those pure seekers-of-knowledge, who had dabbled in other fields including philosophy and languages. That was how Davides had come into contact with him. As far as Davides knew, Bendayan had never shown any interest in politics or social climbing, which made him a safer bet than most for this project.

A prickly sensation edged through his deliberations. Without thinking, he stopped and glanced around. He didn't see anyone he recognized, or anyone who seemed particularly interested in him. Resisting a primal urge to scuttle into the nearest building and hide, he forced himself to meander to his proposed destination, a little place that made marzipan. Stopping occasionally to look at wares being sold by street vendors, he tried to take note of anyone who might be following him. No one stood out or stayed with him beyond a reasonable measure.

Finally, feeling a little silly and a lot paranoid, he ducked into the shop. He picked out an assortment of sweet almond confections that were shaped into flowers and decorated in painstaking detail. It was nice to have a little extra money in his pocket and be able to splurge on something—especially something that would easily buy his way back into Isa and Yaqub's good graces.

When he left the shop, he found that he was still searching for any individual who might be showing an inordinate amount of interest in his whereabouts. *This is getting ridiculous. You're jumping at shadows.* Even so, he took a long, roundabout way back to Ishaq's.

* * *

Davides tapped lightly on the bedroom door, then opened it. Remir was stretched out on the bed, with his hands clasped behind his head and his eyes closed. He appeared to be asleep, but a cautious eye opened and rolled towards the doorway when Davides came in.

"Ready for supper?" Davides asked.

Remir groaned and sat up. "Don't tell me I have to eat again! Your Josefina seems to think I'm malnourished. She keeps plying me with food. If I leave it or tell her I'm full, she threatens to call the physician back or make some hideous folk remedy that will 'settle my stomach'. How am I supposed to get through supper? You'll have to roll me down the steps as it is!"

Davides grinned and took a seat at the desk. "She's probably having flashbacks of me at age fourteen. I was awfully scrawny when I first came to live with them. Took her forever to put some bulk on me."

"Modesty aside, I already have bulk," Remir pointed out. "So, how does one make her stop?"

Davides thought back. "I'm not sure I ever tried. Tell you what, though: tomorrow, we'll get you out of the house, where Josefina can't stuff you full of figs."

"I'd appreciate that. Speaking of being out and about, how did things go at the exchequer?"

"Fine."

"Yeah?"

"Yeah. They accepted the *jizya*. I sent Mateo on his merry way."

Remir raised his eyebrows, doubting, but said nothing.

"What did the doctor say about your leg?" Davides asked, ready to change the subject. He didn't especially want to talk about blackmailing a bureaucrat.

"It's healing well. I'm not supposed to get it wet for a few days, though, which means I can't go to the baths. Oh, and I hope you don't mind, but I used money from the saddlebags to get some purified alcohol, a bundle of bandages, and more of that nasty ointment. If we continue to be 'accident-prone' on this assignment of yours, I figure we might as well be prepared."

"Good thinking. How much did the clothes set us back?"

Remir looked a little sheepish. "Turns out I have expensive tastes."

"Really? I never would have guessed that."

"It's true," Remir admitted, then added, "Of course, I might have been more frugal had I known you also had to pay Ishaq for a mariner's astrolabe."

Davides's eyes found the floor. Remir certainly had a diabolical sense of timing. Even though he had planned on Remir learning of the astrolabe — counted on it, in fact — he still felt thrown off balance.

"Ishaq was apologizing to me for being a negligent host," Remir continued blithely, "but he said he had this project to do for General Haroun. At first, I thought he

140

was talking about the translation, which . . . okay, I can barely fathom a blacksmith doubling as an astronomer, but as a linguist, too? Then, he brings up this 'astrolabe' that would allow ships to sail out of sight of land without getting lost."

"Fascinating concept, isn't it?" Davides inserted.

"Mesmerizing. Only, the last I knew, Seville was not on a coast. So, I had to ask myself: how often does one get lost sailing a ship down the Guadalquivir River? I mean, you can see the banks on both sides, right? Not to mention having the current pull you along. Why would General Haroun need an astrolabe?"

Davides could have given him the line about the fleet in Huelva, but he didn't want to lie. He could have explained that the astrolabe was mostly a cover for the translation, but he wasn't sure that he wanted Remir to know the truth, either. For now, he decided, it would be best to keep things a little ambiguous.

Meeting Remir's gaze, he widened his eyes in mock surprise. "I'm sorry! Were you actually expecting an answer? Um . . . okay, how's this? The General wants to fulfill his dream of sailing the seven seas in his own private dinghy."

Remir scowled. "A simple 'none of your business' would suffice."

"Right," Davides said, with sarcasm, "because you would, of course, immediately drop the subject."

Remir considered his point. "That's probably fair. All right. I'll stop badgering you about the astrolabe if you promise to eat at least half of my supper tonight. Deal?"

"Deal." It wasn't much of a concession on Davides's part: he was famished.

* * *

In the morning, Davides and Remir sought out Bendayan at his residence, where the alchemist prepared and sold herbs, spices, and other substances in order to afford his private research. His white hair was more sparse, his shoulders more stooped, but his mind seemed just as sharp as Davides remembered. Despite the four-or-so years since Davides had last seen him, Bendayan recognized him the moment he and Remir walked through the door. Delighted by the visit, he asked them to accompany him to his study and left his apprentice to tend the front counter.

They traversed a long hallway, passing a number of aromatic rooms to either side. One area had bunches of herbs hanging from the ceiling or drying on racks; another exuded a pungent odor and had alembics, retorts, and other vaguely sinister-looking tools arrayed on long tables; the largest room had shelf upon shelf of clay pots, all carefully marked with arcane symbols to indicate their contents.

Small wonder that some people regarded alchemists as sorcerers.

At the end of the hall was a corner room crammed with a desk, a few chairs, a lectern, a side table, and a bookcase. The bookcase was overflowing with rolls of vellum and parchment, sheaves of loose papers, and a few, precious tomes, which were safely ensconced on the top shelf. On the narrow side table, a long stemmed sebsi pipe was perched on a sandalwood stand, and several thick, green glass jars holding different smoking herbs were arranged nearby.

Bendayan invited them to sit. Then, following an almost ceremonial protocol, he mixed some of the herbs in the sebsi pipe, lit it, and passed it around.

Up to that point, Remir had been acting as a detached bystander, but he brightened at the sight of the pipe. It had been a while since he had had the chance to indulge in that particular pastime. With the enthusiasm of an aficionado, Remir began discussing smoking herbs and their relative merits or drawbacks with Bendayan.

Davides had been carrying the Greek document under his arm. When they sat, he placed it on the desk next to him. Knowing very little about herbs (he was pretty sure they fell into the category of 'plants') Davides patiently listened and smoked, watching as Bendayan's eyes wandered occasionally in the envelope's direction.

Finally, the alchemist could resist no longer. He nodded at the uninformative envelope and asked, "What do you have there, Davides?"

"I'm not quite sure," Davides answered. "It's an old text written in Greek. From what I can tell, it's alchemical in nature, possibly encoded. I was wondering if you'd be able to take a look at it."

The old man's eyes sparkled with intrigue. "Listen to him," he said, giving Remir a nudge with his elbow. "He wonders if I'll take a look." Then, he motioned impatiently with his hand. "Let's see your Greek text."

"It's not exactly mine," Davides said before handing it over. "It comes by way of Seville. I'm to get it deciphered."

Bendayan retracted his hand and contemplated him somberly. "I'd heard you were working for Haroun. Seeing you here with your cousin, I thought maybe you'd given it up."

"Is it a problem?" Davides asked, feeling a tendril of dismay. He had been so certain that Bendayan would be a neutral party.

"A problem? Hmph! It's a waste, is what it is. You have a fine mind, and what are you using it for? Military nonsense."

"That's what I've been telling him," Remir corroborated, with a note of pained frustration in his voice, "but it's like I'm talking to myself."

"See there, Davides? You'd do well to listen to your cousin," Bendayan said, wagging a finger at him.

Davides opened his mouth, then shut it. There was no way he could even begin to explain how misguided that suggestion was.

Bendayan's face softened. "Never mind me. Córdoba was a wondrous place before politicians and soldiers tore it apart. Here it is thirty years later, and I'm still bitter. Let's have a look at it, then, shall we?" With a few creaks, he stood and moved to the desk, where sunlight shone in through a glass pane. "Just so we understand each other, Davides, if this document were yours, I'd have worked on it for the price of making myself a copy. Seeing that it comes 'by way of Seville' . . . well, it's going to cost them."

Davides assented with a small smile. Very carefully, he unfolded the parchment on the desk and weighted down the corners.

The old alchemist bent over the text, scanning it. After a bit, he took a thick, glass magnifying disk from the desk drawer and held it above certain sections. "There are definitely some embedded symbols, some allegorical notations," Bendayan muttered. "It'll take some time to sort them out. Stop by in a few days, and I'll try to have

144

some preliminary understanding of it worked out for you."

"That's great," Davides said. He felt like he was one step closer to being free of a quagmire. "Thank you."

"Hmph," said Bendayan.

It was a fine, fall day: the perfect mixture of cool air and bright sunshine. After leaving the alchemist, Davides and Remir went down to the livery and saddled their horses in order to take a leisurely ride through the countryside. Initially, the two mares had a lot of pent-up energy from standing around in a stall for a day and a half. They chomped on their bits and danced sideways through the crowded city streets. Once they had crossed the Alcántara Bridge, Davides and Remir gave them their heads and let them gallop southwards, back into the olive groves. Eventually, they slowed them to a walk and wound their way through the estates and country houses of the local nobles. In deference to Remir's leg, they kept the ride short, returning to the city in the late afternoon.

Following supper, they spent time with Ishaq and his family. The children had transferred their capricious attentions from Davides to Remir, who knew an endless supply of stories with which to entertain them. Davides played chess with Ishaq, talked about local news, and discussed Ishaq's recent projects, including the mariner's astrolabe. It was a pleasant little domestic scene, and for a short time Davides was able to stop thinking about the chaos that had become his life.

The next morning, Davides and Remir swung by the tailor's, hoping their new clothes would be ready. They were told that their order was progressing nicely, and that everything should be ready by Thursday, or Saturday, or Monday at the latest. With a sigh and a shrug, they resigned themselves to borrowing Ishaq's clothes for a little longer.

After that, Davides began introducing his 'cousin' to a few choice members of Toledo's scholarly community. Being a close-knit bunch, some had already heard of their arrival. Once the initial introductions and pleasantries were over, Davides let Remir do most of the talking. As Davides had occasion to know, Remir had a gift for dissemblance and could glibly fabricate information regarding his pretend past, present, and future to satisfy their questions.

Their last meeting of the day was with the Bishop of Toledo, who extolled to them the academic advantages of monastic life. At a certain point, Davides noticed that Remir was struggling to maintain a serious, reflective countenance. And, who could blame him? Remir, as a monk? Reclused in a monastery and taking vows of silence, poverty, or chastity? It was absurd, not to mention hilarious. They got out of there fast, before either of them burst out laughing.

"Okay. That might have been a mistake," Davides said, when they were well away from the cathedral. It was early evening, and the nearby taverns were beginning to fill up with the dinner crowd. He slowed and looked around. "As long as we're here in the Christian Quarter, do you want to stop somewhere for a drink?"

"Nah," Remir responded indifferently.

"Really?"

"No, not really! Of course I want a drink. Probably several." Remir shook his head in amused wonder. "It's like you don't even know me."

* * *

The city's harvest festivities were fast approaching, which meant that the taverns were extra crowded and boisterous. Wine, ale, and all manner of tasty tidbits were cheap and plentiful. This time around, Davides kept a close eye on his drink and his drinking. He didn't want a repeat of what had happened last Friday. It was tough, though. He kept running into old acquaintances who wanted to toast his return to Toledo, and new acquaintances who were happy to do the same.

Following one such encounter, Davides realized that he had lost track of Remir, whom he had last seen dancing with a very attractive woman. Davides vaguely remembered dark, wavy hair framing a heart-shaped face. Unlike most of the other women circulating in the vicinity, she didn't have the stamp of a harlot, but perhaps she was merely of a more sophisticated variety. Davides flagged down a serving girl, who appeared a trifle put out when he inquired after Remir rather than being interested in her. But, she knew immediately of whom he spoke. Remir was hard to miss.

"Damijana sure took a shine to your cousin," the girl replied, with a wink and a nudge.

"Damijana?" Davides forced the syllables of the unusual name past a throat suddenly tight with alarm.

"Yeah, she runs this place. Almost never mixes with the customers, if you know what I mean."

Davides was pretty sure he did. "Where are they?" he demanded.

His tone made her suddenly wary. She stopped flirting with him and scrunched her face up dubiously.

He fumbled for a coin and pressed it into her hand. "Please. Our grandmother is ill. On her death bed. I need to find him now."

Compared to the other deceptions he had perpetrated recently, this one lacked anything resembling finesse, but the serving girl was not a discriminating sort. Either the story or the coin did the trick. She nodded towards a back door.

Moving as quickly as he could without drawing attention, he made his way to the door and tried the latch. It opened, and he slipped into the storage room beyond. A tallow candle on a wall sconce sputtered out enough light for him to see that there were lots of casks and barrels, but no Remir. It was at that point that he spied another door, which, he guessed, would lead outside to an alley. Pressing his ear against the wooden planks, he listened for a moment but heard nothing. Hard to discern whether that was good or bad. His lips tightened. He drew his knife, took a step back, then kicked the door open.

"Hey!" a woman's voice objected.

Davides chanced a quick look into the alley. It was dark, but he could see a woman sprawled on the ground, her bodice unlaced, in the attitude of someone who has just been tripped over backwards. Damijana, he presumed. She didn't look hurt; only surprised and annoyed.

Remir was standing near her holding a slim blade in his right hand. When he saw Davides, he appeared slightly annoyed himself. Shifting closer to the tavern wall, Remir turned and offered Damijana a hand up. She eyed him cautiously, then let herself be pulled to her feet.

"Careful," Davides warned, stepping into the alley. "She's one of them."

"I thought maybe."

"You thought maybe!" Davides exclaimed in a harsh whisper. "And you came out here with her anyway?"

"Well, yeah." Remir gazed at her wistfully. With a coy smile, she slowly pulled the lacings tight on her bodice. "I wasn't sure; it was just a hunch. I knew we'd been followed today, and," he gestured with the knife, "she had this blade strapped to her thigh. Seemed like an excessive precaution."

"Strange," Damijana interjected. "'Cause from where I'm standing, it weren't nearly enough." She sighed expansively, and the lacings on the bodice slipped a notch. With an effort, Davides pulled his eyes back to her face.

"How did you tumble?" Remir asked him.

"What? Uh . . . her name. Damijana. It's Slavic, like Attab and Jahwar. That seems to be a common thread with this group. Plus, she's not exactly a harlot by trade; I guess she owns this tavern."

"My husband owns it," Damijana said. "I just run it."

"Your husband?" Remir repeated sharply.

She gave a short laugh. "Aren't you cute. I work with a bunch of thugs who want you dead, but your concern is that I'm a married woman."

Remir reconsidered his priorities and smiled sheepishly, but Davides was not amused. Perhaps the discovery that a group of bloodthirsty criminals was plotting to murder them had dampened his sense of humor. He grabbed Damijana by the arm and shoved her up against the wall.

"Easy!" she hissed. "Can't we be civil?"

"Neither one of us has stuck a knife in you yet," Davides retorted. "Under the circumstances, that's pretty civil."

Rather than being cowed by the threat, she lifted her chin defiantly. "Look, you came into my place. I wasn't stalking you. And, if I *had* been setting up your friend, he'd have been dead 'fore you got to us."

That much was probably true, but it didn't let her off the hook. "You honestly expect us to believe this was all pleasure and no business?" Davides scoffed.

Her chin dipped sideways. "Attab was a brute. As far as I'm concerned, the world's a better place without him. But, there's some who want to know why you took him out, and why you're here in Toledo. They smell competition. Are they right?" She sounded hopeful.

That was a twist Davides hadn't considered: they — whoever 'they' were — had constructed a scenario in which Davides and 'Ramiro' were part of a rival criminal organization, muscling in on their territory. If he was reading Damijana right, she didn't deem that a bad thing and was, in fact, shopping for new management.

He released her arm and took a step back. "You and your associates are way off the mark. Attab attacked us. We killed him. End of story."

She pursed her lips and frowned. "Then, who was the other out-of-towner who came 'round asking about you? He talked the talk, so I pegged him as a pro."

Davides and Remir exchanged glances: that sounded kind of ominous.

"I never caught a name," Damijana went on, "but he was young, like you two. Curly blonde hair and brown eyes. Had an *oud* slung over his back."

An *oud*? Davides's mind flashed back to Ambroz, to the crowded common room and the fair-haired minstrel who had accompanied Remir's tales of bears and bandits. Could it be the same one? And if so, what were the odds that he was merely looking them up for old times' sake?

When Davides glanced at Remir a second time, he was expecting confirmation of his own perplexed apprehension. What he saw was something entirely different. For one telling moment, Remir's face went blank, his eyes downcast and focused inwards.

Funny, how sudden enlightenment felt a lot like getting punched in the gut.

* * *

"It's not what you think," Remir began, as the two of them walked briskly down twisting city streets. Damijana had indicated that the *oud* player was staying on the second story of a cheap boarding house off Nogal Plaza. This seemed as good a time as any to pay him a visit.

"Did you know this minstrel prior to Ambroz?" Davides asked.

"Yes," Remir admitted.

"Then, it's exactly what I think."

"But, no! Because running into Julián was pure coincidence. As you say, he's a minstrel. He moves around a lot and sometimes plays at the taverns in Salamanca. That's how we know each other. When I saw him in Ambroz, I told him not to let on we were friends, for his own safety. I didn't know what you or Sajid would do if you realized he was an old acquaintance of mine."

151

"That's it?" Davides couldn't quite believe that Remir's famous poise had been shaken by something so trivial.

"That's it. Well, . . . except that I also asked him to take word back to my father that I was fine, unharmed, and still en route to Seville."

Something failed to add up. "Then, why is he here now?"

"I have no idea. We certainly didn't *plan* on meeting in Toledo. How could we have? The night Julián was in Ambroz was before you offered to ..." Remir searched for neutral words, "to redirect my potential worth to Seville. And, it was way before you were given the assignment of coming to Toledo. I swear, Davides: Julián couldn't have known I'd be here. Not from me."

Davides ground to a halt, then forced himself to keep moving. He was inclined to believe Remir, although those last words opened up a line of questioning that Davides didn't even want to contemplate right now. "Is there anything else I should know about this friend of yours before we knock on his door?"

Another long pause. *Oh, Lord. Now what?*

"In the interest of full disclosure, I probably should mention that Ambroz wasn't the first time I had contact with Julián on our little journey south." Remir took a few pensive strides before continuing. "I've known Julián for a couple of years now, but always in the context of, you know, recreational pursuits. Basically, we hung out in taverns, sang songs, and got drunk together. I didn't really know what he did for a living, beyond him being a fine musician. If I thought about it at all, I guess I assumed he lived off his tips." Remir hesitated again before divulging the next piece of information. "It turns out that

Julián is the front man for a group of — shall we call them entrepreneurs? — that operates around Salamanca."

"*Filho da égua!* He was one of the horse thieves?"

"They didn't know they were attacking me!" Remir insisted. "If they'd known I was with your group, believe me, they would have stayed far, far away. Why do you think the bandits took off, when they clearly outnumbered you and had better position? I got hold of one of them, who knew that Julián and I were friends, and he called off the attack." Remir's voice dropped so that it was barely audible. "Through this other bandit, I sort of prevailed upon Julián for a favor: ride to Ávila and explain Salamanca's predicament to one of my father's friends. Never mind which one. Then, of his own accord, Julián intercepted me in Ambroz to let me know that he had done so."

And, you never suspected a damn thing! Davides was kicking himself with every step, but he was trying hard to focus on more pressing matters than his own ineptitude. "Does your father's friend have ties with Castile-León?" Davides asked, keeping the emotion from his voice.

Remir nodded.

Davides thought back to when they had been training outside Cáceres just before heading east to Toledo. He had assured Remir that Castile-León wouldn't have figured out yet what was happening in Salamanca. But, Remir had known differently. The peculiar expression on Remir's face. The quick decision to assume an alias. Both had been prompted by Remir's realization that he might have made a mistake in alerting Castile-León.

How soon would word have reached Burgos? A lot depended on how many horses a rider went through to deliver it. Using his experience as a messenger, Davides did some quick calculations: the woods south of Salamanca to Ávila, then Ávila north to Burgos. "That means the Castilians know about Seville's plan and have known for maybe two weeks."

"Assuming the message went through, yes," Remir said. He paused briefly, then added, "I had to try, Davides. I didn't want the neighboring lords in Castile-León to think my father was cooperating willingly with the Emir. And, for all I knew, I was going straight to Seville."

"You don't have to justify it," Davides said, with a strained smile. "We kidnapped you. You had every reason to retaliate in any way you could."

Remir gave him a sidelong look. "You're calling it 'kidnapping' these days?"

Typical, that Remir would pick up on the nuance of a single word. In his own mind, Davides had been calling it that for a long time now, but he probably shouldn't have said it out loud. "Yeah, well, 'strategic-relocation-of-a-political-asset' takes too long to say."

They reached Nogal Plaza, with its decaying walnut tree sagging in the center of the small square. The moon had started to rise and was meekly casting whitewashed light into open areas, leaving others seeped in inky shadow. On the north side of the plaza, the small boarding house stood, held together by patches and prayers. Next to it was a newer, taller structure, and sandwiched between the two buildings were the stairs leading to the second story of the boarding house. The main floor was closed up tight, its proprietor having turned in for the night. However, a faint glow of candlelight peeked through the shuttered window

154

upstairs, and the soft twang of a soulful melody drifted through the air.

"I think we've found the right place," Remir remarked.

They skirted the plaza, sticking to the shadows, and minced their way up the broken stone stairs to the landing. Before they had a chance to knock, though, the *oud* made a muffled squawk as a flattened palm silenced its reverberating strings. Remir tapped lightly. A moment later, floorboards creaked, and a tentative voice from behind the door ventured a hushed, "Hello?"

"Julián? It's me." Remir responded.

There was the scrape of a bar latch being lifted, and the door opened. Compared to the pitch-black of the staircase, the room's candlelight dazzled, making Davides and Remir squint and blink as their eyes adjusted.

"Peace and blessings upon you," Remir greeted the minstrel.

For an instant, Julián stood immobile, the backlight hiding his expression. "Likewise," he managed at last, reaching a stiff hand forward for a formal handshake.

Remir took the hand, but pulled Julián into a half embrace and kissed either cheek. "It's all right. He knows we're old friends."

"Oh," Julián said, still wary, but he stepped back with a gesture of invitation. "Please, come in. It's . . . it's really great to see you again. Both of you ..."

Now that Davides could make him out more clearly, it was easy to understand why Julián made a good scout for the horse thieves. He looked eminently harmless. He had a slight frame, and his features were pleasant but unremarkable. The only visible weapon he carried was the all-purpose knife common amongst travelers. He was dressed for riding, with a tunic that came to mid-thigh, trousers, and tall boots. Everything about him implied he was a wandering minstrel who was talented enough to afford a mount.

After assessing Julián, Davides took a quick survey of the room. The second story was one large, open area. There was a warped table, a couple of crude benches, a few pegs on the wall, and a bucket for water. That was about it. Against the far wall were several straw pallets, two of which were already occupied. Both men seemed to be fast asleep.

"Who are they?" Davides asked, keeping his voice low.

"Don't know," Julián whispered in reply. He shrugged and shifted nervously. "They were dead-to-the-world before I got here."

"I hate to cut straight to business," Remir said to Julián, "but do you by chance have news for me?"

Julián gave a single, diffident nod of confirmation.

Remir frowned at the sleeping men. "Considering the circumstances, maybe it would be best if we spoke in your *jerga*. Do you mind, Davides?"

Did Davides mind if Remir and Julián exchanged information in code, using the bandits' argot that had so mystified him earlier? Well, yes. However, none of them wanted random individuals like Julián's temporary roommates to overhear a conversation involving Remir, Salamanca, or the army from Seville.

Davides plunked himself down on one of the benches and looked at Remir. "Go ahead. You'll fill me in later, right?" He wasn't being naïve. Given Remir's talent for subterfuge, Davides expected to get an edited account. But, he would rather have Remir openly keeping

156

information from him than sneaking out alone at some later point to talk privately with Julián, especially when a gang of aggravated criminals was having murderous thoughts about them.

"Of course, I'll fill you in," Remir assured him, taking the seat next to him.

Julián looked at them askance, befuddled by their arrangement. He settled on the bench across from them and, after another moment's hesitation, began speaking.

At first, Davides understood little of what Remir and Julián were saying. He was fairly certain that they started out talking about him, since Julián glanced in his direction a few times, and Remir would need to explain how much Davides knew and to what degree he could be trusted.

After listening for a short time, Davides was able to draw a couple of interesting conclusions. First, Remir was not nearly as well-versed in *jerga* as Julián. The minstrel had to repeat or re-phrase certain expressions, sometimes resorting to more universal terms in order to get his message across. Also, the sentences themselves still followed the syntax of Andalusian Arabic, so when Davides stopped focusing on specific, unintelligible words, he could gather the gist of what they were saying.

Something about speed or urgency. Someone— Castilians, maybe?—had broken into . . . somewhere. There had been a fight, guards were killed. Something had been stolen. No, Davides realized with a start, not some-thing, some-one.

Amira.

He should have pretended that he was oblivious to the meaning of the words and the sudden tension in the air. But, he couldn't stop himself. Of their own accord, his eyes lifted and found Remir's. He couldn't have been more obvious if he had jumped up and down, and waved his hands. Julián had just told Remir that Castilians had abducted his sister.

"When?" Remir asked, staring fixedly at Davides.

"Monday. During morning prayers." Julián replied, without bothering to encode the information. His eyes darted from Remir to Davides and back again.

It was now Wednesday night. Three full days. Davides registered it, but he was still fighting flat denial. *This cannot be happening!* General Haroun wouldn't take any more chances with Remir, his remaining hostage. Three days ago, the General would have dispatched a team to Toledo. They could be here in the city even now. Their mission would be to find Davides and Remir, and then transport Remir directly to Seville.

Only, Remir would no longer go willingly. The threat to his sister had controlled his actions to this point, but those fetters were now gone. That left Davides as the only thing standing between Remir and freedom.

What the hell were you thinking, becoming friends with a hostage!

Davides's mind raced for some way out of the situation that didn't involve violence. "Remir, what if it's not true? No offense to Julián, but how did he even come by this information? Word on the street? For that matter, how did he know to find us in Toledo? Did he come of his own volition, or is someone paying him—or pressuring him—to give you this information?"

Remir raised his eyebrows speculatively and gazed off into space. "All reasonable questions," he murmured, even as Julián lifted his hands in a gesture of indignant blamelessness.

158

Davides let out his breath. *Okay. This will work. Just buy some time to verify the story before —*

Remir sucker punched him.

Had they been standing, that one shot to the jaw might have comprised the whole fight: beginning, middle, and inglorious end. Remir wasn't holding back and had caught Davides completely off guard. As it was, though, Remir had to twist his body awkwardly to throw the punch. The blow didn't end up knocking Davides unconscious, but it landed with enough force to spill him backwards off the bench.

Davides rolled away from the table, then lurched clumsily to his feet. The taste of copper filled his mouth, and he spat out blood. He shook his head and blinked rapidly, trying to bring sudden double vision back into focus.

Two Remirs? Great. As if one weren't enough . . .

The twin Remirs looked irritated. Or maybe disappointed. Displeased, in any case. They swiveled off the bench and came at him.

Unsure as to which of the two images he should dodge, Davides stood still and braced himself. Remir's shoulder caught him at the waist and strong arms wrapped around his legs. Even as his feet left solid ground, Davides was grabbing for the back of Remir's head to help break his fall. The two of them went down together. Once on the floor, Remir slipped Davides's grasp and, using his superior wrestling skill, moved to establish some sort of hold.

Certain holds, Davides knew, could dislocate joints and incapacitate an opponent. Others could make a person black out. If all else failed, Remir could simply immobilize him and let Julián do the rest.

159

The possibilities flashed through Davides's mind and compelled him to frenetic resistance. He arched his back, thrashed his legs, and struck out blindly with his fists. A wild swing connected hard enough to stun Remir briefly, and Davides scrambled back to his feet.

Remir shook off the blow and came up swinging. He delivered a barrage of punches to Davides's lower ribs and solar plexus. Davides would have given ground, if he had had any ground to give. But, the room wasn't that large, and he didn't want to get pushed into a corner. He tucked his chin low and brought his fists up to protect his face, while keeping his arms tight to his sides in order to deflect some of the jabs and hooks. He should have been thinking about going on the offensive. Better yet, he should have been keeping track of Julián.

From behind him, a foot stamped into the back of his right knee, making his leg buckle. Remir pulled back a bit, and Davides caught a flash of movement from his left. Instinctively, he ducked and threw up his arm, just in time to block the bucket that Julián swung at his head. Before Davides could recover from the glancing blow, Remir sprang on top of him, forcing him to the ground. Again.

And, again, Davides struggled with every fiber of his being, narrowly escaping a couple more pinning holds. But, Remir was still on top of him, and Davides knew he couldn't keep it up: Remir was bigger, stronger, and just plain better at hand-to-hand fighting. It was only a matter of time.

Sheer desperation made Davides grab his knife and pull it free. Remir caught sight of the blade and hastily spun away from him. After directing a lackluster feint towards Julián, Davides clambered to his feet and reeled back against the nearest wall.

He held the knife low and forward while he fought to catch his breath, his lungs laboring against his bruised ribs. His vision had cleared, and he noted vaguely that Julián's roommates had vanished, leaving the door wide open on their way out. Julián had taken Davides's feint to heart and had retreated a few steps before drawing his own knife. In the meantime, Remir was circling away from the door, so that Davides would have to split his attention between him and Julián.

Remir's dark eyes had gone opaque. He directed a grim nod towards Davides's knife and asked harshly, "Is that really the way you want this to go?"

Davides stared helplessly back at him. He didn't want 'this' to be happening at all! Were there alternatives he was somehow missing? He couldn't beat Remir and Julián in an unarmed fight. A moment ago, they had been on the verge of overpowering him. What did Remir expect him to do?

Lose the fight. Let them overpower you. Then, Remir goes free.

It was an astonishing thought, one that had reams upon reams of repercussions. Before Davides could even begin to sift through them, however, an odd plume of darkness drifted through the open doorway. For an instant, Davides thought the bizarre image was being conjured by his concussion. Then, he made out black robes, face masks, and an array of blunt and sharp weapons.

Not city guards. Not soldiers from Seville. Damijana had warned them that her associates wanted them dead. Davides just hadn't anticipated that she had meant tonight.

In one deft motion, Davides reversed the grip on his knife. He chose a fluttering shadow who was wielding a sword and stepped recklessly inside his opponent's first swing. Trapping the sword arm with his left elbow, he plunged his knife into the man's lower back. Davides released his own blade and, as the man fell back in agony, twisted the sword away from the other's weakened grasp.

Now, at least, he had a sword.

The next few moments were chaotic in the extreme: a blur of weapons and limbs, a snarl of too many bodies buffeting each other in the close space of the boarding house room. A couple of weapons might have grazed him or glanced off of him, but he was too incensed to take notice. At some point, the table was overturned, and the glow of the candle stub winked out. That was fine by him, since he didn't need light to fight these men: they were all so conveniently within sword's reach.

Whatever these assailants had been expecting, it wasn't the enthusiastic offensive with which they were met. A couple of wounded ones abandoned the fight and staggered out. They were followed by another who evidently preferred his targets to be unarmed and unsuspecting. In mid-parry, Davides found himself suddenly alone, with no one left to fight. Nearby, however, he heard the solid *choonk* of edged metal on wood. Then came the splintering sound of wood giving way under further impact. From the meager light filtering through the shutters and doorway, he made out a figure scrunched into the corner by the table, clutching the remnants of a bucket defensively in front of him as an axe lifted above him for yet another blow.

162

Davides barreled into the side of the black-robed attacker, and the descending blade scraped down the wall. After ducking another swing from the axe, Davides drove his sword through the man's body, then pulled it free. He waited for his opponent to fall, ensuring he was no longer a threat, before turning to Julián.

Julián, still scrunched into the corner, blinked up at him in wide-eyed astonishment. "Thank you?" he hazarded, making his appreciation sound like a question. "That was, um, incredibly decent of you."

Especially when one considered that a few moments ago, the horse thief had tried to brain Davides with the very bucket he had just been using as a shield. Julián had left that part out, but Davides could fill in the blanks. His eyes narrowed: why exactly had he just saved this guy's life?

There was no sound, no warning. Something that felt like a band of iron hooked over Davides's left arm and wrapped around his body. At the same time, a cloth came from the right to cover his mouth and nose, held in place by an unrelenting hand.

How could he have forgotten about Remir? Neglected the fact that their fight wasn't over?

With a sharp twist of his body, Davides attempted to throw Remir off, to no avail. He drove backwards with his feet until the two of them came up hard against a wall. Remir grunted but didn't relax his rigid hold. Although Davides could still breathe, the cloth over his face smelled sickeningly sweet yet sharply bitter at the same time. The vile odor, mingling with the blood that still oozed from the cuts inside his mouth, made his head swim and his stomach churn.

Davides dropped his sword and grabbed at Remir's right hand, trying ineffectually to pull it away from his face. Black beads, deeper than the pervading gloom, swarmed across his vision. The black beads pooled and spread, like spilt ink.

* * *

wake up . . .

Patches of color were shuffling about, but they failed to form any meaningful composite. It couldn't be very important. He let himself drift.

wake up . . .

Why? Why wake up? It was so comfortable where he was, lying snug in a featherbed. Hard to breathe, but so soft.

Wake up.

The tone of the annoying voice was getting sharper. As he wavered between listening and not, his once cozy bed morphed into something else. It became a viscous mire, clinging to him, weighing him down with paralyzing torpor. Suddenly desperate, he struggled to reach the surface.

Wake up!

Davides woke up, but immediately wished he had not. Splintering pain in his head. Bright light searing his vision. To make matters worse, everything reeked of ale. He found himself breathing shallow and fast in a dedicated effort to keep from throwing up.

He was lying on his side, so instinctively he started to roll over—anything to escape the implacable brilliance slicing into his brain—but he couldn't seem to use his body to turn. Oddly, his arms also refused to obey him.

164

They were heavy and unresponsive, as if they had fallen asleep. Prying his eyes open, Davides squinted at his wrists, which were just inches from his face. A strip of cloth was wound around them, holding them together. Very strange.

And . . . sort of . . . alarming.

A jolt went through him, as confusion and fear finally breached a hole in his wall of stupor. He made an effort to move his feet and discovered they were bound as well. *Where am I? What the hell is going on?*

Tall, dry grass stood all around him, its acrid smell nearly obliterated by that overwhelming stench of stale ale. The sun was rising. Or, was it setting? In either case, it was hitting him squarely in the face. There were some squat trees scattered close by that were creating patterns of comically elongated shadows across the landscape. For some reason, it reminded him of the terrain north of Toledo, but he must be mistaken. What would he be doing in Toledo?

Using an elbow to push off this time, he eased himself onto his back. At least his eyes could seek refuge now. As they fled the blazing orb on the horizon, they caught sight of someone sitting nearby, his back against a tree, his head drooping forward as if asleep.

Davides studied the sleeping man for a few moments. Something struck him as familiar. Slender. Not very tall. Blonde, curly hair. Julián? Yes, Julián. An old friend of Remir's.

That thought finally started something in his aching head. An avalanche of memories, like so many rocks and uprooted trees, crashed down on him. They started to lose momentum when they reached the fight at the boarding house and then petered out completely. Try as he might, Davides could not recall how he had gotten from that boarding house in Toledo to some grassy field in the middle of nowhere.

Plodding through the thick haze in his head, Davides rehashed the moments just before he blacked out. The cloth. The cloth that Remir had held pressed to his nose and mouth. It had been soaked in something. Remir had put something on the cloth, something noxious that had made him lose consciousness.

Davides vaguely remembered hearing about a tincture that physicians were using to keep their patients in a deep, unfeeling sleep during surgery. Opium, henbane, and other narcotic plants were steeped in alcohol, then the resulting tincture was poured onto a sponge and held over the patient's nose and mouth. That kind of concoction would explain why Davides had passed out, why he had stayed unconscious (or, at least, unaware) all night, and why he now felt like he was suffering from the world's worst hangover.

Where had Remir gotten such a thing? Probably from the physician who had treated his leg. Davides had been absent for at least two of the visits, and Remir could have spun a convincing excuse for needing it. Remir had even told Davides about buying bandages and salve, and spending an extravagant amount on clothes, both of which had covered up the expense.

How could you have been so stupid!

Avoiding the offensively cheerful sunbeams that had originally awakened him, Davides searched his surroundings again, but he gleaned little new information. Considering the landscape, he was pretty sure he was somewhere north of Toledo. No sign of Remir, though,

166

nor of any horses. No sign of anything except trees, grass, and rocks. And Julián.

Davides tilted his head back until he could see his so-called captor. Julián was still dozing against the tree. If the horse thief was supposed to be guarding him, he was doing a pretty lousy job of it. Although, who was he kidding? Given the way he was feeling, he wouldn't be going anywhere any time soon unless someone picked him up and carried him.

That brought up an interesting consideration: how had Remir and Julián gotten him out of the city? Draped over their shoulders? It didn't seem likely. Last night, the only way out of Toledo would have been the Bisagra Gate. It was manned by city guards, many of whom would recognize Davides—unconscious or not—and then ask inconvenient questions. Surely, Remir wouldn't have chanced that.

Considering the risk involved in getting Davides through the gate, a better question than 'how' might be 'why'. Why bother taking him out of the city? Why not leave him where he had fallen, back at the boarding house?

Because you know too much to be left behind.

Davides knew that Remir had been apprised of Amira's abduction, that Julián had been delivering secret messages, and that Remir had very few resources at his disposal with which to escape. Their armor, weapons, and most of their gold and silver were back at Ishaq's. Their horses? Useless. Anyone looking for them—like soldiers from Seville—would have immediately posted a lookout at the livery.

No money, no mode of transportation, no equipment. Remir's only real advantage was that no one would initially assume that he was being deliberately evasive.

No one except you.

So, Remir couldn't leave Davides behind. But, he also couldn't keep dragging him along as a prisoner. It would slow Remir down when he had to move quickly. And, it would be far too conspicuous when he needed to pass unnoticed.

The smart thing would be for him to bury you out here, where your body will never be found. Then, he can vanish without a trace.

Movement by the tree interrupted Davides's thoughts. That was all right. They had taken a decidedly depressing turn.

Julián had awakened and, discovering that his captive was conscious, had hopped to his feet. They contemplated each other for a moment, then Julián asked, "How are you feeling?" Seeming to appreciate the foolishness of the question, he winced and added, "I mean, we have a little water, if you're thirsty."

Davides realized that he was extraordinarily thirsty. His throat felt so dry he wasn't even sure he could speak. He gave a faint nod of assent, trying not to jostle his throbbing head.

"Okay," Julián said. He picked up a waterskin, but took only a half step forward before jerking to a halt.

"What's wrong?" Davides croaked.

Julián swallowed hard. "I'm not that keen on getting close to you."

Davides breathed a short, incredulous laugh. He was doped up, beaten up, tied up, and he probably couldn't have stood up if his life depended on it. "What could I possibly do to you?"

"Oh, I've seen what you can do to people, thank you very much. Besides, Remir warned me to stay away from you. And, not to talk to you."

Normally, Davides would have pointed out that Julián *was* talking to him, but in his current condition it seemed like a waste of spit. He lay still and did his best to look non-threatening.

Julián chewed on his lower lip, then approached. He stopped about five feet away and lobbed the skin of water so that it landed with an anemic *splat* near Davides's hands. There wasn't much left. Still prone, Davides got the skin unstopped and tipped it towards his mouth. Water spilled unsteadily onto his face and neck before he managed to find a couple of swallows. The trickle of water ended in drips, and Davides let the empty waterskin drop back to the ground.

In the meantime, Julián had retreated to his tree. Unable to stop himself, Davides echoed the single, most-asked question of the past several weeks. "Where's Remir?"

"I'm not talking to you, remember?" Julián sat down resolutely, avoiding Davides's gaze, and picked up the *oud*. Without actually making any music, he began moving his fingers up and down the strings on the neck of the instrument.

Davides sighed. He probably should have been doing something useful, like loosening the bonds on his hands and feet, or plotting a clever escape. Instead, he fell back asleep.

* * *

When Davides awoke again, he felt better on the inside, worse on the outside. His headache and nausea had diminished, but the right half of his jaw was heavy, stiff, and swollen; his left forearm radiated a sick, cold ache; and, with every breath he took, his ribs felt like they were being jabbed by needles.

Then, he realized that something specific had awakened him. Remir was in the process of untying him.

Pulling together a few shreds of bravado, Davides mumbled, "Anyone ever tell you you hit like a girl?"

The taut expression on Remir's face relaxed a fraction. "You've fought a lot of girls, have you?"

Davides smiled wanly with the side of his jaw that still worked and flexed his newly freed arms and ankles. Remir sat down next to him, wrapping his arms around his knees and staring at the horizon. That was when Davides registered what Remir was wearing. Instead of Ishaq's cream-colored tunic with its intricate red and gold embroidery, he had on a worn, tight-sleeved robe that might once have been black or dark brown, hard to tell which. He studied the clothing, intrigued, and wondered if his eyes were playing tricks on him. Gritting his teeth, he pushed himself into a sitting position and found that he was similarly attired. For some reason, they were both dressed like the bandits who had attacked them last night.

"Why are we dressed like the bandits who attacked us last night?" he asked, putting thought to word.

"It's better than being naked," Remir replied obscurely. Before Davides could request clarification, Remir switched subjects. "I sent Julián to find more water."

In other words, he had wanted Julián out of the way. Davides braced himself. Remir rubbed his forehead,

170

but said nothing more. After a moment, Davides asked, "Do you have a plan?"

"Yes."

Another long pause.

"Is sitting here part of the plan?"

"No."

Unsure as to how to proceed, Davides took a moment to survey their surroundings from his new vantage point. A brisk wind was blowing across the grass, creating an undulating effect that made the land look like a troubled, ochre sea. The only thing of note in the choppy sea was a two-wheeled handcart that had been pulled up close to one of the stout trees. From where he was sitting, the handcart appeared to contain a hogshead of ale. Davides blinked at it in confusion. An ambulatory alehouse?

Some of the vapors from that tincture must still be floating in his head, he decided. He wrenched his fanciful attention back to the important issue at hand. Remir was wasting valuable time on his behalf. The least Davides could do was speed things along. "We should get this over with," he blurted out.

Remir's eyebrows drew down quizzically.

"It's fine," Davides continued, feeling an insane need to reassure Remir. "I worked it all out earlier, made my peace with God. I'm all set. Although, I'd appreciate it if you skipped the whole 'staking out for the crows' thing. That's just gruesome."

Remir was staring at him in disbelief. "You think I'm going to kill you?" he demanded at last.

"Well, that's the most sensible thing to do."

"In whose world?" Remir exploded. "What did they teach you in Seville, anyway? I'm not going to kill

171

you! I didn't even want to hit you! But, knocking you senseless was the only way I could think of to have a rational conversation with you!"

"Then, . . . then, why bring me out here?"

Remir shook his head in frustrated wonder. "What was I supposed to do? Leave you lying there, unconscious, at the boarding house? Sooner or later, they would have come back, and then they would have killed you."

"Oh." That put things in a new perspective. Davides had convinced himself that he'd been brought out here to be disposed of; instead, it seemed he had been brought out here to be kept safe. He couldn't help but feel good about that reversal of fortune. "In that case, I suppose 'thanks' are in order."

"Don't mention it," Remir grumbled, then added in a less peevish voice, "It was the least we could do after you saved Julián. Which reminds me, …"

"What?"

"You'll understand if, based on some of your actions, I'm a bit confused as to whose side you're on? Normally, I wouldn't pry, but, given our current situation, it's become relevant."

"Whose side?" Davides repeated.

"Yes, Davides, whose side!" Remir's voice regained its edge. "You can't pretend to be loyal to General Haroun and help me at the same time. Not anymore."

There they were, right back where they had left off at the boarding house, minus the fists and knives. Davides didn't want to go back there. It made his head hurt. He closed his eyes and tried to think.

Whose side? In the moment before the bandits' attack, he had been ready to drop his knife. Ready to let Remir escape. But, was that the same as being ready to switch sides? Switching sides sounded uncomfortably like treason, and Davides couldn't imagine turning traitor on General Haroun. Not after everything the General had done for him. But, even if Davides were in a position to take Remir captive—which he clearly was not—he had already determined that he couldn't go through with it. He couldn't do the job that the General expected him to do. Where did that leave him?

The wind was cutting through Davides's thin robe. He wrapped his arms around his midsection and tried not to shiver. *Face it, you did something wrong. Kidnapping people and using them as leverage is just plain wrong. You knew it at the time, and you did it anyway.*

"I understand if you feel like you need to go back to Toledo," Remir said quietly, in the absence of any verbal response from Davides. "All I ask is that you give Julián and me a day's head start. Then, you can tell General Haroun's men the truth. I had an ally in the city. We jumped you and left you tied up out here. Under those circumstances, no one will blame you for not being able to stop us."

Davides shook his head. "They'll just expect me to go after you. Enthusiastically. I can't pull that off."

"Then, come with us," Remir said, watching him out of the corner of his eye. "Help me disappear. At least until this stupid war is over."

Help Remir disappear. That sounded harmless enough. Remir wasn't expecting Davides to divulge state secrets or take up arms against Seville—just get him out of harm's way.

"Okay," Davides said.

"Okay, what? Okay, you'll come with us?"

"Assuming the invitation still stands. Yes, I'll come with you."

Remir's whole body seemed to slump with relief. "Good. This way, there's a chance people will think we're dead. They might not even bother looking for us."

Davides frowned, perplexed. "Why would anyone think we're dead?"

Remir glanced down, his jaw skewed to one side.

"What did you do?" Davides asked sharply.

Part 4 – The topic of bloodletting might come up

The short answer was that Remir had done quite a lot. In a voice flat with fatigue, Remir relayed his nocturnal activities without his standard embellishments. Nonetheless, the raw facts in and of themselves made for an absorbing tale.

"It would probably be best if I backed up and started from the beginning," Remir said, looking at Davides circumspectly. "Do you suppose you could refrain from interruptions and critical comments until I finish?"

"O-kay." Davides drew the word out, hanging his reservations on both syllables.

"Okay," Remir repeated, more firmly. "The first thing we had to do was get out of the city without drawing attention. Since neither Julián nor I had any bright ideas on how to accomplish that, I went to someone who might."

"You didn't!" Davides exclaimed, guessing who the 'someone' was.

"I said, no interruptions! Or believe me, I'll never get through this. And, yes, I did. I convinced Julián to wait at the boarding house while I made a quick dash back to Damijana's. I gave her what money you had on you in exchange for her help in getting out of the city. The empty hogshead was her idea. Somehow—and I didn't inquire as to the how—she knew that a hogshead was large enough to accommodate the average man. Since she often

175

sends barrels of ale or casks of wine to another tavern north of the walled city, sometimes late at night, she thought we could tuck you into a barrel and pass right through the Bisagra Gate without being questioned."

No wonder everything smelled of ale, Davides thought. He and his clothing must be permeated with the stuff.

"She supplied the barrel," Remir was saying, "but suggested that I find less conspicuous clothing. That's what made me think of changing into one of the robes from the dead Vandals."

"Vandals? Is that what they call themselves?"

"I've no idea. That's what I started calling them to separate them from all the other people searching for us right now. You brought up their whimsical Slavic theme, and the Vandals were the only Slavs I could remember from my so-called history lessons. Something about sacking Rome?"

Remir was talking about one of the pivotal moments of military history as a vague point of trivia. Davides started to draw a deep breath for an indignant retort, but his bruised ribs clutched painfully, and all he managed was a weak cough.

"You sidetracked me," Remir said accusingly. "Where was I? Ah, yes. I got back to the boarding house with the handcart and the empty barrel. By then, Julián was almost frantic. Waiting around at the scene of a fight with two dead bodies and a trussed-up nobleman is not his idea of prudent behavior. After sizing up the bodies, I saw one was near my height and the other was roughly your size, so I figured, what the hell? We might as well disguise you in something less respectable, too."

"Gee, thanks."

176

Remir continued without acknowledging Davides's sarcasm. "Then, Julián brought up a concern: when the owner of the boarding house got round to checking the room in the morning, he would pin the dead bodies on Julián. Now, Julián is unabashedly a thief, but he has avoided doing anything that would draw serious attention. He wanted to dispose of the bodies, in the hopes that no one would realize that anyone had died in the fight. The quickest way to make the bodies disappear, he thought, was to toss them over the wall and into the Tagus.

"It occurred to me that water, especially moving water like a river, does strange things to a corpse. It makes bodies hard to identify. If two bodies turned up a ways downstream, wearing nice clothes like the ones Ishaq loaned us, people might jump to certain conclusions. From the perspective of sidestepping General Haroun's men, it would be a whole lot easier if they weren't actually looking for us. If they thought we were dead.

"The Vandals' hair color was similar to our own. Neither of them had blue eyes like you, but what are the chances that eye color can be made out after a couple of days submerged in water? Or that anyone will check? Julián and I put a few rents in Ishaq's tunics, so that they would match the wounds on the two bandits. Then, we dressed them up and dropped them into the river."

Davides realized his mouth was gaping open. He shut it with an audible snap.

"Getting you out in the barrel was simplicity itself," Remir said. "The guards didn't look twice at us. I pushed the cart, you stayed unconscious, and Julián walked alongside chatting about old times. It was a non-event.

177

"After we had cleared the walls, however, we had to confront our next obstacles. No food. No equipment. No money. The only thing I could think of was to get my hands on the swords and crossbows you stashed under the aqueduct, and later find someone willing to buy them. I left you and Julián here while I took our handy-dandy hogshead for a late night stroll through the olive groves. I hid the weapons in the barrel and brought them back here."

Remir broke off as a mounted figure appeared in the distance, heading in their direction. After a few tense moments, they recognized Julián, trotting along on a mule.

Julián's reappearance reminded Davides of one of his unanswered questions from their encounter at the boarding house. Now might be an optimal time to revisit that concern. "Did Julián ever give you an explanation for why he came looking for us in Toledo?"

"Yes, he did, as a matter of fact. He was afraid to take the Via Delapidata straight south because of General Haroun's army. He figured that anyone riding fast would get picked up for questioning, which meant that going to Seville by way of Toledo would be safer, and possibly faster in the long run. Little did he know how much faster. He stopped in the city for the night, heard your name being tossed around, and decided to make a few inquiries. Otherwise, he might have ridden out this morning, none the wiser."

"Oh." It was a reasonable explanation, one that fit perfectly with Julián's cautious nature. It might even be true. Davides decided to accept it for now and move to another topic. "You said you had a plan?"

"Calling it a plan might be a slight exaggeration."

Davides rolled his eyes.

"Well, it has plan-like aspects," Remir insisted. "A clear objective: namely, me not being used as a political pawn. To that end, I want to stay far, far away from Salamanca, Seville, and Castile-León. In order to do that, we need our own money. In order to get our own money, we need to sell the weapons. In order to sell the weapons, we need a buyer. And, I was kind of hoping you might have some suggestions for finding us one."

Julián stopped next to a nearby tree, swung down from the mule, and tied the animal there. He lifted a bundle from behind the cantle and walked towards where they were sitting.

"What about your sister?" Davides asked. "Where does she fit into your plan?"

"She doesn't," was the surprising response. "I've been thinking about it, and there's no way the Castilians pulled off that 'abduction' without Amira's cooperation. It's entirely possible that she's the one who arranged it. If I'm wrong, I still can't help her by getting myself caught in the same net. Again, the best thing I can do is disappear. That should keep everybody off-balance." Remir welcomed Julián as the latter reached them. "Peace and blessings. I see you found a mule."

Julián, the horse thief, had 'found' a mule? Davides suspected that somewhere out there a farmer was waking up this morning one mule shy.

"And, a little breakfast," Julián said. "It's not much, but it's better than nothing." His eyes lingered a moment on Davides and his lack of restraints. Without comment, Julián smiled winsomely and unwrapped the bundle to reveal a loaf of dark brown bread, a half dozen quinces, and the skin of water, freshly filled.

Davides accepted the hunk of bread that Julián handed to him, but the sawdust texture of his first bite almost made him gag. He finally managed to swallow, but couldn't bring himself to eat more. When Julián extended one of the quinces in his direction, the mere thought of its overwhelming tartness tossed his stomach. Real or imagined, the smell of the tincture-soaked cloth came back vividly. He looked away and put the bread down. "Thanks, but no thanks."

A line of concern creased Remir's brow. "You should eat something. Who knows when we'll find more food."

"I guarantee you that food would be wasted on me right now. You two go ahead."

"So, you're coming with us," Julián said in a neutral voice. "And, do we know yet where we're going?"

"Of course," Remir replied, through a mouthful of bread. "To find a buyer for the weapons."

Still munching, Remir and Julián turned expectantly to Davides.

Right, a buyer. Davides could think of a number of people in the area who would have bought or traded for the weapons, but without knowing how far-flung the search for them would be, it struck him as unwise to approach anyone in the vicinity. All of the honorable nobles and mercenaries would have sympathies with either King Fernando or the Emir, and the less-than-honorable ones might well be associated with the Vandals.

His thoughts drifted outside Toledo to a small, independent city on the frontier by the name of Segovia. Segovia had gone from Muslim to Christian and back again so many times that no one bothered to keep track anymore. She was always gearing up for battle, always in need of weapons, and her relations with the north were no better (or worse) than her relations with the south.

The problem was that Segovia was on the other side of the Guadarrama Mountains, at least a five day journey on foot, maybe longer. What would they live on in the meantime? None of them was a woodsy sort, able to scrounge a meal out of roots and rodents. And, the mountains would be cold this time of year. They would need cloaks, furs, blankets . . .

A fledgling of an idea flapped about awkwardly in his head. His prudent voice tried to squelch the notion, but since that voice didn't bother offering any viable alternatives, he stopped listening to it. If his idea worked, they would deal another blow to the Vandals, and have funds enough to travel to Segovia, where they should be able to sell the weapons. If the scheme didn't work . . . well, his prudent voice was supplying a number of catastrophic outcomes. It wasn't Davides's fault that he wasn't in any condition to heed them.

* * *

Rather than the jeers and objections it probably deserved, Davides's idea was met with wholehearted support from Remir, silent reserve from Julián. They moved the weapons to the mule, and abandoned the barrel and cart. Then, they headed north towards the Guadarrama Mountains. They moved roughly parallel with the road, zigzagging a bit to catch sight of it now and again but avoiding contact with other travelers. The wind continued to whip in from the southwest, creating a constant rush in their ears that was nearly as grating as its chill.

At dusk, they happened upon a shallow river and decided to stop there for the night. On either side of the thin stretch of water, flat white sand lay exposed. The riverbed was parched from the long summer and was awaiting the rains that would soon inundate it. In the meantime, the short, steep banks of the river sat back a good fifteen to twenty feet from the current flow of water.

The banks provided a convenient windbreak for the poorly equipped group of travelers. Remir and Julián, who had been dead on their feet for the last mile or so, stumbled down the bank, burrowed into the dry sand at its base, and promptly fell asleep.

Davides, on the other hand, was wide-awake. Almost jittery. He untacked the mule and hobbled it, so that it could graze without wandering too far. Then, he went down to the river, re-filled the waterskin, and washed his hands and face. In the dim light of the setting sun, he could see the wavering shadows of small barbels feeling their way along the bottom of the stream. If only he had a net, a spear, or some other kind of fishing gear, he might have been able to catch enough of them to make a meal. Since he had none of those things, he tanked up on water in a futile attempt to quiet his growling stomach. Then, he crossed back to where Remir and Julián were sleeping, clambered up the bank, and settled down to keep watch near the dubious protection of some scrub brush.

Not surprisingly, the undernourished bushes did little to block the wind. Davides wrapped the mule's saddle blanket around his shoulders, taking advantage of its tightly woven material to mitigate the cold air. As an added bonus, the pungent odor of dust and sweat from the saddle blanket effectively masked that of his own ale-infused clothes.

Low on the horizon, a harvest moon rose and tinged their surroundings in shades of orange and black. It was about then that a faint movement on the far bank caught his attention. A spotted wildcat slunk down to the water's edge and, as if to underscore Davides's own ineptitude, deftly swiped a wriggling fish from the shallow waters. Flattening its tufted ears disdainfully in his direction, the wildcat turned and vanished into the tall esparto grass.

The cat brought up a good point—not that Davides should be able to catch dinner barehanded, but that he should be ready to shoot other animals that could. Or, better yet, wait for a hare or ibex to come to the river to drink. Why hadn't he thought of it sooner? Digging into the bag next to him, he pulled out two crossbows and a handful of bolts. He loaded them, set them both within easy reach, and waited.

As the night wore on—and no considerate herbivore wandered into sight—Davides's thoughts turned inexorably to the repercussions of his decision to go with Remir and Julián instead of returning to Toledo. He had managed to block out such reflections while they were traveling, but now they wormed their way to the forefront of his mind, demanding more painstaking consideration.

How had 'feigning death' become the best solution to their predicament? Sure, it meant no one from Seville or Castile-León would be hunting them down. But, it also meant that Ishaq and his family would be worried about him. Ishaq would fear the worst, since he knew that Davides was up to his neck in enemies and intrigue. Eventually, Davides supposed he would be able to get word back to Ishaq, but in the meantime, his unexplained absence was distressing people he cared about.

And, what about General Haroun? If the General thought he and Remir were dead, he would be irritated that Seville's plan for controlling Abdur Rahman was unraveling, and he would be very angry at the perpetrators. That, at least, could turn out to be a positive thing. The General's men would make life extremely uncomfortable for anyone associated with the Vandals.

But, if the General discovered Davides was still alive, all of that anger would be directed at him. The General had taken him in, practically treating him like a son, and Davides was repaying him by deceiving him and undermining Seville's war effort. It wasn't premeditated, and it wasn't for profit, but it still smacked of treason.

Maybe he could get the Greek translation back to General Haroun. Retrieving the text wouldn't absolve Davides, but it would show . . . would show what? That Davides didn't hold any ill will towards Seville? The feeling would not be mutual. If his part in Remir's escape were uncovered, he would be executed. It was as simple as that. Nothing he could do would buy forgiveness.

And, nothing he could do now would bring him closer to recovering his family's lands. Either Sisnando Davides had died last night, and any claim to his homestead had been thrown into the Tagus; or, he had betrayed the trust of the one man who could have helped him get his lands back. By pretending to be dead, Davides had failed his family and given up everything, even his name.

All he had left was a half-share in the weapons they were carrying and a beleaguered sense that, in spite of everything, he had made the right choice.

* * *

Davides awoke to a shout of jubilation, followed by a splash, and then more splashing. Still sleep-sodden, he looked towards the river. In the pale light of dawn, he saw Remir standing knee-deep in the stream, a crossbow under one arm, the feet of a limp duck in the other hand. Catching Davides's eye, Remir grinned, gave a short wave with the crossbow, which Davides realized was one of the ones he had loaded the night before, and sloshed his way back to shore.

They built a small fire pit in the sand and used sticks as skewers to cook strips of duck meat over the flames. By that method, a lot of the duck went to waste, but they didn't have time to roast it properly. Even the diminutive, short-lived fire they had was risky, since its smoke might be seen from the road. But, in this case hunger had overridden caution.

Before leaving the campsite, they buried the fire pit, both to keep it from sending up more smoke and to hide the fact that someone had built a fire there in the first place. The remains of the duck got scattered, some into the river and some into the tall grass. They also swept over their footprints with branches, repeating the process on both sides of the river after leading the mule across to the far bank. An experienced tracker wouldn't be fooled by such tricks, but he might be slowed down for awhile. More importantly, (according to Julián, who spoke with some authority on the subject) hiding their trail was a precaution against shepherds or other haphazard wanderers, who might otherwise note their passage and innocently relay that information to the wrong people.

Since both Remir and Davides were new to the fugitive game, they followed Julián's recommendations before resuming their march towards the mountains.

Yesterday's wind had died down, and the clouds had dispersed. As the morning progressed, a stunning, sapphirine sky appeared. In the distance, they could just make out the emergent silhouette of the Guadarrama Mountains. The land rose steadily, while the trees grew taller and the undergrowth became thicker. Eventually, the road they had been using as an occasional landmark turned west, en route to Ávila; but a narrow two-track rambled on due north into the foothills.

It was along that path that they expected to find Alferia, one of the villages that supposedly formed part of the Vandal's criminal organization. Davides's plan was to liberate that village as they had done Manantial. This time, they wouldn't walk into the middle of town, innocent as newly laid eggs. They would be able to assess the community from a distance and come up with a strategy for overpowering the Vandals with minimal risk to themselves and the villagers. Then, the grateful villagers would likely reward them with money or goods, enough to get them over the mountains to Segovia.

By late afternoon, they were all getting weary and unanimously decided to walk on the path rather than fight the terrain. After all, it was a nice path, one which showed consistent use and attempts at maintenance. Deep ruts from heavy wagons had been filled in with pea gravel. Depressions, where muddy pools might have formed during the rainy season, had small channels dug into them to divert water. Low-hanging branches had been pruned back to allow for easier progression. And, trees that had fallen across the way had been cut up and hauled away, leaving only the shorn stumps.

Despite the promising signs of civilization, they had yet to find the village of Alferia. Or any village. As dusk overtook them, they were just resigning themselves to another cold, hungry night when they heard a low whinny coming from off the path ahead of them.

Anticipating trouble, Remir and Julián both jumped for cover; and Davides, who was leading the mule at the time, pulled the animal around in front of him to serve as a shield. Instead of an imminent attack, however, the next thing they heard was a woman's quavering voice: *"Hola? Hay alguien ahí?"*

Still wary of a trap, Davides nudged the mule a few more steps up the trail. From there, he was able to make out the wide blaze and broad frame of a draft horse facing them, maybe a hundred feet off the path. Ears pricked towards them, it neighed another greeting, one equid to another.

"Yes, someone's here," Davides answered cautiously, in the Castilian that the woman had used.

"Thank God!" the voice gasped. "Please! I need help. I'm trapped!"

From his place of concealment, Remir made a rolling motion with his hand, indicating (Davides supposed) that he should keep her talking. Meanwhile, Remir began to work his way silently towards the draft horse.

"What do you mean, 'trapped'?" Davides asked.

"It's some sort of sinkhole, I guess," she replied. "Or underground river. There's only a little water right now, and the hole's not so deep, but with the log on top of me, I can't get out!"

"I don't understand. How did a log fall on you?"

"We were dragging the log back to my village. The earth just gave way beneath us! My horse jumped forward, but I was too slow, and somehow the front end of the log came down on top of me and got jammed there. Now, my horse can't pull it forward, and he can't step back, or he'll be down here with me. And, the ground's too hard to dig around. I've tried. And, ..." The woman's voice was rising with an edge of panic.

By then, Remir had reached the horse. Apparently, the woman was telling the truth, because he stepped into the open and spoke in a calm, modulated tone, mixing Castilian arbitrarily with his Arabic. "It's all right. We'll get you out. What's your name?"

"Mari Carmen."

"Nice to meet you, Mari Carmen. I'm . . . er, Jamal, and my friends are Nizar and Asad. Just give us a moment. We'll figure something out."

Davides joined Remir while Julián, exercising admirable caution, hung back with a loaded crossbow and continued to scan their surroundings. The log was about two and a half feet in diameter and ten feet long, neatly stripped of its branches. The hole where the woman was trapped was a little over five feet deep, with an uneven, V-shaped bottom in which a trickle of water ran. Unfortunately, the log filled the section of ground that had collapsed, leaving only a couple of inches on either side. About a third of the log was protruding from the back, and the front end had dropped down as far as the traces of the harness would allow. As the woman had said, the horse couldn't move forward unless the nose of the log were somehow raised; and if the animal stepped back, it would fall into the hole on top of the log. On top of her.

Davides and Remir switched back to Arabic and discussed the situation. After discarding several ideas due to a lack of even rudimentary equipment, Remir suggested brute force. "I'll lift up the back end of the log. One of you hold the horse's head to keep him from moving when the log shifts; and the other, pull her up."

Davides looked at the log with raised eyebrows. The thing had to weigh at least a thousand pounds. The nose was being supported somewhat by the harness traces and the earthen wall it was snubbed into, but that still left a lot of weight for Remir to lift. Maybe four hundred pounds?

Julián wore an expression of alarmed doubt similar to Davides's own. "Dibs on holding the horse," he declared.

Remir gave a half smile to Julián, then turned to Davides. "Will you be able to pull her up?" he asked, with a nod at Davides's wounded left arm.

Not just his arm. When it came to lifting someone out of a hole, his bruised ribs and aching stomach muscles weren't going to be of much use, either. Rather than admit that, however, he came up with an alternative. "We can tie the horses' lead ropes together to make a safety line. If I take a half-hitch around my waist, my left arm won't have to do much. I can use my weight to pull her up. But, are you sure you can lift that?"

"Pretty sure," Remir said, "although I've usually had a few drinks before I try this sort of thing."

Having more faith in them than she probably should have, Mari Carmen secured her end of the line under her arms. Julián held the horse's head, Davides took up the slack in their makeshift rope, and Remir squatted down and braced his hands under the lip of the

189

log. Remir gathered himself, then with a grunt of effort that turned into a bellow, he straightened his legs, raising the back end of the log. The horse's hindquarters buckled a little as the log's weight shifted forward, but Davides was already pulling and backpedaling. The woman, aided by the steady tension on the rope, scrambled up the side so fast that Davides couldn't keep pace with her. As she gained the top, he fell over backwards. He felt the ground reverberate as the log dropped back into place.

"You did it!" Mari Carmen cried breathlessly. "Amazing! How can I ever thank you?"

Still flat on his back, Davides heard a faint rustle in the undergrowth behind him. Mari Carmen's gushing thanks faded into the background, and he tilted his head back, seeking the origin of the sound.

Standing not two feet from the top of Davides's head was a steel grey *alano* the size of a small horse. It looked down at him from its magisterial height with glittering violet eyes, the same eyes as Attab's attack dogs. However, this enormous creature made the ones in Manantial look like insignificant rat terriers by comparison. Paralyzed, Davides could only watch as the giant jaws parted and saliva dripped from the white spikes of its teeth. Then, a long black and pink tongue lolled out of its mouth. The dog began panting, adopting an expression of idiotic canine contentment.

"Oh, hey, it's Samson!" Mari Carmen's voice sounded carefree as a bird. Then, she picked up on the tension that gripped her rescuers. "That's just Samson. He won't hurt you."

"Is that right?" Davides breathed from his extremely compromising position, belly and throat exposed. Moving slowly, he rolled to his stomach. He got as far as his hands and knees before the dog leaned towards him and sniffed. "There's a good boy," Davides murmured between his teeth.

"Can you call the dog over to you?" Remir asked Mari Carmen in a stilted voice.

"Samson! Come here, boy." The dog transferred his gaze to her and acknowledged her with a *woof* that shook the air. But, he didn't budge. "He won't listen to me," Mari Carmen explained apologetically. "Don't worry, though. Teia should be somewhere close by. Teia?" she called.

Under the circumstances Davides wasn't sure he wanted to wait for the dog's owner to show up. He pushed himself back so that he was balanced on the balls of his feet. Before he could stand up, however, the dog poked his nose towards him again and slid a wet, slimy tongue across Davides's face.

Spitting, sputtering, swearing, Davides surged to his feet and twisted away. A snort of poorly concealed amusement from Remir blended with a gasp of dismay from Mari Carmen. "I'm so sorry. Please don't be upset. That just means he likes you."

Davides's less-than-gracious retort was preempted by a soft tendril of a voice coming from the direction of the trail. "Is my dog bothering you?"

They turned as one to the newcomer. Captivated as they had been with the reincarnation of Cerberus, no one had noticed her approach. The voice — which spoke Castilian with the same, unusual accent as Jahwar — was clearly feminine. Otherwise, Davides might have mistaken her for a boy. She was slender to the point of being wiry. She wore a short, hooded cape, a jersey that came above the knee, and pants banded around the calves.

191

It was typical raiment for both men and women who worked in the woods, but on her it accentuated the lack of distinguishing curvature. She had a leather satchel slung over one shoulder and carried a stout walking stick. When she stepped closer, Davides was able to make out a pert nose, and finely arched eyebrows, features which seemed to belie her timid voice.

"No," Davides answered her, forcing a tight smile. "He's no bother."

"Oh, Teia, you wouldn't believe what happened to me!"

As Mari Carmen began recounting her adventure, Remir and Davides backed up to where Julián stood with the mule and draft horse, ostensibly to re-attach lead ropes, but also to be within easy reach of the swords. It was Davides's first chance to get a good look at Mari Carmen. She was dressed similarly to Teia, but without the cape. Her frank, open face — now smeared with dirt and some dried blood — had a few wrinkles, but she was stoutly built and probably could hold her own against most men in an arm-wrestling contest. Evidently, she did more than lead the horse when it came to logging.

"How fortunate you were passing by," Teia commented, eyes downcast, after Mari Carmen had finished telling of the gallant rescue. "So late, that is. Most people would be camped for the night."

Her words and tone suggested sincere appreciation. Was it just Davides's own suspicions that made it sound like she was insinuating something more?

"The good Lord heard my prayers!" Mari Carmen exclaimed, oblivious to undercurrents. Turning back to them, she added, "You must come back to the village with us. It's only a mile or so further on. We'll make sure you get a hot supper and a warm place to sleep. Oh, and I'm sure Father Bernat will want to meet you and thank you all personally. Right, Teia?"

"I should think so," was the meek, barely audible response.

"Just let me get my horse," Mari Carmen said. She started unbuckling the traces from the hames of the collar, so that the horse would no longer be anchored to the log.

Remir stepped forward to help her. "Does this village have a name?" he inquired lightly.

"Alferia," she piped back, ducking a look at him under the horse's neck as they worked.

"Alferia," Remir repeated. "Nice name."

It didn't come as a surprise. More of a confirmation of what they had already guessed. So much for sneaking up on the place, doing some reconnaissance, taking out sentries, setting up a crossfire. So much for anything resembling a plan.

* * *

On the short walk to Alferia, Teia kept watching them out of the corner of her eye, as if she were wondering what kind of rough stock they were escorting back to town. Julián's attire was still respectable, but the dark robes that Remir and Davides were wearing measured just one small step above rags. Besides that, they had almost no personal belongings with them that weren't weapons. Julián had the *oud*, the waterskin, and a small pack he had brought with him from the boarding house, but that was it. Teia didn't have to be a member of a criminal conspiracy to not like the looks of them.

193

When they reached the outskirts of the village, Teia offered to go on ahead and arrange for their lodging, while they took care of the horse and mule. It was a very thoughtful gesture on her part. Davides and Remir exchanged glances as she walked away into the crepuscular shadows with Samson at her heels, but they didn't object. How could they? What rationale could they possibly give that wouldn't sound crazy or culpable?

With reservations gnawing at them, they arrived at Mari Carmen's house. It was a small, timber dwelling with an attached lean-to shed. She was greeted enthusiastically by a striped tabby that wound around her legs, mewing. After disentangling herself from the cat, Mari Carmen grabbed a couple of empty pails stacked near the back door, then disentangled herself again. "I'll be right back with some water," she assured them and hurried off.

Davides waited until she was out of sight, then murmured, "This doesn't feel right."

"By 'not right' do you mean 'perfectly normal'?" Remir asked. He turned to Julián, who was pulling the bridle off the mule. "The other village felt . . . I don't know . . . desolate. Right from the beginning."

Lowering his voice still more, Davides added, "And I just can't see someone like Mari Carmen collaborating with a pack of criminals. A hard-working, middle-aged woman doesn't exactly fall into their demographic."

"Maybe Mateo misspoke when he gave you the name of this place," Remir suggested, helping Davides ease the heavy collar off the draft horse. "You did have an adverse effect on his nerves, you know."

"So, it's not just me," muttered Julián, from behind the mule.

Remir grinned and hung the collar on the wall. "No, it's not just you."

Davides divided an indignant look between the two of them.

"What?" Remir countered. "Julián associates you with sharp edges and spurting blood. You know what might help, though? If we all went drinking together. Do you suppose they have a tavern here?"

"It's Friday, *Jamal*," Davides reminded him. Remir had once said he didn't drink on fridays. And, since Remir had dubbed them all with Muslim names, it would probably be best if they all followed the same customs.

"Is it really? Damn."

"Speaking of which," Davides began, but he broke off as Mari Carmen chugged back into view. She poured some of the water into a large earthenware basin near the back door of the house, and set the rest in front of the horse and mule. After they had finished rubbing down the animals, they took turns cleaning their hands and faces in the icy cold water.

Davides thought he was doing a pretty good job of acting nonchalant until a sudden gasp from Mari Carmen made him start so badly that he nearly overturned the basin. She was staring at the deep cut on his forearm, which looked black and slightly misshapen in the murky twilight. "I didn't know you got hurt! Why didn't you say something?" she asked.

"This? No. This is old," Davides said hastily. "I fell. A couple of days ago. It's nothing."

Mari Carmen made a disapproving cluck with her tongue. "Supper won't be ready yet, anyhow. We'll stop

195

by the rectory first and have Father Bernat take a look at that. He's the closest thing we got to a doctor."

Seeing the stubborn set to her jaw, Davides knew any protestation he might make would only sound childish. He sighed, resigning himself to some imminent unpleasantness. A meeting with this priest was inevitable; they might as well get it over with. He shook the water off his hands, then slung the bag of crossbows over his shoulder. Julián and Remir picked up the rest of the gear, and they followed Mari Carmen down the dark street that led into the center of the village.

Even at night, when the houses were closed up tight and the streets were empty, the village conveyed a different ambiance than Manantial. The murmur of casual conversation and laughter behind closed shutters. The general tidiness and upkeep of the place. The only off-putting factor was a strong, sulfuric smell that wafted in occasionally with the breeze.

"That's a peculiar smell," Davides commented, fishing for an explanation from Mari Carmen.

"From the bloomery," she responded. "We make wrought iron, and the forge gives off that smell sometimes. Those of us who live here don't even notice it no more."

By the time they reached the rectory — a square, solid dwelling built of the same stone as the church — Davides was beginning to think that Mateo *had* been mistaken. The place was vibrant, thriving. It had its own industry, implying that its people actually worked for a living. From what he could tell, no vultures had picked the bones of this village, leaving only the skeletal remains.

His new theory received an abrupt check, however, as soon as they filed into the rectory. The first thing he saw was Samson, stretched out near the hearth as if he owned the place.

The dog could just be a coincidence, he told himself. The Slavic tribes that had migrated to Hispania hundreds of years ago had brought that breed of dog with them as a weapon of war, but *alanos* were hardly unique to Toledo's gang of violent criminals. Lots of people raised them, although those people were usually wealthy individuals who could afford to use the dogs for sport. Feeding a creature like Samson would cost a fortune.

Davides's attention turned from the dog to Father Bernat, who was the very picture of a jolly parish priest. Short and rotund, he had a wide, smiling face, and he welcomed them with hearty goodwill. "Teia here was just telling me what happened." He motioned to the girl, who was perched on a stool in the corner. "It's a pleasure to meet three such upstanding young men." Father Bernat extended a hand.

Without hesitation, Remir stepped forward and clasped it. "God's peace be upon you. I'm Jamal. This is Nizar and Asad." Remir indicated Davides and Julián, respectively.

At least Davides now knew which of the two aliases belonged to him. He and 'Asad' both smiled and murmured appropriate greetings.

Once the initial pleasantries were over, Mari Carmen wasted no time bringing up Davides's injury. "Father, Nizar here is hurt. He has a nasty-looking cut on his arm from a fall he took. I thought maybe you'd have something for it?"

"Why, of course! Sit down, sit down. Light a couple more candles, would you, Teia?"

With the surety of someone who knew the place well, Teia slipped into an adjacent room and returned a few moments later with two more candles, which she lit from the one already on the table. Davides found a stool and sat, bracing himself for backwater remedies.

As the small flames burned brighter and illuminated the area, Father Bernat frowned suddenly. He shifted in his stool, examining Davides's jaw. "That's an ugly bruise," he observed. Evidently, it was visible despite Davides's overgrowth of whiskers.

"It was an ugly fall," Davides responded curtly. A sharp look from Remir advised him to modify his tone. He forced a smile. "If you think I look bad, you should see the rocks where I fell. They're really messed up."

"I'll bet they are." Father Bernat smiled back, an appraising look in his bright eyes. Without further comment, he rolled Davides's sleeve out of the way and examined the cut. "Yep. It's festering, all right." He beamed at Davides as if this were joyous news. "We'll put some hot compresses on it, which should draw some of that gunk out, then slap some honey on it. That sound okay to you?"

It was better than Davides had expected. He relaxed a little. At least the priest wasn't insisting on bloodletting. Yet. If Father Bernat turned out to be this village's equivalent of Mayor Attab, the topic of bloodletting might come up again.

Odd, though: the name 'Bernat' didn't strike him as Slavic, although it wasn't exactly Castilian, either.

The hot compresses took a while. Luckily, Remir could sustain an inane conversation with practically anyone, even when his knowledge of the language was imperfect. In this case, maybe it helped. He blundered happily along in broken Castilian, and Father Bernat had to focus so hard on understanding him that he didn't seem inclined to pose a lot of questions in return.

Once he had finished treating the cut, Father Bernat asked Mari Carmen and Teia to see if their supper was ready. No sooner had the door closed behind the two women than he slapped his hands decisively on his lap. "Now you boys can tell me why you're really here."

They glanced at each other, startled by the bluntness of the question.

"Why we're here in the rectory?" Davides asked. He knew that wasn't what the priest had meant, but he wanted to glean more information before deciding how to respond.

"You can cut the crap," Father Bernat said, still jovial. "Hildric's been trying to convince me for weeks we need more 'security' up here. Well, you can just trot right back to Toledo and tell him 'thanks, but no thanks'. You boys seem very capable, but we're not interested."

Davides kept his face impassive but lowered his eyes. 'Hildric' *was* another Slavic name. That, combined with the reference to Toledo, proved in his mind that this man, at least, had ties to the Vandals.

"Sorry, but I'm not sure I comprehend," Remir said, his face displaying baffled amusement. "You believe we were *sent* here — to this village — to work for you as hired swords?"

On the surface, Remir's follow-up question indicated that he thought the priest must be joking: why would this humble community need (or be able to afford) mercenaries? For the three of them, however, Father Bernat's conjecture was humorous on another level. Given their volatile past with the Vandals, the last thing

'Hildric' might have done was send them purposefully to Alferia.

"I'm afraid you're mistaken," Remir continued, with a shake of his head. "We're just passing through on our way to Zaragoza. Al-Muqtadir is recruiting again, or so we were told."

"Mercenaries heading for Zaragoza," Father Bernat mused, his eyes narrowing. "If you don't mind my saying, you boys don't appear equipped for that kind of journey."

"We've had some setbacks," Davides said, and he lifted his injured arm as implied evidence of past mishaps. The priest already suspected that his alleged fall was bogus. Now, he could believe that they had lost most of their belongings in the same altercation.

But, Father Bernat was not quite ready to let the subject drop. "Down on your luck, yet still willing to help a stranger in need. Why, if you three aren't the most virtuous mercenaries I ever laid eyes on!"

"Not *that* virtuous," Julián interjected. He had been so quiet, they all turned and stared at him. "I mean, we had our reasons. Sure, we could have stolen the draft horse and left the woman in the hole. In fact, a few well-placed blows with a sword would have made certain she stayed there."

Davides gaped at Julián, appalled. Where the hell had that come from?

Julián avoided his gaze and went on. "But, as you pointed out, Father, we've nothing but the clothes on our backs. We needed food and shelter for the night, not a large, slow animal that's only worth something if you can find a place to sell it."

His explanation for their behavior made perfect, self-interested sense. It also made Davides wonder if

200

Julián had created the rationale on the fly in order to convince Father Bernat, or whether he had actually entertained those thoughts earlier.

The priest took a moment to process Julián's rendition of their motives. "I appreciate your honesty, son," he said finally. "And it don't change a thing. You still did Mari Carmen a kindness, and we are all in your debt. My yammering at you is hardly proper repayment. Let's get you boys some supper!"

Father Bernat heaved himself up from the stool, flung open the front door, and snapped his fingers. Samson stood and stretched lazily. "Oh, and don't go runnin' off too early tomorrow morning. Give us a little time, and we'll round up some food and what-not for you to take along on your journey. Maybe some warmer clothes, too, eh?" He stepped out into the night, with Samson padding along beside him.

"That would be great!" Remir said cheerfully, propelling an apprehensive Julián and a grim Davides through the door after him.

Alferia didn't have an inn, but it did have what amounted to a communal kitchen and bakery. As promised, it was pleasantly warm in the large, open room, and the food—leftover stew—was hot and plentiful. On the downside, there was nothing resembling privacy. Father Bernat, Teia, and Mari Carmen stayed with them to 'keep them company' while they were eating, and waited until they were settled on pallets in front of the massive fireplace before bidding them good-night. Even when the three were finally alone, they knew they couldn't count on being able to talk freely.

With a shrug and a quirk of his lips, Remir offered to take first watch. The villagers shouldn't find it unusual for some wanna-be mercenaries to stand guard through the night.

Chewing on a stalk of wheat, Remir commented, "It looks like we might be getting enough provisions to speed us on our merry way. Do we have any other business here?"

Julián, who hadn't been thrilled about the original plan anyway, shook his head emphatically. Davides was inclined to agree. While Father Bernat was obviously involved in some capacity with the Vandals, the village showed no evidence of being under the oppressive yoke of his greed and cruelty. If they could get food and clothes without resorting to violence, it was a win-win situation, as far as he was concerned.

"Wake me for second watch," he told Remir, as he laid down on the pallet, pulled the blanket up, and closed his eyes.

* * *

"Wake up."

Why? Why wake up? Davides had already taken his turn at watch. A heartbeat later, it occurred to him that the voice wasn't Remir's. Or Julián's. Or even his own meddling, inner voice. The voice belonged to a woman. Intrigued, Davides opened his eyes. The fire had long since died, but the grey light of dawn illuminated the room enough for him to see.

Teia was standing over him, holding a short spear pointed at his stomach. Even as he took in that startling image, a knife skimmed against his throat, forcing his head back. A second person, a second weapon. Davides froze, but his eyes darted to where he had left his own knife, on the floor next to his pallet.

"Looking for this?" Teia asked, with a curl of her lip. She dangled the knife over him from her fingertips.

"Teia," a familiar baritone admonished from somewhere beyond Davides's field of vision.

Teia's lips compressed. Reluctantly, she tucked the knife into her belt, and Davides found himself wondering how a slip of a girl with a pointed stick could be so much more menacing than Jahwar had been with a battleaxe.

"You boys just lie still, and don't do anything that might make us nervous," Father Bernat said, in the same genial tone of the previous night. "Nervous hands tend to shake, and we don't want any accidents, do we?"

"We sure don't," responded Remir in an obvious parody of the priest's provincial accent and incongruent cheerfulness. Davides couldn't see Remir—or much of anything beyond Teia—but he heard Remir suck in his breath suddenly, as if something sharp had just pressed a little deeper. "Um, where's Asad?" Remir continued in a thin voice.

Where, indeed? Davides had awakened Julián a while ago to take the last watch. Why hadn't he warned them?

"Tied up in the back room. He's fine. We just couldn't risk him making a fuss and waking you before we were ready. From what I've been told, you two are the dangerous ones."

"Mostly him," Remir said. "Not me so much."

From his immobilized position, Davides shot Remir a look of outrage.

Father Bernat chuckled. "I like you boys, I really do. That's why I was so distressed when I got word late last night that two fellas matching your description might be lookin' to *kill* me. Seems they went on a bit of a

203

rampage, first in Manantial, then in Toledo. Our associates lost track of 'em after that, but Hildric was concerned enough to send a warning way out here to Alferia.

"Course, I thought of you boys right off, but something didn't quite fit. I mean, if you wanted to kill me, you had your chance last night, sittin' right there at my table. Three against one. Who doesn't like those odds? So, I'm just convincing myself that the messenger must be talkin' about someone else or somehow got it wrong, when he mentions that there's also a minstrel who's involved one way or another."

Father Bernat nudged the bottom of Davides's foot with his toe. "Tell me, does your friend in the back room just play the *oud* . . . or does he sing, too?"

The seemingly trivial question wasn't meant to be taken at face value. Even Davides knew that 'singing' was slang for when a thief confessed or betrayed his friends, usually under duress. Father Bernat was threatening to interrogate Julián. Why, though? He already knew who they were—or, at least, who the Vandals thought they were. And, if the priest considered Remir and him to be so formidable, why risk letting them wake up in the first place? They should be dead.

There could be only one reason for not killing them outright. "What do you want?" Davides asked flatly.

"What do I want?" Father Bernat repeated in a pleased drawl. "Well, now. Funny you should ask."

At a word from the priest, their assailants stepped back. Apparently, Father Bernat had taken Davides's straightforward question as some sort of capitulation. He supposed it was, in a way: he had no intention of trying to fight or lie his way out of the situation, not when Father Bernat seemed willing to negotiate.

Davides and Remir got slowly to their feet, keeping their hands visible. The spears were still leveled at them, and Davides, for one, didn't want to give Teia any excuse to skewer him. The other spear was being wielded by a stocky man in a leather cuirass, who was grinning at them as if they were the butt of some practical joke. The last two men—the ones with the knives—were both wearing deacon's robes.

Nice to see the Church taking an interest in community events, Davides thought caustically.

As an additional gesture of good faith, Father Bernat went to the back room and returned a few moments later with a chagrined but unscathed Julián. Motioning for the three of them to sit at one of the long tables, Father Bernat settled down across from them.

He planted his elbows on the table, steepled his fingers at his lips, and frowned thoughtfully at them. "Before I get to what I want, maybe you boys should tell me what you know about our operation."

"Not much," Remir answered. "You have several small towns including this one that feed into a fence in Toledo. For some reason, the people working for this gang? guild? have a fondness for old Slavic customs: using Slavic names, burning dead bodies, using attack dogs, enjoying acts of senseless brutality, ow!"

Davides had given Remir a sideways kick under the table: a warning to avoid topics like 'senseless brutality' while sharp objects were being pointed at them. "And," Davides picked up where Remir had broken off, "from a couple of references you've made, we can assume the leader in Toledo is someone named Hildric."

Father Bernat stared at them a moment, then said, "That's it? Good God Almighty! For not having a clue, you sure have stirred up a bee's nest." He sat back, mulling something over, then said, "If that's the case, I'd best fill in a few gaps for you, so you know what you're getting yourselves into."

What we're getting ourselves into? Davides wasn't sure he liked the sound of that, but it didn't seem like an appropriate time to object.

According to Father Bernat, Hildric was Castilian, but many of his subordinates originated from the neighboring kingdom of Aragón. During the glory days of the Caliphate, Aragón had been governed by Slavs who had converted to Islam, but political infighting and pressure from the bordering Christian counties had caused the far-flung city-state to dissolve. The criminal organization's Slavic names and customs were a nod to that historic reality, but didn't constitute any sort of agenda. At least, insofar as Father Bernat was aware.

He and his crew came from a region of Aragón called Urgell, known since Roman times for its iron deposits. A little over a year ago, Hildric had approached him about joining in a venture near Toledo. He had sought out Father Bernat specifically because of the latter's background in mining. At that time, the details of the venture were still fuzzy, but (for reasons Father Bernat kept to himself) he was ready if not eager to relocate. To humor Hildric, he had eventually adopted the Slavic name 'Gelimer', but he only used it in his interactions with other members of the organization.

They had waited until King Fernando had moved his army into the region, leaving chaos in its wake, before they had set up shop. Some of Hildric's people went to

Toledo to establish the fence, while others went to Christian communities in the area that had been scouted out the previous year as likely marks.

Rather than the highhanded banditry of other villages or the complex fence of the city, Father Bernat was sent to Alferia with the idea of exploiting the village's production of wrought iron. The plan was for him to supplant Alferia's elderly spiritual leader, and then use the pulpit to turn the gullible villagers into virtual slaves for Hildric's organization.

Contrary to all expectations, his arrival was seen by the community as some sort of miracle. Rather than resenting being replaced, Father Teodoro had embraced him and marveled at the Bishop's wisdom in sending another clergyman to their grief-stricken community to guide the flock during his failing years. In the course of investigating what the old man meant by 'grief-stricken', Father Bernat had learned that things had changed dramatically in the village since Hildric's scouts had gone through: a disastrous mining accident had killed most of the able-bodied men in the community. They had a pitiful yield of wrought iron, and the only real manpower left were the women.

As it stood, the village wouldn't even make the *jizya*, let alone produce the quantities that Hildric expected. And, while the Toledan exchequer might overlook a couple of bags of flour or wheels of cheese missing from the other targeted villages, it was unlikely to do so in the case of Alferia's wrought iron. Father Bernat was ready to ditch the whole operation when some of the women latched onto him and dragged him out to the mines. It didn't take him long to see that the quantity of iron ore was not the problem, but rather the bloomery being used to convert the ore into wrought iron. It was primitive and inefficient, and produced iron of unpredictable quality. What they needed was a Catalán forge. And, he just happened to know how to build one.

He had to pull a few strings with Hildric, but he got the new forge up and running, with its all important *tuyere* (whatever that was — Davides didn't care enough to ask). However, Father Bernat's request for more manpower fell flat. That was understandable at the time, since it was hard to recruit laborers in an area being held by an invading army. Just getting messages and equipment back and forth had been tricky and expensive.

The presence of King Fernando's army gave them a little extra time to make enough wrought iron to pay the *jizya* and thus avoid drawing any unwanted attention to Alferia. In the meantime, however, Hildric was getting impatient, so the priest had made another request: he wanted an engineer to devise a waterwheel for them. Since Alferia was located next to a decent-sized river, he knew they could improve production even more by constructing a waterwheel at the forge to power its drophammers.

About that same time, Father Bernat had done a little investigating on his own and had discovered that, with battles looming on every horizon, the price for wrought iron had risen drastically. The black market price that Hildric was paying them was —

"Criminal?" Remir inserted, with a puckish gleam in his eye.

"Exactly!" Father Bernat said, appreciating the irony rather than being offended by it. "On top of everything else, Hildric comes to us with this notion of Alferia needing more security. What a crock! He's just wanting an excuse to send some of his own men up here to keep an eye on us."

"So, naturally, when we showed up, you assumed we were working for Hildric as spies." Somehow, Davides managed to say the word without flinching. "This has been really fascinating, and I could talk about iron ore all day, but I'd kinda like to get to the part where you explain what you *want* from us."

The priest's eyes narrowed. "I'm gettin' there. First, though, is it true you have connections with one of al-Mamun's blacksmiths and some other intellectual sorts back in Toledo?"

Davides didn't answer. His mind had stopped on 'blacksmith'. He didn't want this conversation going anywhere near Ishaq.

Remir gave a short, amazed laugh. "You want us to go back to Toledo and find an engineer for your waterwheel?"

"And for the drophammers," Father Bernat added, unperturbed by Remir's incredulity. He turned to Davides. "Drophammers are what pound the slag out of sponge iron in order to get your wrought iron. Since you have such a keen interest in the topic, I thought you'd want to know."

Davides's answering smile more closely resembled a snarl.

"Thing is," Father Bernat continued, "it's not just the engineer. Once you're back in Toledo, you can talk to your people about setting up a contract, direct with us, for wrought iron."

Davides was still stuck on Ishaq. "What people?" he asked.

For the first time, Father Bernat appeared doubtful. He studied Davides, intuiting perhaps that he was missing something. "The ones from Seville. The ones who are tearing Toledo apart brick by brick looking for you." He glanced over at Remir and Julián, and his eyes widened as enlightenment dawned. "Ohhh. Not exactly friends of yours, huh?"

"Not exactly, no," Remir answered, with a twist of his mouth.

Father Bernat rubbed his jaw thoughtfully. "Hmph. Gosh, that actually clears up a lot. But, how 'bout your contact at the exchequer? I'd even sell to al-Mamun if I could get a decent price."

Davides snorted. "There's no 'contact'. I blackmailed some pigheaded bureaucrat into accepting Manantial's back taxes, that's all."

Remir faced him, both surprised and amused. "I thought you said it went fine."

"It did go fine. I accomplished what I set out to do, and nobody important recognized me while I was there." He was still rattled about the Vandals having knowledge of Ishaq, or else he never would have made such an unthinking response.

"Recognized you?" Father Bernat asked, politely quizzical.

Davides closed his eyes, but the question didn't go away. He drew a deep breath. "I used to work as a messenger for Seville. Lots of people know me at the *alcázar* in Toledo."

"Really," Father Bernat mused interestedly.

"I don't have any contacts!" Davides insisted, guessing what the priest was thinking. "Not anymore."

"Okay! Okay. I believe you. Still, why not work for us?" Father Bernat let the question hang in the air a moment, then went on. "I hear you clean up good. You speak Arabic. Maybe even read and write? We give you a few pointers on the industry, and I bet you could pass as prosperous iron merchants. And, we don't have to deal with anyone in Toledo. We could try Ávila or Segovia instead. In return for getting us a contract, we'd equip you, pay you a flat rate off the top, plus a bonus if you bring back an engineer. It would get you boys away from the whole mess in Toledo. Solve all your problems."

Not all their problems — not by a long shot — but it would at least put a dent in the most immediate ones. They had been planning to go to Segovia, anyway; now, they could be paid to do so.

But, as iron merchants working for a self-professed conman?

Remir must have been thinking along the same lines. He cocked a dubious eye at the priest. "That almost sounds like honest work."

Father Bernat chuckled. "Honest, at any rate. I don't know how much *work* is involved. Carry a few samples of our iron with you, sit around and talk to folks, use your fancy words and nice manners to open some doors, ..."

"What about Hildric?" Julián asked, casting an uneasy glance at the four henchmen behind them. "Even assuming you gave him a cut, I can't see him being okay with this."

Father Bernat grew somber and nodded grudgingly. "I can buy us some leeway by fakin' another mining accident, claim we got no product. Once I know

211

how much others are willin' to pay for our iron, I'll decide how to deal with Hildric."

"In the meantime, will Hildric keep searching for us?" Davides asked. "How determined is he? I don't want to be looking over my shoulder all the way to Segovia and beyond."

"To tell the truth, I don't know," Father Bernat confessed. "At the moment, you have the fellas back in Toledo stumped. They found the bodies in the river, realized you weren't dressed the way they thought, and had to start the search from scratch. Then, they stumbled on an empty hogshead and cart, which left them wonderin' what you were smugglin' out of the city in such a hurry. They tried to recover whatever you left behind with some alchemist, but they wound up killin' him and torchin' everything, instead of —"

They killed Bendayan?

Davides surged to his feet. Before he got any further, a strong pull on his sleeve sat him back hard on the bench. Davides swiveled his head towards Remir, whose fingers were locked in a tight grip on his sleeve. Remir was staring straight ahead, his face devoid of emotion. Out of the corner of his eye, Davides saw that the spears, which had dipped in a relaxed fashion during the course of their conversation, had once again been brought to bear. Slowly, Remir's fingers uncurled, releasing him.

They sat in tense silence, Davides using every ounce of self-control to remain seated instead of sprinting for the door. They had killed Bendayan and destroyed his life's work on the sketchy assumption that the alchemist might be working with a rival gang. If the Vandals were willing to kill one respected member of the Toledan community with so little to go on, would they hesitate to attack Ishaq? Had they done so already?

Finally, Father Bernat sighed and shook his head, as if to himself. "I'm sorry. The alchemist was a friend of yours, wasn't he? I'd no idea. Guess that changes things a bit, don't it?"

"All it changes is the order in which we do things," Remir countered, before Davides could respond. "First, we go back to Toledo and settle our account with Hildric. Second, we negotiate a new contract for your iron, because by then," he smiled unpleasantly, "you'll need a different buyer. Third, we look for an engineer. For now, we'll take saddle horses for payment. If and when we get you an engineer, we can discuss the bonus." Remir stood and stretched his hand across the table. "Do we have a deal?"

Father Bernat contemplated the open palm, then glanced at each of them in turn, perhaps trying to assess how solid the consensus was among them as to Remir's proposed course of action. It was hard to imagine Julián inspiring a lot of confidence on the matter, but whatever the priest saw in Davides's face — sorrow, anger, worry, more anger — must have convinced him. He clasped Remir's outstretched hand and gave it a firm shake. "We sure do."

* * *

The preparations for leaving Alferia took forever — at least, that's how it felt to Davides. The horses weren't in a stable but rather roaming in a nearby valley. Father Bernat sent the deacons to round up three mounts for them and bring them to a rendezvous outside of town. Next, the priest held a short consultation with Teia and the

213

other spearman. Davides didn't catch a lot of what they were saying, since they were speaking an unfamiliar dialect, but the discussion seemed to involve finding some light armor for their group. Hard to complain too much about that. Teia and her cohort went in one direction; Father Bernat led the three of them in another. Once concealed in a copse of trees, well away from the early-morning stirrings of happily ignorant villagers, the priest laid out what he considered their best chance for confronting Hildric.

According to Father Bernat, the ringleader generally spent nights at a remote manor in the olive groves that belonged to a local noble named al-Qati. He gave them the most recent password, which would get them past the sentries posted along the perimeter of al-Qati's lands. After that, it would be up to them as to how to approach the outbuildings and main house. Besides the ever present *alanos*, they might also have to contend with miscellaneous members of the organization who were at the estate on business. The most difficult part, however, would be getting through the half dozen heavily armed and armored guards with whom Hildric surrounded himself at all times.

The guards were a daunting obstacle, but Father Bernat considered Hildric to be dangerous in and of himself. Even among his confederates, who prided themselves on ruthlessness, Hildric had a reputation for being short-tempered, brutal, and more than willing to get his own hands dirty. Father Bernat described the ringleader as a man in his mid-thirties, with brown hair, a full beard, and a solid, compact frame.

It was all useful information, and Davides was certain he would appreciate it when the time came. At the moment, though, he felt like a branch bent to the point of breaking. He cut short Father Bernat's description of where al-Qati's estate was: he already knew, although he had never been up to the manor itself. He had also heard a thing or two about its owner, and was not surprised that al-Qati and Hildric had found each other. It was precisely the kind of symbiotic relationship that he had expected and dreaded, since even a degenerate like al-Qati enjoyed the protection of his status as a noble.

At long last, Teia and the stocky spearman showed up. They were toting leather cuirasses and a few other supplies, including a purse of silver dirhams. Davides wasn't sure what to make of the priest's generosity: either he was so certain of their success that he was giving them an advance; or, he considered their odds so dismal that he was extending them all the help he could. Regardless, Davides wasn't about to look a gift horse in the mouth. The three of them quickly donned the body armor and strapped on their swords.

The final item was a *litham*. Davides held the long, indigo scarf at arm's length and contemplated it sourly. The *litham* was meant to be worn as a turban, with one end secured across the lower half of the face. It was the traditional head covering and face veil of the Almoravids, the same North African zealots who had razed Coimbra and killed his entire family. There wasn't any group he despised more . . . although the Vandals were vying for a close second.

His own bias notwithstanding, the *lithams* were a good idea. They would conceal their features, making it more challenging for anyone to recognize them. And, since even Andalusian Muslims found the Almoravids to

215

be intractable, intolerant, and just plain scary, most people would give them a wide berth.

With an ease that suggested she had used the ploy more than once, Teia showed them how to wind the turbans and fasten the veil across their face. By then, the deacons had arrived with three horses, which were saddled and ready to go. Davides, Remir, and Julián secured crossbows to the saddles, mounted, and wheeled away south.

Part 5 – Retribution

They galloped most of the distance between Alferia and the highway. When they reached the intersection — where one major artery turned west towards Ávila, and the other continued south to Toledo — they pulled off the road to give the horses a short breather.

Since they had yet to discuss any plan beyond returning to Toledo, Davides suggested they hold a brief council of war. "Although, I'm not sure why we bother," he added. "If the past few weeks are any indication, whatever strategy we devise will be shot to hell before it even gets underway."

"Yeah, about that," Julián began, his tone diffident. "Um, you guys weren't really expecting me to go with you on this venture, were you?"

A glimmer of humor shone in Remir's eyes as he exchanged a glance with Davides. "No, not really. But, I was hoping you would deliver one more message to my father? Nothing complicated. Just that I slipped Seville's grasp, and that I'm doing my best to stay out of harm's way." Remir reached into the purse, took out some silver coins, and handed them to Julián.

"In other words, you want me to lie," Julián joked, pocketing the money.

"It's not a lie," Remir said. "My father is quite familiar with what constitutes my 'best' when it comes to staying out of trouble."

"*Meu Deus do céu!*" Davides stared at Remir in dismay. What had he been thinking? "Remir, you can't go back to Toledo!"

Remir raised an eyebrow. "You mean to say I *shouldn't* go back. You shouldn't, either. Yet, here we are."

"But—"

"But, what? If anyone ought to stay clear of that city, it's you. I only have one group of people trying to kill me; you have three."

"More like four," Julián amended.

Davides looked at him blankly. Who else, besides Vandals, soldiers from Seville, and unseen-but-assumed emissaries from Castile-León?

"Well, I expect Hildric framed you for the alchemist's death," Julián explained. "From what I gathered when I was in Toledo, lots of people know who you are, Davides. By making you the prime suspect, Hildric gets al-Mamun's men to do his footwork for him. And, your sudden disappearance from the city paints you as guilty. It's . . . just a . . . hunch," Julián faltered, as Davides's infuriated glare burned into him.

With an effort, Davides checked his anger, which wasn't truly directed at Julián in the first place. It wasn't Julián's fault that he thought like a criminal. Actually, it *was* his fault, but that didn't make him wrong. Quite the contrary. "No, you're right," Davides acknowledged. "That's exactly the sort of thing they'd do. Thank you for the warning."

Julián let his breath out. "Happy to be of service. And, speaking of service," he nodded deferentially to Remir, "I should leave now, before you two hash out your plans. You know, just in case."

Just in case he got captured between here and Salamanca? Despite himself, Davides had to admit a growing respect for Julián. He might be a gutless, inveterate horse thief, but he was determined to stay loyal to Remir. Ignorance was the ultimate guarantee that he would not betray his friend.

They said their farewells, and Julián goaded his reluctant horse into motion. They watched as he made his way back to the intersection and took the road towards Ávila, the most direct route to Salamanca.

"You really shouldn't be going back to Toledo," Davides reiterated, once Julián was out of earshot.

This time, Remir's response was surprisingly serious, and it became more vehement as he went along. "I might not have known Bendayan for very long, Davides, but I liked him. He was a kind, generous, harmless old man. I don't want what happened to him to happen to anyone else I know and like. Not if I can help it. These Vandals pick on people who can't fight back. But, you and I? We can fight back. So, tell me, do you have a plan or shall I come up with one?"

Davides was used to the laid-back Remir, the one who would rather use wit than a weapon to accomplish his ends. He was also used to safeguarding Remir, so much so that it had become a reflex. He had to remind himself that wasn't his job anymore. If Remir wanted to join him in a suicidal attempt to put an end to Hildric and his operation, then who was he to argue?

"I was thinking of going straight to al-Qati's estate," Davides replied. "If our horses hold up, we can stake out the manor before sunset, maybe come up with ways to pick them apart piecemeal. Otherwise, we wait for darkness. They have to sleep sometime."

It wasn't a very honorable approach, but they weren't dealing with honorable people. If Davides had thought for an instant that he would be allowed to challenge Hildric to single combat, he would have done so. As with any predatory pack, however, this group preferred to hunt and kill en masse. Personal integrity wasn't part of their mindset.

* * *

The slopes of red earth gleamed like polished copper in the slanting sunlight. Juxtaposed to that metallic sheen were innumerable nooks and crannies steeped in purple shadow. Despite the sparse vegetation, the landscape offered plenty of opportunities for cover, but Davides and Remir weren't interested in hiding. Not at the moment, anyway. They rode down the two-track openly, since everything about them—the horses, the cuirasses, the Almoravid head coverings—would suggest to the sentries that they were coming from Hildric's allies in Alferia.

Davides had to admit that the *lithams* had worked like a charm. On their hard ride south, everyone from wealthy merchants to humble farm laborers had tripped over themselves to get out of their way. No one had wanted to inadvertently provoke the temperamental Almoravids, who were obviously in some sort of hurry.

Their sweat-stained horses were now dragging their hooves in the dirt, having been pushed to their

220

modest limits. That was okay, though. They had reached al-Qati's estate before sunset and were now following the lane that led to the manor.

At a point in the narrow road squeezed between opposing upgrades, two lightly armored men with long spears stepped out and barred their way. The sentries examined them in a routine, almost bored fashion, and Davides took a moment to glance around. The main house was not yet visible, nor did he see a crow's nest from which a sentry might alert the manor of impending danger. So far, so good.

When Davides gave the password, the two men moved aside and waved them through. Remir and Davides prodded their horses forward, but as they drew abreast of the spearmen, Davides pulled up and, speaking the Castilian that seemed to be the *lingua franca* for the Vandals, asked, "Do you know if Hildric is here yet?"

"Yes," one sentry responded. "He rode in a while ago."

"And, how 'bout a man on a flashy chestnut, four socks and a blaze?"

The sentries looked at each other. "Doesn't sound familiar," the same one replied.

Remir started to untie his waterskin from the saddle.

Davides scrunched up his face, as if concerned by the absence of the fictitious man on the chestnut horse. "Odd. When did your turn at watch start, if you don't mind my asking."

"We've been here since morning. Trust me, he hasn't come through. Not this way."

That was unfortunate. It meant that the sentries were due to be replaced soon. Davides and Remir would have to act quickly.

At that point, Remir, still trying to free his waterskin, fumbled their purse to the ground. It dropped near the more talkative of the two sentries, and shiny silver dirhams spilled into the dirt. The spearman stared at the money. Remir swore and hopped off his horse. He bent one knee to the ground and began snatching up coins.

"Oh, great!" Davides scoffed. "You better not have lost any, or Gelimer will have our heads."

Davides swung off his horse as if he were going to help his clumsy companion, but once on the ground, he pivoted back towards the spearman nearest him and drew his sword. Predictably, the surprised sentry didn't have time or space to bring the long spear to bear; instead, he rotated the haft sideways to block Davides's blade. Davides feinted low but swung high. The spearman staggered back, blood streaming down his throat, but he clung tenaciously to the spear. Turning the point towards Davides, he thrust it forward. Davides shifted sideways, and the spear slid harmlessly past him. Davides struck again, this time hitting hard enough to breach the leather armor. The sentry went down, and Davides delivered a swift coup de grâce before turning to see how Remir was faring.

The other sentry had fallen over backwards with Remir on top of him, both of them vying for control of the spear. The sentry's arms were already shaking with exertion as he fought to keep Remir from pressing the haft down on his throat.

"Finish him, will you?" Davides hissed, watching the shadows for any sign of movement.

The sentry's muscles gave way, and Remir was able to push the pole against his windpipe. "I still think we should keep one alive for questioning," Remir said.

"He's not going to talk," Davides stepped close and lifted his bloody sword over them. "Get out of my way. If you don't have the stomach for it, I'll do it."

"Wait!" the sentry wheezed and drew a ragged gasp of air. "Please! I'll talk. I swear!"

Davides yearned to put a sword through him, anyway. As far as he was concerned, all of the Vandals in Toledo deserved to die. However, killing this man was not part of their plan, since they wanted to cross-reference and update what Father Bernat had told them. Giving a snort of disgust, Davides withdrew a few steps, leaving Remir to continue in his role of merciful intercessor.

* * *

They used some of the rope that Father Bernat had thoughtfully provided to tie the sentry's hands. Then, they hoisted the dead sentry onto a horse and slipped into a nearby gully. There, they took a moment to finish securing the prisoner. He wasn't carrying anything of interest, but Davides appropriated the spear and the dun-colored cloak. Leaving Remir to conduct the question-and-answer session, Davides stuffed his *litham* into the saddlebags and slung the cloak over his shoulders. Once suitably disguised, he climbed to an outcropping where he could keep an eye on the lane in both directions, yet still overhear the bulk of the interrogation.

As they had guessed, the sentries served mostly as a deterrent for oblivious travelers and inopportune visitors. They didn't have a means of signaling the main house, since anything visible to the manor, like fire or bright flags, might also be perceived from the walls of Toledo. Hildric relied on his personal guard for protection and security.

Al-Qati was not generally on the premises, and tonight was no exception. The estate hadn't been a working farm for quite a few years, so many of the buildings stood empty, some were falling apart. The sentry proceeded to give Remir a description of the manor's layout and the typical schedule kept by Hildric and his men, by the hired help like himself, and by al-Qati's household staff.

That was as much as they had gotten when Davides discerned a wagon approaching from the direction of Toledo. Two men were sitting up front and another was riding in the bed amidst a jumble of barrels, baskets, and bags. None of them appeared to be wearing any kind of armor.

Davides motioned to Remir, who hastily stuffed a gag in the sentry's mouth, grabbed both crossbows, and wove his way into position a little ways down the lane. Davides skirted around to where the original sentries had been posted. When the wagon got close enough, he stepped onto the path.

"Password?" he asked, trying his best to sound apathetic.

The driver and his companion in the front seat looked at him curiously, perhaps wondering who he was or why there was only one sentry on duty. Davides didn't give them a chance to ponder those questions at length. "What's the password?" he demanded, shifting the spear into a more threatening position.

This time, the driver supplied it. Davides lifted his spear and motioned brusquely for them to proceed. Not that he was going to let them get far. Their knowledge of the correct password confirmed their connection to the Vandals. As they pulled abreast of him, Davides leveled his spear and thrust it through the spokes of the back wheel.

"What the — ?" the man in the cargo area started to wriggle up from the soft bag of seeds he had been lounging on. Then, the wagon shuddered to a halt, making him spill over sideways.

The long haft of the spear, lodged between the spokes of the wheel, had revolved up to the flat bed of the wagon and was now acting as an unyielding brake. The mules stopped, waiting for some clever biped to remove the impediment. But, the driver, who probably assumed that the wagon had merely hit a rut, cursed at the team and slapped the reins against their haunches. The disgruntled mules threw themselves against the traces and started the wagon skidding laboriously forward.

Ignoring the man in back, Davides sprang to the hub of the front wheel, grabbed the driver by the collar, and hauled him off the seat. They tumbled to the ground together with the driver still clasping the reins. That jerked the mules to a halt once more. The driver's companion pulled a hand axe from his belt, but before he could take aim at Davides, a crossbow bolt whizzed past him. He yelped and dove off the wagon in the opposite direction.

In the meantime, Davides disentangled himself from the driver and drew his sword. The driver, blustering at him about his sanity or lack thereof, got out a long knife and adopted a stance that showed a certain understanding of close combat situations. But, a knife was a poor substitute for a sword, and the driver's street fighting skills were no match for Davides's martial training. The driver looked perplexed when, a quick step and thrust later, he'd been run through.

Davides didn't wait around to see him fall. Instead, he rolled under the wagon and came to his feet on the other side. The man with the hand axe was scrambling up the nearby slope in search of cover. Just as Davides started after him, Remir shot again. This time, the bolt pierced the man's thigh. He fell with a howl of pain, which turned into a shriek when he saw Davides's sword raised over him. The shriek ended abruptly, and Davides turned back towards the wagon, where the third man still crouched among the cargo.

"Don't come any closer, or I'll kill him!" the Vandal shouted.

So, that was why he hadn't tried to run: they had a prisoner in the wagon. Davides slowed, hit by a surge of panic. What if they had Ishaq?

"Not sure what you're talking about," Remir called back in Arabic, still hidden in shadows. "Hildric sent *us* to kill *you*. We don't really give a damn about anyone else."

The Vandal apparently understood. His expression went from fierce to bewildered to horrified. He didn't even protest. Maybe he and his Vandal buddies had been skimming off the top. What was that expression about honor among thieves?

"I can make it right!" the Vandal said, also switching to Arabic. "Believe me, this will make things right!" He put away his knife and started shoving aside the barrels and bags that presumably concealed the person being held captive.

"Keep your hands where we can see them!" Davides ordered. With an effort, he softened his tone. The man needed to think they were interested in his deal. "Get down from the wagon, and we'll see what you have."

The Vandal hesitated, but then climbed over the side of the wagon.

As soon as the man's feet touched the ground, Davides attacked. He couldn't quite bring himself to kill him—the Vandal had effectively surrendered—but Davides didn't have a problem hitting him, repeatedly, with the pommel of his sword. By the time the man was lying unconscious in the dust, Remir had jumped into the back of the wagon and had finished uncovering the captive. Davides snagged the Vandal's knife from its sheath before finally allowing himself to look over the side of the wagon.

Lying in the cargo area was a man wearing dusty, travel-worn clothes and riding boots. His hands and feet were bound, and his head was covered by a burlap bag. Even with his face concealed, however, they could tell that the captive was not Ishaq. This man was taller and more muscular. Remir pulled the bag from the man's head, and they studied him for a moment in silence. Davides judged him to be in his early twenties. His skin was tanned from long exposure to the sun, except for a faint line—an old scar—that ran from his eyebrow up into the hairline.

"His hair's matted with blood," Remir commented. "Looks like they coldcocked him. Anyone you know?"

Davides shook his head, frowning in consternation. From their admittedly limited experience, the Vandals weren't ones for taking prisoners. What made this guy special? Davides shrugged. "There's not much we can do for him right now besides cut him loose and leave him hidden somewhere. If he comes to, he'll have a decent chance of making it back to Toledo."

Davides went to the back of the wagon and lifted the wooden crosspieces that kept cargo from sliding out. Grasping the booted feet, he slid them towards him, thinking that he was glad he didn't have to move all of that dead weight on his own: the captive was at least as tall as Remir and heavier by a good twenty pounds.

All of the sudden, the booted feet tensed and shoved forcefully at Davides. Taken by surprise, Davides lost his grip and stumbled back. The man lurched forward, out of the wagon. Somehow, the captive had freed his hands. His left arm was spread wide, while his right hand . . . Davides saw the double-edged blade just in time to twist away from a direct thrust, but the left arm succeeded in ensnaring him in a partial clinch. The bulk of the man's weight careened into Davides, forcing him to the ground and pinning his right arm.

The dagger arced back around, this time aimed at his head. Davides shot out his left hand to block it. He felt the sharp burn of the blade's edge against his wrist, but the weapon twisted in the other's grasp and failed to drive home. Desperately, Davides grabbed his attacker's forearm and braced against it, trying to keep the blade from turning back towards him. As his muscles bunched, resisting the other man's raw strength, the old cut on his arm split open once more, and he grunted in pain and exasperation.

By then, Remir had leapt from the wagon and was in a position to intervene. He stepped hard on the man's wrist, then leaned over and wrested the weapon away from him. Apparently, he didn't step hard enough, however. With a single heave the man tore away from Davides's grasp and shouldered into the side of Remir's leg, throwing Remir off balance. Undeterred by the loss of his dagger, the captive-turned-assailant wrapped his arms around Remir's knees and wrestled him to the ground.

If the man's feet hadn't still been tied together, the outcome might have been different. As it was, after a brief scuffle, Remir managed to put him in an armlock. "Knock it off!" Remir ordered in a strangled voice that sounded suspiciously as if he were about to laugh. "We're not the bad guys. We were trying to free you!"

The captive continued to twist and turn in an attempt to break Remir's hold.

"*Deja de luchar, idiota,*" Davides translated (loosely) to Castilian. "*Estábamos para librarte.*"

That, the man understood. He stopped fighting and fixed Davides with a haughty glare—quite a feat, considering he was face down in the dirt, with his feet hobbled and one arm wrenched into an improbable position. Then, his eyes flickered to Davides's sword, which remained in its sheath rather than being poised to inflict any bodily harm. More than anything else, that seemed to convince him. "*Vale,*" he conceded, as if he were doing them some kind of favor.

Remir grinned at Davides and released the captive, who immediately rolled over and reached for the bindings around his feet.

"Here, allow me," Remir said, speaking Castilian this time. He knelt and used the odd little dagger to slit the strands. The blade had the slim silhouette of a

229

throwing knife but with even less length. "Handy weapon," Remir commented and offered it back to him.

In Davides's opinion it was a trifle too soon to be re-arming a man who, just moments ago, had attacked them. The former captive must have been wondering the same thing. He hesitated, eyes narrowed, before finally reaching forward and accepting the dagger. Still sitting, he slid the weapon into the back of his riding boot, where it disappeared into some sort of concealed sheath.

"Please accept my apologies," the man said formally, as if he were addressing two gentlemen instead of whatever kind of riffraff he probably took them for. "From what I heard and could understand, I thought you were with them. Thank you for rescuing me."

"We weren't rescuing you," Davides said curtly. "You just happened to be in the wagon." He ripped a strip of cloth from the dun cloak and clumsily wound it around his forearm, which was now wet with fresh blood.

"You're after the wagon?"

"We're after retribution," Remir said, as he straightened the *litham* on his head and adjusted the face veil. "These men worked for someone who killed a friend of ours."

"All the same, I'm in your debt." The former captive got to his feet. "My name is Rodrigo Díaz. I'm from the North, a village named Vivar."

Davides felt a touch of uneasiness. He wondered where exactly in the vastness of what could be considered "the North" one might find Vivar. Near Burgos, perhaps? He reloaded the two crossbows that Remir had used against the Vandals and kept an eye on the road to the manor. The sun was setting, and new sentries might arrive at any moment.

"I'm Jamal, and that's Nizar." Remir kept the pleasantries going. "What brought you to Toledo?"

"I'm looking for an old friend. He's from Seville, but was last seen near here. Perhaps you've heard of him? His name is Davides, Sisnando Davides."

Even though Davides had half-expected it, his stomach lurched. *An agent of Castile-León. We just rescued a goddamn agent of Castile-León, who went bumbling around pretending to be some friend of mine! Serves him right Hildric's men picked him up . . .*

"Hey, Nizar," Remir said. "Didn't you mention knowing a *dhimmi* by that name?"

Davides could have killed him. He waited a moment before replying to make sure his voice was under control. "Yes. But, I'm afraid I have some bad news, Rodrigo. I heard Davides was dead. A body matching his description was pulled out of the Tagus. I guess he had a lot of enemies?"

The tongue-in-cheek comment was wasted on Rodrigo, but he was astute enough to make a different kind of connection. "Who killed him? The same bastards who just knocked me over the head?"

"I really couldn't say." Davides pulled the spear out from the spokes of the wagon wheel. For a long moment, he considered turning it on the Castilian. Then, they could tie him the hell back up and decide what to do about him later. At the moment, they didn't even know what Rodrigo was after: Remir or the Greek text.

But, what if they didn't make it back? Whatever Rodrigo's mission, it didn't seem right to leave him here, bound and helpless, not with the Vandals and other scavengers roaming about.

Davides pointed northwest with the spear. "Toledo is that way," he said to Rodrigo. "Your best bet is the Bisagra Gate; the others will be locked by the time you get there."

"Wait! Who would know if the rumors about Davides's death are true? There was someone traveling with him, someone who might need help."

Remir and Davides looked at each other. At least now they knew what Rodrigo was after.

"Try the mosque near Bib-al-Mardum," Davides said. "They may be able to help you."

"A mosque? But, Davides was a Christian."

"The imam would have been summoned first, until the body was identified." Davides said. "He should be able to tell you where to go next." Rodrigo would end up at the Cathedral sooner or later, and then he would learn about Davides and 'Ramiro's' long talk with the Bishop, but a wild goose chase would at least buy them some time.

"Again, my thanks. If there's any way I can repay you, you have but to ask. I'm staying at an inn north of the city, a two-storied building with blue and green tiles around the entrance. Do you know it?"

Davides nodded. *Go, already!* They were wasting precious time. "God go with you," he said, hoping the conventional farewell would nudge Rodrigo along.

Rodrigo hesitated but finally responded, "And, with you." He nodded at each of them, then turned and started following the two-track in the direction of the city.

Between the terrain and the smoky gloom of dusk, Rodrigo was soon out of sight. Remir and Davides hastened back to the gully where they had hidden the two sentries. They didn't have time for more questions. Davides wrapped his *litham* back onto his head and

232

discarded the dun cloak. Then, leaving the wide-eyed sentry where he lay, they led their tired horses back to the lane.

* * *

Their plan depended heavily on the element of surprise. Davides would ride in alone as a messenger from Alferia and would try to position himself near Hildric. Using Davides's arrival as a distraction, Remir would sneak onto the roof of the main house and, using the crossbows, take out the men-at-arms posted outside. Once Davides heard the sounds of a disturbance, he would engage Hildric.

The silhouette of the manor rose in front of them. The low house formed one side of the yard while, in a parallel fashion, the farm's old storehouse comprised the other side. The storehouse was the larger of the two structures with a high peaked roof of clay tiles. Stretching between the two buildings was a dingy wall with a gateway in the middle of it. The back of the manor supposedly had a similar wall, but its gate would be closed and barred.

They could hear excited barking coming from the manor. The dogs couldn't have heard them yet—they were too far away—but something had the little beasts riled up. Whatever it was, the unexpected diversion might work to their advantage. Remir tied his horse in a copse of trees and slipped away into the darkness. Davides continued riding down the lane that led to the main gate.

As he rode through the open portal, he spied one of Hildric's men just inside the gateway and another leaning against the post of an awning that jutted out into the yard. Neither seemed to find his arrival out of the ordinary, nor did they appear concerned by the din of snarls, growls, and yowls coming from the storehouse.

Just as Davides was about to dismount, an agonized scream from the far end of the storehouse stopped him cold.

The man leaning against the post smiled at him. "You're new, aren't you?" he asked.

Davides steeled himself as another anguished cry spasmed through the air. "Yeah," he replied, and swung down. "Gelimer sent me with a message for Hildric."

"He's back with the others, training up some pups." The guard nodded in the direction of the ear-rending racket. "You're welcome to go watch while you wait."

"Okay," Davides said, as another scream cracked and fractured into inhuman moans.

He led his mount to the back of the yard, where a makeshift corral housed a few more horses. A third man-at-arms was guarding the back gate. Adjacent to him were the double doors that led into the back half of the storehouse. Trying to act casual, Davides removed his horse's saddle and bridle, then slung the tack over the split rail fence before heading to the building.

Davides cracked open one of the heavy wooden doors and slipped through. Once inside, he caught a whiff of something putrid, like meat past its prime. Several torches were burning, creating wavering patterns of garish light against pockets of deep shadow. Since he happened to be standing in one of those pockets of shadow, he palmed his knife and concealed it in his left hand under a fold of his cloak.

The space before him was some forty-feet wide and sixty-feet deep. Four rough-hewn posts formed the points

234

of a square and supported the rafters high overhead. A half-loft raised chest high off the ground ran the length of the right side with jumbled storage beneath it. On the left wall, two *alanos* (young, but by no means cuddly 'pups') were chained to the wall. They lunged at the limit of their tethers, yelping anxiously, but they were less interested in him than in what was transpiring at the other end of the room.

A wattle-and-daub wall the same height as the loft spanned the back half of the storehouse. It had an iron bow gate that looked like a mock-up of a miniature portcullis, complete with a pulley system for raising and lowering it. Apparently, Hildric took his dog training seriously enough to erect a pen designed to withstand the rigors of bull baiting.

Through the bars of the gate, Davides could see two more dogs tearing into the remains of . . . something. It wasn't a bull. A dismembered hand lay in the dirt, the belly had been torn open so that the intestines spilled out, and the face was an unrecognizable mass of bone and tissue. On the floor of the pen, bright red spatters stood out against larger blotches of dark brown.

The rank smell came from old blood, Davides realized, with the noisome aroma of sadistic ecstasy thrown in for good measure.

Davides averted his eyes before he lost what remained of his composure. He scanned the room and counted four men, all of whom were wearing mail hauberks and swords. The men were so engrossed in what was happening in the pen that they barely spared him a glance.

Davides spotted 'Hildric' with no difficulty, only he knew the man by a different name. The Vandal's ringleader was Ignacio Gonsaluiz, an aide to the Castilian representative in Toledo. They had met—briefly—last Spring. Davides had been sent to Toledo with a message for al-Mamun, urging Toledo to combine its strength with Seville against a possible incursion from the North. Before al-Mamun could pen a response, however, Gonsaluiz had arrived to announce that the Castilian army was already marching on Toledo. The Emir's suggestion had come a little late.

Gonsaluiz's reputation as a knight was in keeping with Hildric's as a crime lord: short-tempered, brutal, and not afraid to get his hands dirty. He often served as champion in disputes between his lord's clan and other noble factions, disputes in which the winner of the duel was declared 'right' while the loser was declared 'wrong'. As far as Davides was concerned, it was a seriously flawed system of jurisprudence. It assumed that God handed down moral judgements through strength of arms, but it failed to take into consideration that the winners of most disputes were the people who could afford the best weapons, the best armor, and the best fighters to champion their cause. It had nothing to do with right and wrong, good and evil. The proof of that was sitting up in the half-loft, cheering on his dogs as they ripped a man's body into smaller and smaller pieces.

Edging closer to the wattle-and-daub wall, Davides inspected Gonsaluiz's men-at-arms. One was standing right next to him, using a long wooden *garrocha* to poke at the two dogs in the pen and antagonize them into more vicious behavior. The other two men were sitting up in the loft on either side of Gonsaluiz, watching the show.

That's when Davides spotted someone else in the loft, squeezed between Gonsaluiz and one of the men-at-

236

arms. On his knees, his face battered almost beyond recognition, was Sajid.

In the wake of Amira's abduction, General Haroun would have sent someone to Toledo who was careful, capable, and acquainted with Davides and Remir. Sajid had been a logical choice. But, whatever trouble Sajid might have been prepared for, he wouldn't have been expecting the Vandals. They had either jumped Sajid, like the men in the wagon had done to Rodrigo, or they had lured him out here. Then, they had questioned him. But, even if Sajid had talked as to why he was looking for Davides and Remir, he wouldn't have been able to satisfy Gonsaluiz's paranoid insistence that they were conspiring to muscle in on his territory. When beating Sajid failed to produce the desired results, Gonsaluiz had set up this demonstration. Watching the slow, grisly death of another human being, knowing he was next, might overcome Sajid's reticence.

Davides shouldn't have been staring. Sajid's eyes lifted and locked onto his own. There was no question as to whether Sajid saw through the *litham* disguise. The soldier's racked despair unfolded into sudden, almost tangible hope. Alarmed, Davides scowled back at him, and Sajid immediately dropped his gaze to the wooden planks upon which he was kneeling.

He thinks I'm here for him.

Sajid wouldn't know that Remir had escaped, or that Davides was helping him. To Sajid, Davides was still a dependable comrade-in-arms who, for all their differences, would never leave him in the hands of these butchers. And, he was right, at least about the last part.

Davides was supposed to wait until he heard a ruckus outside, but he could hardly hear himself think

237

over all of the barking and gnashing of teeth. The man-at-arms beside him stretched forward into the pen to thrust with the *garrocha*. It seemed as good of an opportunity as Davides was likely to get.

He ducked behind the dog handler and drove his knife through the man's exposed armpit. Leaving the blade embedded there, Davides dropped low and upended him into the pen. Without slowing, he unsheathed his sword and slashed the rope that lifted the iron gate. It might take a while for the *garrocha* aficionado to bleed out, and Davides didn't want him or his bloodthirsty dogs to join the fray.

Gonsaluiz and the other two men-at-arms sprang to their feet. Focused as they were on Davides, they didn't notice Sajid collect himself. Awkwardly but effectively, Sajid dove sideways into the man-at-arms standing next to him. Together, they tumbled off the loft. It wasn't a far drop, but the disoriented man-at-arms ended up on his hands and knees. As he was attempting to lurch back to his feet, Davides hacked into the base of his skull, dropping him instantly.

Davides spun around to where Sajid was lying in a heap. One look at the dazed and bloody soldier told him not to expect any more help from that quarter, but Davides felt like he at least had to cut him loose. By the time he had severed the leather strips binding Sajid's arms, Gonsaluiz and the other man had leapt from the loft, weapons in hand.

Gonsaluiz was built like a block, short and thick set. The blade he was wielding was more impressive in its appearance. It exhibited the distinctive, woodgrain pattern of Damascus steel. Davides found himself wondering how many limbs had been severed by that sword, how many lesser swords had been shattered.

"Where are they?" Gonsaluiz jeered at him.

"Who?" Davides responded. He should have ignored the question, but he had other things on his mind, such as how in the world he was going to survive this fight. The odds were decidedly against him. He had ridden all day and had already gone through multiple fights. They were fresh. The leather cuirass he was wearing was better than nothing, but it wasn't nearly as protective as their mail hauberks. His only advantage was his mobility, but the storehouse did not offer much in the way of tactical maneuverability. The wall with the double doors led to more men-at-arms. The wall behind him had two dogs chained to it. The half-loft? He'd need a running start to vault that high. Or a moment to gather himself. Besides, he'd have to get past Gonsaluiz and his lackey, who had fanned out and were closing in on him. Davides backed away from Sajid and into the center of the room.

"You mean you came alone?" Gonsaluiz laughed. Then, eyes glistening with rapacious delight, he attacked.

Instead of retreating further, Davides sidestepped away from Gonsaluiz and swung at the henchman. His first blow cut deeply into the man's weapon arm. Davides kept moving, positioning the man-at-arms between him and Gonsaluiz. His next attack met a wobbly counterstrike from the henchman that forced both of their weapons low but let Davides bring his sword inside. Davides's reverse upward cut bit into the man's leg, just above the knee.

The exchange had taken only a moment, but Gonsaluiz was quicker than his build would have suggested. Davides felt, more than saw, the incoming blade.   He shied to one side, and Gonsaluiz's sword skimmed his head, scraping the *litham* out of place. Davides backpedaled, yanked the trailing *litham* off his head, and flipped the material around his left forearm. The least it could do was give his arm another layer of protection.

Gonsaluiz pressed Davides back, back, back towards the double doors, and Davides sensed he was about to be cornered.   He set his feet and swung hard at Gonsaluiz.   Gonsaluiz swung back harder.   Davides half-checked the blow, allowing the force of it to carry him sideways.   Then, using the same momentum from the blow, he kept his feet moving, away from the double doors and back towards the middle of the storehouse.

Something warm, wet, and sticky trickled down into his left eye. Gonsaluiz's first swing must have opened a cut on his scalp.   The blood running into his eye made it hard to keep track of the wounded henchman, who was approaching from his left side.   Davides had to turn his head to gauge the distance separating them.   At that moment, Gonsaluiz rushed him again.

Davides's sword shuddered ominously as it came into emphatic contact with Gonsaluiz's.   This time, Davides did not give ground.   Instead, he pushed inside and, using the heavy round pommel of his sword, hammered it into Gonsaluiz's face.   The man-at-arms rejoined the fight, and Davides thrust his sword tip down through the man's boot. The man howled in pain, reached for his foot, and toppled over.

Davides leaped backwards, but he wasn't quite fast enough.   The Damascus blade skimmed through his leather cuirass and plowed a searing furrow along his ribs. Sharp pain stole Davides's breath away.   He stumbled sideways, left arm tight to his side. He knew Gonsaluiz was coming, and he knew he had to move quickly. But, before he could force his legs to do anything particularly constructive, the double doors behind Gonsaluiz opened, and a figure stepped through them.

Even in the poor light of the storehouse, Davides recognized Rodrigo's silhouette. *Oh, shit.*

From Davides's patent look of dismay, Gonsaluiz assumed the newcomer was one of his men-at-arms. He slowed his advance and, without taking his eyes off Davides, shouted, "It's about damned time! Flank him, but don't kill him outright! I want to see his face when the dogs rip out his guts and drag them through the dirt."

Rodrigo angled his way closer to them, in and out of the yellow pools of torchlight. Somewhere along the way, he had acquired a more imposing weapon than the small, concealed dagger. He was now holding a sword. "I wasn't expecting to find you here, Ignacio," he said, in a neutral tone of voice.

Great. They know each other. Of course, they do.

Gonsaluiz turned and stared. If possible, he was even less happy — and considerably more surprised — than Davides at the appearance of the other Castilian. "Rodrigo Díaz? What the hell are you doing here?"

Rodrigo stopped so that the three of them formed points of a triangle. "Some men picked me up in Toledo and brought me here," he answered.

"What? What are you talking about? What men?" Gonsaluiz demanded.

"I didn't catch their names. Pablo? Pavel? Something like that ..."

That's it. You two just keep talking. Davides cleared some of the blood away from his left eye with a quick

241

swipe of the *litham*. He didn't know why Rodrigo had obfuscated how he had come to be there, and at the moment, he didn't care. Their exchange was giving him a desperately needed breather. The pain in his ribs had subsided to a dull throbbing, he was starting to get his wind back, and his heart no longer felt like it was going to burst from his chest. Soon, he might even be able to lift the tip of his sword off the ground again.

"Never mind," Gonsaluiz said. "Whatever you're doing here, it'll have to wait. I'm in the middle of something."

"Yes, I heard. Something involving this man's guts. Frankly, he doesn't look like much, but he seems to have given your men some trouble."

"Don't let the rags he's wearing fool you," Gonsaluiz said. "He's been well-trained. One of General Haroun's pets."

Rodrigo frowned in Davides's direction. "He works for Haroun? Are you saying he's a spy?"

"Yes, that's right. A spy." Gonsaluiz seemed to savor the word. It would make a pat justification for killing Davides without Gonsaluiz having to answer a lot of pesky questions. "His name is Sisnando Davides. Ever heard of him?"

Davides didn't wait to see Rodrigo's reaction to the news. If it was news. Maybe Rodrigo had already figured it out or had known it all along. In any event, Rodrigo struck him as the lesser of two evils. He attacked Gonsaluiz.

Davides's sudden assault caught the knight off guard, and his first blow ripped into flesh. It was a satisfying moment, but Davides's initial burst of energy waned rapidly. Gonsaluiz got off his heels, his strength fueled by fresh outrage. After a few more strikes and counterstrikes, Davides's arms began to feel heavy and sluggish. Then, a sudden wave of dizziness made the room career. The floor seemed to surge upwards and smack into him, jarring his sword from his grasp.

By the time his vision had cleared, swords were clashing directly over top of him. Metal rang and shivered. Booted feet jostled him on either side, and blades bit into the floor beside him.

It took a moment for him to realize that Rodrigo was fighting Gonsaluiz. On his behalf. He watched in confused wonder as Rodrigo's sword deflected Gonsaluiz's once again, frustrating the enraged knight's attempt to land a crippling blow on Davides's prone form.

Move!

Davides shook off his astonishment and began squirming his way out from under the two combatants. Before he could get far, a spatter of blood rained down on his face, and a body heavy with mail armor sprawled across his legs. Repulsed, he struggled to extricate himself from Gonsaluiz's floundering form. He kicked free just as Rodrigo's blade descended again and severed Gonsaluiz's neck.

Davides drew his feet under him and scrambled back a few paces, grabbing his sword in the process. He stared wide-eyed, first at the dead knight, then at Rodrigo. "You killed him," he said. It was a stupid thing to say, but saying it out loud somehow made it more real.

Rodrigo lifted his gaze from the headless body and the rapidly forming puddle of blood. "I owed you," he said, by way of explanation. "Now, we're even."

"Okay," Davides said. It seemed an extreme way to repay a debt, but who was he to argue with Rodrigo's sense of honor?

"Besides," Rodrigo faced Davides, his expression resolute, "I needed you alive, not in pieces."

Davides had liked Rodrigo's initial rationale better; this last one sounded a lot like a threat. He blotted more blood from his left eye and tightened his grip on his sword.

At that moment, however, a sound from the deep shadows near the half-loft caught their attention. Rodrigo shifted his stance, poised for another fight, but then his eyebrows drew down in puzzlement. "That's . . . not Jamal."

At first, Davides assumed the person in question was Remir. Remir. Jamal. The names and faces were getting fuzzy. But, when Davides turned to look, he saw Sajid. The soldier was on his feet once more, holding one end of the *garrocha*. The other end was embedded in the man-at-arms who had withdrawn from the fight. Sajid twisted the point in deeper, spat on the writhing body, and yanked the *garrocha* out. No, it most certainly was not Jamal. Jamal was that good-natured youth who had wrestled Rodrigo to a standstill and then politely offered him back his knife. This man with the *garrocha* was cut from entirely different cloth.

Sajid began hobbling towards them, the blood-stained *garrocha* scraping in the dirt behind him.

What now? Davides's head spun. Sajid still thought they were on the same side. If he had seen Rodrigo kill Gonsaluiz, he would think they were all on the same side. One big, happy family. Sajid was about to find out how wrong he was.

244

Let Sajid and Rodrigo fight it out. Maybe you and Remir can get clear in the confusion.

It was a practical approach, but not very honorable. Sajid was already hurt, and, as Davides had cause to know, Rodrigo was a formidable adversary. Why had Davides bothered trying to save Sajid from Gonsaluiz if he was just going to turn around and sacrifice him to Rodrigo?

Davides pitched his voice low, so only Rodrigo would hear him clearly. "You and I are old friends."

"Pardon?" said a perplexed Rodrigo.

"You and I are friends." Davides insisted, knowing that the most Sajid would pick up from the Castilian in which they were speaking was 'friends'. He put a derisive edge on his voice. "Come on, Rodrigo. It's not like it's the first time you pretended to be an old friend of mine."

Rodrigo, caught between confusion, mistrust, and perhaps a little guilt, stood his ground but didn't move to attack either Sajid or Davides.

Sajid reached them and grimaced, which was about as close to a smile as Sajid ever got. "Peace be upon you," he greeted them in Arabic.

"And, on you be peace," Davides responded. Out of the corner of his eye, he saw Rodrigo's sword waver, then lower.

"I never thought I would be so happy to see you, Davides."

Since Davides couldn't bring himself to return the sentiment, he said, "Sajid, this is my friend, Rodrigo. I'm afraid he speaks Arabic about as well as you speak Castilian. Rodrigo, Sajid."

No sooner had Davides made the introductions than another bout of giddiness hit him. Not the elated kind of giddiness. The unsteady, about-to-fall-down kind. He didn't realize he was actually swaying until Rodrigo grabbed hold of him and rightened him.

What happened next was like a bizarre dream. Instead of attacking each other like the natural enemies they were, Rodrigo and Sajid calmly discussed their next move. Most of what one said the other couldn't understand, but through pantomime and a few shared words, they came up with a plan. They decided to move to a more defensible position and hole up for the night.

Davides could have translated, but he kept quiet, content to lean on Rodrigo for support. He was afraid to disturb the odd truce by adding any clarity to the situation. For the moment, muddy was good.

Sajid exchanged the *garrocha* for Gonsaluiz's sword and, despite his own injuries, took the lead. He eased one of the doors open, checked outside, then motioned for them to follow. Rodrigo stretched Davides's arm across his shoulders and helped him towards the double doors. He maneuvered Davides through the doorway and into the yard.

The horses were massed in one corner of the corral, ears pricked towards them and nostrils flaring. The guard at the back gate was lying face down on the ground, an irregular stain of blood spread under him. The guard from the awning was crumpled in the middle of the yard with two crossbow bolts protruding from his mail hauberk.

Aside from the crossbow bolts, there was no sign of Remir.

Recalling what he knew about the layout of the manor, Davides gestured towards the door that connected the awning and the main house. It was close to the kitchen, and the kitchen should have water and a fire.

Sajid stayed in the lead. He pushed at the door, which opened into a dark hallway. Unable to see much beyond the rectangle of sparse light that emanated from the opening to the kitchen, they inched their way down the hallway, past a couple of closed doors. Davides expected to run into servants or off-duty sentries, but no one appeared.

When they reached the kitchen, they saw that it had been only recently vacated. A low fire was burning in the hearth, and a pot of stew still hung from the trammel hook. Several earthenware plates with bits of stew and crusts of bread had been left on the long, wooden table, along with a clay pitcher and some cups. One of the cups had tipped over, leaving a trail of liquid on the table that disappeared through a crack between the boards. A back door, which led to a garden, stood ajar.

Sajid, his limp increasingly pronounced, summoned enough strength to cross the room, close the back door, and drop the latch into place. Then, he slumped onto a stool near the table.

Rodrigo swung the hallway door shut with his foot and propped Davides against the wall. It was a nice, solid wall, Davides thought. Unlikely to list unexpectedly. Rodrigo took Davides's sword from his hand and, before Davides quite realized what was happening, set it on the table behind him. Davides started after it—he needed that sword—but Rodrigo kept him pinned against the wall.

"Easy, old friend." Rodrigo smiled a faint, mocking smile and nodded at the cut across Davides's ribs. "Let's see how badly you're hurt."

Davides glared back at him. He had just been disarmed and was now being told—in so many words—to take off his armor. He was getting the impression that he had somehow surrendered . . . without the part where he had ever actually surrendered. Grudgingly, Davides fumbled at the straps of his armor until he had loosened them. Rodrigo pulled the cuirass off and let it fall to the floor, then steered Davides over to the hearth.

"Lie down," Rodrigo said.

The direct order should have rankled, but the sad truth was that Davides wanted nothing more than to lie down. He lowered himself next to the warm bricks that extended out from the fireplace and stretched out. Finally, he could rest.

Or not. Without warning, Rodrigo peeled Davides's shirt back from the cut across his ribs. Fresh, scalding pain made Davides suck in his breath sharply.

"It doesn't look too bad," Rodrigo reported after a moment. "Your insides are still inside, anyway."

"*Ótimo*," Davides said between gritted teeth.

Rodrigo unwound the *litham* from Davides's arm and pressed it lightly against the wound as an improvised bandage. "Your friend appears to have fallen asleep, or to have passed out."

It took Davides a moment to put together that Rodrigo was talking about Sajid. They were all tossing that 'friend' term around rather loosely. He rolled his eyes in Sajid's direction. Sajid was still on the stool, but he had cradled his head on the table with one arm while the other arm held the sword across his lap. His face had the laxness indicative of deep sleep.

"Who is he?" Rodrigo asked.

"A soldier."

"From Seville?"

Davides nodded.

Rodrigo sighed in disgust. "I knew I should have killed him."

Davides nodded again. He didn't have the mental energy to be clever or cagey. "He would have tried to kill you if he had found out who you were."

"You found out who I was," Rodrigo observed. "Back at the wagon. Why didn't you kill me when you had the chance?"

Davides shook his head. He didn't know why he hadn't killed Rodrigo. He didn't care. He was so tired. His eyes closed.

A spasm of acute pain racked Davides back to consciousness. Rodrigo was leaning hard on the bandage, on the gash across his ribs. Davides's fingers closed on Rodrigo's sleeve, but he lacked the strength to make the arm move.

"Davides," Rodrigo said, his voice calm but remorseless, "where is Remir being held?"

"He isn't," Davides said between gasps. "He escaped."

The pressure and pain eased slightly. "How did he manage that?" Rodrigo asked. "Was Gonsaluiz helping him?"

Davides almost choked at the thought. "No."

"Then, what brought you out here? Why else would you and Jamal and this Sajid character take on someone like Gonsaluiz?"

"We told you. Retribution." The last word was slurred, diminishing whatever *gravitas* it might have otherwise conveyed. Davides was fading fast, too fast this time for Rodrigo to stop him. Or, maybe this time Rodrigo made no effort to keep him conscious. Maybe this time Rodrigo had other concerns.

From what seemed a very great distance away, Davides heard Rodrigo say, "I was wondering when you would show up."

* * *

Wooden wheels ground over hard packed dirt. The road's uneven surface caused friction at the skeens, which in turn sent miniature shockwaves along the axel-tree and throughout the entire frame of the wagon. When a pebble happened to be more on the scale of a rock, or a depression was actually more of a crater, the wagon's unpleasant vibration was interrupted by a single, bone jarring jolt.

One such jolt had awakened Davides. Another had prompted him to push back the prickly, woolen blanket covering his head and look around. The sun was climbing, its warm beams moderating the brisk autumn air. He was in the back of a wagon. Crates, barrels, and burlap bags surrounded him, obstructing his view of the (very slowly) passing landscape. Behind the wagon ambled an unfamiliar, dappled grey horse, its lopped ears and half-closed eyes indicating its boredom with the wagon's plodding pace.

"He's up," said a voice in Castilian. Rodrigo's voice.

Damn. It wasn't just a bad dream.

Davides tilted his head back so he could see the front of the wagon. He squinted against the sun, trying to pull into focus the two figures on the front seat. Rodrigo and Remir. Davides squinted harder. Remir and Rodrigo?

250

Rodrigo now wore mail under a loden cloak, and his hand rested casually on the pommel of a sword at his belt. Remir was driving. Instead of the *litham*, Remir had donned a wide brimmed straw hat, the kind favored by farm laborers and their mules.

Remir glanced back at him, and white teeth shone through a face caked in dust. "You look like hell," Remir said cheerfully.

"Really? 'Cause I feel great." Nothing so bad a little sarcasm wouldn't help.

There were things Davides wanted rather badly to know, such as *why is Rodrigo here? why did he follow us to al-Qati's?* and *does he know who you are?* All good questions, none of which he dared ask. Finally, he settled on a noncommittal, "Where are we going?"

"Alferia," Remir answered, while at the same time pulling hard on one rein in an attempt to steer around some obstacle in the road. The mules, obdurate, continued straight ahead. The front wheel of the wagon hit yet another rock, subjecting them to yet another violent lurch.

"It's like they do it on purpose," Remir grumbled.

"They can't turn as fast as a mounted animal," Rodrigo explained. "You have to watch ahead and start moving them over well in advance."

"They didn't turn at all!" Remir pointed out.

"You're not accustomed to driving mules, are you?" Rodrigo asked.

Davides shifted until he could lean against a bag of seeds—the same bag of seeds that the lazy Vandal had been sitting on earlier, when transporting Rodrigo to al-Qati's. It was the only thing Davides could see in the wagon with any potential for absorbing shock. But, the

251

effort of moving even that tiny bit wore him out. He closed his eyes to rest, just for a moment . . .

* * *

When the shuddering of the wagon roused him a second time, the sun was considerably higher in the sky. Remir was now on the passenger side of the front seat, and Rodrigo was driving the mules. *Does that have meaning? Is Rodrigo the one in charge? Or, was Remir just that bad at driving mules?* Remir wasn't acting like he was being taken somewhere against his will. Of course, Davides reminded himself, Remir had some practice in that area.

As if sensing Davides's gaze on him, Remir turned in his seat. This time, his smile was more subdued. "Peace and blessings," Remir said.

"And, on you," Davides replied. Then, since Rodrigo didn't appear to object to them conversing in Arabic, Davides asked, "What happened?"

"You passed out again. This is a habit verging on a vice with you."

"I mean, at al-Qati's. What happened?"

"Hey, don't blame me! You started the fight before I was in position. I had to—"

"No, I mean," Davides paused and looked pointedly at Rodrigo's back. "what happened at al-Qati's? He knows who I am."

"Oh, that. You weren't awake for that?" Remir asked.

"Not so much."

"Well," Remir thought back, "I overheard part of your conversation in the kitchen, and I realized he had

252

somehow figured out who you were. I didn't know what else to do, so I walked in and told him the truth."

"You did what?" Davides asked in disbelief.

"I also convinced him there was no way in hell I was going back to Burgos with him."

"How did you manage that?"

"I said, 'there's no way in hell I'm going back with you'. Not my best rhetorical style, I'll grant you, but he seemed to appreciate the sincerity behind the words. It may have helped that he had other matters on his mind. When he explained to me who Hildric really was, we both thought it best not to linger at the manor. We left before daybreak and reached Toledo early this morning."

"You went back to Toledo?" It struck Davides as a tremendously risky thing to have done, given the number of different parties still searching for them.

"It was either that or dump Sajid by the side of the road somewhere," Remir said mildly.

Davides felt a pang of guilt. He had forgotten about Sajid. In his own defense, he had been unconscious for quite a long time. "What, um, did you end up doing with him?"

"We took him to Rodrigo's inn."

At the mention of his name, Rodrigo turned his attention away from the road and gave each of them a quizzical look.

"Davides was asking about Sajid," Remir switched back to Castilian. "I told him we took him to your inn."

Rodrigo nodded. "Your soldier friend was in rough shape, Davides. We roused a physician and claimed that Sajid had been beaten and robbed by bandits, which, as I understand it, is the literal truth."

253

"We also implied that he was a stranger to us and that we were simply acting as good Samaritans," Remir added. "We didn't want people to wonder why we were leaving without him."

"And, Sajid was okay with all of that?" Davides asked.

"He had worsened during the night," Rodrigo said. "He wasn't conscious when we got to the inn, much less in a position to argue the matter. The physician wouldn't venture to say whether or not he would pull though. Regardless, we paid for his medical care and a couple of weeks lodging for him. I hope that was adequate?"

Neither Remir nor Rodrigo had had any reason to help Sajid. Quite the opposite. To them, Sajid was the enemy. Things being what they were, Davides probably should have been thinking of him as an enemy, too. Sajid wouldn't have hesitated to stick a sword through him if he had discovered what Davides was doing.

"Yes, more than adequate. I guess now I owe you a debt."

Rodrigo gave a short, humorless laugh. "Last night, I was interrogating you, Davides, torturing you for information. If it's all the same to you, let's just go back to being even."

Rodrigo's words surprised Davides. He hadn't been harboring any special resentment towards Rodrigo, although he supposed things might have gotten ugly — uglier — if Remir had not made his appearance when he had.

"Fair enough," Davides said. He hesitated, then asked, "Is that why you followed us to the manor last night? To square your debt with us?"

"It figured into my reasoning," Rodrigo replied, giving each mule a tap with the whip to keep them moving along, "although there were other factors. For one, I wanted to know why you were so anxious to get rid of me, especially when I had offered to help. I also wanted to know where those men in the wagon had been taking me, and why they had abducted me in the first place. All of the questions seemed to lead me down the same path."

"I'm still surprised you didn't go back to Toledo first, for your armor, your weapons, your men?" Davides couched the last words as a question. Rodrigo was a Castilian knight, he was certain, even though Rodrigo had never admitted as much. So, where were his men-at-arms?

A long pause followed his query. Finally, Rodrigo said, "For being half-dead, you're not doing a half-bad job of questioning me. For your information, I came alone. And, I have given Remir my word that I will not attempt to force you or him to return with me to points north. Does that put your mind at ease?"

"It helps." As Davides had occasion to know, Rodrigo took his honor very seriously. Giving his word was tantamount to swearing an oath on the Bible.

Davides relaxed a little and took a moment to look around the wagon. The dappled grey must be Rodrigo's mount, retrieved from a stable when they had stopped in Toledo. Most of the cargo consisted of empty crates and barrels, which had originally concealed Rodrigo's presence from curious passersby and now masked his own. Then, he spied a few items that were not mere camouflage.

Wedged under the front seat was an ironbound box roughly two feet square, with an impressive padlock guarding its hasp. Next to it, lay Gonsaluiz's sword, the blade chastely stowed in a battered leather scabbard.

"You brought the sword," Davides remarked. Of course they had. It wasn't the sort of thing you left lying around. A sword like that was worth a small fortune. Maybe not a king's ransom, but probably a count's.

"Yes," Rodrigo said, "but if I were you, I'd get the cross-guard and pommel switched out so it won't be so easy to recognize."

"Me? You won the fight. The sword is yours."

Rodrigo shook his head. "You keep it. The last thing I need is to be carrying around a sword that ties me to Ignacio Gonsaluiz's death. I have enough enemies at Court without adding his clan to the list."

"Far better that Davides add them to his list," Remir inserted wryly.

"That's not what I meant. Damascus steel is extremely rare in Castile-León. Even disguised, the blade would be noticed. People might draw conclusions — appropriate ones — about when I showed up with that sword, and when Gonsaluiz went missing. However, Davides's reputation as a soldier of fortune from Seville gives him a much wider range of possibilities for possessing such a weapon."

A soldier of fortune. In other words, a mercenary. A month or so ago, Davides would have been insulted, but a lot had happened since then. He still wasn't enthused about being thought of as a hired sword, but he was more realistic about his actual prospects in life.

"Speaking of which, Davides," Rodrigo went on, "if you're looking for a job that makes better use of your talents than selling iron, I know people who would be interested in hiring you."

"As a mercenary? I don't think so, Rodrigo. I don't want to kill people for a living."

"It's not always about killing people," Rodrigo said, undeterred. "More and more, it's about convincing them. Negotiating. You speak Castilian and Arabic fluently. You know the ways of both Christians and Muslims. You're literate. You're versed in politics. And, you've learned warfare from one of the best commanders in all of Hispania. Do you have any idea how rare that combination is? You could name your price."

It was hard for Davides to imagine himself being an asset to anyone for any reason when he was too weak to stand. "You seem to know a lot about me," he commented.

"A lot of people know a lot about you, Davides. More than once, I've heard talk about approaching you and bringing you over to Castile-León."

If Rodrigo thought his words were encouraging in any way, he was mistaken. Davides had a sudden, mental image of faceless men meeting behind closed doors and discussing ways to subvert him. "Were those your orders?" Davides demanded. "Find Remir. Oh, and while you're at it, get Davides to switch sides?"

Rodrigo shook his head, impervious to Davides's sharp tone. "No. After I found Remir, I was supposed to kill you."

"Whoa!" Remir interjected. "That's not what you told me! Unless I somehow misunderstood, you said that you were supposed to rejoin the Castilian troops in Zamora once you had gotten Amira out of Salamanca. Those were your orders. But, my darling sister asked you to look for us, instead."

Amira had sent Rodrigo?

257

"Well, yes," Rodrigo admitted. "To be precise, the Lady Amira was the one who asked me to find Remir and kill you."

Davides's mental image morphed from the faceless, conspiring lords to Amira's fiery gaze. Back in Salamanca, she had vowed to have him hunted down and staked out for the crows. She hadn't wasted any time following up on her threat, had she?

"How did she know where we were?" Davides asked, mystified.

"She guessed," Remir said, in a tone of mild, brotherly exasperation. "Somehow, she found out that you and I had fallen off the map near Cáceres. Everyone else was searching the roads south, but she knew you had connections in Toledo and speculated that you might be hiding me there."

Rodrigo had ridden all the way to Toledo on Amira's speculation? As incredible as it seemed, that scenario explained why Rodrigo had been traveling alone, why Gonsaluiz hadn't known Rodrigo would be in the area, and why Rodrigo might now be willing to return to Castile-León empty-handed.

It suddenly occurred to Davides that, while Rodrigo had given Remir his word not to force them to go north, strictly speaking he had said nothing about whether or not he felt obliged to kill Davides. "It sounds like she gave you a very specific directive," Davides said.

"Very specific, yes," Rodrigo agreed, and turned a weathered smile first towards Remir and then back towards him. "But, I'm not honor-bound to kill you, if that's your concern."

"Glad to hear it." An undertow of sluggishness pulled at Davides. He fought against it by posing another question. "Where did the strongbox come from?"

"I found it while I was searching for some *aguardiente*," Remir answered.

"You people have the strangest practices," Rodrigo observed. "Perfectly good liquor, and he empties it over your wounds."

"We're inscrutable," Davides acknowledged. "Any idea what's inside the box?"

"About ten times the silver and gold that Attab had stashed away," Remir said. "There's also a letter inside addressed to 'Hildric'. It was written in Aragonese, so Rodrigo had to decipher it for me, but the money was earmarked for hiring mercenaries and buying more weapons. Strange, don't you think?"

Strange, yes. Davides suspected he should care but couldn't quite bring himself to do so. Remir and Rodrigo must have cared, though, because they kept talking about it.

"I'm thinking that Hildric's corruption went deeper than we had supposed, which was already pretty damn deep," Remir went on. "If Hildric was a knight from Castile-León, why did he bring Aragonese with him to set up his organization in Toledo? Last I knew, Castile-León and Aragón weren't on the best of terms."

"True," Rodrigo confirmed.

"Then," Remir continued, "Hildric outfitted at least some of these Aragonese with armor and swords, gear that is usually reserved for soldiers. He was pushing Alferia for high yields of wrought iron, a commodity prized by warmongers. And, he had a treasure trove destined for still more hired swords. What was he planning to do with them all?"

"Are you suggesting that he was conspiring with someone in Aragón against King Fernando?" Rodrigo asked.

"It would explain a lot, don't you think?"

Even in his dazed state, Davides could see that it would, although he failed to understand why it should matter to him and Remir. Internal conflicts between Castile-León and Aragón were not their problem.

Or, were they? He and Remir were heading for Alferia, and Father Bernat was one of the people Gonsaluiz had brought from Aragón. The priest had *claimed* he wanted 'Hildric' out of the way so he could turn a fair profit. He had *claimed* he needed Davides and Remir to market Alferia's wrought iron and find an engineer. But, Father Bernat was an accomplished liar, who had already duped them once with his bumpkin-like charm. His self-serving arrangement with them did not mean that he wasn't part of a larger, political conspiracy in which they were being used as pawns. And, as everyone knew, pawns were expendable.

"Probably shouldn't mention the letter when we get to Alferia," Davides managed to articulate.

"Agreed," Remir said.

"A better solution might be to skip Alferia altogether and head for Ávila instead," Rodrigo suggested.

A brief moment passed, then Remir said curtly, "It's too far."

Rodrigo looked back at Davides with an appraising eye. What he saw didn't seem to encourage him. He faced front again without comment.

"You mean, too far for me?" Davides asked. "I'm fine."

"No, you're not," Rodrigo said bluntly. "You need bed rest and a physician. And, the only healer outside of Toledo whom Remir trusts — if I can still use that word — is this pretend priest. So, we go to Alferia."

"Not 'we'," Remir amended. "If there's any chance that Father Bernat is involved in some conspiracy with Aragón, it would be a mistake for you to go there, Rodrigo. Tomorrow morning, when we reach the road to Ávila, you should leave us. And, take the letter with you. Or burn it, I don't care. So long as no one finds it on us."

"My intention was to see you to safety," Rodrigo said.

"And, my intention was to avoid intrigue and live my life in peace. Looks like we both lose."

* * *

They spent the night on the side of the road in a spot that, due to its natural amenities, had seen many a traveler before them. A shallow creek gurgled nearby — the same one they had crossed with Julián two days earlier, only this time they were further downstream, just off the road. The area was level, clear of stumps and rocks, and large enough for several wagons to pull in. A stand of columnar junipers provided shade in the summer and windbreaks in the winter.

These amenities were lost on Davides. He woke up long enough to be helped from the wagon and deposited next to their campfire, whereupon he once again fell headlong into sleep.

When Davides awoke the next morning, he felt chilled and shaky despite the heavy blanket wrapped around him. He dozed fitfully as they continued their journey and barely registered Rodrigo's departure later that morning. When the vibration of the wagon finally stopped, a small, distant corner of his mind realized they had reached Alferia.

By then, Davides wasn't thinking about the potential danger they might be facing. He wasn't thinking about conspiracies, Aragón, or Gonsaluiz's mercenaries. He wasn't thinking about kidnappings, Salamanca, or General Haroun's army. His thoughts, clouded by fever, went only so far as to thank God they had made it.

He spent much of the next week in bed. For the first several days, he was only dimly aware of the comings and goings of other people: Remir, Mari Carmen, Teia. Mostly, he remembered Father Bernat applying poultices, lancing his wounds to let pus run, and coaxing him into taking a vile medicine that tasted like onions gone bad. By the time he had the wherewithal to be on his guard, it seemed a wasted effort. Father Bernat had brought him chicken soup. How evil could he be?

* * *

"Welcome back!" Father Bernat's booming voice traveled past the closed door and into the bedroom where Davides was resting. It was Father Bernat's own room in the rectory, which he had given over to Davides upon their arrival in Alferia a week ago. The bed in which Davides was laying dominated the room. The rest of the space was occupied by a stool, a large trunk, and Samson, who was sprawled next to the bed on a worn, woven rug.

Sunlight filtered past the edges of the heavy shade that covered the window, creating a halo effect.

"God's peace be upon you," said Remir.

The sound of Remir's voice brushed away some of Davides's somnolence. Remir and Teia had left Alferia several days ago to 'check on things' in Toledo. No one had consulted Davides as to whether this was a prudent move—or maybe they had, and he simply didn't remember. Either way, he had had to keep his qualms to himself. Father Bernat and his associates knew them as 'Davides' and 'Ramiro', alias Nizar and Jamal, who had fled trouble in Seville only to find more of it in Toledo. They didn't need to know who Remir really was, or what he might be worth to certain, interested parties.

"Come on in and sit a spell," Father Bernat continued. "I'll fetch us something to drink."

"How is he?" Remir wanted to know.

"Better," Father Bernat said, his voice followed by the dull clunk of clay mugs on the table. "The fever's down, and his wounds are mending. But, he's still weak from blood loss and sleeps most the time. Did you find the fixings I wanted?"

"I think so," Remir said. More clunks on the table. "Haliver oil, dried beef liver, tincture of yellow dock root, and clover honey. Please tell me you don't mix it all together."

Father Bernat let out a guffaw, and Teia said something in a voice too soft to pass through the door. The screech of chair legs on the stone floor further drowned out their conversation. For a time, their voices were indistinguishable murmurs. Then, Father Bernat spoke again.

"To tell the truth, I'm not surprised. Framing you two for that alchemist's murder smacks of subtlety. Hildric was many things, but subtle weren't one of 'em. Still, it's good to know you boys aren't wanted outlaws in Toledo. It might reflect poorly on us virtuous folk here in Alferia." He chuckled a little before continuing, "What's that in the satchel, Teia?"

Davides lost most of her answer and wondered crossly why she couldn't speak up, just a little? He supposed he could have joined them, or asked them to come to him. But, lately, he had gotten the impression that he was being sheltered — in the way that parents shelter their children — from matters of importance. Everyone walked softly around him, talked softly. No one wanted to say or do anything that would aggravate him. So, like a child, he resorted to eavesdropping to stay informed.

Remir's voice intermittently traversed the door. "... can translate it to Castilian . . . will purchase whatever quantities the town produces . . . less than you asked, but you only have to transport it to Toledo."

"You got a contract? Well, aren't you a wonder! Who's the buyer?"

Remir's reply was inaudible.

"Must be some well-to-do blacksmith!" Father Bernat exclaimed.

Davides felt the blood drain from his face. He didn't need to hear Ishaq's name to know with certainty to whom they were referring. What other blacksmith did Remir know well enough to negotiate a contract in so little time? He sat up in bed, threw aside the cover, and swung his legs to the floor. Only to have them land on the dog, instead. Samson yelped in surprise and scrambled sideways, an injured expression on his face. The door to

264

the bedroom opened, and Remir poked his head inside. Davides, still sitting on the side of the bed, glared at him.

Remir fixed a smile in place before doing a quick about-face to address Father Bernat and Teia. "He's awake. Isn't that great? I'm just going to catch up with him a little, if that's all right?"

Remir didn't wait for an answer. He came into the bedroom, closed the door behind him, and stood eyeing Davides warily. After a long moment, he crossed to the stool and sat down. "Just hear me out," he said, switching to Arabic.

"How could you get Ishaq involved with these people?" Davides struggled to keep from shouting. "*Pelo amor de Deus*! After what they did to Bendayan! What were you thinking?"

"Would you give me a little credit for — gee, I don't know — thinking? I did not do this on a whim, Davides."

"It doesn't matter! You knew I'd be against it."

"Yes, because where Ishaq is concerned, you tend to use your heart more than your head."

"Says the resident expert!"

Remir's eyes rolled skyward as if looking to God to grant him patience. It struck Davides suddenly that that was his look, when Remir's antics had required extraordinary measures of forbearance on his part.

"It's done," Remir said finally. "Now, do you want to hear my reasons for doing it, or do you want to yell at me some more?"

Davides wanted to yell some more. But, he had already demanded answers from Remir twice — *How could you? What were you thinking?* — and all that popped into his head were iterations of the same.

"Giving someone permission to yell at you takes all the satisfaction out of it," Davides grumbled.

"Yeah, I figured that out when I was about five years old."

"It worked on your father?" Davides asked, with skepticism.

"It works on practically everybody."

"Okay," Davides said, exaggerating a calm he did not yet feel. "Tell me, then, what were you thinking?"

"I knew Ishaq would be worried about you, and I thought he deserved to know what happened. But, I needed an excuse to seek him out that would make sense to Teia. That's how it started.

"When Ishaq saw me, I honestly wasn't sure whether he was going to hug me or punch me. He had heard rumors about the two dead bodies in the river, and, well, he thought we were dead. Seeing me alive-and-well brought him hope, but seeing me without you . . . Let's just say, I talked fast. I told him about Julián, my sister's escape, our fight at the boarding house, Alferia, Bendayan, al-Qati's. Everything."

"I take it Teia wasn't with you?"

Remir smirked. "No. I waited for Ishaq at the baths. Even Teia can't pull off that good of a disguise."

It wasn't the complete disaster Davides had been imagining—assuming Remir's 'everything' had truly encompassed everything. Past precedent suggested that it probably had not. "I still wish you wouldn't have involved Ishaq with . . . with what's going on here."

"He wanted to help you, Davides. I convinced him not to come rushing out with al-Mamun's personal physician, but he refused to sit idly by. The contract was a compromise. It gives him an excuse to be interested in

Alferia. In fact, he's sending an apprentice here shortly to look at the quality of Alferia's iron and draw up some plans for the waterwheel. The apprentice will also be able to report back to Ishaq on how you're faring.

"And, not everything is about you, you know." Remir rocked back on the stool and assumed a critical expression. "Ishaq got a really good deal on this iron. Not to mention the fact that, unlike the Vandals, he will use it to make hinges and doorknockers and astro-thinga-majigs. Not swords."

Davides snorted. "Brilliant rationalization."

A hint of Remir's familiar, mocking smile played about his lips but failed to manifest. His eyes shifted.

If Remir had been doing nothing more than rationalizing, he would have looked Davides straight in the eye. The fact that Remir wouldn't hold his gaze suggested first that Remir was serious about not wanting the iron to go towards making weapons, and second that he felt a little embarrassed about having a strong opinion on the subject. Maybe Remir wasn't accustomed to the feeling. When they had left Salamanca, he hadn't seemed to have a strong opinion on anything.

Davides nodded towards the satchel, which was still tucked under Remir's arm. "Is that the contract?"

Remir's eyes came back up. "What? Oh. No. The contract's out on the table. This is something Teia found." He held the satchel out.

Davides took the leather bag hesitantly, wondering what venomous creature would strike from within if he opened it to look inside.

"They're some of Bendayan's notes," Remir said. "Teia heard about someone trying to fence them, and she picked them up. I guess the shop got looted, you know, after the fire burned out."

Davides stared at the satchel, more genuinely afraid of its contents than before. It was almost like seeing a ghost.

"They're just scraps, for the most part," Remir went on. "A page or two from a book. Fragments of scrolls. But, 'it' is in there. What's left of it, anyway."

By 'it', Remir had to mean the Greek text. Davides had assumed the document was lost forever. He had come to think of it as one more casualty in his and Remir's war with the Vandals.

Davides opened the satchel, and the pungent smell of smoke stung his nostrils. He leafed past fragments of water-stained clothpaper and charred parchment: Bendayan's personal library, reduced to less than one cubic foot. Then, his fingers found the stiff edge of the envelope that had protected the Greek text. He drew it out carefully.

Like practically everything in the satchel, it was scarred by fire. He opened the vellum envelope and withdrew the folded piece of parchment. Seared by heat, it was stiff and brittle, and Davides doubted he could unfold it without having it break into a thousand tiny bits. He turned the parchment over in his hands, and a leaf of clothpaper that had been stuck to the back fell away. Notes, in Bendayan's own hand.

They were written in Greek, minus the encryption and allegory that had complicated any understanding of the original text. However, irregular blotches of burnt brown now stained sections of the notes, leaving Davides only slightly more informed about the document's contents than before.

"What's it say?" Remir asked.

Davides started. He had been so absorbed in trying to understand Bendayan's notes that he had lost track of where he was and how much time might have passed. He took a deep breath. "It's talking about some substance. The original word is in Persian, I think, but Bendayan translated it as 'fire powder'. He mentions there are various formulae for making this fire powder depending on the desired effect, but I can't make out the exact ratios of the components anymore." He pointed to a word that had escaped obliteration. "That means sulfur. And, that," his finger skipped down to where a line of words was still visible, "something, something 'burns with a purple flame'. Whatever that last component is, Bendayan references the East as its point of origin, and I don't think he was talking about Damascus. Further east.

"Down here, it describes packing the fire powder into containers and igniting them through . . . through a siphon of some sort? The fire powder is then supposed to produce a . . . rending, I guess, that's capable of breaking through soil and stone."

"Rending?" Remir repeated, sounding both dubious and appalled.

Davides read it over again. "That's the gist. Something made of fire, but having a force—maybe like a lighting bolt?—that can break through solid surfaces."

"And, here I thought the document would reveal 'how to turn base metals into gold', or 'how to prepare an elixir of longevity'. You know, the usual bullshit."

"More like 'how to breach a castle wall'," Davides said. "Even if this fire powder can't go through stone fortifications, I bet sappers could use it to tunnel underneath."

Remir's mouth took a sour turn. "Sometimes I hate the way your mind works."

"Me, too," Davides agreed. "No wonder General Haroun was so anxious to get it translated."

"What are you going to do with it?" Remir asked.

What was he going to do with it? Part of him wanted to finish the job of burning it. If not for that damned document, General Haroun wouldn't have sent them to Toledo, they wouldn't have gotten mixed up with the Vandals, and Bendayan wouldn't have been killed. But, even as he thought it, Davides knew he was misplacing blame. Bendayan's death was not the document's fault. It was his. He was the one who had chosen to walk through the alchemist's door. Besides, Bendayan had loved knowledge, had loved the written word that preserved knowledge. What would Bendayan think of him deliberately destroying such an artefact?

Without the exact formulae, the document itself was useless. A curiosity. A puzzle box that couldn't even be opened. Bendayan's notes were more informative. They revealed the existence of a substance with any number of useful—and potentially destructive—applications, and suggested the very real possibility that somewhere in the world this 'fire powder' was already in use. That much knowledge had been preserved.

Preserved, but to what end?

* * *

Remir and Davides sat at Father Bernat's table, playing *alquerque*. A few more days had passed, and Ishaq's apprentice had come and gone. The Greek text was back in the leather satchel, about as easy to ignore as a deeply embedded splinter.

Davides was spending more and more time out of bed as he became stronger. But, with strength came restlessness. This morning, in particular, he had felt an odd anxiety building inside him. He wondered if it had anything to do with the fact that, in over a year, this was the longest he had stayed in one place at one time. His distraction had been to Remir's advantage. Remir had won three games in a row.

The door to the rectory opened, and Teia slipped inside. It wasn't until she turned to face them that Davides noticed the flush in her cheeks, the perspiration that dampened and matted stray hairs around her face, and the rapid rise and fall of her chest. She had been running and was out of breath. That didn't bode well.

"Armed men on horseback. Maybe fifty," she said.

Remir arched an eyebrow, but kept his eyes on the board. "Any idea what they want?"

Teia scowled at him. "That's what I need you two for." Without another word, she crossed to the bedroom and went to a large crate wedged into the corner. The crate had arrived with Ishaq's apprentice. In it were all the belongings that Davides and Remir had left at Ishaq's when they had fled Toledo: armor, swords, clothes, money, . . . Teia lifted the cover.

"Hey!" Davides protested.

Ignoring him, she pushed a few things aside and pulled out Davides's mail hauberk. "Put this on. Quick." She let it slump to the floor and began rummaging for the various pieces of Remir's leather armor.

271

"Okay," Remir said, "let's skip over how you knew what was in that crate and get to the part where you tell us what you expect us to do?

"Stop them at the bridge. Find out why they're here."

"Stop them," Remir repeated, and clucked his tongue against his teeth. "Twenty-five to one odds are a little long, don't you think?"

Teia stopped moving. Her sudden stillness was almost as unsettling as her earlier flurry of activity. "Why, from your stories, Davides alone can fight off forty bandits." She widened her eyes in an obvious mockery of innocence. "Twenty-five to one should be cake."

Davides extricated his gambeson from the now jumbled mess in the crate. "You've been telling stories about me?" he asked Remir, as he put his arms through the sleeves of the quilted jacket and did a quick job of lacing it.

"I've been practicing my Castilian," Remir explained, donning his own armor.

"You couldn't have used other material?"

"I could have," Remir said, breaking into a wolfish grin.

Teia shifted impatiently from one foot to another. As Davides finished lacing the gambeson, she picked up the hauberk and heaped it over his head.

"Where's Father Bernat?" Davides asked, his voice muffled as he struggled into the hauberk. If the armed men were in a predatory mood — and armed men roaming the backwoods often were — the priest's cheerful guile would serve the village better than Davides and Remir's swords. And, if these men had been hired by the late

'Hildric', they would be expecting to speak to 'Gelimer', not to two strange, Muslim-looking individuals.

"At the mines," Teia answered. "Too far, if there's trouble."

Davides belted on his sword, the supple leather sliding into place with comforting familiarity. Both the armor and the sword felt reassuring. They also felt heavy. Heavier than Davides remembered. He still had a ways to go before fully recovering from the fight with Gonsaluiz.

"How far away are these men?" Davides asked.

"Opposite end of the valley, last I saw. Wait for them at the bridge. The deacons should already be in place."

"In place to do what?" Remir asked, but Teia was already gone, flitting back out the front door.

Davides and Remir made their way toward the bridge north of Alferia, their gait purposeful but unrushed. If the horsemen were observing the town from a distance, it would be better if he and Remir appeared confident and in control. Their demeanor would give the horsemen pause for thought and would have the additional benefit of keeping the villagers from panicking.

They reached the bridge and took up their position in the center of it. It was a solid, wooden bridge about twenty feet in length that was just wide enough for a wagon to cross. Symbolically, the bridge represented the access point to the village if one arrived from the north. In the literal world, however, the creek was low enough that a horse and rider would barely have to slow to cross it. Mud and the rise of the south bank might have been considered obstacles if the village had had its own militia. Instead, it had two men on a bridge.

273

Davides resisted the temptation to look around for the deacons. Oak trees were scattered along both sides of the riverbank, as were a few tangles of underbrush. The bridge itself offered cover, if one were willing to stand in knee-deep water and hide beneath it, but there was little chance of escape should the encounter turn ugly. Somehow, Davides couldn't see the deacons putting themselves in that position.

The horsemen cleared the valley and reined in a hundred yards or so from the bridge. From that distance, Davides could make out a few details. The type of horse they were riding reminded Davides of the ones Gonsaluiz and his coterie had at al-Qati's: large-boned, with blocky heads and low-set necks. They weren't fast, and they lacked the style and grace of Andalusian horses, but they were sturdy, dependable animals. Typical light cavalry mounts from the North.

The men wore armor. Some had mail, some had leather, some had a hodgepodge of both. A few carried lances or spears, others carried bows, all of them had swords. Most of the shields were blank, but one man in front had what looked to be leather stretched over the shield, hiding a heraldic sign, an indication that he didn't want to be recognized or that he had been dishonored.

"You should probably do the talking," Remir said. "While the Christian women here seem to find my accent irresistible, I'm not sure it would have a positive effect on these gentlemen."

Davides smiled wryly. "You're assuming they're going to be interested in talking."

"As ridiculous as we look standing out here by ourselves, they won't be able to resist saying something."

"Maybe they don't share your appreciation of the absurd," Davides said.

The horsemen urged their mounts into a trot and headed towards them, then halted again about thirty yards from the bridge. The man with the covered emblem on his shield signaled for the others to wait while he proceeded alone.

Davides let out his breath. "You were right. Any guess as to what he might say?"

"'Is this the Way of St. James?'," Remir said, in a parody of Castilian-accented Arabic.

"That's probably it," Davides agreed, amused despite himself. "They look just like a group of pilgrims on their peaceful and pious way to Santiago."

The approaching rider was wearing a helmet, which concealed his features to a degree. An unkempt, rusty-brown beard bristled out from beneath the helmet, and down-turned eyes, set in a perpetual squint, scanned up and down the riverbank, watching for danger.

When the rider had closed the distance to ten yards, Davides spoke. His words said 'Good afternoon. What can we do for you?', but his tone said 'Stop where you are and explain yourself'.

The man stopped. He looked them over one more time, then jerked his head in the direction of the village. "Is that the village of Alferia?"

"It is."

The rider nodded. When he spoke again, his eyes looked upwards, as if he were reciting something from memory. "I'm looking for a couple of old friends. They're from Seville, but they were last seen near Toledo. Maybe you've heard of them?"

The words were strikingly familiar.

"Unbelievable," Davides muttered. He still didn't know who the horsemen were, or why they had come to Alferia, but he had a pretty good idea of who had sent them.

"Do these friends have names?" Remir prompted the rider, forgetting or setting aside his original plan to remain silent.

"Oh, yes! Yes, they do. Of course, they do." The rider's eyes went up again, back to the script. "Nizar and Jamal. They're young, like you two, and one of them — Nizar, I think — has blue eyes," he focused on Davides, "like you. He didn't mention the armor, though."

"He didn't, huh?" Davides said. The rider didn't seem to realize he had just referenced a third party.

"No. In fact, he said you would look like a couple of no-accounts."

"Rodrigo said that about us?" Remir asked, sounding deeply wounded.

"He was describing what you would look like, not what ..." The man trailed off and grimaced. "Ugh. I told Rodrigo I have no gift for these games, but he warned me to tread softly. He said you might be under duress."

Only from you and your fifty-odd followers.

"My name is Velasco Flaínez. Vela will do. Rodrigo said you were in need of mercenaries and would pay in honest coin, not false promises."

Davides tried not to let his surprise and confusion show. "Er, did he happen to mention what the job was?" Davides asked.

"Well, we're mercenaries," Vela said, shifting in his saddle, "so it usually involves attacking or defending something."

Coming from just about anyone else, the words would have been laden with sarcasm, but Vela seemed merely to be stating a fact for their benefit: mercenaries attacked and defended things. Before Davides could decide how to respond, Vela withdrew something from his belt that resembled a scroll. He extended it towards them. It was a piece of birch bark, which had been rolled tight and tied with a narrow strip of leather.

"Rodrigo said to give you this in lieu of a proper letter of introduction. We met on the road," Vela added apologetically, "so this was the best he could do."

Davides took it and unrolled the coarse, white and black cortex to reveal the paper-thin pink layer inside. The message was addressed to Nizar and Jamal. The words were smeared, having been written with a charred stick, but Davides could still make them out: *Jamal's hometown is unoccupied. Hawk your iron there. Vela can help.* And, a signature, which Davides deduced to be Rodrigo's, scrawled across the bottom. He stared at the brief missive, knowing that Rodrigo couldn't care less about their iron enterprise, and wondering if there were any way he could be misinterpreting the note's actual meaning.

"And?" Remir asked, eyebrows raised.

"And," Davides replied, looking past Vela to the group of mercenaries, which now seemed small and inconsequential, "Rodrigo is suggesting we use these mercenaries to take back Salamanca."

* * *

Vela came from a minor noble family whose holdings were near Burgos, along the Arlanzón River. Like many of his fellow knights, he had devoted most of his life to the art and practice of war. As a boy, he had served as a page, graduated to squire, and eventually won his spurs in battle. He had happily served King Fernando as a knight ever since. Until recently.

Last spring, Vela was sent to collect tribute from a number of frontier towns who were under Castilian "protection". Somehow, the gold and goods he ultimately delivered to his liege didn't quite match the tally sheet. According to Vela, it was a simple clerical error, not deliberate embezzlement. Regardless, Vela was sent into exile, his property seized by the Crown. Under penalty of death, he could not return to Castile-León unless King Fernando pardoned him.

Vela had fought alongside Rodrigo on numerous campaigns. They had a history of protecting each other's backs, not just from enemy soldiers, but also from those Castilian nobles who resented the places of honor to which the two men had risen. For the moment, Vela had fallen, but Rodrigo maintained his position. And, an impressive one it was. He was the *alférez* for King Fernando's eldest son. The captain of the Prince's private guard.

Odd, Davides thought, that Rodrigo had failed to mention his close connection with Prince Sancho.

That tidbit of knowledge illuminated something that had been nagging Davides for some time. The decision to extract Amira from Salamanca had been a reckless one, one that was completely out of character for King Fernando. But, Davides could imagine the Prince ordering his trusted and talented *alférez* to liberate Abdur-Rahman's daughter, whatever the cost. General Haroun, who knew the workings of King Fernando's mind well, had not anticipated the brash and potentially lethal maneuver. Which is probably why it had succeeded.

If Amira's abduction/rescue had not formed part of King Fernando's official response, then Rodrigo might already be on shaky ground with his King, even assuming he had been following the Prince's orders. Small wonder he preferred to stay away from any and all things related to Gonsaluiz. Rodrigo should have stayed far away from Vela, too. The King would exile Rodrigo in a heartbeat if he found out that he had lent aid to the disgraced knight, even if that aid had been in the form of a cryptic message with an illegible signature.

Rodrigo knew that Vela needed a job. Vela's retainers, loyal men that they were, had followed him into exile, but now it was up to Vela to make sure they didn't all starve. Finding work was not a problem. You couldn't shake a stick without hitting someone in the market for hired swords. The tricky part was finding a job that didn't pit Vela and his men against their King, and that wasn't purely speculative in nature (*Help us take that castle over there, and we'll give you a cut of whatever might be inside . . .*).

Rodrigo also knew about the cache Remir had taken from Gonsaluiz: gold and silver sitting in a war chest, just waiting for a purpose.

* * *

Davides and Remir watched as the small roll of birch bark curled, crumpled, blackened, then burst into flame. The fire in the hearth danced high for a moment, then settled back to red-tinged coals.

Evening had fallen. They had spent the intervening time arranging for Vela and his men to camp on the north side of the river. Fifty-some horses had needed access to food and water in a valley where the villagers usually kept

279

their livestock. Fifty-some men likewise needed food and, well, some kind of drink. It hadn't seemed wise to leave a pack of mercenaries to their own foraging devices so close to the village, so Davides and Remir had made the necessary arrangements and had footed the bill for their meals.

Towards the end of these arrangements, Father Bernat had arrived, still covered head to foot in the black soot of the forge. He was all smiles and goodwill towards Vela, while Davides and Remir were on the receiving end of a few hard, questioning looks.

Vela—a devout man, as it turned out—had been delighted to see the priest. He and his men had not been to Mass since the order for exile had been handed down, initially because they had had to leave the borders of Castile-León within a short time frame, then because they had been riding through Muslim territory and had been avoiding towns. Vela had entreated Father Bernat to hold a special Mass for him and his followers. They needed his intercession, his spiritual guidance . . .

That was when Davides and Remir had decided it was time to leave, before one of them coughed, choked, or said something regrettable. Now, they were settled back in the rectory, staring at the embers that were consuming the last traces of Rodrigo's message.

Remir broke the silence. "That night at al-Qati's, I'd heard enough to know Rodrigo had figured out who you were. But, I didn't know how badly you were hurt, or how far Rodrigo would go to get information from you, or whether his orders were to kill you, regardless. In the process of assessing the situation, it's possible I oversold your change of heart regarding the war. I wanted Rodrigo to see you as an ally, not an adversary. I'm sure that's why he suggested you hire out to the Castilians. And, now this."

And, now this: a cavalry unit on their doorstep, along with a proposal for a madcap mission.

"I don't expect you to come along," Remir went on. "It was one thing—"

"You're considering this?" Davides interrupted. Not that Davides hadn't also considered Rodrigo's suggestion. He had considered it and had promptly dismissed it as unfeasible. "What happened to the notion of you staying 'far, far away' from Salamanca, Seville, and Castile-León?"

Remir shrugged.

Concerned that he hadn't driven home his point, Davides continued, "You would be using Castilians to attack Sevillians in Salamanca."

"Yes," Remir said, undeterred.

After a moment's silence, Davides said, "You realize Salamanca is not actually 'unoccupied'."

"I assume Rodrigo meant that the main army has marched north on Zamora. But, General Haroun will have left behind enough men to control the city: make sure supplies go through without a hitch, make sure the army has a defensible position to which they can retreat, if need be. See? I was paying attention to your boring lectures on military strategy back in Cáceres."

Remir was trying to make light of the situation, but Davides would not be distracted. "Forget about the risk to you personally, Remir. Anything you do to Seville's forces might endanger your father's life. He's the only hostage they have left."

"And, maybe they've already killed him. Or have him chained in a cell somewhere. I think it's high time I found out."

"But, you're up against impossible odds! Fifty men are not enough."

A lopsided smile sketched across Remir's face. "You're really going to talk to me about impossible odds?" He stood up, the look in his eyes daring Davides to continue down that line of argumentation.

Remir was right: Davides had no room to talk, not after charging pell-mell into the fight with the Vandals. His gaze dropped back to the embers.

"I'm going to make the arrangements with Vela," he heard Remir say. "We'll leave tomorrow."

Davides nodded, abstracted, and Remir turned and left.

* * *

It was the old conflict plaguing him again: his friendship with Remir at odds with his lingering sense of loyalty to General Haroun. Davides was trying to sleep, but his thoughts were as hapless as twigs floating down a rushing river. They raced with the current, slammed into rocks, got sucked under, only to bob back to the surface further downstream. Finally, in the darkness before dawn, he could lie still no longer. He got up and went outside, thinking to wander aimlessly and let his mind do likewise.

As he left the rectory, he saw a dim glow coming from the church and headed in that direction. The main entrance had a recessed, arched doorway with a small, wheel window above it. The door yielded easily, and he went inside.

It was a simple church with an aisless nave. The semi-circular apse on the opposite end had a muted fresco depicting the Epiphany. Its centerpiece, the Star, shone in beaming yellow contrast to the earthy tones used throughout the rest of the painting. Along one side of the nave, long banks of candles flickered in the wake of the draft from the door.

It was an unusually large number of candles for a church this size. Vela and his men, desperate for divine intervention, must have paid for prayers to be said on their behalf. Father Bernat was having a good night, fiscally speaking.

Davides watched the tiny flames and thought how nice it must be to know what one wanted. No, that wasn't quite right. What people wanted was not necessarily what they *should* strive for. He had wanted his family's title and lands back. He had wanted them so badly that he had ignored his better angels and had accepted the assignment General Haroun had offered him. In his case, knowing what he had wanted—what he thought would have pleased his parents—had only led him to his current predicament.

The sound of the front door's latch lifting interrupted his uninspired ruminations. The door swung open, and Father Bernat's broad frame filled the portal. He had an armful of fresh candles in assorted shapes and sizes. When he saw Davides, he stopped short.

"Well, good morning," Father Bernat said. His voice, typically ebullient, was tempered. Soft and mellow.

"Good morning," Davides said. "Sorry. I'll get out of your way."

Father Bernat walked over to the banks of candles and began to switch out the ones that were sputtering with fresh ones. "Don't let me interrupt you. That door stays unlocked for a reason. You're welcome here as long as you like."

"I'm good, thanks," Davides said, and turned to leave.

"You sure? When's the last time you confessed, Sisnando?"

The question caught Davides by surprise, as did Father Bernat's use of his real name as opposed to 'Nizar'. It had seemed a tacit agreement that they did not discuss religion or aliases.

"None of your damned business," Davides said.

Father Bernat faced him, his expression somber but not in any way offended. "If I was in your line of work, son, I'd want to make sure I stayed current."

Davides made a show of looking around his immediate surroundings. "And, to whom would I give a confession?"

"No reason I can't take it."

Davides could think of so many reasons. He gave a harsh laugh. "No offense, but I don't plan on giving my confession to a fake priest."

"Whoever said I was a fake priest?"

Davides waited for the punchline, the booming laugh, something to indicate that the conman was putting him on once more. None of the above happened.

"Bullshit," Davides said.

"Hand to God, I am an ordained priest. But," he sighed, "back home, some of my ideas were too unconventional for the bishop's tastes. We didn't much get along."

"By 'ideas' do you mean larcenous tendencies?" Davides inquired.

That won him a hearty chuckle. "No, no. That came later. A man's gotta eat," he said, patting his round belly affectionately.

Davides couldn't help but admire his effrontery. That didn't mean he had any intention of sharing his most intimate secrets with someone whose interpretation of the Commandments seemed sketchy at best. "All the same, I think I'll pass."

"Suit yourself. But, I doubt you'll get a chance running with those mercenaries."

"I won't be . . . I mean, I'm not going with them."

Father Bernat's lips pursed. He stepped closer, and tiny orange pinpoints of reflected candlelight shone in his eyes. "Now that you mention it, Jamal was a touch vague on that point. I know it's 'none of my damned business', but why not? Jamal never struck me as any kind of soldier. You, on the other hand, ..." He trailed off meaningfully.

"Conflict of interests," Davides said, hoping to put a quick end to the topic.

"You disagree with what he's fixing to do?"

"Actually, I don't," Davides admitted. "In his place, I'd do the same thing."

"Then, where's the conflict?"

"I used to work for the people he's going after."

"Ah. So, you're thinking to recuse yourself. Stay neutral."

"Yes," Davides said, relieved to have the situation put succinctly without having to go into further detail.

"I don't envy you, Davides. Pick one side, and you let down the other. But, if you stay neutral, both parties

285

have cause against you. You're in for a world of guilt no matter what you do."

So much for feeling relieved.

Father Bernat gathered up the old candles and headed for the door. "Well, the Lord be with you, whatever you decide," he said.

"That's it?" Davides demanded. "No words of wisdom? No priestly advice?" He recognized the hypocrisy behind this request, since it came mere moments after calling Father Bernat a fake priest. But, he was willing to take counsel from anyone, even from a charlatan, if it gave him a way out of his dilemma.

Father Bernat paused and looked back, amused. "You've got a good head on your shoulders. You'll figure something out."

Part 6 – Nothing if not resolute

Morning found Davides putting on his armor and packing his saddlebags. In the long list of reasons for and against his present course of action, one had finally eclipsed the others. If he helped Remir return to Salamanca, he would at least come close to atoning for his part in Remir's abduction. He would right his original wrong, even if it meant being viewed as a traitor by Seville. Even if it meant throwing in with a lost cause.

Davides traversed the still-sleeping village in the pre-dawn grey and crossed the bridge to where Remir, Vela, and the mercenaries were readying their horses. Remir greeted him without apparent surprise. He even had a mount set aside for Davides. If Davides wasn't mistaken, it was one of the northern chargers left ownerless by Gonsaluiz and his men.

Davides looked at the waiting horse, then at Remir, who had just swung up on his own mount. "Am I really that predictable?" he asked.

Remir smirked. "Let's hope not, or this little foray will be doomed before it gets started."

Davides tied his scant belongings to the saddle, tightened the girth, and mounted. "What did you tell Father Bernat?" he asked, sticking to Arabic to minimize the chance of being overheard.

"Not much. He wanted Vela and his men gone and didn't care about the 'particulars', as he called them."

"And, what did you tell Vela?"

"That we're paying him and his men to cut Seville's supply lines. He seemed pretty enthused about the prospect."

"I'll bet. But, then what?" Cutting the supply lines would annoy Seville considerably, but it wouldn't get Remir back into Salamanca.

"Then, we find Julián."

* * *

They rode west. They were using packhorses for their supplies instead of a wagon so that they could avoid roads and prying eyes. They wended through the northern foothills of the Gredos Mountains, where green had given way to autumn's yellow and burnt orange foliage. Off their left shoulder loomed grey, granite mountaintops, drizzled at their peaks in white snow.

The distance separating Alferia from the Via Delapidata was only about a hundred miles. Still, it took them the better part of a week to reach their destination: the 'cursed' woods south of Salamanca where once upon a time, according to Remir, the physician Gabirol had met an untimely death at the hands of a treacherous *dhimmi*. Remir didn't mention the curse this time around. Vela and his men had enough reason to be jumpy without his adding to it.

Davides and Remir left the mercenaries camped in the woods just off the Via Delapidata. Vela's orders were to attack the next military supply caravan that came through. If any Sevillian troops retaliated in force, it was up to Vela to decide whether to engage or fall back. In the meantime, Davides and Remir would search for Julián.

288

* * *

Without great expectations, Davides pulled back the flap of coarse jute fabric that covered the entrance to yet another *shisha* bar. Over the past two days, he had visited two inns, four taverns, and five *shisha* bars—make that six—all within a day's ride of Salamanca. Remir was too well known to let himself be seen, but Davides could pass as just another traveler looking for a hot meal or a pipe.

They had had a couple of close calls with patrols, whose purview seemed to include the same areas that Davides and Remir were searching. Had the patrols actually been looking for them, they would have had to give up their quest to find Julián. But, the Sevillian soldiers' main purpose, it seemed, was to be visible: to remind everyone who was in charge and thereby preempt any rebellious notions that might be brewing in the countryside. They were looking for groups of peasants armed with pitchforks, not Abdur Rahman's son.

It was late, and the *shisha* bar was nearly empty. Davides squinted against the gloom and the smoke, trying to make out the scattered forms and faces. The owner began waving him off, saying they were closed, and Davides toyed with the idea of asking him, straight out, if he had seen the minstrel recently.

"He's with me!" a voice called.

Davides turned and saw Julián, not ten feet away, sitting cross-legged on the floor amidst a swirl of smoke. Before he had time to fully appreciate his spectacular fortune in finding the minstrel, Julián opened his mouth again.

"Davides, my good friend! Come, sit!" Julián thumped a nearby cushion, sending a cloud of god-knew-what fine particles billowing into the clogged air.

At the sound of his name – his real name – being advertised to the world, Davides scanned the room again. No hostile eyes. No undue interest. He let out his pent-up breath and crossed to Julián, who looked up at him with a serene smile. That was when Davides realized that Julián was good-and-truly stoned.

Davides forced a stiff smile. "The man wants to close up for the night. Let's take the party elsewhere."

Julián thought it over. A sober Julián would have thought it over much longer. "Okay," he said agreeably, and allowed Davides to pull him to his feet and usher him outside.

Davides felt like bashing him over the head with the *oud*. How could Julián be so careless? Blurting out Davides's name. Being under the influence of euphoric drugs in the first place! Davides couldn't help but wonder what other information Julián might have shared with the world while he was enjoying the stupefying effects of *hashish*.

Julián's horse was tied outside. They swung up double and rode to the open fronted sheepfold where Remir was hiding with their two mounts. It wasn't a party, but Julián seemed delighted to see Remir, anyway. Then, he started to cry.

* * *

"Cut me some slack," Julián protested the next morning, when he was clearheaded enough to explain himself. "The last time I saw you two, you were about to wage a private war against organized crime in Toledo. Frankly, I wasn't expecting either of you to survive."

They were still encamped in the vacant sheepfold, which was probably only used by sheep and their shepherd during the worst of the winter months. Despite that, the small structure had been surprisingly well-maintained. With its leak-free thatch roof and solid, waddle and daub walls, it officially constituted the nicest campsite they had had in the past week.

"Plus," Julián's voice faltered a bit. "I failed you, Remir. I never got the last message to your father. I tried. I tried to get into the *alcázar* like I did before: just a spinner of stories, singer of songs, come to entertain those who were willing to pay. This time, though, Sevillian guards stopped me and questioned me. I don't know if they recognized me from before or were just being cautious. Either way, I knew I was in trouble.

"Hoping to God they thought Davides was still on their side, I told them I was one of his old schoolmates, that he had run into some trouble in Toledo, and that he needed help. At first, it almost went sideways. The guards didn't believe me, I guess because they didn't know Davides had been sent to Toledo in the first place. But, I stuck to the story, and eventually they took it to someone higher up. Much higher up.

"The man had that air about him, you know? Like soldiers would fling themselves on their spears just because he ordered them to do it. Still, I almost had a heart attack when the guards addressed him as 'General'."

Davides experienced a slight, cardiac arrhythmia of his own. "General?" he repeated, through a mouthful of breakfast. "As in, General Haroun?"

Julián nodded and took a pull from their wineskin. "Your General asked the guards some questions about me, then ordered them out. After they left, he starts grilling me: when did you study in Toledo, where did you stay, how long were you there, how did we meet? I must have answered okay, because next thing, he draws close, lowers his voice, and asks me what I know about your current whereabouts."

Davides swallowed hard. "And, what did you tell him?"

"I was too scared to do a good job of lying, so I stuck close to the truth. I told him how we met up in Toledo. How some men attacked us one night. We fought them off. Then, we dressed two of the dead bodies to look like you and your 'cousin', and dumped them into the Tagus. I skipped everything to do with the Vandals and Alferia, and instead went with the notion of 'mystery assailants'.

"The General must have had his own list of likely culprits, because he didn't press me about the 'who' or the 'why'. He was more interested in hearing that we had sneaked out to an abandoned villa near Toledo — a villa that belonged to one al-Qati — until you could figure what to do next. In the meantime, you had sent me to get word back to him in Salamanca.

"From the General's reaction, I think he already knew you had left Toledo, and maybe even knew something about the bodies in the river. But, I was the first to tell him you were still alive." Julián turned back to Remir. "I'm sorry if I screwed up, Remir. I know you wanted to stay 'dead' for as long as possible. 'Course, for all I knew, you'd gotten yourselves killed fighting Hildric."

"You did great," Remir assured Julián, giving him a reassuring clap on the back. Then, he turned to Davides with a grin. "Can you imagine if General Haroun sent men to question al-Qati? I would pay money to see that."

Davides was grappling with too much new information to fully enjoy the thought. First and foremost, unless something had changed since Julián's visit to the *alcázar*, General Haroun didn't know that Remir had slipped Seville's grasp. That meant that Abdur Rahman didn't know, either. If neither man knew Remir was free, the General would still be using the threat of violence against Remir to leverage Abdur Rahman into cooperating with him. That opened the possibility that Remir's father might not be imprisoned, after all.

Also, if Abdur Rahman and General Haroun didn't know about Remir, they wouldn't know about Davides's defection. Davides's stomach sank. He had assumed that piece of dirty work had been done for him.

"How long ago was this, when you had your little chat with General Haroun?" Remir asked Julián.

Julián counted backwards on his fingers. "Ten days."

Ten days? Something didn't quite add up. Davides and Remir had gotten Rodrigo's pithy, birch-bark message ten days ago. Presumably, Vela and Rodrigo had crossed paths several days before that, at which time the army had already left Salamanca. Unless Rodrigo was prescient and could divine the future, at least two weeks had passed since General Haroun's army had headed north, so Julián couldn't have spoken with the General just ten days ago. He must have smoked his way through a few extra days, lost in oblivion.

"Have you heard who was left in charge of Salamanca when the main army pulled out?" Davides asked Julián. He knew all of the commanders, either personally or by reputation. He knew their strengths and their weaknesses. Finding out who was giving the orders in Salamanca would help him and Remir shape a viable plan.

"I told you already. General Haroun."

"No, I mean, who was left in command of Salamanca when the others went north."

"That's what I'm saying. My 'chat' with the General came after the main army left. He is the one in charge of Salamanca."

"That's not possible," Davides said, shaking his head in flat denial and thinking to himself that General Haroun would never leave this critical offensive on Castile-León in the hands of one of his commanders.

"I'm afraid it is," Julián maintained. "General Haroun got hurt a couple of weeks ago. He took a bad fall with his horse. Apparently, it was very dramatic: he and his bodyguard were at a full gallop when his horse stepped in a hole and broke its leg. It somersaulted, crushing him in the process. They say he's lucky to be alive."

"The General doesn't believe in luck," Davides said tonelessly. "'It is as God wills it to be'." He had heard the conciliatory Muslim expression a thousand times before, but this was the first time the words demoralized him so completely.

A thick silence followed. Davides stared at the ground, unable to meet Remir's eyes. Not yet, anyway. He was too close to panic. Despite everything, he still respected General Haroun, still felt a measure of devotion he couldn't seem to shake. He and the General just happened to disagree—fatally—on the tactics employed in this one, particular campaign.

Julián fidgeted uneasily before saying, "I don't understand. Why is it such a big deal that General Haroun is in the city?"

Remir gave a snort of humorless mirth. "We would have rather dealt with someone else."

Julián looked from Remir to Davides and back again. "You sound as if you were planning on buying textiles from him or something."

Remir gave him a tight smile. "Or something."

Julián's eyes went wide. "Oh, no! No, no, no, no! Are you crazy!" It wasn't so much a question as an assessment. "You can't go back to Salamanca! It's not just General Haroun, you know. They left a small army behind."

"How small?" Remir asked.

"I don't know! Enough to still be called an army!"

"What about my father's men?"

"They've all been disarmed and reassigned to general labor. Give it up, Remir. Whatever you had in mind, just give it up."

Davides felt Remir's eyes find him. Julián's followed. He had to say or do something.

"I should declare myself," Davides said, thinking out loud. He tossed aside his half-eaten crust of bread, having lost his appetite. "I should ride in and explain my position to him. I've dodged this responsibility long enough."

"O-rrr," Remir drawled, "we could think of plan that won't get you drawn and quartered on the spot."

Davides groaned and dropped his head into his hands. "Like what?" he asked desolately behind his phalangeal shield. "We needed a weakness in Salamanca's operations to have any chance of this working. The General doesn't have weaknesses."

"Except you," Julián suggested haltingly. "If everyone including General Haroun believes you're still working for Seville, that would be a huge weakness, right? You could ride in, welcome as can be, and arrange a private meeting with the General. Then, — "

"No!" Davides exclaimed, appalled.

"Why not?" Julián asked. "You'd have a coup with no casualties."

"I can't." Davides cast about for a way to explain himself. "I can't deceive them like that." *I can turn against them, but I can't deceive them? What sense does that make?*

Remir cocked an eyebrow. "We knew before we left Alferia that we'd have to resort to some sort of deception, since we don't exactly have the manpower for a frontal assault or a siege. Besides, and don't take this the wrong way, Davides, but ever since I've known you, you've been involved in deceiving somebody about something."

Davides winced. Remir was right. *What does that say about me?"*

"It's not deception *per se* with which I take issue," Davides said after a moment. "Yes, I knew if we got this far we would need some ploy to get inside the *alcázar*. But, the ploy can't be me, acting as a trusted messenger of General Haroun. It would be . . . I don't know . . . ignoble. I'm prepared to fight them, Remir, I really am. Just don't ask me to stab them in the back."

Remir blinked at him. "Ignoble?"

"Yes, ignoble. Despicable. Morally reprehensible."

"I know what it means," Remir said, eyes sparkling with amusement. "It's just a ridiculous-sounding word. Plus, I enjoyed seeing how many synonyms you could come up with off the top of your head."

"You're mocking me? I'm baring my soul, and you're mocking me?"

"Well, yeah. What else am I supposed to do when you're way up there on the moral high ground? Tell me, does the air start to get thin where you stand?"

"Yes, as a matter of fact, it does," Davides retorted.

"An overabundance of morality," Julián mused. "Thank God I don't have that problem."

"So," Remir said decisively, "we need to be sneaky without sinking to the state of ignobility."

"You're not going to let that go, are you?" Davides asked.

Remir flashed a smile and went on. "I could get myself inside the *alcázar* without being noticed by guards—I've done it dozens of times—but that doesn't help us much. We need to get Vela's men inside, as well as provide weapons to my father's men."

Remir thought for a moment, lips pursed and eyes distant. "Will we have to contend with those North African mercenaries, the ones who came over the walls that first night and took control of the *alcázar*?"

"I doubt it," Davides replied. "Those men were too dangerous and too expensive to leave guarding a relatively quiet place like Salamanca. General Haroun would have sent them with the army's vanguard to use as shock troops. The occupying force should all be Sevillian soldiers."

"So, Vela and his men should match up well with them," Remir mused.

"Except for the part about being significantly outnumbered," Davides said.

"Yes, but what if we lured some of the troops outside the city? General Haroun might be the world's most capable commander, but that should make his responses to routine situations predictable, for someone who knows him well. For instance, what would the General do if his supply trains going through Salamanca were being targeted by bandits?"

Davides frowned, thinking that Vela and his men could never be mistaken for ordinary bandits. "By bandits or by Castilian mercenaries?"

Remir's gaze slid in Julián's direction. "By bandits."

* * *

Julián took some convincing, but he eventually agreed to contact his horse-thieving compatriots and rendezvous with them in Gabirol's Woods. In the meantime, Davides and Remir caught up with Vela and his men, who had managed to find something worthwhile to attack: Sevillian drovers and their livestock, destined for the frontlines. The Castilians were now enjoying some well-deserved lamb chops. Vela had sent a man south to check for more supply trains, and knew that another one would be rolling through in a couple of days.

The new plan, as they informed Vela, was to have Julián's horse thieves attack the next supply train (with some covert help from Vela's men) in exchange for the bulk of the livestock, horses, and supplies such an attack might yield. They would allow a few guards on horseback to escape and reach Salamanca. When the General heard about the attack, he would send out a patrol to deal with the "local" bandit problem, at which point Vela would ambush the patrol. Julián's horse thieves would lie in wait and close off any escape to ensure that this time no one made it back to Salamanca. They would then collect the patrol's shields and weapons in the hopes of being able to get them to Abdur Rahman's men.

Davides estimated that around three hundred Sevillian soldiers would have been left behind in Salamanca. At any given time, one-third of them would be off-duty, unless there was a clear and present danger. Bandits waylaying supplies should not put them on high alert within the city walls. If the first stage of their plan was successful, another fifty or so Sevillian troops would have been ambushed by Vela in Gabirol's Woods and would no longer be a threat. That left one hundred men to patrol the city wall and around fifty men to guard the *alcázar*.

The tricky part would be getting Remir, Davides, and Vela's men all into the *alcázar* itself before the real fighting began. Remir intended to sneak into the *alcázar* alone at night, find some of his father's trusted men, and get them to alert others: there would be weapons in marked wagons coming the next day, and there would be a distraction. They had to be ready to take advantage of it. Then, before dawn, Remir would hide away in the stables and wait for their arrival.

They — Davides, Vela, and his men — would be in the wagons, along with the aforementioned weapons. Those who spoke at least some Arabic would be posing as Sevillian teamsters; the others would be hidden among the cargo, concealed by the oilcloth covers that many of the wagons had stretched over the beds to protect the contents from wet weather conditions. Despite the risk of being recognized, Davides would have to be one of the teamsters and do most of the talking, since he was the only one capable of producing a convincing Sevillian accent. In any case, the goal would be to keep moving, so the Sevillian soldiers would not have the opportunity to ask a lot of questions or examine them closely.

If they succeeded in properly executing all of the above, they would still find themselves surrounded by fifty guards in the fortified palace. They would need one more act of misdirection to have any hope of success.

* * *

Salamanca's golden-hued walls rose before them. Squinting through the dust that billowed from churning hooves and spinning wheels, Davides could make out the forms of Sevillian guards spaced along the parapets of the outer walls. So far, the guards had not closed the main gate, which meant the guards believed that the eight wagons were part of one of their supply trains, and that the wagons were making a desperate bid to gain the safety of Salamanca's walls from some unseen but imminent threat.

The wagon bucked and lurched beneath him as the horses, unaccustomed to pulling wagons at a full gallop, struggled to move as a team. Their progress was punctuated by the crack of his driver's whip overhead, urging the horses to maintain their headlong flight.

Soon, Davides could distinguish the faces of the soldiers on the wall. Bows at the ready, they looked out past the small wagon train towards the line of trees in the distance. Julián's friends had been schooled on the range of those bows, and they stayed within the trees, no more than menacing shadows. The wagons raced through the gatehouse unimpeded and slowed but did not come to a complete stop.

"We were attacked!" Davides shouted to a nearby soldier. "Where's the Captain?"

The soldier pointed wordlessly toward the *alcázar*. Before anyone could object, the driver's whip whistled through the air, and their team of horses scuttled forward up the cobblestone street. They pushed through Salamanca's busy thoroughfares at a reckless pace that had pedestrians cursing them and jumping for safety.

As the forbidding portcullis of the *alcázar* came into view, Davides reviewed the coaching (or criticism) he had received from Julián on how to get through this next part: *You look like a teamster on the outside, but if you're not careful, you'll still come across as . . . well, as you. They'll recognize you by your manner. Don't use fancy words. Don't ever look the officers in the eye. And, for heaven's sake, don't stand so straight. Slouch a little. You do know how to slouch, don't you?*

The driver reined in the team in front of the gates, and the seven other teams pulled up behind them in a long row. The soldiers stationed here had seen the commotion at the outer walls, and they had converged at the gate towers to examine the lathered teams of horses, the arrows sticking artistically out of the wagons' oilcloth covers, the bloodstains on wagon seats where a second teamster should have been.

Slouch a little. Fighting the impulse to do the exact opposite, Davides rounded his shoulders and drooped. "We were attacked," Davides called up to them. His

301

throat felt parched, and his voice came out raspy. "About four miles south. Lost some wagons and some men."

They waited, the horses dripping sweat. Davides glanced at his driver, Pedro, whose face had the complexion and approximate flexibility of latigo leather. Pedro was sweating, too, but he sat unflinching before the prospect of driving the wagon into a fortress full of the enemy. Vela's men were nothing if not resolute.

A great clanking of massive chains announced the raising of the portcullis, and a small contingent of soldiers filed through the opening. Davides identified the officer in charge, a man he had seen on occasion but with whom he had had no personal interaction. He hopped off the wagon and ducked his head in a servile manner, not letting his eyes stray above the man's chest. *Please, God, nobody in the wagons sneeze.*

"You said you were attacked four miles south of here," the Captain said without preamble. "Were these attackers mounted?"

"Yes, sir."

"How, then, did you escape with the wagons?"

"We had an escort. They bought us some time. We're carrying supplies for the front." Davides extended a rolled-up piece of vellum sealed with wax. He had carried enough of these in his lifetime to have done an adequate job of forging one. "Our orders."

At a nod from the Captain, an aide took the scroll, broke the seal, and read the contents. "Sir, it says they are not supposed to unload their cargo here. We are to supply them with fresh horses, and they are to continue on to Zamora. It also says there were twelve wagons."

Davides felt the Captain's eyes turn back to him. "What cargo was in the wagons that were lost?" The man's voice had a distinctly accusatory tone.

Davides felt a stab of indignation. How could the Captain blame him, a lowly teamster, for losing those wagons? The fact that Davides was directly responsible for their loss was beside the point. The Captain didn't know that.

He slouched some more in what he hoped might be taken for a cringe. "One had salt, sir. Barrels of salt. The others had iron parts. I don't know what for." Actually, he did know: iron hardware for constructing siege engines. But, he didn't feel a need to admit that.

"Did you see any sign of Sevillian cavalry in the area?"

"Sir?" Davides pretended to be confused by the question.

"You should have gone right past fifty of our men!"

"I'm sorry, sir. We didn't see anyone."

"They didn't just vanish into thin air!" The Captain snatched the orders from his aide and scanned them quickly. "Pull your wagons through the inner bailey and around to the stables. You can switch out your horses, but don't leave yet, understand? There is no guarantee you won't get attacked again on the north side of the city. Stay with them," he ordered his aide. "I'm going to see how the General wants this handled." He turned on his heel and stalked off.

Davides climbed back onto the wagon seat. "You heard the Captain," he said to Pedro, whose Arabic was limited. "Drive around to the stables."

Abdur Rahman's stables were modest both in size and construction compared to the Emir's labyrinthine shedrows back in Seville. The horses here were housed in a long, clearspan building of cut stone walls. Wooden rafters rose to a peak above a center breezeway and were partially covered in thatch. At the ridge, the roof was open to the sky, both for light and ventilation.

They pulled the wagons around in a circle in the stableyard. Davides jumped down from the wagon and took the horses' heads while he surveyed the area more closely. The aide stood fidgeting nearby, squinting at them in the bright, afternoon sunlight. A few guards were scattered around the stableyard and lounging near the water trough, but they barely gave the supply wagons a second glance. Not far away, a blacksmith was shoeing a horse. Davides welcomed the sharp clanking of his hammer on the anvil, since it would mask any small, inadvertent sounds that might emanate from their wagons.

Once Pedro had finished unhitching the horses, Davides led the horses, one on either side of him, into the stable. A wide breezeway of crushed limestone ran down the center of the building and crunched underfoot. Wooden mangers lined both walls, and iron rings jutted out from the wall every eight feet or so. Horses of varying shapes and sizes were tied to the rings, about fifty in all. A good many bore the stamp of Sevillian chargers. They stood in beds of heavy straw, dozing and swishing their tails at flies. Above the horses were lofts that stored the hay and straw.

"Where do you want these two?" he called out, a little more loudly than was strictly necessary.

"Keep your shirt on!" spat back a gnarled man, who limped towards him from the opposite end of the stables. "You Sevillians, always in such a rush."

"Maybe you'd like to get shot at by bandits," Davides retorted, trying to stay in character. "See what kind of rush you're in."

"Would to God they had found their mark," the man muttered under his breath, as he took one of the horses.

"What?"

"I said, praise God they missed their mark." He led the horse back down the breezeway where a gap in equine bodies suggested an empty tie ring.

Davides waited for the stablehand to return, breathing in the pungent aroma of manure and pine tar, and trying to act natural. Pine tar was a familiar scent in stables, since it was a popular means of improving the condition of horses' hooves. It was also extremely flammable.

Out of the corner of his eye, he saw the fire racing along the back edge of the loft to his left. Rather than sounding an alarm, he turned towards the horse he was holding and patted its sweat-stained neck. "Easy, now," he said in a soothing voice. "Just be patient." They needed that fire to be burning out of control . . .

"Fire!" The gnarly stablehand shouted from the other end of the stable. "We've got fire! Quick, get the horses out!"

The horses sensed the blaze at about the same time. They shifted nervously and gave anxious whickers. Davides grabbed the leads of the nearest two horses, along with that of the horse he was still holding and trotted them back out to the stableyard. He thrust their lead ropes into the hands of the astonished aide (horses had an annoying habit of running back into burning barns, so there was no point in turning them loose) and motioned to Pedro to help get more horses out.

Black smoke began oozing from the open roof. Stablehands and onlookers — some of whom, Davides hoped, were Abdur Rahman's men-at-arms — scrambled into the stableyard to help. The soldiers who had been lounging at the trough were pulling water from the well and forming a line of buckets, but Davides knew that would be a wasted effort. This was no ordinary barn fire, and a few buckets of water didn't stand a chance of extinguishing it.

No one cared about the newly arrived supply wagons anymore. With everyone's attention focused on the stable and the horses, Davides slid the Damascus sword, wrapped loosely in a blanket, from under the wagon seat. He walked around the circle of wagons, giving light taps on them: a signal to Vela's men that things were going according to plan and to stay put for a little while longer. Then, he hurried back to the stable.

It was harder to breathe and see than he had expected. The heat and the smoke stole air from his lungs and stung his eyes. He weaved through a press of horses and people, searching for a side door that was supposed to be near the back of the stable. He had just made out the door's outline when a hand grabbed his arm and spun him around. The blanket came loose, revealing the finely honed edges and wavering pattern of Damascus steel.

"You need to get out of here!" A Sevillian soldier was shouting at him, over the crackling flames. "The roof's coming down! Come on!" His exhortations stopped abruptly as he caught sight of the finely crafted sword in Davides's hand.

At that point, a rafter gave way. It struck the loft first and then careened to the ground, sending a spray of embers in their direction and igniting some of the straw where horses used to be.

Davides jerked his arm free from the soldier's grasp. He hastily reversed his grip on the sword and swung the pommel into the soldier's jaw. The blow staggered the man, but Davides had to hit him a second time before he fell to the ground, unconscious.

The weight of smoke and heat pressed down on Davides. His lungs seized up, and he coughed, over and over, unable to draw in any fresh air. He grabbed the soldier by a limp arm and dragged him toward the door. Eschewing stealth, he flung the door open, took the man by both arms, and hauled him through.

The air was only marginally more breathable outside. They were in a small, weedy area surrounded by low buildings that housed the stablehands. At the moment, it was empty since all of the stablehands were helping with the fire. Nearly empty, that is.

Remir stepped out from behind a clothesline full of laundry, a knotted rope coiled over one shoulder. He divided a sour expression between Davides and the inert soldier.

"He thought he was saving me," Davides explained, equally disgusted at the situation. They didn't have time for prisoners. They didn't dare risk exposure at this point. The last thing in the world they needed was a witness. "I couldn't leave him to burn."

"I suppose not," Remir grumbled. He took hold of the soldier and began towing him toward the opposite end of the yard.

Davides trailed after them, still coughing. "That pine tar . . . may have worked . . . a little too well."

"I soaked some of the straw in water last night. That should slow the fire down. But, you're right. We need to move fast, before our distraction wears thin."

They left the soldier lying in the yard, and Davides hoped he would have the decency to stay unconscious for a good, long while. Remir led the way through sections of the *alcázar* seldom seen by visitors: laundry, rubbish pile, more servants' quarters. They didn't encounter anyone. News of the fire at the stables had spread—one could hardly have missed it, since smoke now lifted in the air like a great black plume, and its stench permeated the air—and the workers that would have populated these areas had gone to help put out the fire or to watch the spectacle.

They came to a ten-foot wall, a partition rather than part of the *alcázar's* fortifications. It had not been constructed to deter climbing. Remir went up the wall with barely a break in speed, as he had probably done a hundred times before. Davides had to secure his sword behind him first and then search for the right handholds and footholds to make it to the top. The wall was a good ten inches thick, but it was pitted and uneven. Davides carefully placed one foot in front of the other with arms partially outstretched for balance.

Ahead of him, Remir moved with enviable ease to the corner of an adjoining building whose roof was about eight feet higher than their wall. Once he stood next to the building, Remir vaulted towards the roof, much as he had done to gain the loft of the inn back in Manantial. His chest and elbows hit the edge of the eaves, and he swung his legs up. Then, he stayed crouched against the low-pitched, tiled roof and waited for Davides.

Davides looked down at his narrow footpath, then up at the roof, then at Remir, who was motioning for him to hurry. Right, hurry. What was the worst that could happen? He could drop eighteen feet onto a cobblestone surface. That would hurt, but it wouldn't kill him. He scuffed his feet closer, flexed his knees, and sprang towards the roof. He had a moment of panic as the sword got in the way of his legs swinging up, but Remir grabbed him by the back of the shirt and hauled him the rest of the way up.

"I told you that thing was going to get in the way," Remir hissed.

It had been a point of debate: swords or no swords; armor or no armor? Any scheme that involved loping around on rooftops benefited from a lack of encumbrance. But, eventually they would come down from the rooftops, and unless they happened upon a serendipitous stash of weapons and shields, they would be easy prey for Sevillian soldiers. In the end, Remir had decided against both armor and a sword, since his nocturnal activities would require secrecy above all else. Davides had opted to wear the light leather cuirass typical of the teamsters and had insisted on bringing a sword, despite its impediment to his movement.

He followed Remir in a careful jog along the red, clay tiles. It felt weird doing this sort of thing in broad daylight—it felt weird doing this sort of thing at all—but the smoke from the stable fire had settled into a low-hanging haze around the *alcázar*, like a moderate fog. It concealed them completely from afar and, from a closer vantage point, turned them into incorporeal shadows flitting across the rooftops.

They jumped across a narrow alley to another building, then crossed to the opposite side of the structure where an adjoining roof with a much steeper pitch rose in front of them. After scrambling to its peak, they tightrope-walked their way along the roof's ridge to a wall. There, they had to repeat the process of leaping vertically to reach the next rooftop. By that time, Davides had stopped calculating how high up they were or how much it would hurt if he fell. He wasn't looking up; he wasn't looking down. He was simply following Remir.

At last, they reached the roof of the uppermost level of the *alcázar*. They were at the outer edge of the palace and there was a straight drop of about forty feet to a balcony that overlooked a narrow garden. Brick chimneys protruded from the roof at intervals, and Remir stopped at the third of these. He pulled the coil of rope over his head, knotted one end around the chimney, and tossed the other end so that it hung down to the balcony.

They both froze when they heard renewed shouting and the clang of steel against steel coming from the direction of the stables. Vela's men. Remir shot Davides an anxious look: they had wanted to have his father out of the building before the fighting began. Otherwise, the General could still use him as a hostage.

Without further delay, Remir took out a thin, tapered metal shaft that was bent slightly at the point—a sewing awl for repairing saddles—and put it between his teeth. Then, one hand following the rope, he slid down to the eaves and dropped out of sight.

Davides double-checked the knot securing the rope to the chimney. Then, he too followed the rope down the roof, but he stopped when he reached the eaves. He scanned the wall across from them, the balcony, and the garden below. Everything looked tranquil here, despite the fact that he could hear the clamor and din of battle as if it were occurring right next to him. He peered downward.

Remir had lowered himself to the top story of windows and hovered there, high above the ground, his feet locked around one of the knots. He took the awl from his teeth and reached it towards the intricately carved, lattice shutters of the window. He flicked the curved point of the awl upwards through the slight gap between the shutters once, twice, three times before something gave and the shutters parted. Swaying slightly from the effort of tripping the latch, it took Remir a few more moments to hook the awl through a hole in one shutter. He opened it wide, then grabbed the top edge of it and used that to pull himself toward the window. A moment later, he had slipped inside.

Then, it was Davides's turn. He took a firm grip on the rope and lowered himself over the edge of the roof. Using the knots to control the speed of his descent, he slid towards the balcony. He kept expecting to hear sounds of a scuffle emanate from the window through which Remir had disappeared. Not that there was anything he could do, were that to happen. His job was to get to the balcony and ensure they had an escape route.

When he reached solid footing, he pulled his sword free and backed up flush against the wall. Then, he sidled over to the nearby archway and chanced a quick look through it. The passage beyond was empty. It would lead them towards a terrace that overlooked the inner bailey. If Abdur Rahman and Remir could stand together on that terrace, they could rally his men—weapons or no weapons—and hold the gate against the Sevillian soldiers stationed out on the city wall.

The dangling rope slithered like something alive, and Davides looked up. Abdur Rahman was coming down, followed closely by Remir. Davides felt his exhilaration go up another notch. In all honesty, he hadn't expected they would get this far. Abdur Rahman dropped the last few feet, with the control and balance of a much younger man, and backed out of Remir's way.

Despite his agility in getting down the rope, Abdur Rahman appeared frailer than he had before, his face more drawn. Anger, frustration, and worry had taken their toll over the past weeks. Seeing his son again might have diminished some of the frustration and worry, but his anger was alive and well. At the sight of Davides, acrimony sparked in the depths of his eyes.

Davides held his gaze for only a moment before looking away. "No guards, I take it?" he said, to fill the tense void.

Remir hopped down next to them and took it upon himself to answer. "Not inside his chambers, anyway. Give him your knife, would you?"

Davides pulled out his knife, a long single-edged blade that had come with the teamster's outfit, but Abdur Rahman looked pointedly at the Damascus sword in Davides's other hand.

"I'd rather have that," he said in a voice that made the comment a command.

Davides hesitated. Give up his sword? What good was he to anybody without a sword? Besides, given the look in Abdur Rahman's eyes, Davides couldn't be certain that Abdur Rahman didn't intend to use the sword to run him through. Right there on the spot.

"Trust me, Father," Remir said, "if someone tries to stop us, you want Davides to have the sword."

Abdur Rahman kept his eyes locked on Davides. "I'm not convinced that I do."

"He's a friend," Remir insisted. "And he's an excellent swordsman. If anyone can make sure we reach the terrace, he can."

Abdur Rahman turned his attention back to his son. "Fine," he said, in a tone that suggested the very opposite. "But, after this is over, you and I are going to have a talk about your choice of friends." He snatched the knife from Davides's hand and went through the archway with long, purposeful strides.

Remir gave Davides an apologetic smile as they started after him. "Don't be offended. He's just on edge."

Davides was pretty sure that Abdur Rahman had meant to offend him. "It's all right. The last time he saw me, I was taking you hostage."

"There's that, too, I suppose," Remir acknowledged.

They turned down the passage, the soft-leather soles of their shoes making little noise on the polished flagstones beneath them. Abdur Rahman stayed in front, with Remir and Davides flanking him. They cut through a large, dark room with a vaulted ceiling, and picked up a narrow hallway on the other side of it. A square of bright light shone ahead of them, and Davides guessed they had almost reached the other side of the palace, which would then open to the inner bailey.

The sunlight in front of them was suddenly blocked out. A door had opened, and men began filing into the hallway. At first, all Davides could make out were silhouettes: men with crested helmets, *adarga* shields, and spears. Another man joined them, walking with the help of a cane and declaring in his stentorian voice: "… pure coincidence? Don't talk to me about bandits! This isn't the work of bandits. This is something else."

General Haroun broke off as he and his men became aware they were not alone in the hallway. His injury might have slowed him down physically, but his mind was as quick as ever. He took in the scene — Abdur Rahman slightly fore, Remir on his right, Davides on his left. Without visible emotion, he focused on Davides and in a voice as hard as granite said, "How much? Whatever he's paying you, I'll double it."

The demeaning offer stung Davides in a way that expressions of anger or incredulity never would have.

"This isn't about money," was all Davides could think to reply.

"No? Pity. Kill him," The General said to his bodyguards. "Then, bring the other two to me." Having arranged the situation to his satisfaction, he turned and hobbled the other way, motioning for two of his men to accompany him.

Davides shook off his chagrin, pushed past Abdur Rahman, and stood between them and the remaining four bodyguards. "Find another way. I'll hold them here."

"You sure?" Remir asked. His voice did not exude confidence.

They both knew it was crucial that Abdur Rahman and Remir appear together on the terrace overlooking the inner bailey. If Abdur Rahman's men didn't commit to the fight, the day would be lost. "Positive," Davides said. "Go!"

Davides heard Remir and Abdur Rahman's footsteps fading back, then the sound of a door opening and closing.

"I don't remember you being this arrogant," one of the bodyguards observed, his lip curled in a sneer.

"You don't? Maybe you've taken too many blows to the head. You should consider retiring, Umar. In fact, now might be a good time."

Not so long ago, Davides had trained next to these men: Umar, Farid, Kadeer, and Rasul. They all knew each other. They had ridden together, eaten together. He had even met Kadeer's family . . .

Which wasn't to say that they all liked each other.

"Let's back him up," Umar said contemptuously. Umar and Farid joined shields, leveled their spears, and stepped forward in unison.

Davides wasn't about to be 'backed up'. He liked his narrow hallway, which was just wide enough for two people to stand abreast of each other or for one person to swing a sword. He stood his ground, the matte finish of the Damascus blade making it nearly invisible in the gloom of the hallway. When the two bodyguards had closed the distance between them, his sword flickered twice. Its keen edge made short work of the spears, leaving one spear point completely severed from its wooden haft and the other dangling uselessly. Umar and Farid dropped their broken spears, and Kadeer and Rasul wordlessly handed theirs forward. This time, Umar and Farid made Davides's job a little more challenging, but the end result was the same: the spears lay broken on the ground.

"Davides!" Kadeer yelled from the back. "You know you're done the moment we get a crossbow!"

Was Kadeer warning him, threatening him, or simply pointing out the obvious? Davides had no cover in the hallway, but he had hoped it might not occur to them, in the heat of the moment, to resort to projectiles.

"So, go get a goddamn crossbow!" Davides shouted back.

Kadeer hesitated, then darted back through the open doorway next to him.

Meanwhile, Umar and Farid drew their swords, crouched low behind their shields, and rushed him. They couldn't swing their swords in the hallway, but they meant to drive him back into the large vaulted room, where they could then surround him. Instead of falling back, Davides slid to the floor. It was not normally where one wanted to be in a fight, but at the moment his opponents' only vulnerable areas were their legs, and his lightweight armor would make it easy for him to bounce back to his feet. His first strike cut through Umar's boot and bit into the ankle. That momentarily stopped their advance, but Farid chopped down with the edge of his shield, clipped Davides on the shoulder, and knocked him flat on his back.

Davides brought his sword around to deflect Farid's blade. Still prone, he thrust upward, cutting into Farid's inner thigh. Farid jerked back, and Davides rolled away even as Umar's sword jabbed down at him, missing him by a hair's breadth. He sprang back to his feet, dismayed to notice he had lost a good eight feet of hallway in the process.

Farid had staggered back against the wall, blood pooling on the floor beneath him. Umar started towards Davides, but Rasul reached him first. Rasul delivered a barrage of precision attacks that kept Davides on the defensive and cost him another few feet of precious ground.

"What are you doing, Davides!" Rasul demanded.

Strike. Counterstrike.

"Trying to stay alive," Davides retorted, although he knew that wasn't what Rasul meant.

"How could you turn on the General!"

Rasul's anger at Davides's betrayal began to show in his fighting. More power, less precision. Davides was still waiting for an opening when the two blades collided with such force that Rasul's sword shattered, leaving him with nothing but the grip and a jagged stump. Rasul flinched as a steel shard nicked his cheek, and Davides took advantage of the distraction to land a blow against the side of Rasul's helmet that sent him sprawling to the floor.

Before Davides could regain any lost ground, Umar's shield slammed into him, knocking him against the wall. If Rasul had been angry, Umar was beyond furious. He took a swipe at Davides's unprotected head. Davides ducked, but that might have been what Umar had been waiting for: his shield rammed into Davides again, this time bashing his head against the stone wall. An explosion of pain from his nose blurred Davides's vision, and for a moment the wall and Umar's shield were the only things keeping Davides from dropping to his knees.

"You son-of-a-bitch!" Umar spat at him.

The pressure of Umar's shield against him yielded, and through the pain and tears and sudden flow of blood from his nose, Davides sensed the impending swing from Umar's sword. He diverted it, barely, and Umar's sword left a long, jagged scar along the wall next to him. Davides quickly sidestepped to put some space between him and

Umar. When Umar tried to follow, hampered by the bad ankle, Davides brought his sword around in an arc that found the gap in armor between Umar's neck and shoulder. It sliced through muscle and sinew until it hit bone.

Both men stood shock still for a moment, neither quite believing what had just happened. Then, Davides jerked his sword free, and Umar crumpled to the ground.

The hallway was quiet. Rasul hadn't regained consciousness. Kadeer hadn't come back.

Davides crouched down next to Umar, thinking to appropriate the bodyguard's shield, but he had only begun the process of loosening the enarmes when Kadeer surged into the hallway with not one, but two loaded crossbows. Kadeer's eyes widened with surprise and alarm at the scene before him. He brought one of the crossbows to his hip and pulled the trigger. It was an awkward way to shoot a crossbow, and the bolt ricocheted harmlessly off the wall.

With no shield and no reasonable options, Davides rushed Kadeer, trying to cross the fifteen feet that separated them before the bodyguard could bring the second crossbow to bear. He failed. At the last instant, Davides twisted sharply sideways. The loosed bolt embedded itself in his armor and burrowed into his flesh. Davides faltered a stride but kept going. The bolt stung, and anger spurred renewed strength into him. He reached Kadeer, knocked the crossbow aside with his sword, and used his free hand to shove Kadeer against the wall. Before Kadeer could draw a weapon, the edge of Davides's sword was indenting the flesh of his throat.

"Davides," Kadeer gasped, then stopped. He was trying very hard not to move, not to swallow, not to breathe. But, his eyes were eloquent.

"What?" Davides snarled at him. "Now you want me to spare you? You *shot* me!"

"I was . . . following orders."

In other words, it was nothing personal. Kadeer had merely been following orders. *Sound familiar?* Davides's rage abated. Deep down, he didn't want to kill Kadeer. He backed the sword off slightly and checked over his shoulder: Umar, dead; Farid, unconscious or dead; Rasul, stirring. *Damn.* If Rasul got back to his feet, he wouldn't have much choice.

"Surrender," Davides commanded.

Kadeer blinked at him, unsure. Before Kadeer could respond one way or the other, they heard running feet and jangling armor approaching. Then, a man's voice called out, "Nizar?"

The Castilians? It had to be the Castilians. No one else here knew him by that name.

"*¡Acá!*" Davides shouted back.

Five of Vela's men including Pedro burst into the hallway, bristling with armor and weapons. They cast about the room for something to attack. Two of them went to stand over Rasul, who had made it to a sitting position but was still unsteady and disoriented.

"*Jamal nos envió a ayudarlo. Nos dijo que estaba en apuros.*" Pedro sounded vaguely recriminatory, as if Remir had somehow exaggerated Davides's plight.

"*Llegasteis a buena hora,*" Davides assured them. He backed away from Kadeer, who promptly raised his hands and fell to his knees in surrender.

319

* * *

They were trying to move quickly and get to the fight at the gate, but there were a couple of matters that had to be worked out first.

For one thing, the Castilians didn't want to take prisoners. Prisoners required guards, manpower they could ill afford. Also, in the intense, early moments of the battle, while Abdur Rahman's men had been scrambling to get weapons out of the wagons, Vela and a number of the other Castilian mercenaries had fallen. Consequently, the Castilians were feeling even less kindly than normal towards Sevillian soldiers. They wanted to execute the bodyguards and move on.

Davides could sympathize. He remembered how he had felt after Hatim had been killed in Manantiel. And, he remembered how Remir had kept him from cutting down a defenseless man who had surrendered. Since Davides couldn't very well threaten the Castilians with bodily harm if they persisted in killing the General's bodyguards, he instead appealed to their practical nature: the two bodyguards belonged to important families back in Seville and would bring a tidy ransom, which they could then send to the fallen men's families. Wasn't that what Vela would want?

Davides's argument won grudging support, but then there was the matter of Davides's injuries. Nothing much could be done about his nose, which presumably would stop bleeding in its own time. The crossbow bolt was of greater immediate concern. Pedro was kind enough to extract it for him, and did so with about as much care as one might use to remove a sliver from a thumb: he took hold of the protruding end and yanked really hard.

Pedro peered at the wound through the small, irregular hole left in the leather armor. "*Un rasguño, nada más,*" he declared.

Just a graze. Davides would have another scar to add to his collection, but at least he wouldn't be bleeding out any time soon. Pedro handed him one of the *adarga* shields, and Davides strapped it onto his arm as they headed towards the inner bailey, herding Kadeer and a groggy Rasul along with them.

They paused when they reached the large, semi-circular terrace that overlooked the gate and inner bailey. Smoke from the stable fire still hung in the air, giving everything a muted, grey cast. To their right, broad steps swooped in a gentle curve to ground level. Scattered on the ground before them were the dead and injured, a confused jumble of Sevillians, Salamantines, and Castilians. There had been no battle lines, no phalanx, just a chaotic free-for-all. Loose horses milled around, intent on escaping the smell of blood and fire, but they had nowhere to go.

An arrow whistled into view from beyond the wall and plunged downward. It skittered across the cobblestones without finding a mark. Then, Davides heard a familiar voice shout his name and saw Remir pelting up the steps towards him. For once, Davides noted, Remir had actually acquired a sword during the course of a fight instead of losing one. By the looks of it, he had had to use it, too: the edge was nicked and bloodstained.

Remir joined them in the shelter of the hallway. He glanced at Rasul and Kadeer, but refrained from comment. "The soldiers on the outer wall are shooting blindly into the *alcázar*," he said. "Pretty soon they'll figure out that we're out of arrows, and that they're just sending us more, but in the meantime keep your heads down. Speaking of which, what happened to your nose, Davides?"

"I kept my head down," Davides said, with a slight grimace. "Besides being out of arrows, what's our status?"

"The soldiers outside the *alcázar* are finally getting organized and are calling up the off-duty troops. They've been trying to get the gate open. We've been keeping it shut, mostly thanks to Vela's men. They've some experience with sieges, I guess.

"Most of the fighting within the *alcázar* is over. There's a group of Sevillian soldiers holding out near the armory, but my father's men should be breaking those ranks soon. Then, we'll have access to the weapons stockpile and be able to equip more men for our side."

"That's great, but none of it will matter unless we get the General," Davides said.

Remir nodded agreement. "My father's assembling some men now." He hesitated, and Davides braced himself to hear whatever it was that Remir was reluctant to say. "Davides, we need you to stay at the gate and coordinate things here. Right now, there's no single person in charge. But, you speak Castilian and Arabic, you know battle tactics—"

"Theoretical knowledge," Davides interrupted. "I've never been in an actual siege before."

Remir jerked his head towards the Castilians. "They have. They can help you."

"Okay." Davides couldn't argue with Remir's logic, even though he had expected to be more directly

322

involved with the final stage of their plan. "Your father knows he can't kill the General, right? For this to work, we need him alive."

"I know," Remir said quickly, starting back towards the steps.

"But, does your father know?" Davides insisted, remembering the internalized ire he had seen in Abdur Rahman's eyes.

Remir waved a hand to indicate ... something. No worries?

Davides turned towards Pedro, wondering where to begin.

"Your orders, don Nizar?" Pedro asked in Castilian, using the honorific *don* with a forgivable amount of irony. For all Pedro knew, Davides had about as much business leading them as Julián did.

Davides gave Pedro a taut, self-deprecating smile in return. "How about this: you and your men do whatever it is you normally do to hold a gate. I'll take cues from you and translate them into orders for Abdur Rahman's men."

Pedro nodded with a grim smile. "Yes, sir."

* * *

Three days had elapsed since they had won back Salamanca. Three days since the General had been forced to surrender. Under the circumstances, Abdur Rahman's terms had been generous. The Sevillian soldiers had been disarmed and expelled from Salamanca and the surrounding areas. General Haroun's officers and bodyguards would be released when Seville negotiated a reasonable ransom for them. And, as a way to safeguard

Salamanca's sovereignty, General Haroun would remain a prisoner in the city until the war between Seville and Castile-León resolved itself, one way or the other.

Considering that the General had not been in any position to bargain, the terms had been munificent. However, that didn't mean that the General would harbor warm, fuzzy feelings towards Abdur Rahman. Or, towards Davides.

Davides stood immobile in front of the closed door, his feet and hands having suddenly turned leaden. There was nothing ominous about the door itself. It looked exactly like a half-dozen others that were spaced down the hallway: oaken planks, rounded at the top, held together by wrought iron *clavos*, and supported by long strap hinges. Pleasant, well-made doors. As with so many things, the difference between this door and the others was not in the door itself, but in what lay beyond.

He steeled himself, lifted a heavy hand, and rapped on the door. From inside, a voice asked for the password before Davides heard the clicks of locks turning. The door opened. A guard stood blocking his path. The man's eyes swept over Davides, searching for anything resembling a weapon, and they paused pointedly on the well-worn saddlebags Davides was carrying. Davides handed the saddlebags to the guard, who accepted them with a cool nod and stood aside, granting him entrance into the General's quarters.

Except for two, well-armed guards and an excessive number of locks, the room looked nothing like a cell. Against one wall was a large bed with a trunk at its foot and a wash basin in the corner. A mahogany desk, equipped with paper, quill, and ink, was situated near an open window. A slight breeze wafted through the room, making the paper flutter gently beneath a brass weight.

The General was sitting by the desk with his injured leg propped on a stool, perusing some written material by the sunlight beaming through the window. He did not look up when Davides entered, but said casually, "I could have sworn I told my men to kill you."

"You did. They tried."

"My own fault, I guess," the General mused, as if to himself. "I trained you too well."

The General's comment grated on Davides. It was as if he were taking the credit for his own defeat. "Or, I was trained just well enough, depending on one's viewpoint. But, I'm not here about that." Davides gestured towards the saddlebags held by the guard. "I came to return those to you," he said.

The General's eyes finally lifted from the papers, curiosity overcoming his contempt. When he spied the saddlebags, he shifted in his chair and sat up straighter. The guard rolled a quizzical look at Davides, then turned out the contents of the saddlebags on the bed: two bags of coins slumped from one side, a stiff, badly scorched envelope slid from the other.

The only thing missing was Bendayan's clothpaper notes. When deciding what his obligation was with regards to the Greek text, Davides had settled on the blank slate approach. He would return the manuscript and the gold the General had sent for the translation. It would be up to General Haroun to devise a way to open the burnt parchment without its complete disintegration and to find someone capable of deciphering it.

The guard poked at the contents a little and double-checked the empty interior of the saddlebags before packing them up and handing them to General Haroun.

The General cautiously extracted the envelope and traced the blackened areas with light fingers. "What happened?" he asked, forgetting for the moment his scorn for Davides.

"I left it with an alchemist in Toledo. Some men burned down his shop. The alchemist was killed, but we were able to recover that."

"Why on earth would they set fire to the place if they were trying to retrieve it?"

"They weren't looking for that; they were looking for me. Thugs sent by Ignacio Gonsaluiz."

"Gonsaluiz? Why was he looking for you?" the General asked, sounding genuinely baffled.

It shouldn't have been baffling. A Castilian knight rooting out a Sevillian spy in Toledo should have been the most normal thing in the world. A ghastly thought struck Davides. "Don't tell me you were allied with that *filho da égua!*"

"Not allied, no. It was more an enemy-of-my-enemy kind of relationship."

In other words, General Haroun and Gonsaluiz had shared a common enemy: Castile-León. The revelation didn't come as a surprise to Davides, since Remir and Rodrigo had speculated as much while discussing the motives behind Gonsaluiz's illicit activities in Toledo.

"You mean to say that Gonsaluiz was plotting with Aragón against King Fernando," Davides clarified. "Working to start a war on a second front."

"Now, how would you know about that?" the General inquired, his eyes narrowing. "You were spying for the Castilians, weren't you? That's why Gonsaluiz lashed out at you."

Davides might have been guilty of a great many things, but spying for Castile-León wasn't one of them. "All we did was ride into the wrong godforsaken village! Remir and I stumbled into the middle of Gonsaluiz's operation and would have stumbled right back out again, completely unwitting. But, no! He convinced himself we were a threat and wouldn't stop coming at us. He killed an old man whose only offense was to accept the job of translating that cursed document for me. He tortured and killed your men because they had the audacity to show up in Toledo and ask for me. He was a sadistic fiend who enjoyed tormenting others. He didn't need much of an excuse to lash out at someone."

The guards were staring at him wide-eyed. The General was looking at him in a much different way. "'Was'?" he repeated, his voice lingering on the word in a significant way.

Davides looked at him levelly, but said nothing.

"Rasul said you fought them using Gonsaluiz's sword. I told him he must have been mistaken. But, he wasn't, was he?" The General shook his head in wonder. "I can't believe how badly I underestimated you."

And, Davides couldn't believe how long this conversation had lasted. He had wanted to return the document and money, and be gone. In and out. "I had help," he said curtly, not wanting the sole credit for Gonsaluiz's demise. He backed up a couple of steps towards the door. "Anyway, I just came to return the saddlebags."

General Haroun didn't move but was watching him with an imprecise expression: wary and reflecting and somber all at once. Davides's hand was on the door latch when a barely audible question from the General froze him in place, "When exactly did I lose you, Davides?"

How could Davides explain to him that there was no exact moment? That he had tried to ignore his conscience. That he had sought rationalization, half-measures, and simple avoidance; but, none of those had been able to rival the magnitude of the wrong he was perpetrating. That somewhere along the way, his capacity to tolerate tyranny had stretched until it had snapped. That his actions were less about the General losing him than they were about him finding himself.

But, he couldn't possibly say all of that. It sounded too sappy.

"What would you have done if I had told you, back in Seville, that I objected to using Abdur Rahman's children as leverage?" Davides asked finally.

"I would have told you to mind your own business. I wasn't paying you to have scruples or an opinion."

"And, if I had persisted?"

"Then, I would have found someone less thin-skinned to do the job."

"That's what I thought," Davides said. "And, that was when you lost me."

* * *

Remir was waiting for him out in the hallway, leaning a shoulder casually against the wall. Davides glanced at him but kept walking. Distance. He wanted some distance between himself and that door.

"How'd it go?" Remir asked, falling into step with him.

"Fine."

"Hmph. I knew you'd say that."

"Then, why'd you ask?"

"Insatiable curiosity." Remir shrugged. "I can't help myself."

They descended a flight of stairs and emerged onto the gallery that led to their rooms. The gallery overlooked the patio where Sajid and Davides had once waited for Remir to prepare for the long trip to Seville. With the cold autumn nights, the colorful flowers had shriveled away and died, but potted evergreens still broke up the monotony of the buff-colored stonework. Davides stopped and turned into the small room that he had been occupying for the past three days.

Remir came in behind him and propped himself on the edge of a side table, next to a bowl of shelled almonds. "We're arranging to bring Amira home," he said.

"Thanks for the warning," Davides responded with heartfelt sincerity. He dropped into a chair, feeling physically and mentally drained. "I'll be sure to clear out before she gets here."

Remir frowned slightly and popped a few almonds into his mouth. "Where will you go?"

"I thought I would check on Ishaq. You know, make sure everything is okay between him and our friends in Alferia." After that, Davides didn't know where he would go or what he would do. Once again, he was penniless. All of the money from the Vandals had gone to pay the Castilian mercenaries. "Did Vela's men agree to stay on for a while?"

"They did. But, . . . I guess they're looking for a new leader."

"Why doesn't Pedro do it? He seems very capable."

"Funny, that's what Pedro said about you," Remir said, tilting his head slightly.

"Me? Pedro thinks I'm your valet."

"Well, as valets go, you're apparently very impressive in a fight. Pedro wanted to know what your background was, so I told him. He thought you would be a good fit."

Davides snorted. "Maybe to join them; not to lead them."

"I don't know. Look at it from their standpoint, Davides. They're in a land where they don't know the language or the customs, but you do. They already know you and trust you. Besides all of that, they rode into exile with Vela, so they can't go back home unless someone advocates for them and convinces King Fernando to pardon them."

"And, they think a displaced Portuguese noble can somehow help their cause?"

"They think *you* can help their cause. You heard what Rodrigo said: there are people in Castile-León who know who you are. Like it or not, all this time they've been keeping track of you. You're the best chance Pedro and the others have of going home someday. And, who better than you to understand that desire, that aspiration?"

Davides felt his resistance crumbling, but he still saw a glaring problem. "I can understand why Vela's men might think this is a good idea, but I can't imagine your father trusting me with a flock of sheep, let alone with a small band of mercenaries."

Remir smiled ruefully. "It's true, my father is not in a particularly trusting mood right now. But, he does realize that you sacrificed more than you could possibly hope to gain when you decided to help me. And, he knows that I trust you. He's already agreed to the arrangement. The only one who still needs convincing is you."

Davides shook his head. "Not the only one. What about your sister? Won't she take exception?"

"Nah," Remir dismissed the concern.

Davides looked at him skeptically.

"Yeah, okay, maybe," Remir amended, after a moment. "But, she'll come around. Think of all the other people — just since I've known you — who have started out wanting to kill you and ended up liking you."

"Is that supposed to be comforting?"

"You're not dead. That should be comforting."

It was, if one were inclined to look on the bright side of things. That seemed to come much more easily to Remir than it ever had to Davides.

Still, it would be comforting to know that he would have food, shelter, and clothes on his back for the next few months. It would also be comforting to be around people who weren't trying to kill him, to remain in one place for longer than a week, and to be engaged in a worthwhile endeavor like protecting Salamanca.

"Okay," Davides said.

"Okay, what? Okay, you'll do it?"

"Assuming the offer still stands. Yes, I'll do it."

THE END

331

Made in the USA
Middletown, DE
10 April 2017